THE
NIGHT
OF THE
CRASH

Jessica Irena Smith is a glass artist from County Durham and has a BA in Glass & Ceramics and an MA in Glass, both from the University of Sunderland, where she was based at the National Glass Centre. Jessica's writing is inspired by many things, but she loves podcasts, especially true crime, which she listens to while cutting glass and loading kilns. In 2016, Jessica won a Northern Writers' Award; in 2017, she was awarded a TLC 'Free Read' by New Writing North; and in 2020, she was longlisted for Mslexia's Novel Competition.

Also by Jessica Irena Smith

The Summer She Vanished

THE

NIGHT

OF THE

CRASH

Jessica Irena Smith

HEADLINE

First published in 2024 by Headline Publishing Group

1

Cataloguing in Publication Data is available from the British Library

ISBN 978 1 0354 0521 3

Typeset in 11/15.25pt Adobe Garamond Pro by Jouve (UK), Milton Keynes

Printed and bound in Great Britain by Clays Ltd, Elcograf S.p.A.

Text Design © Shutterstock

HEADLINE PUBLISHING GROUP
An Hachette UK Company
Carmelite House
50 Victoria Embankment
London EC4Y 0DZ

www.headline.co.uk
www.hachette.co.uk

Dark corners. That's where secrets lie. They can be big, they can be little. Sometimes they need piecing together, for things to make sense and stories to form. Sometimes they lie undiscovered for years, waiting to be found, as dark as the corners they hide in.

But dark corners are also where the truth lies: they just need a little light.

And that's where I come in. I'm Steppy Corner. You're listening to All the Dark Corners: The Disappearance of Shaunee Hughes.

I

Now

Polystyrene ceiling tiles. I can't pinpoint the exact moment I come round, but when I do, that's what I see. I've a feeling I must've been drifting in and out for some time now, because those tiles feel vaguely familiar. My tiny New York apartment doesn't have polystyrene tiles, thank God; yet still, when I wake finally – properly – I'm certain that's where I am. As my eyes trace over the contents of my would-be home – the generic prints on the walls, the wood-veneer furniture, the wall-mounted television – none of it mine, I somehow believe that it is, all of it: the bed I'm lying in, the cannula in my arm with the line coming out, the IV bag hanging from the stand beside me. My dad, asleep in a chair in the corner of the room.

Dad.

I do a double-take, such as my eyes will allow, for they throb with even the slightest movement.

Why's he in my apartment?

I blink, feel more pain. 'Dad?' I croak, unsure if anything's come out.

He wakes with a start, scrambles from his chair, the open book in his lap toppling to the floor, and I wonder again what he's doing in my apartment – *how'd he get in?* – all the while knowing this is most definitely *not* my apartment.

'Thank goodness you're awake.' He's at my bedside now. For a doctor, he seems remarkably ruffled. His eyes are red-rimmed, like either he's been crying – I've never seen Dad cry before – or up all night. The whole thing unnerves me.

I brace myself with my elbows, try to sit up. Don't have the strength. 'Where am I?'

'Hospital, sweetie. You've been in an accident.'

I have? I try to remember, close my eyes – maybe that will help – but the pounding in my head only grows, and there's something else too: voices, loud yet indistinct, like more than one radio station playing at once.

Shit-shit-shit-shit-shit . . .

Don't-die-don't-die-don't-die . . .

I put a hand to my head and recoil when I feel stubble, have a sudden flashback: me and Garrett as kids, running through freshly harvested fields, shorn wheat, stubbly like plastic drinking straws . . .

Stay with me . . .

Jesus!

I can't tell if the voice is male or female, one voice or many. I open my eyes again.

'Where am I?'

Dad sighs, not impatiently. 'Hospital. You've been in an accident.'

'What kind of accident?'

'Car,' he says. 'You were driving and, well . . .'

'I was driving?' I can drive, sure, but I don't own a car. Not in New York.

'A hire car.'

I close my eyes again – *No-no-no-no-no . . . Stay with me . . . Christ!* – open them just as quickly. A woman's voice, I'm sure.

'Where am I?' I ask.

'Hospital, sweetie.'

'No.' I feel like I'm on a hamster wheel. '*Where* where?'

'Oh.' Dad looks relieved: *right*. 'The city.'

'New York?' Has to be.

He shakes his head. 'The Springs.'

'Colorado?'

'You came home for Thanksgiving a few days ago. I had them transfer you here.'

'Wait . . .' My head's splitting. '*Home* home? Heartsick?'

I have the sudden urge to laugh, probably would if my head didn't hurt so badly, because I'm quite certain Heartsick's the last place I'd *choose* to visit, especially on Thanksgiving. These days, my Thanksgivings are spent with Travis and his family. Then it comes to me, a little voice in my head, my own this time: *not any more*.

'You lost control,' Dad's saying, 'went off the road.'

That makes no sense. Crashing cars is something Garrett does, not me. I'm a careful driver. Bit rusty, sure, but careful.

'This.' I touch a hand to my head again, tracing my fingers along the jagged ridge that stretches front to back, held together by parallel strips of metal, like rungs on a ladder. It feels alien, like it's a part of someone else, not me.

'Easy,' Dad says. 'You've got a nasty scar. Tree branch through the windshield.'

'I'm in hospital,' I tell him. 'How long have I been here?'

'A couple days.'

'And Mum?' I feel like she's around somewhere, am sure I've already seen her, yet the look on Dad's face when I ask, the fact he doesn't answer right away, makes me panic. Something's very wrong. 'Was anyone else in the accident?' I demand. 'Anyone in the car with me?'

Dad answers too quickly this time. 'No. Not in the car,' which is a weird thing to say, but then this whole situation is weird, and before I can ask what he means, he asks me, 'What's the last thing you remember?'

My last memory is being home in my apartment, one night last . . . when? A few days ago? A week? I squeeze my eyes tight shut – *Don't-die-don't-die-don't-die* – feel a sudden, all-consuming fear, want to say *I'm frightened* but all that comes out is a squeaky 'I don't know.'

'Steppy, sweetheart,' Dad says gently, 'there's something I have to tell you.' He waits a beat. 'It's Mum.'

Mum? I open my eyes, half expecting to see her here, right in front of me, wherever *here* is.

'Where am I?' I ask, but I don't think Dad hears me.

Instead he says, 'I'm so sorry. Mum's dead.'

2

Then

Seven days ago, I'd never heard of Casey Carter. It was somewhere after 2 a.m. on a Sunday and I was home alone, trying to resist the urge to pop a sleeping pill. It had been a particularly rough day. Following months of back and forth, punctuated with periods of complete radio silence, Travis had finally come to collect the rest of his shit.

'How's Paige doing?' I'd asked, eyeing him – *had he been working out more?* – as he surveyed the bags and boxes filling the living room.

I hadn't quite gone so far as shredding his clothes or dousing them with bleach, though I'd thought about it; had instead taken particular pleasure in stuffing his custom suits into garbage bags like rags.

'She's good.' I watched him open a couple, peer inside, felt a childish pang of satisfaction. He straightened up. 'But you've gotta stop calling her.'

That hit me like a gut punch. It was the way he said it, like I was calling all the time, like I was the one who'd done something wrong. Travis was good at that: flipping the script, making himself the victim. He'd had months of practice.

'I mean' – he was slinging garbage bag after garbage bag out the apartment door – 'what do you think's gonna happen?'

I knew the spiel well, was saying it along with him in my head, inwardly rolling my eyes, waiting for the dramatic pause.

'Seriously.' Travis stopped throwing bags, looked at me. 'You think you and Paige can just go back to how things were, be best friends again?'

I had a sudden urge to punch him in the face, but instead I took a deep breath. 'Why don't I grab the last of your stuff? You go ahead, call the elevator.'

He looked at me, wondering what the catch was, then shrugged, disappeared out into the hallway, while I grabbed a nearby Sharpie I'd been labelling boxes with and, after removing the lid, dropped it into one of the remaining garbage bags – the one with all Trav's linen suit jackets – smooshed it right on in there, then slung the bag out the door with the rest of them.

Now I was in bed, googling myself, or, more accurately, *All the Dark Corners*, which wasn't as big-headed as it sounds, more a form of self-harm, something I'd taken to doing when I couldn't sleep. I'd lose hours trawling the *Dark Corners* Facebook fan pages, falling down rabbit holes on Reddit or online newspaper comments sections. I say a form of self-harm because although most of the stuff written about me was complimentary, that almost made it worse. To the outside world, I was Steppy Corner, creator and voice behind true crime podcast phenomenon *All the Dark Corners: The Disappearance of Shaunee Hughes*. To the outside world, it seemed I had my shit together. I'd been asked to pen articles, or been the subject of such articles, for publications that pre-*Dark Corners* I could barely afford to subscribe to, would have struggled to find work answering calls in their ad departments. People – and by *people*, I mean people who have people to do things for them – were now calling *me*; people who previously wouldn't so much as have returned my calls, would probably have blocked my number. I'd been profiled in print, done television interviews, radio phone-ins. I'd gone from struggling would-be journalist to darling of the true crime podcast world. There was talk of a book deal; an appearance was currently being brokered for the inaugural true crime convention the following year – something called CrimeCon. All thanks to the runaway success of *Dark Corners* and the now-solved mystery of Shaunee Hughes.

But although a second season of *Dark Corners* was guaranteed – sponsors were already lining up to put their name to it – therein lay the problem. *My* problem. I had no idea what season two was going to be about, what case I'd cover, though not for lack of suggestions: I'd been inundated. Everyone from local journalists to retired cops, bereaved family members to plain old do-gooders knew someone whose uncle, best friend, pseudo-niece or nephew had been the victim of some terrible unsolved crime. Even those with no direct connection to a case had an opinion on what I should cover, which grisly murder/mysterious disappearance/heartbreaking miscarriage of justice/decades-old cold case – or a combination thereof – should provide their next true crime fix, the one they'd discuss around the water cooler at work, speculate about on the very Facebook fan pages, Reddit forums and online newspaper comments sections I was now trawling through.

But try as I might, nothing grabbed me.

Not like Shaunee's case.

I sighed – an especially melodramatic sigh, though there was no one around to hear – clicked a link someone had posted, cringed at the sound of my own voice. Cue the catchy theme tune I knew so well – so popular now it had its own Facebook page – the one synonymous with

Dark Corners. Then my voice again: 'When Shaunee Hughes left her Murdoch home on March 17, 1990, her mother waved her goodbye. Her father – just arrived home from the grocery store – watched her disappear round the corner at the end of their quiet small-town street. Little did her parents know it would be the last time they'd see her. You see, Shaunee, a fun-loving ten-year-old, as bright as that sunny spring day, left the house on her shiny red bike and seemingly vanished into thin air. Twenty-five years on, her case remains unsolved . . .'

I didn't feel a connection to Shaunee's case above all others just because, thanks to *Dark Corners*, it had been solved. It wasn't because her killer had been apprehended, or because her remains had at last been found and given a proper burial. With Shaunee, there'd been something deeper. Before my family's move to the UK, the year after Shaunee vanished, when I was four and my brother, Garrett, two, we'd lived in Murdoch, the very same town as the Hughes family. At the very same time. I was too young to remember, of course, but when I looked back, I'd wondered if Shaunee Hughes – her disappearance – was the reason Dad took the job offer in London, uprooted us and didn't return to the US for over a decade.

But if what happened to Shaunee Hughes had been behind my parents' decision to up sticks and relocate, I could hardly blame them. Even though I'd been blissfully unaware of Shaunee's existence, had no comprehension of her disappearance at the time, the one thing I'd learned making *Dark Corners* was the feeling of unease this sort of crime sows in the places it occurs, the doubt it casts in people's minds. Everyone and no one is a suspect. Was it the neighbour from a couple houses down, the one who had a wife, children, the one you only knew to say hi to, though he seemed like a nice guy? Or was it the I-always-thought-he-was-a-bit-of-a-creeper store clerk, the overfriendly teacher, the busybody mailman, the geeky guy from the video store?

So despite the fact that I lived the first four years of my life in Shaunee's hometown, and though she may have been the catalyst for my family's move abroad, the first I heard about her was last year, 2015, thanks to one of those sliding-door moments, a chance encounter that almost didn't happen.

It was the weekend and Paige had been in town, staying with me and Travis. The three of us were due to go to a party, but Paige was feeling off-colour so decided not to go. I'd offered to stay home, keep her company, but she insisted I didn't, mostly because Travis had started whining about how Kyle would be 'totally bummed' if I didn't go. (Truth was, Kyle wouldn't have given a shit.)

When we'd arrived at the party, Travis had promptly abandoned me. He was holding court in another room, so I'd fought my way through a crowd of guests, sought sanctuary at the makeshift bar, began making small talk with another guest. To my relief, my new acquaintance was only slightly drunk. She told me she loved my accent, asked me where I was from.

'It's complicated,' I said, which was what I always said. 'But I was born here.' She looked surprised. 'Not *here* here,' I clarified. 'A small town in the Midwest. Murdoch?'

I wasn't expecting much – most people had never even heard of Murdoch – but the girl began flapping her hands, almost spilled her drink.

'Holy shit,' she exclaimed. '*Murdoch*? No way! That's where I'm from!'

'Oh,' I said quickly. 'I only lived there till I was four. We moved to London in ninety-one.'

'Right after Shaunee Hughes,' she said. She'd gone all serious, nodded sagely like it figured. 'My family thought about moving, too. Like, nothing was the same after that.'

She'd given a shake of her head and I'd nodded in agreement, like I knew who the hell Shaunee Hughes actually was.

When our conversation ended, I'd excused myself and gone to the bathroom, got my phone out, googled *Shaunee Hughes Murdoch*. The search yielded old newspaper articles mainly, headlines like *MURDOCH COLD CASE REMAINS UNSOLVED A DECADE ON*, and *TWENTY YEARS ON, FAMILY OF SHAUNEE HUGHES STILL SEEK ANSWERS*.

The rest, as they say, was history. When Trav and I got home, I'd googled the shit out of the case, wondered why it had never been solved. That night, as I'd lain awake in the dark, I'd decided to return to Murdoch with a view to making a single podcast episode about Shaunee Hughes's disappearance. Podcasting was something I'd always fancied trying, ever since I'd listened to the first season of *Serial*. My journalism career wasn't going so well – wasn't going at all, actually – so I used the little savings I had to buy the best recording equipment I could afford, nothing fancy, then, next day, handed in my notice at my PA job. Two weeks later, I'd packed some clothes, hired a car, driven all the way to Murdoch – on little more than a whim, Travis kept reminding me, with a look that said he thought I'd be back in New York by the end of the week, tail between my legs – and checked myself into a motel.

After two days on the road, having arrived late at night and exhausted, my motel room door closed behind me and I stared at my temporary home, wondering what on earth I'd done. Though I could barely remember Murdoch, I'd naively assumed that when I got there, the memories would come flooding back. They didn't. I felt no connection to this strange little town, no sense of nostalgia as I drove past the local football field or elementary school; had no recollection of the gas station I filled up at; felt no bond with the

Murdoch-born-and-raised waitress who served me at the diner I stopped at for a late supper.

In short, as I lay on my motel bed with its shades of brown linen, surrounded by furniture that made me feel like I'd been transported back to the seventies, right down to the rotary dial telephone, I realised I had no 'in', no link to Murdoch other than four pre-school years I couldn't remember, no contacts I could hit up, no long-lost connections to rekindle. All I had was my instinct, an interest in the case and my determination, the latter admittedly driven mostly by a desire to prove Travis wrong.

So, after feeling sorry for myself and more than a little homesick, I grabbed the pad of motel-headed notepaper beside the phone and made a list of all the people in Murdoch connected to Shaunee Hughes I thought I should speak to. I didn't have high hopes, but over the next few days, the list grew, and as it did, I discovered that Murdoch residents fell into two camps: those who were willing to talk, and those who weren't. The important thing was, though, enough people *were* willing to talk, including cops who'd worked Shaunee's case at the time – many now retired, all still haunted by it – as well as some who'd come after, cold-case detectives.

I guess it was like a snowball effect, or maybe a self-fulfilling prophecy, but the more people I talked to, the more people seemed willing to talk. Starting with those closest to Shaunee, I worked my way outwards, interviewing family, friends, witnesses – even suspects. People were surprisingly open; organisations incredibly generous. I spent hours in freezing-cold archives; disorganised police evidence rooms; sweltering small-town courthouse basements. I dug through boxes of material, read and reread hours of hard-to-decipher notes and transcripts. I pored over the evidence piece by piece, worked out timelines. I double-checked tip-line information, ran down leads, tracked down tipsters. I worked all day, barely slept at night. I hardly ate, lost weight. My hair started to fall out. But my perseverance and patience paid off: in early summer, I released my first hour-long podcast episode, and slowly but surely, new leads began to trickle in.

By fall 2015, Murdoch had the answer it had sought for over twenty years. Shaunee's body was recovered. Her killer was not, as many townsfolk had hoped, a stranger, but had lived right under their noses all these years. Evil had a name: Larry Polk, the father of Shaunee's best friend, Kara. Before my arrival in Murdoch, he hadn't even been a suspect. Irony was, it was Larry who, on hearing of *Dark Corners*, had approached me, keen to talk; Larry who'd inserted himself into the investigation, willing to do anything he could to help.

In the end, it was a simple conversation that did it, inconsistencies in his story that at first I put down to the passage of time. But there were other signs, too. He imparted information he wanted to impart; answered questions I didn't ask; avoided those I did. Larry's story, and with it Larry, began to unravel, and when, ultimately, he got wind that police were issuing a search warrant for his home, he'd panicked, returned to Shaunee's burial site to dispose of trophies he'd kept all those years – a friendship bracelet his daughter had made for her; some items of her clothing. He led the police straight to her.

People lauded me for cracking the case, but in all honesty, I felt like a fraud. All I'd done was shake some trees, shine a light in dark corners. The Hughes family were grateful, but for them it was far from over. The prospect of a trial hung over them: Larry Polk would plead innocent.

As news of the podcast and Shaunee Hughes's story spread, so too did media coverage, which until then had been fairly local. Now it was national. International.

Though these days the initial buzz surrounding the case had

somewhat died down, there were still periodic updates. I sat a little more upright in bed, got comfortable against my pillows and clicked the link on the most recent online news article: *MURDOCH CASE DELAYED AGAIN AS POLK DEFENSE SEEKS TO RELOCATE TRIAL.*

My heart ached for Shaunee's family. I was still in touch with Mr and Mrs Hughes and Shaunee's two older brothers, both now married with children not dissimilar in age to Shaunee when she disappeared. Mrs Hughes, Patti, had recently been diagnosed with a particularly aggressive form of cancer. It was doubtful whether she'd live to see the man accused of abducting and murdering her ten-year-old daughter make it to trial. But ever gracious and pragmatic, she was remarkably philosophical about the whole thing.

'At least now I know what happened to her,' she told me in one of our off-the-record chats at her kitchen table, her hand on mine. 'At least I can stop wondering.' She'd been able to lay her daughter to rest, she told me. Soon, she'd join her. She'd have hated to die without knowing.

I scrolled through the article until I reached the end and hit the comments section, but against my better judgement, I kept going. There were all the usual suspects – *Burn in hell!*; *Bring back the death penalty in Wisconsin!!!*; *My heart goes out to Shaunee's family*; *#prayforshauneehughes* – but as the words whizzed by, I thought I saw a name I recognised, not Shaunee's, or one of her brothers', or Patti's, or any of the Hughes family's. Not even mine. I slowed down, scrolled back up to double-check, and there it was in black and white: *Garrett.*

But why would Garrett's name pop up in the comments section of an article on Shaunee Hughes?

Garrett. My two-years-younger baby brother.

Fun Garrett.

Garrett, who was always up for a laugh, could drink his friends under the table, skied all winter like a pro, golfed all summer equally well.

Garrett, who collected friends like some people collect baseball cards or Pez dispensers; who always had a good-looking girl on his arm. Any girl he wanted.

Garrett, who'd dropped out of college so many times I'd lost count; who'd never held down a job because he couldn't stick at anything.

Garrett, who'd show you the best night out but make you pay for it.

Garrett. Whom we all knew had a dark side.

Yes, that was my brother.

And that was why the post made my heart sink, made another name pop unbidden into my head: *Paige*.

I thought back to that night at the start of the year, the night I was still trying to get to the bottom of months later while also trying so hard to forget it. The night that blew a hole in everything, as surely as if Garrett had taken a hand grenade, pulled the pin and lobbed it into the centre of my life.

That was where it had all started, for although I'd always known what my brother was like, that night had made me wonder what he was truly capable of.

I stared at the comment at the bottom of the article.

Anon87: Hey, anyone else heard the rumor about that missing girl? The one from Heartsick CO? That Steppy Corner's bro Garrett is somehow involved?

3

Now

After Dad tells me Mum's dead, I vomit – a shock reflex, I think – pure liquid, thanks to a two-day-empty stomach. I turn my head just in time, despite the pain it causes, manage to aim over the side of my hospital bed. Though I don't know where I am, or why I'm here, I've a horrible feeling that somehow I'm responsible for Mum's death. Something about an accident.

Dad rushes to my side with one of those kidney-shaped cardboard dishes, thrusting it at me seconds too late, but I take it from him anyway, hold it feebly beneath my chin before collapsing back onto my pillows, white and shaking, head bursting, acid burning the back of my throat. He leaves the room to fetch a nurse, but all I want is Mum, even though we aren't – *weren't* – close. I start to cry, think of Paige, wonder if anyone's called her. Paige will know what to do. Paige, who was at my bedside when I woke in hospital after surgery for appendicitis when I was a student; Paige, who, with Travis out of town, met me in the emergency room at three in the morning after I was mugged on the subway. Paige, who held my hair as I vomited into the toilet bowl for two solid hours after I got food poisoning at a clam bake. Paige, who drove all the way from the south of England to collect me in Scotland after my rust bucket of a car broke down.

She's probably on her way right now, scrambled to book the first available flight. Or maybe she's borrowed a car, is speeding cross-country, driving through the night just to get here.

Then I remember we haven't spoken in months, and I cry even harder.

After a nurse has cleaned up, helped me into a fresh hospital gown and changed my sheets, Dad comes back in, tells me something about a home invasion gone wrong. Mum was home alone. Someone broke in and killed her. Still numb, I barely say a word.

'Does Garrett know?' I ask when he's finished. I'm trying to remember if I've seen my brother since I've been here.

But Dad avoids the question. 'The police. They want to speak with you. I'll try to put them off, but, well, once they know you're awake . . .'

'Why do the police want to talk to me?' I can't remember anything – don't *know* anything.

'Sweetie,' Dad says softly. 'The night of your accident.'

I rack my brain. *What accident? How long have I been here? A few days? A week?*

'It was the same night Mum was killed,' he goes on. 'You were on your way to the house when your car went off the road.'

I open my mouth to say something, but there's a knock at the door and another nurse pops her head around.

'Dr Corner,' she addresses my dad, 'I'm sorry, but the police are here. Is now a good time?'

'I already told them.' Dad sighs, irritated. 'She's too confused. They'll have to wait.'

The nurse nods, about to close the door, but I call, 'Wait.' She stops. I look at Dad. 'Let's just get it over with.'

Dad wants to stay while the police talk to me, but I insist I'm fine. After a visit from the doctor – I get the feeling from the way he speaks to me that we've met before – he and Dad leave the room, and two strangers in suits enter, a woman and a man. I barely glance at either; it hurts too much. Instead, I close my eyes, repeat in my head, *I've been in an accident*, over and over and over, like a child prepping for a test.

'Hey, Steppy,' says a voice.

I open my eyes, see a woman by my bed. She's short, has grey everything: hair, pant suit, pallor . . .

'I'm Detective Krauseneck,' she tells me. *So she's a detective.* 'How're you feeling?'

'Like I've been hit by a Mack truck.'

I'm not meaning to be funny, but she gives a small smile, nods like she understands what it feels like to be hit by a Mack truck, then takes the chair Dad was sitting in, drags it across the floor to my bedside with a noise that makes my head ring.

'So.' She sits, takes out a notebook, and I wonder if she's a cop. 'I'm sorry about your mom,' she says. 'Your dad's told you. About what happened to her.'

I can't decide whether it's a statement or a question, though I answer reflexively, 'I've been in an accident,' know as soon as I say it, from the expression on her face, it's not what she's looking for.

She shifts in her seat, says, '*Oh-kay*,' draws the word out, and I wonder what she's doing here – this is a hospital, after all – wonder if *she's* been in an accident too. 'How about we start with that evening.'

I get the feeling this *is* a question, that *that evening* is supposed to mean something to me, but the woman's already on to the next thing.

'. . . the twenty-seventh,' she's saying.

I nod like I know what she's on about, but I don't even know what month we're in, never mind what day. Then I hear a voice in my head: *You came home for Thanksgiving a few days ago.* Who said that? Dad?

'Can you run us through what happened that evening, Ms Corner?' the woman asks. 'From the time you left?'

'Left where?'

'Your cabin.'

I look blankly at her.

'You've been staying in Heartsick,' she explains. 'Rented a cabin. You arrived' – she consults a notepad – 'six days ago.'

I'm trying to concentrate on what she's saying, but I've just noticed her fingernails – they're bitten right down – and now they're all I can focus on. 'I'm sorry?' I ask, embarrassed.

The woman glances over her shoulder, and I notice, for the first time, that there's someone else in the room. A man, standing by the door. He's younger than his female counterpart, taller, too.

'I was saying,' she says, and I think how exasperated she looks, wonder what's rattled her cage, 'that you gotta rental place outside town. Nice little cabin, edge of the forest. You don't remember?'

I furrow my brow, try to squeeze a memory from it like the last drops of juice from an orange, give a feeble shrug. *Sorry.*

'And the accident?' She sounds like someone not holding out much hope.

'I was in an accident,' I agree.

'Okay . . .' The woman jots something down in a notepad I've only just noticed, turns towards the door. 'Anything you'd like to ask, Detective Luck?'

I look up, head pounding, see a man by the door. For a split second

I think it's the grim reaper, but then he steps forward, our eyes meet and I see a face I recognise.

'Lucky?' I ask. 'That you?'

Nathaniel Luck raises a hand, a small half-wave, clears his throat. 'Hey, Steppy.'

It's funny: I don't wonder what Lucky's doing here so much as how he and this strange woman at my bedside know each other. 'My brother and Lucky went to high school together,' I explain to the grey woman. 'It must be . . . God, I don't know' – I turn to Lucky – 'how long since we've seen each other? Years.'

He gives me a weird look. 'What's the last thing you *do* remember, Steppy?'

'Being home in New York?'

He exhales. 'Okay,' he says. 'How about we do this a little different. How about I tell you what we know, see if it jogs your memory some? Then, if you remember anything – *anything* – you just butt in, 'kay?'

I shrug. 'Okay.'

'Sunday morning, twenty-seventh, day of the accident,' he begins, 'you paid a visit to Heartsick PD.' He stops, takes out a notebook, flicks through a few pages, which seems weird. Why would Lucky be carrying a notebook? 'We know from your cell phone data,' he goes on, 'that afterward you returned to your rental cabin. Garrett stops by at some point in the afternoon . . .'

'He does?'

'. . . doesn't stay long,' Lucky continues, 'then you're there the rest of the day, till eight forty-one p.m., when you get a call from him.'

He pauses and I stare at him. I'm still stuck on Garrett stopping by. The last time I spent any time with my brother was . . . when? The start of the year? He came to stay with me and Travis in New York, and I swore never again.

'But see, here's the thing.' It's the woman at my bedside again. 'As well as knowing *when* exactly Garrett made that call to you, we also know *where* he was when he made it – his cell phone was pinging the tower nearest your parents' place.' She stops dead, like she's waiting for the penny to drop. When it doesn't, she says, 'We know your mom was killed sometime between eight and eight forty that evening.'

Mum's dead. My lip begins to quiver. I bite the inside of my cheek until I taste blood. 'How . . . how do you know the time she . . . she died?'

'Your mom was on the phone to a friend' – the woman has a notepad in her lap, flicks through it till she finds what she's looking for – 'a Deb Franklin?'

Not a friend, I think, Mum's literary agent. But okay.

'Ms Franklin called her at seven thirty-five that evening, and they spoke till just before eight. Garrett arrives at the house sometime after that, and right before he calls you, he places a call to 911 at exactly' – she consults her notepad again – 'eight thirty-nine.'

'Garrett was there?' I ask, horrified. 'Is he okay?'

The woman shoots Lucky a look I can't read. I reckon they know each other. 'See,' she says slowly, 'we know what time Garrett made these calls and where he was when he made them. What we don't know is *why* he called you. What he said to you. Do you remember?'

'No.' I shake my head, and it feels like it might split in two. Garrett texts me once in a blue moon, but he rarely calls me. We're not that close.

'Call lasted less than a minute,' Lucky says, like that might explain it. 'Right after that, your phone powers off.'

'Garrett calls me, then my phone powers off,' I repeat.

'Any idea why that would be?' the woman at my bedside asks. I think she might be a cop.

'Why what would be?'

'Your phone. Why it went off. After he called you.'

'My battery died?' I hazard. Standard Steppy, letting her phone die. This I do know. It's kind of comforting.

The woman writes something down – she's got a notepad, I notice – nods to herself. 'Okay, well, whatever your brother *did* say to you in that call, seems it was enough to make you leave the cabin then and there, jump in your car, head up the mountain pretty fast.'

'Your car went off the road around nine p.m.,' Lucky adds.

I was driving? I can drive, sure, but I don't have a car. Not in New York.

'So,' the woman interrupts my thoughts, 'here's what we're thinking. Your brother calls you, panicked, says he's up at the house – your parents' place – Mom's dead.' Her bluntness makes me flinch. 'He hangs up, or you hang up, get cut off – whatever – and you don't know what to do. Maybe you go to call your brother back, find you can't – battery's dead – panic, because whatever he said to you in that call . . .'

She's speaking so fast I can barely keep up, let alone take in what she's saying.

'Steppy,' a voice says.

I look up. *Lucky?*

'Whatever Garrett said to you,' Lucky's saying, and I wonder if he's an apparition; wonder, if not, why he's here, 'made you leave in a hurry, head straight for your parents'. We think that phone call may hold the key to what happened that night.'

'Guess you can see why we're so keen to know what he said,' says the woman at my bedside, and I wonder if she's a detective. She's certainly acting like one.

'You really don't remember?' Lucky asks, not accusingly.

'No,' I tell him. I squeeze my eyes tight shut – *Don't-die-don't-die-don't-die* – open them again. 'Can't you just ask Garrett?'

'That's just it,' Lucky says. 'We can't. No one knows where he is.'

'Any ideas?' the woman asks.

I almost laugh – why would I know where Garrett is? – feel a sense of déjà vu, rack my brain, trying to remember when I last saw him – New York? – for some reason think of Paige . . .

'Steppy,' a voice says. I look up, am surprised to see Lucky, wonder what he's doing here. 'You okay?'

'I've been in an accident,' I tell him.

'You have,' he says gently. 'Do you remember we were talking about Garrett?'

There's a woman at my bedside and I wonder how long she's been there. She opens her mouth, like she's about to butt in, but Lucky puts a hand on her shoulder – I think he knows her. 'When Garrett dialled 911,' he says, 'he didn't actually wait for the call to be answered.' He removes his hand from the woman's shoulder and she slips something from her pocket – looks like a recording device – lays it on the edge of the bed.

'Most people,' she says, 'know that 911 calls are recorded.'

I do know this, so I nod more vigorously than my body will allow.

'Thing is,' she goes on, 'what most people *don't* know is that soon as you even dial 911, moment it starts ringing – before the operator picks up – call starts recording.' She lets her words hang. 'Anything the caller says during that time – *anything* – long as they're on the line . . .' she gives me a long, hard stare, 'well, it's recorded.'

She reaches out, presses play, and I hold my breath. It feels like the woman and Lucky do too.

There's the familiar tone of a call ringing, then, a split second later, a voice, equally familiar. 'What've you done? Shit-shit-shit.' Garrett. My blood runs cold. There's a rustling sound, a clunking, like the handset's been put down – not hung up, but placed to one side. Then

Garrett's voice again, more muffled but still audible. 'They're coming for you now, buddy, oh yeah. *Fuck!* What did you do? What did you fuckin' do?' More rustling. Scraping. The jangle of keys, like they're being scooped up from a counter top. The line goes dead.

I'm not sure what I've just heard.

'Steppy,' Lucky says gently, looks at me with such sympathy I feel it like a physical pain. 'No one's seen Garrett since that night. Not since the night of your accident. Not since your mom was killed.'

'I don't understand,' is all I can say.

Around me, my world shrinks to the size of a pinhole.

Lucky hesitates just long enough, and the woman at my bedside seizes her chance. 'There's a warrant out for Garrett's arrest,' she says. 'Your brother's the prime suspect in your mom's murder.'

4

Then

Welcome to Heartsick! screamed the sign at town limits. *Small-town heart, big-town amenities!*

My stomach dropped as I passed it. Today, November 23, 2016, was the day before Thanksgiving. For the first time in almost a decade, I'd be spending it with my family.

'You're what?' Mum had said when I'd phoned to say I was coming. 'Thanksgiving?' She sounded as happy about it as I was. 'Why?'

'I'm not allowed to spend time with my family?' My tone was indignant, my indignation genuine. I'd managed to convince myself my decision to go home for Thanksgiving had nothing to do with Casey Carter. I was most certainly not returning to Heartsick to investigate her disappearance. Rather, I was going home for some respite after a busy, somewhat traumatic year, because I needed a break from the frenetic pace of city life and a technology detox (though I had, of course, brought my cell phone and laptop).

'Of course you are, Stephanie,' Mum had replied. 'I just wish you'd given us more notice, that's all. Garrett's around' – she said it like the two of us being home together was mutually exclusive – 'and, well . . .' she paused, lowered her voice, 'your brother's been through a hard time these last few weeks.'

She didn't elaborate and I didn't ask, just let the silence hang – something I learned doing *Dark Corners* – hoped Mum would bite, say something like *There's a missing girl. People think Garrett has something to do with it.* But Mum was smart, had played me at my own game, and in the end, I'd caved. 'Well, you don't have to worry about hosting me. I've booked a cabin.'

Dad was already at his weekday home in the city when I phoned him Sunday evening, hot on the heels of my call to Mum. 'You're driving?' he'd asked, his usual laid-back self. 'Why not fly? I'll pick you up. You can hire a car once you get here.'

Flying would have been the smarter, quicker option, but the mere thought of being cooped up with screaming infants, excited families returning home for Thanksgiving and college kids and ski bunnies headed out for the first fall of snow made my head ring. I made a noise that implied I'd consider it, but I'd already decided. Having read about Casey Carter late Saturday, by Monday morning I'd hired a car and hit the road. Driving would be better, I told myself, give me the chance to clear my head, process everything I'd learned over the weekend. Part of me also hoped that by the time I reached Heartsick, Casey Carter would have turned up. Alive, preferably. So although it seemed a long shot – by this point she'd been missing twenty-one days; I hardly needed reminding of the stats – I decided to drive the sixteen-hundred-something miles.

Heartsick. The name was neither as dire as it sounded, nor as romantic. A corruption of Hartsick, itself a corruption of Hartsock, the town was named after its nineteenth-century founder, Herbert Hartsick. Whatever the story behind the name, though, it was the gift that kept on giving for headline writers, who until recently had been mostly positive: *Heartsick, A Hidden Gem*; *The Rockies' Best-Kept Secret*; *The Ski Destination For People Who Don't Do Ski Destinations.*

Visit Heartsick, they all cried, *the beating heart of the Rockies!*

But over the last couple of weeks, the headlines had begun to change, grown darker and more sensationalist: *HEARTACHE IN HEARTSICK*; *SMALL TOWN AT HEART(SICK) OF TRUE CRIME MYSTERY*; and *WOMAN'S DISAPPEARANCE GIVES HEARTSICK HEADACHE.*

I'd come across such headlines myself when I'd googled Casey Carter after finding the comment mentioning my brother, and his alleged – rather tenuous, I thought – link to her. By then, Casey had already been missing over two weeks, last seen late on the night of October 31 – or possibly the early hours of November 1 – supposedly in Garrett's company. I wasn't sure what I expected to find online, but the photos that greeted me made my stomach drop more than the *Welcome to Heartsick!* sign, made me wish I hadn't googled Casey Carter at all. You see, beautiful Casey Carter, with her long dark hair and big brown eyes, was exactly my brother's type.

Aged twenty-two, the papers said, she worked two waitressing jobs, one in town, the other a short drive up the mountain at a local ski resort; had only lived in Heartsick a little over a year, moved there the end of last summer from, of all places, sunny Florida. The most recent photos, the ones that came top in Google Images, were a mix of those presumably released to the press by her family and ones from Casey's social media. One of them, the photo most of the news articles ran with, was a selfie showing her in costume, one half of her face painted with a colourful Day of the Dead skeleton design, a crown of red and white fabric roses atop long, glossy brown hair, which tumbled in waves over her shoulders. Her non-cell-phone-holding hand showed a glimpse of matching red and white nails. Round her neck she wore one of those friendship necklaces that transported me back to the nineties and my school days in the UK: a half-heart pendant, jagged along one edge so as to look broken, on a silver chain. One of the many incarnations of the photo, the only one apparently uncropped, revealed that it had been taken in a bathroom mirror with another girl around Casey's age, a similar but less good-looking version of her. Dressed in identical costumes, heads tilted towards each other, the girls beamed at the camera, no hint of what was to come.

The *Heartsick Enquirer* had covered Casey's disappearance since the start.

Efforts to find Missing Heartsick Resident
Enter Second Week

Mystery continues to surround the whereabouts of twenty-two-year-old Heartsick resident Casey Carter. At a press conference held by local law enforcement, Ms Carter's mother, Loreen Skinner, who flew in from Florida after learning of her daughter's disappearance, appealed to anyone with information to come forward.

'I knew straight away something was up,' she said. 'That first day Casey didn't return my calls. It was so unlike her. We speak every day. If someone out there has her, or knows where she is – knows anything at all – I'm begging you, come forward.'

Local police say they aren't ruling anything out at this stage, and are currently investigating a number of leads, but they're also facing difficult questions surrounding their response to initial reports of Casey's disappearance. When asked about the length of time that elapsed before a missing persons report was filed, Heartsick PD spokesperson Officer Lester Melville said it was 'regrettable, though not uncommon in this type of case'. Officer Melville has stressed that such criticism is unhelpful, as it diverts public and media focus away from the important task of finding Casey.

The last known sighting of Casey Carter was just before midnight on October 31, when she left a Halloween party at Buddy's Bar, a popular local hangout. It's understood that Heartsick PD were called to do a welfare check at Carter's residence around lunchtime, November 1, but an official missing persons report wasn't made until two days later.

Police are particularly interested in speaking with Buddy's patrons from the night of October 31, or anyone with information on Casey's car.

'Tracking down Halloween partygoers, most of whom were in costume, is no mean feat,' Officer Melville said. 'We're asking anyone present at Buddy's that night who hasn't already come forward to do so, whether they remember seeing Casey or not.'

Officer Melville went on to confirm local rumor that Casey's car is missing. 'Casey got a ride to the bar that night with friends. Her own car, a 2011 dark grey Toyota Camry, last seen parked outside her condo on the night of October 31, is also missing, so we're appealing for information on that.'

Regarding internet-based interest surrounding the case, he stressed that while locals should remain vigilant, they should 'refrain from becoming involved in speculation which can be both harmful to the investigation and upsetting to Ms Carter's family'.

Anyone with information on the case should call the Heartsick Police Department direct, or the dedicated tip line.

Judging by the article's accompanying comments, it seemed Officer Melville's plea regarding speculation had had little impact on the people it was aimed at.

ross_61: You no whos guilty AF!!! He was the last one seen with her.

Truecrimefan_No1: *ross_61*: Totally agree. Cops are in on it to if u ask me.

ross_61: *Truecrimefan_No1*: Yeah hole thing stinks of a coverup.

Nicole.T: don't think theres a coverup bt wud be helpful if the PD would be more open. Like we all no who there talkin about garrett Corner. If police wud give more info we cud decide 4 ourselves.

I'd skim-read a few more articles – *COME HOME CASEY!*; *A VANISHING IN HEARTSICK*; *HOW ONE WOMAN'S DISAPPEARANCE HAS A WHOLE TOWN ON EDGE* – but there was no new information. As far as I could find, Garrett had been named neither a suspect, person of interest or formal witness, though his name appeared frequently in comments sections; and although consensus among armchair detectives seemed much the same – he'd already been tried and convicted in the court of public opinion – I couldn't help but feel relieved: even if he was the last person seen with her, that was all there appeared to be on him. There was no evidence he'd done Casey harm; nothing, in fact, to say a crime had even been committed.

That first night, the night I found out about Casey, I'd logged into Facebook, searched Garrett's two-thousand-plus Facebook friends, but although he was 'friends' with several Caseys, male and female, and a good few Carters, there was no Casey Carter. Garrett accepted Facebook friend requests like they were going out of style, so it made me question if he even knew Casey, let alone whether the rumours about him being the last person seen with her were true. I looked her up on Facebook too. There were, of course, hundreds of Casey

Carters, but *the* Casey Carter was easy enough to find, as so many people were tagging her in posts. Her profile, however, yielded little of interest aside from a few photos, most of which I'd already seen. Her friend list wasn't visible, she had no relationship status, location or workplaces to show and – although it seemed she'd once been a prolific Facebook user – over the past few months, she'd barely posted anything.

People had posted on her timeline, though – *Where are you Case? Come home soon! Praying for you girl* – and someone had set up a 'Find Casey Carter' page, which already had ten thousand followers, each of its posts gaining more likes and reposts than the last. When I clicked on the name of the page's apparent founder and de facto admin, Brooke Morgenstern, her profile revealed her to be the Casey lookalike in the Halloween selfie. It had been Brooke who'd posted the original photo to her Facebook page on the evening of October 31, captioned it *Besties ready for Halloween!*

At every motel layover, rest stop and roadside diner I broke my journey at, I continued to google Casey Carter. Initially her disappearance hadn't garnered much press attention, but over the last week or so, coverage had snowballed, doubtless thanks in part to social media. Things seemed to reach a critical mass the weekend before I travelled home: what had started as a local story went statewide, then national, reporters dispatched to Heartsick from all over to gauge the feeling of locals, document search efforts and generally keep anxious readers and viewers up to date, even if there was nothing new to report.

On the second day of my journey, somewhere in Illinois, I read that they'd found Casey's car. I'd stopped to stretch my legs and use the rest room, had gone online to check for updates, poring over my tiny phone screen, found the internet abuzz.

Holee shit they found her car!!!!
You guys hear yet?
Where'd they find it anyone no???
Can guess who's prints will be all over it lol
I'll bet Caseys bodies sumwhere nearby

After trawling through the usual illiterate comments and streams of consciousness, I'd managed to find a news clip from a reporter who'd been at the scene earlier that day.

'We're a couple hours' drive from Heartsick,' she was saying – face all earnest, standing on what looked like a gravelly track surrounded by trees. There was no sign of Casey's car, but a little further down, just visible, yellow police tape flapped in the wind – 'on a remote logging road, where police have confirmed that earlier this morning, following a call from a member of the public, they've recovered Casey Carter's car. A number of sources claim it was found by members of Casey's own family, in Heartsick since her disappearance, although police have yet to comment on this. They have said, however, that a thorough search has been conducted with no sign of Casey, and that they'll be making no further comment until they have results of forensic tests carried out on her vehicle. Questions remain, though, on this cold November day, as to why it's taken three weeks to find the missing car, and why, ultimately, it was her family and friends, conducting their own search, who found it.'

At every stop-off on my journey, I also tried phoning Paige, regardless of Travis's warning, but kept getting her voicemail: 'Hey, it's Paige! Leave a message! Or don't!' (I didn't.)

Yet despite being secretly relieved that she didn't pick up or return my calls, I kept on calling, because while my logical self knew it was silly, asked what I was hoping to achieve, what possible link there could be between my ex-best friend and Casey Carter, I knew there *was* a link – Garrett – and that the question nestled at the back of my brain like a tumour was still there: what really happened between Paige and my brother that night in New York?

I finally arrived at my Heartsick rental late Wednesday evening. The cabin was pretty much as small as you could get, a timber A-frame building with an open-plan living/kitchen space and separate bathroom downstairs; a gallery bedroom accessed via a ladder-like staircase in the eaves. Modern, clean, comfortable and chintzy, in the best of ways. I said a silent prayer of gratitude: owing to a combination of Thanksgiving, ski season and an influx of reporters descending on the town, it had been the only option available at such short notice, and only then thanks to a cancellation.

The porch light was on to greet me, as were the lights inside, and it was warm and cosy, even without the wood burner lit. There was a fruit basket in the living room with a note – *Welcome, Steppy! Enjoy your stay!* – and some basic provisions – a loaf of bread, some tea and coffee – on the kitchen counter top.

After carrying my stuff in from the car, I threw my coat onto the couch and flopped down. It'd been a long day's drive. Three long days' drive. I checked my cell phone – just after 8 p.m., no messages – noticed the battery was low, got up reluctantly to find my charger, couldn't – typical Steppy – so made myself a cup of tea instead. While it brewed, I did some light unpacking, failed to locate my charger, had a moment's panic when I couldn't find my sleeping pills either – the ones I'd been trying not to take, though I'd popped one every night since discovering Casey's story. Sleeping pills found and crisis averted, I stood on the porch in the open doorway, hands wrapped round a mug of tea, staring into the darkness. I knew that beyond the driveway – well, the small turning circle at the end of the road leading to the cabin – was the forest, but it was so black I couldn't see further than my rental car, and even that was only a hulking silhouette. Where are you, Casey Carter? I wondered. Are you out there, somewhere, lost?

It had been late when I'd driven through the centre of town to get here, so the view of the Rockies that framed it like a theatre backdrop had been lost in the night. Still, just as I knew that trees lurked beyond the cabin, so too I knew the mountains were out there, bearing down upon the town, hiding its secrets, and as I'd hit Main Street, with its festive decorations and twinkling lights, I'd felt uneasy. Something was lurking beneath the Hallmark Christmas movie facade. At the sides of the road, squeezed between the parked cars, the trucks and family SUVs, satellite vans, the type used in remote TV broadcasts, sticking out like sore thumbs; on every lamp post, stop sign and store window, posters.

I'd come to a halt at a stop light, squinted through my windshield at the nearest. *CASEY CARTER*, it yelled, in bold black letters. *MISSING: HAVE YOU SEEN HER?* Beneath the text was a black and white shot of a smiling Casey, though not the Halloween one so many of the newspapers had run with. I watched the poster whip back and forth in the wind, wondered how long it could go on fighting the elements, how much longer before it would be gone.

Gone like Casey.

Someone in the car behind had honked their horn. Startled, I saw the stop light had turned to green, hit the gas pedal.

5

Now

The following week passes in a haze. I sleep often but feel permanently tired. I struggle to focus or retain information, frequently have a headache. Day and night bleed into one, and I alternate between thinking I'm home in my New York apartment, or a guest at some swanky hotel. In more lucid moments, I remember – *I'm in hospital. There's been an accident. Mum's dead* – though I need reminding at regular intervals, and even then it still doesn't feel quite real.

By day five or six, the heavy fog I've been under since I woke – post-traumatic amnesia, according to the doctors – begins to lift, and after another round of scans – CT and MRI, both of which I apparently had on admission, though I've no memory of them – I'm deemed fit for discharge, though with a whole host of provisos and a big bag of meds.

But although the post-traumatic amnesia's much better, the retrograde amnesia – the gaping black hole in my memory where the days preceding my accident once lived – is a different story. Those memories, I'm told, may never return, which leaves me with a sense of both relief and unease.

Nathaniel Luck, my brother's old high school friend, pays me a visit the day before I'm discharged. I haven't seen him in years. At least that's what I think, what I tell him, my face lighting up in surprise and recognition when he knocks on my hospital room door, pokes his head round and asks, 'Okay to come in?'

Lucky's a cop now (detective, actually, he explains), which apparently I already know: he and his partner, also with him, a Detective Krauseneck – I repeat her name in my head, an attempt to commit it to memory – visited me here a few days ago. I stare at Krauseneck, hoping for some spark of recognition, but draw a blank. All I can focus on is how incongruous she looks next to Lucky, but then this version of Lucky, all grown up in suit and tie, is incongruous too. The Lucky I remember, Garrett's best friend (*ex*-best friend, I remind myself), wears jeans and a baseball cap, works weekends at the video store . . .

'How's this doing?' He taps his head with a pen, and I'm back in the room.

I mirror his gesture, touch my hand to my head, feel my way gingerly along the scar that snakes its way from front to back. I'm only just growing used to it.

Lucky and Krauseneck exchange glances, and something about it tugs a thread in my memory.

'You seem better,' he says, and I wonder, better compared to what? 'You were still pretty out of it when we saw you a few days ago.'

He recaps what he and Krauseneck apparently told me when they were last here, and we quickly establish I not only have no memory of that, but still no memory of the days preceding my accident either. Before they leave, Lucky swabs my mouth for DNA (elimination purposes, he says – apparently I was at my parents' for Thanksgiving dinner three days before everything went down) and gives me his card.

'If anything comes back to you – anything – or you hear from

Garrett' – why on earth would *I* hear from Garrett? I wonder – 'here's my number.'

Detective Krauseneck looks on impassively.

I'm discharged from hospital the following day, though it feels more like a release from prison. I step blinking into the daylight as if I've done a seven-year stretch, not nine days in bed in a room with a picture window and wall-mounted TV.

'It's not too late to change your mind,' Dad says as he helps me into his car. 'Stay here with me.'

For a moment, I swither. New York's off the table, doctor's orders – too far to travel. Staying here, at Dad's Colorado Springs apartment, would be the sensible option, and close enough to Heartsick to be acceptable to the cops. Though Lucky and Krauseneck didn't say so explicitly, I got the strong impression I should stick around.

But for the past few days, as I've lain in my hospital bed, information finally starting to stick, the one question among many I keep coming back to is what on earth I was doing in Heartsick in the first place. I ask people, of course, from Dad to the doctors and nurses, even Lucky and Krauseneck, but they all tell me the same thing: 'You came home for Thanksgiving.'

But I know me and that doesn't sound right. I mean, technically, yes, I apparently was in Heartsick for Thanksgiving, and technically, yes, maybe that's what I told people. But now I know for sure my suspicions were right: that Thanksgiving was merely an excuse, I had an ulterior motive. And now I know too what that ulterior motive was. Because before Lucky and Krauseneck left yesterday, they warned me not to watch TV. Silly, really – like telling me not to think of a pink elephant – because having had no urge to watch television these past few days, it suddenly became all I could think about.

I switched the TV on, began scrolling idly through channels, recoiled as an image flashed up in front of me, filling the screen: my parents' house. In front of it, a coiffed reporter, cold but determined-looking, mic between gloved hands, snow falling around her.

'. . . That's right, Brad,' she was saying.

I froze, the remote in my hand still pointing at the screen.

Behind the reporter, yellow crime-scene tape flapped in the wind, a flimsy barrier between her and the house.

'It was here, just eight days ago, at this stunning but remote home, that Dr Jayne Corner was brutally slain. The body of the *New York Times* bestselling author, known in her native Scotland as the Morningside Therapist' – she says *Scotland* and *Morningside* slowly and with emphasis, like she's speaking a foreign language – 'was found by police, who were at the property to conduct a welfare check following a 911 call . . .'

Slain. Brutally. The words echoed in my head. I thought back, tried to remember if Lucky and Krauseneck had told me how Mum died. If they had, I'm sure I'd remember, so I don't think they did, and for some reason I hadn't asked. Maybe I'd been too afraid to.

The reporter was still speaking. She touched a hand to her ear, leaned into the camera against the snow. 'That's right, Brad,' she went on (Brad was presumably the news anchor, out of shot in the comfort of the studio). 'We understand she was home alone, her husband, Dr Reid Corner, having returned to the city Sunday afternoon, before events at the property, which sources close to police describe as *bloody*' – I flinched at the word – 'unfolded. But whilst police *are* remaining tight-lipped about how exactly Dr Jayne Corner died, we can reveal that in a shocking twist, the victim's daughter, Stephanie Corner' – my photo flashed up on screen – 'was involved in a horrific automobile accident, apparently while rushing to the scene. Ms

Corner – Steppy, as some viewers may know her – is an investigative journalist and host of the most successful true crime podcast of the past couple years, *All the Dark Corners*. Though these days it's thought she lives in New York, word locally is that she's been in town investigating another case . . .'

Huh? My ears pricked up. She must have it all wrong. There's close to home and then there's too close.

'. . . that of missing local woman, Florida native Casey Carter.'

Who the . . .? I just had time to wonder, before the picture cut to a brightly lit studio, so bright it hurt my eyes, and a news anchor, presumably Brad.

'We understand, Dana,' he said, all tan, teeth and hair, 'that in yet another shocking twist, police have named Ms Corner's brother, Garrett Corner, the son of the victim, as a person of interest in his mother's murder.'

Just like Lucky and Detective Krauseneck said. A photo of my brother flicked up on screen. My stomach flipped.

The camera cut back to Dana, still outside my parents' house. 'That's right, Brad,' she said, hand to ear. 'But that's not all. In a truly tangled story – one worthy of its own true crime podcast – we can reveal exclusively that Garrett Corner is also the local man at the heart of weeks of speculation that says he's somehow involved in Casey Carter's disappearance – the same case his own sister's reputedly investigating!'

Another photo flashed up on screen. This time a beautiful young brunette, dressed in Halloween costume, half her face painted in a colourful skeleton design, a crown of roses adorning her flowing tresses. As I stared into her brown eyes, something in the deepest, darkest corner of my memory stirred.

But before I could reach in there, pluck it out, the image cut abruptly to the studio, and Brad again. 'So it's fair to say, Dana, that police must be keen to speak with Garrett Corner?'

'Correct, Brad. As of right now, though, it seems that Mr Corner's whereabouts are unknown, and while police remain tight-lipped about many details – are refusing even to say if they believe Dr Corner's murder and Casey Carter's disappearance are linked – a warrant *has* been issued for his arrest. But whether or not you believe he's the prime suspect, one thing's for sure: police in Heartsick are hoping that twenty-five years from now, they don't find themselves the subject of a true crime podcast about not one, but *two* unsolved cases.'

'I'm sure, Dana, I'm sure . . .'

Shaking, I pressed the remote to shut off the TV. It had been bad enough to learn that police suspected Garrett was guilty of killing Mum. When Lucky and Krauseneck had told me, apparently for the second time, I hadn't quite believed it – hadn't wanted to. But that my brother was linked to some missing girl, that I'd come home to investigate, that I couldn't remember any of it?

'Steppy?' Dad's looking at me, concerned. 'I said it's not too late to change your mind.'

I nod like he's right, yet I know that it *is* too late, that I have to return to Heartsick. To finish what I started. Whatever that is.

Although snow threatens the further we drive from the city, the first flake has yet to fall.

We spend the journey studiously avoiding the topic of Mum or Garrett, and we certainly don't discuss the missing girl (Dad doesn't even know I know about her). When we break the journey at a roadside diner, we both order food, though neither of us eats, and as we nurse our coffees, staring out the window at the highway, Dad clears his throat, slides something across the table to me.

'I've been making funeral arrangements,' he says. 'Thought maybe you'd like to help.'

It sounds dumb, but my first thought is: *Funeral?* It's not like I've forgotten Mum's dead, but I still can't get my head around it. A funeral sounds so final.

I look down, am slightly horrified to see before me a brochure of urns: *The Memorial Collection*, the glossy front cover reads. To humour him, I begin to flick through, stop on a page with a wooden urn, its surface adorned with intricately carved owls.

'What about this one?' I say, spinning the brochure around. 'Mum loves – loved – owls.'

'No,' is all Dad says. 'No owls.'

The roads are slick, and by the time we reach Heartsick, daylight is fading, the town's mountain backdrop reduced to ominous black shapes in the gloom. It's that in-between, twilight time, shops closing for the day, restaurants and bars beginning to stir, but there's something different about the place I can't quite put my finger on. A sadness, perhaps. I try to recall the last time I was here – a couple years ago at least – before reminding myself that according to what everyone says, I was here a few days ago, though all I can conjure when I think back is a yawning black hole.

As we drive down Main Street, street lamps glowing to life and festive lights twinkling, we slow to a halt at a stop light. I catch sight of a poster whipping to and fro in the wind, just have time to glimpse a black and white image of a girl – young woman, really – remember the TV news report, the photo flashing up on screen, the beautiful young woman with brown hair and eyes.

'Is that . . .?' I begin.

The light turns to green.

Beside me at the wheel, lost in his own thoughts, Dad says, 'Huh, sweetie?'

But it's too late. The moment's gone, we've already set off again, the poster just a tattered old piece of paper in the rear-view mirror.

It turns out Lucky and Krauseneck are right: home while I've been in Heartsick is a small rental cabin outside town, nestled in forest, accessed via a tree-lined dirt track. The tarmacked highway has long since given way, becoming narrower and more pothole-ridden the closer we get. At last it opens into a small clearing revealing a tiny wooden house surrounded on all sides by spruce.

Since I've no memory of even booking it, let alone having set foot inside, the first thing that occurs to me as we pull up, the place in darkness but for the car's headlights, is how isolated it seems. This strikes as me both good and bad, sends a bolt through me like an electric shock, fear and thrill, and I put a hand to my head, wonder with a feeling more of intrigue than anything else if the accident's caused some kind of crossed wires in my brain.

We find the key in a lock box on the porch, the first flakes of snow beginning to fall as Dad carries my stuff inside: an overnight bag he's furnished me with; some groceries we bought en route; an old-style clamshell cell phone into which he's programmed his number.

What happened to my own phone was a mystery to me until yesterday, when Lucky took from his pocket a clear plastic evidence bag. Inside was a barely recognisable lump of melted plastic – all that was left of my phone after the fire that apparently engulfed my car, moments after I was dragged unconscious from it.

'A little memento,' he said gravely, and I swallowed. 'If you hadn't been rescued from that car when you were . . .'

If you hadn't been wearing a seat belt . . .

If the couple driving in the other direction hadn't seen you go off the road . . .

If the branch that pierced the windshield had been any bigger . . .

Of all the refrains I've heard these past few days since information's been sticking, it's the what ifs that stay with me the most.

'You sure you'll be okay?' Dad asks for the hundredth time, and suddenly I doubt myself, wonder how he'd feel, having driven all the way here, if I changed my mind, said, *Actually, Dad, now that you mention it . . .*

But I don't. Instead, I reach up on tiptoe, kiss him on the cheek. 'I'll be fine,' I say, 'honest.'

And even if I can't be sure that's the truth, I know it's the right decision. I have to be here. Besides, although Dad's returning to the city for now, so *some stuff at the house* can be taken care of (I shudder to think what), he's on leave. He'll return to Heartsick soon, to the home he and Mum shared, for her funeral.

I stand in the doorway and watch him go, listen to tyres fading as they crunch their way down the frozen mud track, watch tail lights disappear into trees until they're swallowed by the night. When I can no longer hear the car, I close the door, silence ringing around me, and survey the cabin. It's actually pretty neat. Small but perfectly formed, cosy and traditional yet clean and modern. It's cold and dark, though, so I light the wood burner in the living room, switch on every lamp I can find.

It's not until I'm unpacking my provisions in the kitchen that I feel the draught, find that the source isn't the back door, leading out to a wood pile at the back of the cabin, forest beyond, but one of two little kitchen windows, the bottom halves of which are hung with cutesy gingham curtains. The nearest one twitches slightly, and I draw it back, feel a blast of cold air, find the window's been left open a crack. I close it with a shiver.

The whole of the downstairs is open-plan, so I make myself a cup of tea, check the food situation – some out-of-date milk in the fridge, a stale loaf of bread on the kitchen counter – cross back to the living room with its sofa, coffee table and TV. Next to the TV there's a fruit basket, the contents of which look okay, probably thanks to the cabin's temperature over the last few days. In addition to my overnight bag, which Dad's left by the door, I find a holdall I recognise as mine, filled with my stuff.

There's a pen on the floor and, weirdly, some tiny scraps of paper scattered about, which, when I pick a couple up, turn them over, are blank. Also on the coffee table is a half-drunk mug of something, an oily film covering its surface, along with a USB cable, a TV remote and, thank goodness, my laptop. The battery's dead, so I find my charger and plug it in, and the laptop whirs into action. Pushing the cold mug away, I set my tea down while I wait for the login screen to load, then punch in my password, get a *Password Incorrect* message. Thinking little of it – I probably made a typo – I try again, but get the same message. I try a third time, still no luck, check caps lock – not on – try a fourth, fifth – type slower, one-fingered – sixth, seventh and eighth, but every one's the same: *Password Incorrect*.

I'm certain the password is correct – I've used the same one for years, for all my devices – so I must have changed it. But why? And to what?

My head's splitting. Overwhelmed and frustrated, I slam the laptop shut, close my eyes, push the heels of my palms into them.

Shit-shit-shit-shit-shit . . .

Don't-die-don't-die-don't-die . . .

I exhale, open my eyes, and that's when I notice it, the corner of a scrap of paper poking from beneath my laptop. I pull it out and find a hand-written list of names:

> Evan Coombs
> ~~Brooke Morgenstern~~
> Loreen Skinner
> Rebecca Johnson
> Luke ?

All but one of them, Evan Coombs, is in my writing. The second name, Brooke Morgenstern, has been crossed out. There's an internet router on the sideboard, and I instinctively reach for my laptop again, intending to check my search history, before remembering I can't. I can't get internet on my melted-blob-of-plastic cell phone either, nor on the stand-in Dad's lent me: it's too old.

I have to work with what I've got. I look around again. Place looks like the *Mary Celeste*, which, even without the knowledge I now have about the alleged phone call from Garrett, would suggest I left in a hurry. For a moment I picture myself on the couch – possibly holding the pen I found on the floor, possibly working my way through the list of names – imagine my cell phone ringing, see myself answering, hanging up, leaping from the couch, pen falling to the floor, perhaps along with some of those scraps of paper. I imagine pulling on my sneakers, scooping up my car keys, grabbing my phone . . .

But what did Garrett say in that call? What did he tell me that made me leave in such a rush, head to my parents', drive so fast that I didn't make it?

Frustration threatens to engulf me again. I've always had a good memory – it served me well on *Dark Corners*. That, and an eye for detail, was what ultimately cracked the Shaunee Hughes case. But now, no matter how hard I try, I can't remember.

My head hurts so badly I feel sick, so I take some of the painkillers I've been discharged with, begin unpacking the rest of my things from hospital. Along with a pharmacy bag of rattling meds, the overnight bag contains a wash bag with basic toiletries; some brand-new socks and underwear (which I know Dad's secretary, Betsey, was dispatched to buy); my melted cell phone, still sealed in its clear plastic bag; and another, larger clear plastic bag, this time containing my clothes from *the night of*. What's left of them, anyway. Without taking them out, I recognise my jeans, cashmere hoodie – a treat to myself after the success of *Dark Corners* – and T-shirt. From the looks of it, they're unsalvageable, as not only are they torn, they're covered in mud and something else: dark red splotches. So dark they're almost black. Dried blood, I realise with a shudder. It's alarming how much there is, and it conjures up a sudden intrusive image: blood, my blood, drip-drip-dripping. I remember something Dad said years ago, when we were little and Garrett had split his head open – doing something he shouldn't have, no doubt – and Mum was freaking out: *Head wounds bleed*, he said. *A lot.*

I open the bag, slide my clothes out piece by piece, realise that even if with all the blood and dirt and snags and tears they were somehow salvageable, each garment has been cut down the seams – presumably by the EMTs or at the hospital – leaving ragged raw edges. The dried blood has made the fabric crisp, like old papyrus scrolls that threaten to disintegrate in my hands. I sigh. I loved my cashmere hoodie.

I'm not sure why, but I begin going through the pockets like I would before laundering them, checking for errant tissues, grocery store receipts. The large centre-front pocket of the hoodie is empty, but when I reach my jeans, to my surprise I fish a small scrap of card from the back pocket. No, not a scrap of card but a matchbook, *Buddy's* printed across the front, an ad for a tattoo studio on the back. Since I can't remember anything of the days preceding my accident, it's entirely possible I picked it up along the way, a souvenir – I don't smoke – from some roadside bar or diner I stopped at for a bite to eat. If that was all it was, a plain old matchbook, I'd probably have forgotten all about it, tossed it in the trash. But that's not all it is. When I open it, in addition to twenty unused matches, I find a hand-written string of numbers on the underside of the flap, a drop of dried blood partly obscuring the last two digits so I can't quite make them out.

0327092912150109

I count them, eighteen digits total. But what do they mean? A phone number? Some kind of code?

What puzzles me most about them, though, is the handwriting. I recognise it immediately. But something's different about it here, something that to someone who didn't know mightn't be noticeable. Because while there's no doubt whose the carefully honed cursive script is, it's less neat than usual, has a hint of desperation about it.

Like it's been written in haste.

6

Then

I slept badly that first night at the cabin. The wind had picked up, and though I was snug indoors, the howling and shrieking as it wound its way round the building, threaded through the trees, was unsettling. Then, in the early hours, I was jolted awake by an animal's cries. Tossed around on the wind as they were, it was not only impossible to tell where they came from, but how near or far they were either: one minute they seemed right outside, the next I could barely hear them.

I awoke next morning to a scrabbling at the cabin door. My first thought was that it might be a bear, before I remembered that any self-respecting bears would be hibernating, so, feeling emboldened, I crept downstairs. The wind had died, and as I crossed the living room to the cabin door, I hesitated, listening. The scrabbling stopped. As quietly as I could, I unlocked the door and opened it a crack. The moment I did, something small and furry shot through the gap at my feet. I whirled round, heart hammering, found myself staring down at a cat, which in turn stared up at me. I'd never owned a cat, didn't quite know what to do with one. Growing up, whenever I'd asked for a pet, Mum would reply, 'We're not pet people, Stephanie.' The only time she'd relented was when Garrett asked for one, and she'd let him get a hamster. But within a week, and under mysterious circumstances, the hamster was dead, and not even Garrett could persuade Mum to let him get another.

I crouched down slowly and stretched out a hand, in much the same way you would with a dog. The cat was ginger and white, one of those long-haired types with a fine burst of whiskers, but although it was quite beautiful, when I touched it it felt deathly skinny beneath its thick coat, and its fur was damp and matted, stuck with twigs and leaves. It craned its neck towards me, then, with a suddenness that made me almost topple backwards, began butting its head against my hand, purring loudly.

'Was that you outside last night?' I asked, but it only purred louder, tipped its chin, smiling, eyes squeezed shut. 'I guess you're hungry, huh?'

But what did I have that a cat would eat? Not a fruit basket, for sure.

The few provisions I'd picked up before I hit town yesterday hadn't included cat food, so I rooted through spotlessly clean kitchen cupboards until I found a single can of tuna fish, which I dispensed into a saucer at my feet. The cat polished it off, purring loudly, as I filled a bowl with water, placed that next to the now empty saucer.

After seeing to the cat, I texted the cabin owner – *Quick question: does the cabin have a cat?* – tried calling Paige again – no luck – then frittered the rest of the day away, so that by the time late afternoon rolled round, I was running behind. I only just had time to shower and change, crack open a kitchen window for the cat, before, phone battery low – I still hadn't located my charger – firing off a text to Dad as I rushed out the door, letting him know I was going to be late.

Once I hit the road, I realised I'd forgotten to get a gift, so pulled off the highway at a gas-station-cum-grocery-store, apparently the only place open on Thanksgiving. After surveying the sad offering of bouquets on the forecourt, I grabbed a somewhat past-it bunch of lilies from a plastic bucket, then pushed through the store door, past another Casey Carter poster, this time publicising a vigil.

Inside was deserted but for a down-on-his-luck-looking old guy paying for what appeared to be his weekly shop in small change; another guy behind the counter sporting a drooping seventies-style moustache, a trucker cap and a Grateful Dead T-shirt.

To a soundtrack of Muzak, I scoured the aisles in search of other suitable gifts, quickly ruling out gas station candy, a six-pack of beer or anything – hats, key chains, fridge magnets – on the revolving display stand of Heartsick souvenirs. Lilies it would have to be, I thought, making a quick pit stop at the pet section to grab some cat food and a sack of kitty litter.

'Happy Thanksgiving,' the guy at the counter wished me, eyes on his cell phone.

'Happy Thanksgiving.' I let my armful of cat goodies slide onto the counter, placed the sad lilies next to them.

Close up, the man was younger than he'd first appeared, his retro look belying his age. He was probably early twenties at a push, was covered in tattoos, and had flesh tunnels in his ears the size of cotton bobbins.

'No problem.' He put down his phone, began scanning my groceries, all the while watching me, to the point I was beginning to feel uncomfortable. It was only when he'd finished and I held out my card to pay that he looked at it, said, 'Hey, I thought I knew you from somewhere! It's the voice!'

I smiled. My hybrid accent. Mostly British, but with an American twang that deepened depending on where I was, who I was with, whether I'd had a drink . . .

'You're that podcast girl, right?'

'That's me.' I held up my hands, *guilty as charged*, only thankful it was 'podcast Steppy' he recognised, not 'Garrett's sister Steppy'.

'No way.' He began bagging my purchases. '*All the Dark Corners*.' He shook his head. 'Love that shit!'

I couldn't help but laugh.

'Hey, I couldn't have a selfie? My girlfriend – Ashley? – she's like your number one fan. I'm not even kidding.'

'Sure, why not.' But before I'd even got the words out, he'd scooted round the counter, put his arm round me, snapped a photo of us together, grinning upwards.

Before *Dark Corners*, I don't think I'd ever taken a selfie. Before *Dark Corners*, if a stranger had approached me, asked me for one, I'd have been horrified. These days, although it happened less often over the past few months, I'd grown somewhat used to it.

'Man,' the guy said, looking at his phone, shaking his head, 'Ashley's gonna freakin' die when she sees this. She's the one got me into *Dark Corners*, see. I mean, I'll be honest, when she told me I should listen, I wasn't sure. But man – that first episode? I was totally hooked.' He barely drew breath. 'Ashley said she knew it was that Polk done it from the start.'

I nodded politely. I'd grown used to that too: the number of armchair detectives who claimed retrospectively they'd always known it was Larry Polk.

'Honestly, though?' He lowered his voice. 'I think she just says that to make herself look good. Don't tell her I told you that, though.'

I laughed again, made a zipping motion across my lips.

'Hey.' The guy turned serious all of a sudden. I felt the atmosphere shift. 'You heard about that missing girl? Casey Carter?'

'Hard not to,' I said, trying to keep my expression neutral. 'Big news around here.'

He nodded gravely. 'So big they cancelled the Thanksgiving parade.'

'That right?'

'Yeah. You in town looking into it? Like, for season two?'

'Why?' I asked, before I could stop myself. 'You know something?'

'Nuh-uh,' he said quickly. 'Don't even know Casey. Your brother did, though, right?'

Shit. So he did know I was Garrett's sister. I guess I shouldn't have been surprised: small towns like Heartsick, nothing stays secret for long. 'Not that I know of,' I answered honestly. 'And no, I'm not looking into it.' *Not officially.*

'Oh,' he said, disappointed. 'Well, if you change your mind, you should speak to Evan.'

'Evan?'

'Bartender. At Buddy's. Here . . .' He tore some paper from the PDQ machine, scribbled something on it. 'It's the bar Casey Carter was last seen at. With your brother?' He handed me the paper. 'Not that I'm saying it means anything,' he added quickly. 'But that's why you should speak to Evan, right? See, everyone's looking at your brother–'

Everyone? Really? I turned the paper round in my hand. *Evan Coombs*, the guy had scribbled in boyish writing.

'. . . but, see, Evan,' he went on, 'he dated Ashley's older sister, Tiffany, for a while? That's how I know him? Anyhow, he says it's not your brother cops should be looking at.'

'He did, huh?' I arched an eyebrow. 'So who should they be looking at?'

'Oh, I dunno. Evan's got some story about some girl.'

'Someone Casey Carter knew? Someone with motive?'

The guy shrugged. 'Guess you'd have to speak with Evan.'

I held the paper up – 'I'll speak with Evan' – slipped it into my back pocket, then scooped up my paper shopping bag, hoisted the sack of kitty litter onto my hip.

'Hey! Thanks again for the selfie,' the guy called after me. 'I'm Jesse, by the way.'

I turned, arms full. 'Nice to meet you, Jesse,' I called back, reversing my way through the gas station door. 'Thanks for the tip.'

7

Now

I'm at Mum's funeral. Beside me sits Dad, stoic and silent. Garrett . . . well, Garrett's nowhere to be seen. The officiant is talking, but I don't hear what he's saying because all I can focus on is Mum's coffin, and all I can hear is the scratching noise coming from the underside of the lid, fingernails on wood . . .

For a millisecond when I wake, everything feels normal. Then I remember, *Mum's dead*, and for the first time it really dawns on me: nothing will ever be the same again. I break down, blub like a baby for at least ten minutes.

It's the sound that finally makes me stop. It's not loud – in fact, I think I imagine it at first, think it's some remnant of my dream crossed over into the real world – but when I listen, hear it again, my whole being turns cold: fingernails on wood.

I climb from my bed and pull on a sweatshirt. My body aches from top to toe and I feel like I've slept with my head on a concrete block, though after spending much of the night tossing and turning, unable to find a comfortable position, I'm surprised I slept at all.

I pad cautiously downstairs, only then noticing how quiet it is. The scratching's stopped, the air filled with the sort of thick, all-enveloping silence that comes with a fresh snowfall, pale blue light creeping in from the edges of the blinds, confirming this. Hailing as I do these days from the city, total silence is a rarity I usually welcome. Now, though, it makes me realise how horribly alone I am, amplifies every negative thought I've ever had, every bad decision I've ever made. I wonder what my therapist would make of this, cringe even thinking it. I'm not a therapy type of person, but I've been going quietly, once a fortnight for the past three months, have told Dr Englund it's because of Shaunee Hughes and *Dark Corners*, have told myself this too. But if I'm totally honest, my need for therapy has more to do with Travis and Paige. I've told Dr Englund some of it, of course – bad break-up; ex-boyfriend who resented my success, left me for my best friend – and though I think she suspects there's more to it, she knows better than to push.

I'm at the bottom of the stairs when the sound comes again, brings me back to reality, and for a moment I'm rooted to the spot, bare feet on cold wood. The sound's coming from outside. I tiptoe across the room and open the door. The moment I do, a ginger and white cat, long fur spiky with snow, shoots through the gap. I close the door and turn, find the cat smiling up at me like an old friend.

I exhale with relief. Almost smile. *Claws* – claws scratching on a wooden door, not fingernails on a coffin lid.

'Um, hey,' I say. I'm not used to conversing with cats. Paige would know what to say – she's a cat person – but me . . .

I reach down, touch its ice-cold fur. It must belong to someone, I think, as it has a collar on – a new-looking glittery red one with a funny little silver bell. No ID tag, though. Maybe it's lost, has wandered too far from home, got turned around in the snowstorm.

It begins purring, winds its way round my legs.

'Okay, I'll see what I can find, but I don't have any cat food,' I warn it, heading to the kitchen, stopping dead when, inside the second cupboard I try, I find several cans of cat food and an open bag of kibble. 'Oh.' I hold out some of each. 'Which would you prefer?'

I give it a mix of the two, then go to fill a bowl with water, before finding there's already one on the floor on the far side of kitchen.

'Maybe you come with the cabin?' I wonder aloud.

The cat glances up but doesn't stop eating.

After I feed it, I don't shower – I'm not supposed to get my head wet yet – but I use the bathroom and brush my teeth. I've tried to avoid mirrors since leaving hospital, but now, looking at my reflection in the light of the tiny bathroom, I'm pretty horrified. A nurse helped me dress before I was discharged, showed me my face in a mirror so it wouldn't be too much of a shock later. Still, it is. Almost half my head is shaved, an angry-looking scar running front to back, and I have two black eyes, just starting to turn a garish yellow, matching-coloured bruises at seemingly random points over most of the rest of my body. I look so different from the Steppy I know that it comes almost as a surprise that there are parts of me I still recognise: my tattoos – a full sleeve on my right arm, shoulder to wrist; a twisting vine winding its way down my left, onto the back of my hand – the sprinkling of freckles on my nose, barely noticeable in winter; the little scar above my left collarbone, which, with its ghostly impression of stitches, reminds me of a pond skater; the tiny callus on my lip, the bit I chew subconsciously when I'm thinking, the one you wouldn't even know was there unless you were me. I've never really given much thought to those features that make me unique until this moment. Now, I cling to them like my life depends on it.

Though I'm not hungry, I make breakfast and eat in silence, too afraid to turn on the TV for fear of what I might see. The cat keeps me company, then licks my milky cereal bowl clean, purring gratefully. After that, since I can't access my laptop or get online, I decide there's only one thing for it: I have to venture into town. But I don't have a car. There's a local cab company, but I don't know its name or number, nor do I have internet access to look it up. I dig in my overnight bag, the one I brought from hospital, pull from it the card Lucky pressed into my hand before he left. *DET. NATHANIEL LUCK*, it reads, *HEARTSICK PD*. There's an email address and phone number. I grab my cell phone and dial it.

Lucky's tied up at work till mid afternoon but comes as soon as he can. He arrives wearing a suit like the one he wore at the hospital, a bulky winter coat lying across the passenger seat.

'Let me get that,' he says, grabbing it, stuffing it into the back as I climb in beside him, side-eyeing me as I do. 'You look,' he says brightly, then hesitates. 'Uh, better.'

'You for real?' I arch an eyebrow at him. The car's warm, so I unwind my scarf though keep my coat on. 'I look like shit. And why didn't you tell me about the missing girl, Lucky? I saw it on the news.' I can still see her image flashing up on screen, her dark eyes and pretty smile, the colourful face paint, crown of roses.

'Okay, you got me.' Lucky holds up his hands. 'You look like shit. But I thought I told you not to watch TV.'

'Stop trying to change the subject.'

'I'm not,' he says. 'There's just nothing to tell.' He starts the engine. 'Nothing that has anything to do with your mom – with Garrett – anyhow.' We begin crawling down the snow-covered track. 'That *is* why everyone's saying you were really in town, though – investigating Casey Carter's disappearance.'

'Everyone?'

'Internet, mostly.'

'Great.' *Fucking internet.* I roll my eyes, which hurts, ask, 'So, what's the story?'

'Casey Carter?'

I nod.

'She vanished, Halloween. Or possibly the early hours of November first, or sometime thereafter. No one quite knows. But' – Lucky glances at me, presumably trying to gauge my reaction – 'Garrett was the last person to see her.'

'Last person to *see* her, or last person seen *with* her?' I cringe as I say it. It's the kind of smart-ass distinction Garret would make.

'Last person seen with her,' Lucky clarifies. 'He and Casey left a bar together just before midnight – Buddy's?'

Buddy's. It takes me a second to remember: the matchbook. So Buddy's is a bar. The last place Casey Carter was seen.

'They went back to his place?' I ask. Did my brother even have a place? As long as I've known him, he's tended to flit between our parents' home and couch-surfing at friends'.

'Hers,' Lucky says. 'But he didn't stay, said he dropped her home, drove straight to your folks'.'

'*Said*?'

'Uh-huh.'

'You think he's lying?'

He shakes his head. 'Mighta done initially. But we ruled him out.'

'How?'

He looks at me from the corner of his eye. 'You know we discussed all this the day of your accident? When you came to see me?'

'*That's* what I was doing when you said I'd visited Heartsick PD? I saw you?'

'Yup. And it was your brother's cell phone that ruled him out.'

'Garrett let you have it?'

'Didn't have to. Gave us permission to access his data.'

'Cell tower pings?'

'Initially,' Lucky says. 'But also his Google Location History.'

I nod. That was ultimately how Larry Polk was caught. After his story changed, when I interviewed him for *Dark Corners*, the police got a search warrant for his home. But Larry somehow got wind of it and, late one night, drove thirty miles out of town to dispose of personal items of Shaunee's. Police got a warrant for his cell phone data – something he hadn't had to worry about all those years before – which led them to a remote hunting cabin that had once belonged to his family. Nearby, they found Shaunee's grave, along with the items Larry had buried recently. The cell phone data tracked him all the way, within a few metres.

'Well, luckily for us – and Garrett – his was switched on,' Lucky continues. 'Tracked him like a GPS system from Buddy's to Casey's place, to your parents' – where he spent the rest of that night and most of the next day.'

'Mum and Dad were there?'

'Your dad wasn't – he was in the city – but your mom was home, backed Garrett's story. Apparently she was pretty pissed, him showing up so late.'

That sounds – *sounded* – like Mum. 'So you're certain Garrett has nothing to do with Casey's disappearance?'

'My personal feelings about your brother aside, the evidence against him doesn't stack up. And it's not just the phone data,' he says. 'There's other stuff, too.'

'Like what?'

'The fact his fingerprints were nowhere to be found inside Casey's condo, for one. Then there's her car.'

'What about it?'

'Well,' he sighs, 'I'm limited in what I can say, but I guess this is public knowledge, so . . . Casey got a ride with her friend to the bar on Halloween, left her own car at her condo. But when her friend goes to check on her next morning, it's gone. Still gone when police do a welfare check at her address that same day. Car turned up a couple weeks ago, three weeks after she vanished. Remote logging road outside of town.'

'So either Casey drove it there or someone else did.'

'Right.' Lucky nods. 'But we know Garrett drove Casey home in *his* car, then drove to your parents', so he can't have taken it.'

'Anything else?'

'Only that Casey was in costume for Halloween that night and the headband she was wearing – a flower one? – was found on the table inside the front door, like she'd come home, taken it off. Plus her keys were gone, her wallet . . .'

'So it *looked* like she got home then left again. Do you think it was staged? Someone took her wallet and keys to make you think she left of her own volition?'

'Possibly,' he says. 'We never found the clothes she was wearing that night – they weren't at her condo – and her bed didn't look like it'd been slept in. Yet we've got information suggests she definitely got home and to bed safe that night.'

'Information?'

'Look,' he says, 'I've already said more than I should. We've an independent witness, that's all, but we've not gone public with what they told us yet. More than that I can't say.'

An independent witness who knows Casey got home and to bed? What Lucky's telling me is as frustrating as it is mysterious, but I don't want to push, so I change tack. 'So if I was here in Heartsick investigating Casey's disappearance, had I found anything out?'

'No idea.' Lucky laughs. 'When we met, you were the one trying to get information outta me.'

'Are there other theories about her disappearance? Like, could she have left town without telling anyone, done a *Gone Girl*? And suspects. The internet and its theories about my brother aside, are there any?'

'Whoa there.' Lucky pulls his head back. 'One question at a time. So, the leaving town thing. I *guess* she could've done that. I mean, she'd lived in Heartsick less than a year, didn't have many ties, so it's certainly possible, 'specially since someone – maybe Casey herself – took her car.'

'But it was found abandoned,' I point out. 'If Casey had been planning to leave, she'd need it. Why dump it?'

'True, but who knows what frame of mind she was in? I mean, if, to use your words, she was pulling a *Gone Girl*, staging her own disappearance, maybe she abandoned it on purpose, wanted to make us think something *had* happened to her.'

'What about bank accounts? Credit cards?'

'Nothing. No one's accessed her account or used her cards since before she vanished. Which is, of course, exactly what someone pulling a *Gone Girl* would do if she wanted to throw people off, make it look like she'd vanished without a trace.'

'You don't think so, though.'

Lucky shakes his head. 'Of all the theories, I think it's the least likely. I mean, she'd have to have cash to live off, means of travel, somewhere to stay. And then there's the text.'

'Text?'

'Early hours of November first – one forty a.m. – Casey's mom gets a text from her phone.'

'What did it say?'

'Something about Casey leaving town for a few days, needing to clear her head. Her mom didn't see the text till she got up that morning, but it was enough to alarm her, make her call Casey's best friend, have her go check.'

'You said "a text from her phone". You don't think Casey sent it?'

'Casey's mom certainly doesn't. She thinks someone else did, someone who wanted to make us think Casey left of her own accord.'

'What do you think? That maybe Casey went up into the mountains to harm herself, that it was like a suicide note?'

'Seems unlikely from what her friends say. That she was suicidal, anyhow. I mean, she'd been through it the past couple years, but everyone we spoke to said she'd come out the other side. She was in good spirits Halloween.'

'So,' I say, 'if Casey didn't leave of her own accord, and Garrett's in the clear, you think someone else abducted her after Garrett dropped her home?'

'It's something we're looking at. But they'd have needed transport. Her car was missing, don't forget. If someone abducted her, took her car, abandoned it in the mountains, how'd they get back? Plus, where was *their* vehicle all that time? Not parked outside Casey's, that's for sure – somebody would've seen it.'

'God, it's so confusing.' My head aches. 'So what other theories are there?'

'Well, her friends say it wasn't uncommon for her to take her car up into the mountains, go for a jog or a hike, so maybe something happened on the road. Maybe the text from Casey's phone to her mom really *was* from Casey. What if the text was just that: she was hungover, not feeling great. Maybe she *did* just need to clear her head, had gone for a drive.'

'At two a.m.?'

'Friends say she's a night owl . . .'

'But she'd been drinking.'

Lucky shrugs. 'People don't always make good decisions.'

'So you think she went for a drive in the middle of the night and someone chanced upon her? Abducted her?'

'Possibly. Maybe she had car trouble. Or maybe someone else pretended they did, flagged her down. Then they could've taken her and her car, abandoned it somewhere it wouldn't be found straight away, hiked back to theirs. Casey's car wasn't found for three weeks, remember, the area was so remote. But we'd also been looking in the wrong place: that last text pinged a cell tower miles from where her car was eventually found.'

'What state was it in when you found it?'

'Driver's-side door open, keys in the ignition, Casey's purse and house keys inside. Looked kinda staged.'

I get chills. 'So,' I say, 'back to suspects. Let's say Casey hasn't done a *Gone Girl*, or been abducted by a stranger, and it's not my brother. Who does that leave?'

'There's an ex-boyfriend back in Florida,' Lucky says. 'Seems Casey ended things with him a bunch a times. Apparently, after the last break-up, things got so bad she moved here to get away from him.'

'Says who?'

'Casey's friends, her mom. This ex has a pretty extensive rap sheet – assault, mostly. On Casey, another ex. His own mom.'

'Does this ex have a name?'

Lucky shoots me a look that says, *Nice try.* 'Come on now, Steppy, you know I can't tell you that.'

I don't push it. 'Can I ask if you at least spoke with him?'

'Sure did. He was pretty cut up about the break-up, for sure. Had been for months. He's been in town since, helped with some of the searches.'

'Doesn't make him innocent,' I say. I think of Shaunee Hughes, of Larry Polk. Larry helped organise searches.

'Doesn't make him guilty, either. We checked his phone data – like Garrett, he was pretty open, gave us full access. He *was* in Colorado Halloween, but nowhere near Heartsick. We ruled him out.'

We sit in silence for a bit, everything I've just learned – possibly for the second time, I realise – buzzing round in my head. I watch the snow falling outside the car, the trees beginning to thin the closer we get to town. Lucky's got the heat on, and a combination of that, plus the motion of the car, makes me feel sleepy.

Don't-die-don't-die-don't-die . . .

I jolt from my micro-sleep.

Lucky glances over. 'You okay?'

'Just tired,' I lie, then change the subject. 'So, Heartsick, huh? Small world. How'd you end up here?'

'Just the way the cookie crumbles, I guess. My mom lives the next town over. Her health's not so good, so when I heard Heartsick needed a detective . . .'

'Detective at twenty-seven. That's young.'

'Not that young,' he tells me. 'But twenty-eight, actually.'

I should have remembered. Lucky's ten months older than Garrett, though it might as well be ten years. He's always been more mature.

'You ever run into him around town?' I ask.

'Who? Garrett?' Lucky shrugs. 'I see him around, that's about it. We're not exactly catching up over coffee, if you know what I mean.'

'Okay,' I say at last, 'I'll bite. So you've ruled Garrett out in this girl Casey's disappearance – even if the rest of the world hasn't – but what about Mum? I mean, I know you have to start with the immediate family, the spouse, but Dad didn't do it . . .'

I don't know what makes me pause here, but for some reason I do.

I expect Lucky to jump right in, tell me, *Of course he didn't*, but he doesn't, and as the silence grows, I feel like I'm missing something.

'Dad *is* in the clear?'

'Absolutely,' Lucky replies, a beat too late.

'And Garrett? Even if he was at the scene, had opportunity, I can't see what his motive would be. My mum – my parents, really, but especially Mum – always protected him. Why would he want her dead?'

Lucky shrugs. The snow swirls in front of the windshield at a dizzying pace. 'Those sorts of reasons aren't always so clear-cut.'

'Oh, come on.' I say it with a vehemence that surprises us both, makes my head pound. 'Sorry, Lucky, that's just not good enough.'

His demeanour doesn't change. He continues to stare at the road. 'Look.' He sighs. 'I really shouldn't be telling you this, but word on the street—'

'Word on the *street*?' I laugh, it sounds so absurd. Where does he think we are?

'Word on the street' – Lucky ignores me – 'is your brother owed money.'

'What do you mean, owed money?'

'Drugs,' he says simply.

'He's always smoked a bit of weed,' I admit.

'It's more than weed, Steppy.'

'All right,' I concede. 'But I still don't get how that gives him motive. Not for killing Mum.'

'Your mom had lent him money before, right?'

I swallow. Nod. Mum lends – *lent* – Garrett money whenever he asked for it. Which was pretty much all the time.

'Well,' Lucky says through a sigh, 'maybe he hit your mom up one last time, but she refused. I mean, even though we cleared Garrett in relation to Casey's disappearance, it still brought a lot of negative attention on your family. Maybe your mom had just had enough.'

I'm not sure. Mum would have gone to the ends of the earth for Garrett. But Lucky's also right: that doesn't mean she wouldn't get sick of him asking – for favours, money, doors to be opened. It doesn't mean Mum and Garrett never rowed. They did. And when they did, things could get pretty heated . . .

'Dad said it was a home invasion gone wrong.'

'Apparently some cash was missing. Not a lot – your parents didn't keep much, your dad says – but your mom's purse had been gone through. Her cell phone was missing, too.'

'So it *could* have been a burglary.'

Lucky pulls a face. 'No sign of forced entry.'

'But why would Garrett take that stuff?' I ask. 'I mean, like you say, it wasn't a lot of cash. I know Mum's phone's worth something – it's the same as mine – but not that much. If Garrett wanted money, he only had to ask her.'

'Look, Steppy. I wanted to avoid telling you this, but your mom's death, it was pretty brutal. If you're asking me, whoever killed her knew her. It was personal. Plus we found traces of blood in Garrett's bathroom sink. Looks like he tried to clean himself up before he left. Then there's the 911 call and the call he made to you. It doesn't look good.'

'And there's still no sign of him yet?'

Lucky shakes his head. 'Was gonna ask you the same question.'

I laugh. 'I'm pretty sure I'm the last person Garrett would contact. Have you tried tracing his cell phone? Mum's?'

He shakes his head again. 'Seems your brother's wised up since last time, switched off his location data. Ironic, really, given that the same cell phone data exonerated him in Casey's case. I mean, we know he was at your parents' right around the time your mom was killed – his cell phone puts him there – but as for your mom's cell, her location history wasn't on, so it's not traceable like Garrett's was the night of Casey's disappearance. Plus, both your mom *and* Garrett's phones powered off shortly after she was killed. See, your dad happened to call your mom a little after nine, right after we reckon Garrett left the scene. Garrett had already switched his own phone off, but let's just say he *did* take your mom's, he would've heard it ring when your dad called, probably panicked – realised it could be traced – and shortly after that, her phone powers off too. All this happens right around the time of your car accident, so one theory is he ditched it at the crash site—'

'Wait,' I interrupt. 'Crash site? Garrett was there?'

'Oh shit, yeah,' Lucky says. 'You don't know. Well, see, after Garrett calls you, you're racing up the mountain, trying to get to him, to your parents', when you go off the road. Meanwhile Garrett's driving *down*, opposite direction, sees there's been an accident – probably doesn't even know it's you right away; you're in a hire car – and the couple flag him down.'

'The couple who saw me go off the road?'

'Right. They were headed down the mountain that night, a little ways ahead of Garrett. They saw your headlights coming towards them, saw you lose control, go off the road, down an embankment into the trees.'

'They called 911?'

'Wife dials 911, husband – along with Garrett, who's also stopped by this time – drags you from the car. Just in time, thank God.'

I have a sudden flashback, the drip-drip-drip of blood, mixed with something else. Gasoline? There's a burning smell. Voices – voices! That would explain them, I realise: not EMTs or police, but the couple who stopped at the scene. Passers-by who saved my life.

'You know how remote that road can be, 'specially that time of night,' Lucky's saying. 'Lord knows what would've happened if the McKinleys hadn't come along.'

'But Garrett stopped to help too,' I say. 'You really think those are the actions of someone who's just killed their mum? A murderer fleeing the scene stops to help at the scene of an accident? I mean, you said yourself he wouldn't have known it was me in the wreck. Why not just keep driving?'

'Yeah, he stopped . . .' Lucky pulls a face. 'But someone literally ran into the road, flagged him down. Besides,' he adds, 'he left before the EMTs showed, was long gone before anyone realised who he actually was. Now he's on the run.'

'We don't know he's on the *run*,' I say. 'Not exactly.' Garrett has a tendency to do that. When stuff gets too hot to handle, he splits. 'Look, I know he doesn't always make the right choice – scratch that, he *rarely* makes the right choice – but that doesn't mean—'

'I know it's hard to hear, Steppy. Trust me, I'd give anything *not* to be having this conversation . . .'

'So don't.' I laugh nervously.

'. . . but you have to admit,' he carries on, 'it's not looking good for Garrett.'

I can't admit it, not aloud, but deep down I know Lucky's right.

'Look,' I tell him, 'I don't exactly disagree. But there must be other people you're looking at for Mum's . . .' I can't bring myself to say the M word. *Murder*. 'You must have other suspects?'

'Your mom had enemies?'

'Not enemies. Not exactly. Just people who didn't like her, I guess. She didn't have many friends. Hell, I didn't like her a lot of the time.' That last sentence just sort of slips out. I glance at Lucky, but he has his poker face on. 'Look, what I'm trying to say is, my brother's a lot of things. But a killer?'

There's a pause. I can tell Lucky wants to say something, so I wait. Eventually he bites. 'You know what happened with Garrett and me, right?'

'You mean in high school?' I don't. Not really. I was at uni in the UK by that time. Only home in vacations. All I knew was, when I did come home, Lucky didn't come around any more. 'Guess I just thought you'd grown apart.'

'That's one way of putting it,' he says, nodding slowly, eyes on the road. 'Garrett never said anything?'

'No,' I answer honestly. No one did, though I should have suspected.

'You remember Jenna, though,' Lucky says.

I nod. Jenna and Garrett dated back in high school. I didn't really know Jenna well, only met her once or twice. But I liked her, which meant she was too nice for Garrett.

'They'd been going steady a few months, Jenna and your brother, but I guess, in the end, she couldn't take the way he treated her. He was controlling, told her what she could and couldn't wear, who she could socialise with. All the while, he was going behind her back.'

'Sounds like my brother.'

'Well,' Lucky goes on, 'Jenna and Garrett had been broken up a while. He'd tried to get her back, but she wanted nothing to do with him. See, in the meantime, *me* and Jenna had gotten closer . . .'

'Ah,' I say. Garrett wouldn't have liked that.

'So, after we've been seeing each other a while – in secret – we decide to make things official, decide it's best to be upfront. So I go to Garrett, tell him everything.'

'And he wasn't happy.'

'I mean, you'd think, right? But it was like the opposite. I guess you could say he gave us his blessing, stupid as it sounds.'

'Maybe he'd just moved on.' Garrett likes to dwell on things, hold grudges, but he can also compartmentalise, cut things – or people – from his life without a second thought.

Lucky taps his finger on the steering wheel. 'That's what Jenna thought. Me, I wasn't so sure. There was always something at the back of my mind, telling me it couldn't be that easy.'

I have a sinking feeling.

'So,' he continues, 'like, a couple weeks later, I'm leaving work – the video rentals store? The one by Subway?'

'I remember it.'

'Well, it's past midnight and I'm going to my car – parking lot's deserted – and I get jumped by three guys. Beat me up real bad.'

'God. Do you know who they were?'

'Nope. Didn't recognise them – they were wearing ski masks. But they were older. Not high school kids.'

'So not Garrett,' I say, relieved.

'Right,' Lucky says. 'Garrett was smarter than that. Knew not to get his hands dirty.'

'You're saying he set you up?' I'm genuinely taken aback.

'I couldn't prove it,' is all Lucky says.

'Did you go to the police?'

'Didn't have to. Hospital called them. I was beaten so bad I ended up in ICU. Was completely outta it two whole days.'

'Christ,' I say. Why didn't I know? I was away from home, yes, but it was a pretty major thing. Why wouldn't Garrett, or Mum, have mentioned it? 'Did Garrett say anything? When you saw him at school after?'

Lucky shakes his head. 'I was outta school a few weeks. After that, my parents had me transfer to another high school.'

'Jesus, Lucky, that's fucking awful.' I shake my head in disbelief. 'I always thought you and my brother were so close. I just can't imagine he'd . . . what, put a hit out on you?'

'I know he's your brother, Steppy, but Garrett can be dangerous. I mean, I was one of his best friends, but I always felt like I was on borrowed time, like an outsider.'

'You don't mean because . . .'

'Because I was the only black kid in the group? That was definitely part of it. I think Garrett thought that because he chose me, kept me around, I owed him. Being in his group, I was protected. You know what high school can be like.'

I nod. I hated high school. I was sixteen when we moved back to the US. Starting a new school was bad enough, but in sophomore year? To say it was a baptism of fire was putting it mildly. Garrett, on the other hand, a freshman, sailed through like he was born into it.

Lucky's still talking. 'For your brother, everything's real black and white: you're either with him or you're not. Ride or die. Sounds crazy, I know – I mean, shit, we were high school kids. But once you cross him – hell, not once you cross him, once he *thinks* you've crossed him – that's it.'

'I'd no idea,' I say. 'I'm so sorry.'

'Hey.' He shrugs. 'It's not your fault. But I guess what I'm saying is – and look, I don't wanna sound like I'm dissing your brother, 'specially now . . .' He trails off. 'When you came to see me at the police department,' he begins again slowly, 'you asked me if I really thought Garrett was capable of being involved in Casey Carter's disappearance.'

'What did you say?'

'I told you it didn't really matter what I thought. That we'd already ruled him out.'

'But if you had said?'

'Truthfully? See, that's the thing. Truthfully, I don't know what your brother's capable of. He has a dark side, Steppy.'

'We all have a dark side.' I laugh nervously.

'Maybe we do,' Lucky says, laughs too. 'But Garrett's dark side? It's different from yours and mine. Garrett's dark side? Well, it scares me.'

I don't answer, because I know he's right.

Because if I'm honest, Garrett's dark side scares me too.

8

Then

Don't do it, I told myself sternly. Casey Carter's disappearance was too close to home. I wasn't here to investigate. But back in the car, I googled *Buddy's Bar* on my phone. Reception was a bit spotty, but as the search results loaded and my phone screen filled with headlines, I knew I'd found the right place.

> *LOCAL BAR AT CENTRE OF GIRL'S MYSTERIOUS DISAPPEARANCE*
> *BUDDY'S PATRONS COULD HOLD KEY TO WOMAN'S DISAPPEARANCE*
> *WOMAN DISAPPEARS AFTER HALLOWEEN PARTY AT HEARTSICK BAR*

Above the headlines was a Google business listing with a thumbnail showing an innocuous-looking building and a section of Google Maps. Beneath that, the opening hours: Monday through Sunday, 4 p.m. till 2 a.m. But were they open Thanksgiving? I dialled the phone number given, but it just rang out. That didn't necessarily mean they weren't open, though. Maybe the phone had been left in the office. Maybe they were so run off their feet, serving customers on a busy holiday, that they didn't have time to answer it.

At the exit from the gas station back out onto the highway, I put my right blinker on, then hesitated. I was running late. Turn right and I'd continue on the road to my parents'. Turn left and I'm headed back into town, back towards Buddy's. Mum would be so mad if I was late. But I was already late. What did I have to lose?

The first thing that struck me as I pulled into Buddy's parking lot was that it didn't look hopeful: mine was the only car. The second thing that struck me was that it was a weird place for my brother to be drinking – run-down, out of town, on the side of a busy high-way. Garrett usually frequented the city bars and clubs rich kids favoured; the cosy, chic après ski resort ones further up the mountain; or Heartsick's laid-back, trendy downtown bars. Buddy's was none of these. It was, as the photos had suggested, a drab-looking dive bar, across the highway from another gas station; on the adjoining lot to the Mountain Gateway Motel, a shabby two storey strip-style building. It had a neon sign out front, which, unlike the motel's towering neon sign, was unlit, the place in darkness. The only light in Buddy's lot came from passing headlights on the highway and the next-door motel.

I climbed from the car, picked my way carefully across the uneven gravelly lot and up the few steps to the bar's front door. I tried it – locked – then made my way along the porch to the nearest window, but it was high enough off the ground that I had to stand on tiptoe to peer between the tiny faux-leaded diamond panes, and I could see little in the darkness beyond the layer of grime-covered glass.

Though the place clearly wasn't open, I decided to try my luck round back, but if the front of the bar was dark, the back, with a thick line of trees beyond, was pitch black, so I had to use the flashlight on my cell phone to guide me. Holding it up, I surveyed the yard: a couple of big plastic dumpsters either side of a windowless back door; a jumble of white plastic garden furniture, stacked haphazardly.

As I made my way round front again, still guided by my phone and doing my best to avoid the potholes, a voice from the darkness made me jump.

'They don't open Thanksgiving.'

I turned. On the adjoining lot, at the nearest end of the motel, I saw a floating rectangle of light: a phone screen. I peered through the dark, made out the silhouette of a woman holding it.

'Thanks,' I called back.

The woman gave a nod, hollered, '*Rocky!*' then pocketed the phone like she was about to leave.

'Wait!' I called. 'Maybe you can help?'

The figure froze.

'I'm looking for someone.' I began walking towards her. Even at a distance and in the dark I could sense her hesitancy, could see her shoulders tense. I picked up my pace. To hell with the potholes. 'A bartender at Buddy's. Evan Coombs?'

I'd reached the border between the two lots – a row of low cement blocks I was lucky to spot in the dark – the woman waiting beyond, shrouded in shadow under the motel's overhang. Lanterns were strung the length of the building between the two storeys, but as I drew closer, I noticed that a good few of the bulbs were out. Closer still, and a shadow, large and low to the ground, darted across my path, making me jump – a dog, I realised. German shepherd. It cocked its leg on one of the wooden corner pillars, began weaving its way deftly around patches of weeds that sprouted between the veranda and the gravelly lot. The woman didn't bat an eyelid.

'Dunno any of the bartenders,' she said. 'Only know they don't open Thanksgiving.'

Now that I was closer, I saw she was wearing track pants, sneakers and a T-shirt – no coat, despite the temperature – and was hugging her arms round her for warmth. She looked down at the dog, said, 'Let's go, boy,' and as she uncrossed her arms, my breath caught. On her T-shirt was a photo of Casey, the Halloween one I'd become so familiar with, the half-painted face, crown-of-roses one. Emblazoned above Casey's image were the words *#FindCaseyCarter*, and I suddenly realised who the woman was. She was bigger than she'd appeared online – face heavier-set, build chunkier – and minus all the glamorous nail acrylics and make-up, save dark, tattooed-on-looking eyebrows, which I guessed must be permanent. If she was the same age as Casey, she could only be early twenties, but here, even in the dark, she appeared older than the carefully curated social media photos. Nevertheless, I was sure: it was the girl from Facebook – the Find Casey Carter admin; Casey's less-good-looking-though-nonetheless-lookalike friend. *Besties ready for Halloween!*

My brain scrambled to recall her name. 'Brooke?'

She stopped, unsure. At her side, the dog sat down.

'You a reporter?' she asked.

'God, no,' I said quickly, relieved that, unlike gas station Jesse, she didn't seem to recognise me.

'Well who then?'

'My name's Steppy,' I said. 'I was wondering—'

'You gotta be shitting me.' Brooke cut me off. 'Garrett Corner's sister?'

So she did know. How could she not? 'I'm not here to cause trouble,' I assured her.

'Then butt out.' She widened her eyes at me.

'Look,' I said, praying it wasn't already too late, 'your best friend's missing. Everyone's saying my brother was the last person seen with her. I get why you wouldn't trust me. But I'm just trying to find out what happened – the truth.'

'Nice try.' She made to leave again, and the dog got to its feet. 'See ya.'

'I like your necklace,' I said quickly, in sheer desperation. One last shot.

The comment seemed to throw her, and she stopped, hand going instinctively to her neck, touching the silver half-heart pendant with the jagged edge. The mirror image of the one Casey was wearing in the Halloween photo.

'It's a friendship necklace, isn't it?'

Brooke didn't reply, looked surprisingly defensive, tucked the pendant down the front of her T-shirt.

'Casey had the other half,' I continued, undeterred. 'You must be close.'

At this, her expression softened. 'Real close.'

'You look so alike, you and Casey.'

'Really?'

'God, yeah,' I said, hoping I wasn't overdoing it. 'Like, if I hadn't known, I'd've thought you were sisters.'

Her face lit up. 'We were close as sisters.'

Behind her, in the nearest motel window, a curtain twitched.

When I looked back, Brooke's expression had changed again. She looked downcast.

'I wish we'd never come here,' she said.

'You're not from Heartsick?'

She shook her head. 'Florida. Only moved here 'cos of Casey.'

I'd read online that Casey hadn't lived in Heartsick long. 'You moved here together last year?'

'*Casey* moved here last year,' she corrected me. 'Upped and left Florida, didn't tell no one 'cept her mom and brother. She'd gone through a real bad break-up,' she added, as though, without that explanation, I'd doubt the strength of their friendship.

'Why Heartsick?' I asked.

'Why anywhere?' She scowled at the ground, scuffed the dirt with the toe of a threadbare Converse. 'Stuck a pin in a map? It was the opposite of where we came from? I dunno.'

'So you followed her here?'

'I didn't *follow* her,' she said, defensive again. 'Like, once Casey had gotten settled, she reached out, let me know where she was. It was her idea for me to move here.'

'And that last night. Halloween.'

'We went out together.'

'So you were there that night' – I nodded in the direction of Buddy's – 'at the bar, with Casey. How did she seem?'

'Like, okay, I guess.' Brooke shrugged. 'Just normal.'

'And my brother gave Casey a ride home?'

'That's what the cops said. She'd been s'posed to get a ride with me . . .'

'Why didn't she?'

'Bar was real busy. I was our designated driver, but me and Casey had gotten separated. I tried calling her cell phone a couple times, but she didn't pick up. Guess I just figured she'd gotten a ride with a friend.'

'Do you live together?'

'Nuh-uh,' Brooke said. 'I got my place, Casey's got hers. Like I said' – there was that defensiveness again – 'Casey moved to Heartsick before me. Her condo's only one bed. I mean, we were *gonna* get a place together, planning on it, like, after our leases were up . . .'

'Right,' I said, sensing it was best to move on from the topic of living arrangements. 'So, uh, you and Casey know Garrett?'

'Nope. Met him the first time that night.'

'So when'd you realise something was wrong?'

'With Casey? Next day. Her mom called me real early, said Casey wasn't answering her phone. She'd got this text, see, in the middle of the night – like two a.m. or something. It was from Casey – her phone, anyhow.'

'You don't think Casey sent it?'

'Dunno.'

'Do you know what it said?'

She thought a moment. 'Something about her needing space to work things out, clear her head.'

'So her mom asked you to go round?'

Brooke nodded.

'And when you got there?'

She shrugged. 'She wasn't there.'

'Did you try calling her?'

'Course. But her cell phone was off.'

'So you called the police?'

She looked guilty. 'Didn't think I needed to. Just assumed she'd gone for a run. I mean,' she added, like she was only just thinking about it now, 'she *was* more of a night owl than an early bird . . .'

'The news reports said her car was missing.'

'Yeah.' She nodded. 'It wasn't there when I got over there.'

'She'd do that?' I screwed up my nose. 'Take her car to go for a jog?'

'Sometimes, I guess.' She didn't sound so sure. 'She'd drive up into the mountains, then hike or run from there.'

'So, her place,' I said. 'Did you go inside?'

'Don't have a key.'

I wondered if this wasn't a bit strange: two best friends, each living alone but planning on moving in together, not giving each other a key. 'So what did you do?'

'Called her mom back, told her Casey wasn't there.'

'I read the police did come out that day, though, so someone must've called them.'

'Casey's mom,' Brooke said. 'She was pretty rattled over the text message, so she called them and they came out, did a welfare check. But I guess, like me, they didn't think anything was wrong.'

'So when did you realise something *was* wrong?'

'Couple days later, when I still hadn't heard from her.'

A couple of days? Before everything with Paige went down, if she hadn't called or texted me in two days, hadn't returned my calls or texts and I couldn't locate her, felt the police weren't taking it seriously, I'd have organised a search party myself.

'Casey's mom was still bugging me . . .' *Bugging me.* It seemed a somewhat insensitive turn of phrase for a frantic mom, worried about her daughter. '. . . then someone from the restaurant she's a server at called me, said Casey hadn't showed up for work in two days.'

'That was unusual?'

Brooke nodded. 'Casey likes to party – we both do – but she worked two jobs. She'd always show up for them, no matter what.'

'So *you* called the police this time?'

'Right.' She nodded again. 'Well, first I called her mom. Then the police. That's when they made it official, filed the missing persons report.'

'Is Casey's mom still in town?' I remembered how the newspaper article said her mom had travelled from Florida. 'I was hoping to speak with her.'

'She was,' Brooke said, 'till a couple days ago. But she left, went back home. Too many people asking questions. Too many reporters wanting a story.'

'So,' I said. 'What do *you* think happened to Casey?'

'Really?'

I sighed. It was impossible to ignore the elephant in the room. 'You think my brother had something to do with it?'

'Sorry,' she said, like she wasn't sorry at all.

'Look,' I told her, 'I know there's been a lot of stuff online, but if all they've got is that he was the last person seen with Casey . . .'

Brooke glared at me. 'It's not just that.'

'Then what?'

She paused. 'Name Amy Johnson mean anything to you?'

'Should it?'

'You know your brother was in Thailand, right?'

I swallowed, felt a pit in my stomach, gave the smallest of nods. Last year, after ditching yet another job, Garrett had announced he was going travelling. South East Asia.

'Well, Amy Johnson was vacationing there too.'

'And?'

'She was staying on some island, same one as your brother, and she disappeared. Wound up dead.'

'Okay,' I said. 'But what's this got to do with Garrett?' More to the point, what did it have to do with Casey? But even as I asked that first question aloud, I had a sinking feeling, the one that seemed to go hand in hand these days with my brother's name.

'Amy Johnson,' Brooke said. 'Your brother was the last person seen with her as well.'

9

Now

Lucky drops me outside the library in the centre of town.

As I'm climbing from the car, about to pick my way across the now snow-covered sidewalk, he leans across the passenger seat, calls, 'Wait up! I forgot to give you these!'

He hands me a set of old VW car keys on an *I Heart Heartsick* keychain. I look at him questioningly.

'Jenna's not into driving in the snow,' Lucky explains, 'what with being pregnant and all.'

'What?' The cold air nips at my exposed scalp. *'Jenna?'*

'You don't remember.' He smiles, holds up his left hand, and I see the slim gold band on his ring finger. 'We're still together.'

'You're kidding,' I say, though he's obviously not. 'Congrats.' If anyone deserves a happily-ever-after, it's Lucky, though I doubt my brother would feel the same. 'Does Garrett know?'

'Probably,' Lucky says. 'He wasn't invited to the wedding, though, that's for sure.'

I hold up the car keys. 'So what's the deal?'

'When I told Jenna you'd been discharged from hospital, had come back here, didn't have a car, she said you should use hers. It's in the parking lot behind the veterinarian's office. Next block? You can drive a stick shift, right?'

I *can*, but I'm thinking of the list of instructions I was discharged with, am pretty sure not driving's one of them . . . 'You sure it's okay with Jenna?'

'Sure I'm sure,' Lucky says. 'She can ride with me as long as you need it. Just promise me one thing.'

'Anything.'

'Well, two, actually. One, you'll have dinner with us – me and Jenna. She's a huge fan of that podcast you do, won't ever forgive me if I don't ask.'

'Deal.' I nod. 'And the second?'

'Drive careful,' he says, without a hint of irony. 'These roads can be treacherous.'

Heartsick's library is modern and swish. Although I've only been out of action nine days, my legs are shaky and weak, and after climbing the steps to the entrance, I feel like I've ascended Mount Everest. As I stop to catch my breath, the automatic doors parting before me, I'm struck by how noisy it is for a library, and while that's something that wouldn't have bothered me before, now it feels almost overwhelming.

There's a pre-school story-time session in full flow, toddlers and babies seated on their moms' knees and on colourful squashy mats, and though I keep my head down as I cross to the main desk, I still get a few stares. The librarian I ask about accessing the internet throws me a wary look before showing me to a bank of computers, and I choose one in the furthest, quietest corner.

I check my emails first, have prepared myself for the fact that I may not be able to log in, but unlike on my laptop, my password works fine. What I'm not prepared for, however, is the scores of unopened emails that greet me. Hundreds in a little over a week, some from names I know, others I don't recognise, clearly journalists looking for a scoop. Starting with the most recent, I begin opening them one by one, but their content's much the same.

So very sorry about your mom, Steppy.
If there's anything I can do . . .
Oh my goodness, I just saw about your accident on the TV.
Are you OK??
Please email me or phone when you get the chance.

It's not long before the words start to swim in front of me and I'm gulping down tears. Everything feels so real all of a sudden, as if before I was viewing things through an out-of-focus lens, and now it's in macro. I only read a few more emails before I stop. I can't face the thought of opening any more, let alone replying, so I log out.

Next, against my better judgement, and telling myself I'm only checking to see if my password still works, I log into Facebook. Turns out my Facebook password's working fine too, and I'm met with a similar sight in Messenger: concerned friends, well-wishers and complete strangers all wanting to know how I am, wanting me to contact them. Scattered among them, however, are some messages that, going by the portion visible above the fold, contain sentiments that aren't so kind.

U shud of died in that car crash . . .
Fucking deserve everything you get . . .
Good luck with season 2 lol . . .

Ask your bro where casey is . . .
It's called karma. Hope you rot . . .

I sink lower in my chair as I realise how much this whole thing has blown up, wonder if the strange looks I've been getting are less to do with my alarming appearance and more to do with people recognising me from all the coverage. I'm only thankful that, after the advent of *Dark Corners*, when fans started to search me out, I changed my Facebook settings so people could no longer post on my timeline.

As with my emails, I do a quick scroll-through. Right at the start of the unopened messages, I see a name that catches my attention: *Paige Foster*. Next to it, *10 d*. Ten days ago? I double-check the date in the bottom corner of the computer screen, count backwards. Wasn't that the day of my car accident, the day Mum . . .?

I stop, try to think instead why my best friend – *ex*-best friend – would be messaging me at all, never mind recently. Given the date it was sent, I might have assumed she was being the bigger person, reaching out to check how I am. I know she isn't, though, as I can see the first part of the message without opening it, and it looks like a response to something. A response, presumably, to a message I sent.

Appreciate that. But I've been th . . .

Even though a part of me knows I'll probably regret it, I have to know what it says, so I open the message to reveal the rest.

27 Nov 2016, 19:57

Appreciate that. But I've been thinking and have decided it would be best if you don't contact me again.

The coldness of it takes my breath away – I can't help but feel it's got Travis's name all over it – but it's when I scroll up, see my message to Paige, the one that precipitated her response, that I'm truly floored.

I meant what I said earlier. I'm sorry.

According to Facebook, I sent it the same day – the day of the accident; the day Mum died – around forty minutes before Paige replied.

But what does it mean? Apart from the obvious – that I appear to be apologising to Paige. *Apologising* to her. Me. Surely it should be the other way round? Frantically I scroll up further to see if I can get some – any – context; hope the coloured text bubbles reveal a thread that will help me decode what on earth's gone on. But the preceding messages are from months ago and completely unrelated – December 2015, right before Paige came to stay with me and Travis at New Year's, when Travis was still *my* boyfriend, Paige my best friend.

But why I'm apologising to Paige isn't the only mystery, I just don't realise it straight away. Once I get over the shock of my apology, of Paige's abrupt response, the significance of exactly what I've written dawns on me: *I meant what I said earlier.* That means I've spoken with her.

Recently.

The frustration of not being able to remember swells inside me until it threatens to swallow me whole. My breathing grows rapid, my chest tightens, and I grip the edge of the computer desk with both hands, close my eyes to escape.

Shit-shit-shit-shit-shit . . .
Don't-die-don't-die-don't-die . . .

The noise of the library brings my surroundings flooding back. The wail of a baby, the beep of books being checked out. Whispered conversations. A telephone ringing at the front desk; the clack of a nearby keyboard. I gulp it in like I've been drowning, finally made it to the surface for air.

Get a grip, I tell myself. I have to stay focused. But if I came to Heartsick to look into Casey Carter's disappearance, without access to my laptop – without access to my own memory – I've no idea what, if anything, I've discovered. I'm back at square one, except now there's an added element: Mum's death. It's obvious the cops think Garrett's involved. Then there's what Lucky said about my brother's dark side.

'*Jesus*. Did your mom drop your brother on his head as a baby?' Travis asked once, after Garrett had pulled yet another of his dumb stunts.

I laughed, knew he was only half joking; had, in truth, wondered myself sometimes: where did it all go wrong with Garrett? He'd been a colicky baby, a fractious toddler, a sickly preschooler. Even when he grew out of it, became a rambunctious, hard-to-control child, Mum continued to overindulge and mollycoddle him. Maybe it was as simple as that.

But surely there's a huge leap between Garrett *possibly* having got some guys to jump Lucky, back in high school, and murder, and I can't help but wonder if it's not all too convenient: my brother conclusively ruled out of Casey Carter's disappearance, only to be implicated in Mum's murder. Sure, it doesn't look great for him: he has motive (if Lucky's to be believed), means and opportunity. And now he's nowhere to be found. Not the actions of an innocent man. But what if he *is* innocent? What if whoever's behind Casey's disappearance is also behind Mum's death? What if Mum's been killed to create a smokescreen – cast suspicion on my brother – in an effort to divert attention, not to mention limited small-town resources, from Casey's disappearance? What if whoever's responsible thinks that if my brother is ultimately apprehended and charged with his own mother's murder, everyone will simply assume – whatever the contrary evidence – he's guilty when it comes to Casey, too?

Which leads me to the question: if I can get to the bottom of what happened to Casey, will it also lead to Mum's killer?

I can't be certain, but if I'm at least going to try and untangle the mystery, I have to treat it like I'm making a podcast, be objective and thorough. And since the list of names I found at the cabin is the only tangible thing I have right now, it seems like a good place to start. I take it from my bag, set it next to the computer in front of me.

Evan Coombs

~~Brooke Morgenstern~~

Loreen Skinner

Rebecca Johnson

Luke ?

I draw my finger down it, hoping to feel something – a jolt of recognition – but of course I don't. If I *was* looking into Casey's disappearance before my accident, it's probably safe to assume these names are linked to her. So, just like with Shaunee Hughes, I begin with an internet search, my intention to read every newspaper article I can find on Casey Carter. In the fraction of a second it takes the search results to load, I steel myself, then begin working my way through them. After the shock of the TV news report, I studiously avoid the ones on Mum's death peppering the results, reasoning that if my hunch is right and the two cases are connected, it won't do any harm, for now, to focus my efforts solely on Casey.

The online news articles reveal that the story of Casey's disappearance is pretty much as Lucky described, so I turn my attention back to the list of names, establish pretty quickly that Loreen Skinner is Casey's mom. Hailing from Florida, she's quoted frequently in news articles and appears at police press conferences in several grainy YouTube videos I watch with the sound off, making desperate pleas for information. She doesn't cry, just looks broken, and I'm reminded of Shaunee Hughes's parents, her mom especially; of the toll not knowing takes.

Casey's mom is on Facebook, too, a quiet and dignified presence. Her profile is private, but she pops up every now and then, liking the odd Facebook post in a group called Find Casey Carter, which in the weeks since her daughter's disappearance has garnered over twelve thousand followers. Loreen never comments on posts, nor does she get involved in online speculation or gossip. She doesn't join the frequent pile-ons involving the criticism of my brother or the cops; nor the rows that break out regularly between obstinate strangers with opposing views and unshakeable bat-shit-crazy theories – the ones posting typo-ridden, often illiterate streams of consciousness.

I continue searching for the remaining names on my list with little success. There are hundreds of Evan Coombses and Rebecca Johnsons on Facebook (Rebecca's name rings a faint bell, for reasons that feel just out of reach), but none have any apparent link to Casey, and I strike out on general internet searches for them, too. Unsurprisingly, the mysterious first-name-only Luke is also a bust. I do find Brooke Morgenstern, though, the self-proclaimed bestie of Casey Carter and founder of the aforementioned Facebook group, on which she maintains an active presence.

In one of her more recent updates, a post that's been liked over a thousand times, Brooke has shared a photo from a candlelit vigil. It's night-time, so hard to see, but it looks like the shot's been taken in a residential street. A large crowd of people, most with their backs to the camera, are huddled close together in bulky winter clothes, so that they look like one big mass. The only colour in the shot comes from the yellow-white of candle flames, dotting the picture like fireflies. I peer closer, hoping I'll recognise someone, wondering if I'm among them, but amid all the faceless people, it's impossible to see. Brooke has captioned the image: *November 26. Thank you to everyone who turned out last night! We will keep praying until Casey is returned safe to us!*

Most of the other posts are status updates on the case – reports on searches, both official and unofficial – and general appeals for information, punctuated with more photos of a smiling, happy Casey. Among these images is an uncropped version of the one that many of the news outlets have run with, the one so obviously from Halloween. In it – a bathroom mirror selfie, I see now, featuring both girls – Casey and Brooke have their faces painted in the same colourful half-skeleton design and wear matching flower crowns; around her neck, Casey wears one of those friendship necklaces with a silver half-heart pendant.

I stare at Brooke's face a while, willing myself to remember. If the lists I made during *Dark Corners* were anything to go by, the fact that I've crossed Brooke's name out most likely means I've either tracked her down and spoken to her or exhausted all efforts without finding her. The fact that I've found her online so easily now suggests the former, but there is also a third option: I could have crossed her out because I tracked her down but she wouldn't speak to me. *Do I recognise her?* I wonder. She does look vaguely familiar, but maybe that's because she looks a lot like Casey.

Casey's own Facebook profile is also easy enough to find, because so many people are tagging her. There's little to be gleaned from it, though, no sign of a boyfriend – ex or otherwise – very few photos and no useful posts. In fact, it seems that Casey's posted nothing at all since – I scroll through, double-check – summer 2015.

There are plenty of posts on her page from other people, though, hundreds in just a few weeks. They're from people who know her, people who don't, but they all want to know the same thing: where's Casey?

But Casey's whereabouts aren't the only mystery right now, and though I've had more than my fill of Facebook for one day, I resist the temptation to log out, bring my brother's profile up instead, immediately wish I hadn't. For although *I* had the foresight long ago to change my settings so people can't post on my page, Garrett has not. And now everyone, it appears, from old high school buddies to complete strangers, wants to throw their two cents in, their comments a mix of pseudo-psychology, threats of violence and everything else in between.

But it's not just posts about my brother, and they're not only limited to Garrett's Facebook page. Unable to stop myself, I go from social media page to social media page, forum to forum and blog to blog. The feeling, it appears, is universal.

Alana Winter: Omg you guys! Anyone hear? Garrett's sis Steppy's been in some kinda car accident. Like real serious.
Jax Johnson: *Alana Winter*: It's called karma lol
Chuck aka Chip Hudson: Sorry *Tracey Jeanette Moyer* but I have to agree with *Gordy Masterson*. There's no way Steppy didn't know her brother's got something to do with Casey's disappearance, no matter what the cops say. She came back to Heartsick to investigate FFS.

I read only a handful before I stop scrolling, my hands shaking. I feel sick. How has this happened? I've gone from hero to villain in a matter of days. I wouldn't mind, but I never wanted to be the hero in the first place: *Dark Corners'* focus was supposed to be Shaunee, her unsolved case. Not me. I didn't ask for all the attention it brought; didn't invite it into my life.

I have a sudden flashback. I'm alone in bed, in my New York apartment. It's late, a Saturday, and something tells me it's been a particularly rough day. I'm trawling the internet, falling down rabbit holes, hoping I'll chance on a new subject for season two of *Dark Corners*, but I've found an article on Larry Polk instead, am scrolling aimlessly through the comments section. And that's when things start getting a little hazy. But not before I'm certain I glimpse my brother's name . . .

The memory cuts out, a cassette tape ribbon snapping, and I'm back in the library, trying to put the pieces together. I know I've been desperate to find a subject for the second season of *Dark Corners* for some time, something I feel a connection to, like I did with Shaunee Hughes. Was I so desperate for that connection, I wonder, that I alighted on something too close for comfort? Was I so desperate for that connection that now here I am, tangled up in something I've no control over, nor memory of?

Because there's personal, and then there's personal.

And maybe, just maybe, I should have been careful what I wished for.

IO

Then

Though not music to my ears – my brother the last person seen with two girls, one dead, the other missing – it wasn't exactly a smoking gun, either. After all, I only had Brooke's word for it that Garrett *was* the last person seen with this Amy Johnson in Thailand. When I'd asked her how she knew about Amy, she said, 'Facebook,' and when I'd pressed her for more, she said, 'Amy's sister, Rebecca. She reached out to me. You should speak with her,' insisted on giving me Rebecca's email address.

But as I climbed back into my car in Buddy's parking lot, I felt uneasy. Something about Brooke was off. Her story just didn't hang together. Not the Amy Johnson bit – that I'd have to look into separately – but what she'd told me about Halloween, the night Casey disappeared. It wasn't unreasonable that alarm bells didn't ring when she went over to Casey's condo the next day – it was entirely possible that she genuinely believed nothing was wrong, that her best friend had simply taken her car, gone for a hike or jog, especially if that was what she sometimes did. But Brooke had said it herself: Casey was a night owl, not a lark. How usual would it have been for her to go out jogging so early, particularly the morning after a big night out? There could, of course, have been other explanations for her absence. She might simply have woken up, found she'd no milk in the refrigerator for her morning coffee, so jumped in her car and gone to the grocery store.

But then there was the text, the one from Casey's cell phone to her mom's, the one sufficiently concerning that with Casey uncontactable the next morning, her mom had called Brooke instead. If the text *had* been sent by Casey, and if Brooke was right about what it said – that Casey needed space to clear her head – then that alone was enough to cause alarm; but if it had been sent by someone *pretending* to be Casey, well, that cast a whole different light on things. A far more sinister one. Either way, Brooke hadn't been overly concerned, hadn't contacted police until two days later.

And then there was what Brooke was even doing at the motel in the first place. Wasn't it a little too coincidental that I turned up looking to speak to a barman at the place Casey was last seen, and her best friend – one of the last people to see Casey the night she vanished – happened to be hanging around?

Once we'd finished talking, when Brooke had made it clear she'd no more to say, I'd thanked her for her time and left.

As I'd crossed the makeshift divide to the Buddy's side of the parking lot, I'd turned, called, 'Hey, I meant to ask – there's a vigil?'

There was a pause, like a lag on a phone line, then Brooke had shouted back, 'Nine p.m. tomorrow, outside Casey's place, Watson Street.' Through the dark, I could sense she was scowling. 'You should come.'

I'd felt her eyes on me all the way to my car. Inside, I glanced in the mirror in time to see the door of the endmost motel room – the one with the twitching curtain – close. Brooke and the dog were gone.

I watched for a minute but she didn't reappear, so I flicked the car's interior light on, stared at the email address for Amy's sister, Rebecca, lit up on my phone screen. I wouldn't email yet, but maybe I'd do some digging. Though I hadn't said anything to Brooke, Garrett *had* mentioned something about a girl who died while he was in Thailand – 'some British chick' – and if my memory was correct, it happened right before his return to the US. Could this be Amy Johnson? An initial internet search yielded only articles and a Wikipedia page on the pioneering twentieth-century British pilot of the same name, so I tried *Amy Johnson Thailand* instead. Bingo: a handful of newspaper articles, mostly British, from the end of 2015, beginning of 2016 – exactly when Garrett had been in Thailand.

Family of Missing Amy Johnson Fly to Thailand to Join Search

The devastated family of Tunbridge Wells gap-year student Amy Johnson, missing from the Thai island of Koh Tao, have flown to the country to help with her search and appeal for information. Amy, 19, missing since just after Christmas, had travelled to the island from nearby Ko Pha-Ngan. Friends said she had decided to spend New Year on Koh Tao, as it was known to be more peaceful than its Full-Moon-party-hosting counterpart. The last confirmed sighting of Amy was on a ferry to the island on 28 December, and someone using her name and matching her description checked into a hostel on the island the same day. Police have also since recovered items, identified as Amy's, from the hostel.

'Amy's disappearance is completely out of character,' her sister, Rebecca, told reporters yesterday, before she left for Thailand with her parents. 'She's travelled extensively in her gap year but always keeps in touch, wherever she is, by phone or email. We last heard from her on Christmas Day. When we didn't hear anything after that, we knew something was wrong.'

Describing her sister as quiet but streetwise, Rebecca Johnson said she hopes her family's trip will stir up interest in the case. 'My sister isn't a partier. She doesn't really drink and she definitely doesn't do drugs. She's careful. This isn't just a case of a Brit who's drunk too much, fallen in the sea or met with an accident, like a lot of people are saying. If anyone has any information, no matter how insignificant, please, please come forward.' Rebecca stressed that her family would particularly like to hear from people who saw Amy right before she vanished, even if they've since moved on or returned home. 'We're keen to build a picture of her movements, try and fill in those last few days, as no one knows exactly when or where she went missing.'

According to friends, Amy had been travelling in Thailand for a couple of months, ending up in Ko Pha-Ngan for Christmas. 'Amy had been to a Full Moon party the month before, which she hadn't really enjoyed, but her friends were keen to go again, so she agreed,' Rebecca said. Asked whether her sister had travelled alone to Koh Tao, she said her family weren't sure, though they knew that none of her close friends had gone with her. 'Amy's friends were having fun on Ko Pha-Ngan, so Amy told them, and others at the hostel, that she was planning to go alone. But that didn't mean she didn't go with someone else, or that she didn't meet someone along the way – she'd made a lot of friends among the other travellers, people from all over the world.'

Amy, an aspiring journalist, blogged regularly about her travels. Her final entry was the morning of December 25, her last contact with family the same day. Thai police say they are keeping an open mind about her disappearance and are not ruling out foul play, though there's currently no evidence suggesting she's met with any harm.

I remembered the name Ko Pha-Ngan, was sure Garrett had been staying there. I wasn't sure about the other island, though, thought back to January and that first night he'd returned home, staying at mine and Trav's apartment.

'Thailand's dope, Step,' he'd told me, beer in hand, as I rolled out the futon on the bedroom floor.

'Why'd you come home early then?' I'd asked. Last I'd heard, he'd been planning on staying at least through spring.

He'd shrugged, fiddled with those stupid leather bracelets he wore. 'Some girl died,' he'd said, quite matter-of-factly. 'British chick.'

'A girl died?'

I'd finished with the futon, and Garrett and I had joined Paige and Travis in the tiny kitchen, where they were preparing dinner – not takeout, for once – the four of us crammed in like sardines. At the mention of a dead girl, they looked up.

'Place was crawling with cops,' Garrett said, hoisting himself onto a worktop. 'Put a real fuckin' downer on things.'

'Jesus, Garrett, *really*?' Even for my brother it was tasteless.

'What?' he said, indignant. 'I'm just telling it how it is. They found her body on some beach.'

Travis, his back to us at the stove, asked, 'You knew her?'

'Nah.' Garrett took a swig of beer, wiped his wrist across his mouth. 'Never met her.'

'How'd she die?' Paige asked, wide-eyed. 'Was it . . . was it an accident?'

'Nuh-uh.' He'd leaned in close, whispered in her ear, loud enough so we all could hear, 'She was murdered.'

Paige had gasped, put a hand to her mouth, and I'd drawn a deep breath, said, 'Fuck's sake, Garrett,' reached around him to a cupboard. 'That's not funny.' Paige had moved aside, but Garrett didn't take the hint. 'Move,' I told him.

But he hadn't budged, had laughed, said, 'Fuck's sake, Steppy, lighten up,' jokingly mimed throttling me.

I went back to my phone, kept scrolling through the news articles. There was a flurry around the same time, covering Amy Johnson's disappearance, her family flying out to Thailand, then, for a week or so, coverage died down, until 13 January.

Body Found in Thailand Search for Missing British Backpacker

Thai police have today confirmed that a body has been recovered on the island of Koh Tao in the search for missing woman Amy Johnson, last seen on December 28. The body, discovered by locals in a remote spot, hasn't yet been formally identified, but Amy's parents and sister, who travelled to Thailand to help with the search, have been informed.

Two days later:

Body Found in Thai Island Search Identified as Missing British Tourist

Police have confirmed that a body found on the Thai island of Koh Tao on 12 January is that of missing Amy Johnson. The 19-year-old gap-year student had been missing for two weeks, after checking into a hostel there after Christmas. Her partially clothed body was discovered by locals in what police are describing as a shallow grave. A murder investigation has been launched, though police have yet to make public the cause of death.

I read on. Another few days later:

Local Man Arrested for Murder of British Tourist on Thai Island

Police have arrested a 24-year-old local man on the island of Koh Tao in connection with the death of British tourist Amy Johnson. Her partially clothed body was discovered by locals on a remote beach two weeks later. Sources say she'd been strangled.

So a local man was arrested – I skim-read the rest of the articles – and went on to be charged with Amy's murder. Why then did Brooke insinuate that Garrett had something to do with it? And why did something about the whole situation not add up, something I couldn't quite put my finger on?

I continued scrolling for a while, had almost given up when I came across a blog entitled *Not the Flying Amy Johnson!* The home page had a photo of Amy – I recognised her from the news articles – and the caption: *Gap-year student from the UK, blogging about my travels in Thailand. Living and loving life!*

The last entry was dated December 25, 2015 and covered Christmas Day, Full Moon parties and plans for New Year. At the end of the post was a photo of a young girl giving the peace sign. Late teens, with big brown eyes, a smiley face and long brown hair – equally long tanned limbs – she was wearing shorts and a bikini top, Christmas tree deely boppers on her head. *Christmas wishes from Thailand, peeps!* the photo was captioned. She was naturally pretty, but with the air of someone who didn't know it, which made me a little uneasy. Why? I wondered. Because that made her Garrett's type? But other than what Brooke had said, I'd no proof she even knew Garrett, let alone that he'd been the last person seen with her.

I scrolled down to the comments beneath. They contained the usual outpouring of grief and emotion (*Omg just read about you in the news. Praying they find you!!!*) mixed with a good dose of trolling (*Wot does she expect to happen to her looking like that lol! Like u would wouldnt u*).

When it came to cases like Amy's, the internet – with its armchair detectives, do-gooders, conspiracy theorists and trolls – was a double-edged sword. Cases that might otherwise have received little attention could go global, but that exposure often came at a price. There was a darker side. For every helpful piece of information there were ten thousand useless ones. It could be hard to sort the wheat from the chaff. And from behind the safety of a keyboard, people could be thoughtless at best, cruel and unkind at worst.

I sighed, rubbed my neck, scrolled back up to the top of Amy's blog, where I'd spied a link to a photo gallery, was about to click on it when my phone pinged, making me jump. Dad.

Where are you?

Shit. I'd completely lost track of time. If I was late before, I was super late now.

Cursing some more under my breath, I dropped my phone into the cup holder, flicked off the interior light and, with a final glance in the mirror – Brooke long gone – set off again.

II

Now

I don't realise I've dozed off until, from somewhere over the other side of the library, someone announces, 'Fifteen minutes till closing!'

I jolt upright, rub my eyes, my head pounding, neck stiff and sore, and look around. The place is almost empty.

I've got no choice but to call it a day, but before I do, I return to the internet, google: *how to access a laptop without a password*. The consensus, according to the web, is that it depends on the laptop. I jot down a couple of things to try, though am not filled with hope. There's a computer repair place somewhere downtown – I've checked online – but because I don't know why I changed my password – what might be on my laptop, what I might have been protecting – I'm reluctant to hand it over to a stranger. The other thing that occurs to me is that maybe I *didn't* change my password. After all, I've used the same one for years. Most people who know me could probably work it out, and my laptop's been unattended at the cabin while I've been in hospital. The thought sends a shiver through me, though I quickly dismiss it: why would someone go to all that trouble? Why not just take the laptop?

The second thing I do is check my old cell phone account. Just because my phone's toast doesn't mean I can't get information on my activity over the last few days. I hold my breath as I log in, my heart lifting when my password's accepted, sinking again when I'm confronted with a long list of meaningless phone numbers. There are so many; without names, there's no way of knowing who they belong to. My heart sinks further when I realise that although I know from Lucky and Krauseneck that Garrett called me around 8.40 the night of my accident, I can't get his cell phone number: there's no record of incoming calls. But there is something in my outgoing ones, a number I appear to have called numerous times in the days leading up to my accident and Mum's death, each call lasting only a few seconds, the last the day itself. On impulse, I fire off a text to it from my new cell phone: *Hey. Who's this?*

It's dark by the time I leave the library and walk the couple of blocks to the parking lot at the back of the vet clinic, where I find Jenna's car, a V W Bug, the old kind. After clearing the windshield and kangarooing my way out of the parking lot, heaters blasting out cold air, my hands are shaking so badly I have to remind myself to breathe. Strange, I think: my brain recalls nothing of my accident, yet my body seems to. Muscle memory.

It's snowing heavily, and by the time I hit the highway I've a line of cars on my tail, so, even though I've got half a tank of fuel, I pull in when I see a gas station up ahead.

The cold hits me as I step from the car, but I breathe it in. It feels surprisingly good. There are two other cars in the forecourt, so I take my time pumping gas, let those customers go ahead before I follow at a distance into the store. The gas station door – another Casey Carter poster in its window – gives a two-tone beep as I enter. One of the customers is at the till, paying for his gas, the other picking up groceries, so I pretend to be shopping, go up and down the aisles, head down, trying to look inconspicuous, feeling anything but.

When the other customers have left, I glance around – I must look shifty as hell – make sure the coast is clear before I approach the counter.

'Just this,' I say, placing an acrylic beanie hat down, *Heartsick Stole My Heart!* embroidered in big letters across the cuff. I'm not sure I'm supposed to cover the scar on my head, but if it makes people stare less, I really don't care. 'And the gas.'

The guy behind the counter looks up and his mouth drops open. 'Holy shit,' he says. 'I mean *ho-lee* shit. Steppy. That you?'

Up close, he looks little older than a kid, but he has a drooping retro-style moustache – looks straight out of a seventies porno – a dirty old trucker cap, a Grateful Dead T-shirt, and flesh tunnels the size of dimes in his ears.

I shift on the spot. 'I'm sorry. Have we met?'

'It's Jesse.' His eyes grow wide. 'You don't remember?'

I bite my lip, shake my head. 'I was in a car accident?' I say it like a question.

The guy, Jesse, nods, a little too eagerly. 'I know,' he says, then, 'Shit. I'm sorry. About your mom.'

I mumble a thanks.

'I didn't recognise you,' he tells me, 'not at first. You look pretty different.'

'The car accident?' I say again. 'I just got out of hospital. I've, um, I've been here before?'

'Uh-huh.' He nods. 'Thanksgiving. You picked up some groceries.'

He stares at me like a kid fascinated with a bug. I feel awkward, push the beanie closer to him, make a pretence of looking in my wallet.

'Oh, yeah, right.' He picks the beanie up, about to scan it, then hands it to me. 'On the house,' he says, like that somehow makes up for my car accident and my dead mum. But I know he means well, so I thank him, and he snips off the tag without asking while I pay for the gas.

'Hey,' he says, as I make to leave. 'You, uh, you manage to speak with Evan? Before your . . . uh, before the . . . you know?'

'Sorry?'

'Evan. When you were here Thanksgiving, I told you you should speak with him.'

I'm already a few steps from the counter, pulling the beanie on. I turn to face him – I must look ridiculous – take the list of names from my pocket. 'You wrote this?' I hand it to him.

'This one.' He points at the topmost name, Evan Coombs, hands it back. 'Not the rest of 'em.'

'I know,' I say, 'I wrote those. Look' – I decide honesty's the best policy – 'I know it's crazy, but I've no memory of anything. Not the last few days – the ones before my accident.' I don't say *the ones before my mum was murdered*.

The guy takes a deep breath. ''Kay,' he says. 'So, like, me and my girlfriend, Ashley, we're totally into *Dark Corners*?' He stops, waits for a reaction, maybe hoping what he's said will jog my memory.

I shrug apologetically.

'Anyhoo,' he goes on, 'me and you get to talking – when you were in on Thanksgiving? – and I tell you me and Ashley are fans – like, *huge* fans – and I ask if you're in town looking into Casey Carter's disappearance. You know about Casey Carter, right?'

I nod. 'What did I tell you?'

'You said you're not,' he goes on, 'not for a second season, anyhow, but, like, you still seem interested – I guess with your brother an' all – and I tell you you should speak with Evan.'

'Evan Coombs.'

'Right.'

'Because . . .?'

'Oh, right, yeah. You can't remember. So, like, my girlfriend's older sister – Tiffany? – she used to date Evan. Still does, kinda. And Evan bartends at Buddy's – the bar Casey was seen leaving on Halloween with your brother. Uh, you know about your brother, right?'

I'm not sure exactly what he's checking I know, but assume it's the fact that Garrett was the last person seen with Casey, so I nod.

'Well, Ashley said Tiffany said Evan said it's not your brother the cops should be looking at. Said something about some girl Casey got in a fight with.'

'That night? Someone Casey knew? Someone with motive?'

'You asked me pretty much the same thing on Thanksgiving,' he says, 'but you'd really have to ask Evan. I told you that then too.'

'But you don't know if I've done it already?'

'Sorry.' It's Jesse's turn to shrug apologetically. 'But Buddy's is only a little ways along the highway, so maybe . . .'

'Okay,' I tell him. 'Thanks for the info.'

'Um, hey?' I'm turning to leave again when Jesse calls after me. 'They, uh, they found him yet? Your brother?'

'Not that I know of.' I'm at the door. I pull my new hat lower, brace myself for the cold. 'No one knows where he is.'

My phone pings in my pocket and I take it out, almost drop it when I see the message, am still staring at the screen when Jesse's voice makes me jump.

'Not even his wife?'

12

Then

I didn't drive the rest of the way to my parents' as carefully as I should nor as fast as I might have, considering I was running so behind. This far down the mountain, there'd been no snowfall yet, but the roads were slick, and I breathed a sigh of relief as I reached the final leg of my journey, turned up the long driveway that cut a swathe through the forest, glimpsed the house at the top, lit up like a beacon, all glass and wood and stone.

My parents' house had never really been my home. Having moved to New York with Travis a year or so after graduating from uni, I'd long since flown the nest when they bought the place four years ago. Had Garrett actually stuck college out, it shouldn't have been his home either, but when my parents moved here, he'd sort of tagged along. At times, I wondered why on earth they chose this place, so remote, nestled in a crook of the mountain and surrounded by forest, but in truth, it was Mum who'd been the driving force behind the move; Mum, who professed to love solitude and the winter the way most people profess to love puppies and the ocean. She'd already been winding down her therapy practice for a while, wanted somewhere peaceful to write, was more than ready to give up city life. But while for her this was the perfect home, Dad's work, still in Colorado Springs, meant a lengthy commute, so the compromise was a small apartment in the city, near the hospital, where he lived during the week.

Remote though it was, there was no denying the house was stunning. Three storeys, including a basement, the ground level built from stone that looked as though it had been hewn from the surrounding mountains; the upper storey warm brown timber. There was a magnificent central apex with huge picture windows – much of the upper storey was glass – and a balcony running the width of the house. The living quarters were upstairs, benefiting from the spectacular view, the bedrooms downstairs, Mum's office in the basement.

As I climbed from the car, I saw Dad silhouetted in the light of the open door.

'Welcome home,' he greeted me, something he always said when I visited.

He hugged me, batted away my apologies for being late, because the drive had taken longer than I remembered, the roads were slicker; because I'd had to stop for gas.

'Your mum and I have been keeping up with all your articles and TV appearances,' he said as we made our way upstairs to the living room. 'We're so proud.'

We? I was about to say, before, as if on cue, Mum appeared. She was dressed, as ever, all in black, something fifty-ply – or so it seemed – cashmere. It had been a while since I'd seen her, and though we didn't always see eye to eye, there was something vaguely comforting about those heavy-rimmed tortoiseshell glasses she always wore, her striking red hair, which these days came from a bottle.

'You look good,' I told her as she hugged me.

She paused for the briefest of moments, a hand on each of my shoulders, and I smiled to myself, knew that as she took in the soft feel of my sweater, it must have dawned on her she wasn't the only one sporting cashmere. Following the success of *Dark Corners*, I'd graduated from Zara and J.Crew to Rag & Bone and Club Monaco, albeit on more of an Outnet budget than a Net-a-Porter one. But if I was expecting a compliment from Mum, I was in for a disappointment, and as I handed her the gas station bouquet – 'For you, Mum. Happy Thanksgiving' – she replied, 'Lilies. Always make me think of funerals,' before carrying them from the room at arm's length, like a baby needing its diaper changed.

'The flowers are beautiful, thank you,' Dad said quickly.

I widened my eyes at him – *Really?* – wished that for once in his life he'd stand up to her, but he only smiled, embarrassed, ran a hand through his hair. Dad still had good hair, silver-fox-soap-star or American-president-level good. He was blonde, like Garrett, but unlike Garrett, his sandy waves were now greying.

'Something smells good,' I said, changing the subject.

'It should do.' Dad winked at me. 'Your mum's been watching Eduardo slave over dinner for hours. Get you a drink, sweetheart?'

'Water's fine.' I crossed to the floor-to-ceiling apex window, stared out into the gathering darkness. 'Thanks.'

Dad got me a water, poured himself a finger of whiskey. 'Not celebrating with Travis and his family this year?'

Oh God. I cringed. Hadn't he heard? 'We broke up a few months ago,' I said, glad I wasn't facing him. 'Mum didn't tell you?'

Mum and I didn't exactly phone each other up, have girlie chats, but I had told her about me and Travis. 'Men don't like their partners being more successful than they are. It's emasculating,' was her take on the matter. I suppose I should have just been happy that, in a roundabout way, she was acknowledging the success of *Dark Corners*, though I'd replied, 'It had nothing to do with that,' more than a little defensively, then stopped myself. I couldn't bear to tell her the real reason.

'That's too bad.' Dad nodded sympathetically. 'I always thought you guys were good together.'

'Funny,' I said, my back still to him. 'Me too.' It was all I could do to keep the bitterness from my voice.

Outside, I thought I saw something move in the darkening tree-line, wondered what lurked beyond. This far out of town, my parents didn't bother drawing blinds, didn't even have them in this room. But when night fell, with the house lit up like a Christmas tree, you could see right inside. Like a doll's house you've taken the front off. I shuddered, thought of Casey again, wondered if she might just have gone for a jog, got lost or met with an accident. It was perfectly possible, especially at this time of year. Even without snow, the weather up here was difficult, unpredictable. The mists came down as if from nowhere, snaked silently along the roads and through the trees. Then, almost as quickly as they descended, they'd lift, like cockroaches in a dark room, scattering when the light's turned on. Yes, it was easy to get turned around out here, lose your bearings . . .

'No Garrett?' I asked, tearing myself from the window.

'Guess he's running late too,' Dad replied.

I rolled my eyes. It was fine for Garrett to be late. Garrett had been late for his own twenty-first birthday party – the one my parents had thrown him at great expense – having spent the previous night in the drunk tank. He'd been late for the only wedding where the groom had been dumb enough to make him a groomsman, after he and the groom woke up in a dry riverbed, miles outside town, with no memory of how they'd got there and Sharpie-drawn handlebar moustaches on their faces. He'd missed the flight for our parents' anniversary vacation because he'd been picked up by police for trespassing on a local golf course and firing off a potato gun. He'd *even* missed our grandmother's funeral, after getting into a six-man brawl at a biker bar on a road trip back from Coachella. Yet somehow, in Mum's eyes, at least, these indiscretions were more acceptable than me running fifty minutes late for Thanksgiving dinner.

Tonight, the prodigal son rocked up in his beaten-up old Jeep an hour after me, looking like the handsome sociopath in every movie you've ever seen and reeking of weed, though no one said anything. He was easily the biggest presence in any room, so it took a second to register that he'd brought a plus one: a few steps behind, just inside the doorway of the living room and looking decidedly uncomfortable, stood a young woman. I looked over at Dad, trying to gauge if he'd known Garrett was bringing company. I couldn't tell.

'Aren't you going to introduce us, Garrett?' Mum had materialised again.

'Oh, hey, sure,' Garrett said. 'Mum, Dad, sis, this is Taylor. Tay,' he looked at his date, grinned, 'this is everyone.'

It went without saying that like all Garrett's dates, Taylor was extremely good-looking. She bore an unsettling resemblance to Casey Carter – *missing* Casey Carter – though she lacked Casey's girl-next-door glow, was much thinner, too – too thin – with the look of someone who knew the calorie count of everything she ate. Even so, no one could say my brother didn't have a type.

'So *this* is the lovely Taylor,' Mum said, in a voice that told me she didn't think Taylor was lovely at all.

I was surprised she managed to avoid that thing she always did, though, that thing so many women do when they meet other women for the first time: the looking them up and down, sizing them up in a way they think is incredibly subtle, when in fact it's incredibly obvious. Maybe Dad had had a word after all, laid down some ground rules.

While Mum disappeared off to the kitchen again, Dad fixed Taylor a Diet Coke, tried his best to engage her in conversation, and so although I'd rather have conversed with a rat in a dark alleyway, I found myself stuck with Garrett.

'Hey, sis. Haven't seen you since New York.'

Though my brother had been home for months, he had the air of someone who'd only recently returned from backpacking round South East Asia – the mussed-up hair, the permanent tan, the totally unsuitable clothing (it was winter, he was wearing Jesus sandals), those stupid leather bracelets. He gave me a playful punch in the arm, hard enough that it hurt, though he might as well have sucker-punched me in the stomach. *New York?* He was really going to go there? That whole few days had been a dumpster fire, and he was going to bring it up like he was talking about the weather?

Things didn't improve as the evening progressed.

'I hear they cancelled the Thanksgiving parade,' I said innocently, during a lull in the already stilted dinner conversation.

My words sent a ripple round the table, like a glum Mexican wave. Mum looked irritated, Dad on edge, Taylor more uncomfortable than ever. The only person who didn't look bothered was Garrett.

'Come on, guys,' I said, when no one replied. 'What's the story?'

'Steppy . . .' Dad shot me a look that said I was treading on thin ice. Not so much a rebuke, more a warning I chose to ignore. It irritated me that he never checked Garrett or Mum, yet here he was checking me, simply for addressing the elephant in the room.

'There is no story,' Mum said, though the vehemence with which she speared a carrot with her fork said otherwise.

'Since when was a missing girl no story? She's been gone, what' – I totted it up in my head – 'three and a half weeks already?'

'*She's been gone three and a half weeks already*,' Garrett parroted in a whiny voice, a supposed imitation of mine, something he'd done throughout our childhood. 'For someone who's pretending not to know a lot about it,' he said, 'you seem to know a helluva lot about it.'

'Hard not to,' I shot back. 'There are posters up all over town.'

Taylor coughed. Mum took a deep breath, was about to say something when Garrett stopped her. 'Mum, just chill,' he told her. 'It's okay. Steppy's just interested, aren't you, Step?'

I didn't reply.

'You been on your little forums, Steppy?' Garrett asked. He looked directly at me, a challenge. His tone was light and he was smiling, but there was an edge to his voice. There was always an edge with Garrett.

'I've read stuff online, if that's what you mean.' I held his stare. A tension had settled over the table like a cloud of toxic dust. 'Like, that you were the last one to see her.'

'Last one seen *with* her,' Garrett said, exactly the kind of smart-ass distinction I'd expect him to make. 'There's a difference.'

'Tomayto, tomato,' I said.

'Well, lucky for me it doesn't matter. Pass the potatoes?'

'Oh? How come?'

'Because,' he said, scooping vegetables onto his plate, 'I dropped her home, came straight here, stayed the whole night. Cops've cleared me.'

I was about to ask how, exactly, but Mum got there first. 'This is *not* appropriate Thanksgiving dinner table conversation.'

'Mum's right,' Garrett agreed smugly. 'I'm more than happy to have this talk with you, Step, but now's not the time.' He raised his glass. Mum followed swiftly, as did Taylor and Dad, then, with all the reluctance of someone being led to the gallows, me. 'To family!' he toasted, then, 'Hey, I know. Let's go round the table' – he paused, looked at each one of us in turn, lingered on me – 'and say what we're thankful for.'

Dad looked sceptical, like he knew Garrett was up to something, but Mum just smiled, tipped her head. 'Garrett, that's such a lovely idea.'

'I'll start.' Garrett jumped back in before anyone else had the chance. 'I'm thankful for two things this year. First' – he looked at Mum and Dad, pointedly ignored me – 'I'm thankful for family.' I wanted to vomit. 'It's not been easy, but you guys – Mum, Dad – well, you've really been there for me lately.' He turned, reached down beside him, took Taylor's hand. Her discomfort evaporated and she beamed up at him. 'And the second thing I'm thankful for,' he said, 'is my beautiful wife, Taylor.'

I almost choked on my turkey. Dad practically spat out his wine. Next to him, Mum's fork clattered to her plate. *'Jesus Christ!'* I was sure I heard her hiss under her breath.

There was an excruciating silence and I almost expected Garrett to go, *Kidding!* but he didn't. My eyes went instinctively to Taylor's left hand – the one Garrett's now enfolded. Was she wearing a wedding ring? If she was, how the hell hadn't I noticed? Because, I saw now, she wore rings on almost every finger, including her thumbs, those trendy stacking types, a mixture of silver and gold.

Following my gaze, Garrett held up Taylor's hand, showed it to the table. Sure enough, on her left ring finger was a slim gold band. 'I mean, this is just till we get something better.'

'Oh, I don't need anything fancy,' Taylor said quickly.

Dad cleared his throat. 'Well,' he said, forcing a laugh, 'I can't say it's not a little unexpected . . .'

'Lord give me strength,' muttered Mum, though she wasn't remotely religious.

Taylor looked down at the table again.

There were some mumbled congratulations – me and Dad – some

mumbled and not so mumbled thanks – Taylor and Garrett respectively – before we all returned in earnest to our meal. For a few minutes, all that could be heard was the clink of cutlery and glassware, until the silence was no longer awkward but unbearable.

'So,' Mum said, and the huge mahogany dining table round which we were seated, the one she'd insisted be shipped from the UK when we moved back, twelve years after we'd left, suddenly felt uncomfortably small. 'When did this' – she held up her fork, circled it in Taylor's direction, drawing an invisible frame around her – 'happen?'

I wasn't clear whether she meant the marriage or Taylor, but even for Mum it was beyond rude, and though I wouldn't usually stick my neck out where Garrett was concerned, Taylor looked about to burst into tears, so I said, '*Mum.*'

But she ignored me and Garrett ignored us both. 'Week ago today,' he said, like he hadn't just dropped the most almighty bombshell. 'Me and Tay took a little road trip to Vegas. Drove there Wednesday, married Thursday, home Friday.'

'My God.' Mum put her head in her hands, then looked up, straight at Taylor. 'You're not pregnant, are you?'

'Christ, Jayne,' Dad said.

Taylor hadn't been drinking alcohol, I'd noticed. But then neither, uncharacteristically, had Garrett.

Mum glared at him. 'I have to ask.'

Taylor flushed, squirmed in her seat, looked like she wanted the ground to open up and swallow her. Garrett just looked amused. 'Jesus, Mum, you're so funny.'

'So, uh, how long have you been together?' I tried. This was the first I'd heard of Taylor, but it didn't mean they hadn't been going steady for a while. Then I reminded myself this was Garrett we were talking about.

'Four months three days,' Taylor said – almost the first words I'd heard her utter all evening – right at the same time Garret shrugged, said, 'Few weeks.'

Taylor flushed again.

'Sounds pretty serious.' Mum's voice dripped with sarcasm.

'Well, what is it they say?' Garrett threaded the fingers of his right hand through Taylor's left, rested them interlocking on the table. 'When you know, you know.'

Taylor glowed. Mum radiated irritation, opened her mouth to say something, but thankfully Dad got there first.

'Well,' he said, 'congratulations, both of you. And Taylor' – he raised his glass. Garrett, Taylor and I followed. This time Mum was the one a beat behind – 'welcome to the family.'

13

Now

I'm back in Jenna's car, on the gas station forecourt, staring at my phone.

It's Paige. Who's this? the reply to my text reads.

The mystery number. But why on earth had I been calling Paige? I'm too much of a coward to reply for now, though, so instead I text Dad – *Garrett's married??? No one thought to tell me???* – then Lucky – *WTF Lucky. Garrett has a wife???*

I feel like I'm living in some sort of parallel universe – one where I'm back speaking to Paige, where Garrett's married – and when, moments later, my cell phone rings, in the second before I see Dad's name on caller ID, I think it might be Paige, feel happy and sick all at once.

'You don't remember?' Dad asks when I answer, then, when I don't reply, 'You don't remember.'

'When did this happen?'

'Recently.'

'Jesus Christ.' I have so many questions, though there's one thing I'm sure of. 'You know what they'll be saying online when they find out?'

'I do,' he says after a pause.

'Do you? Really? Garrett's the prime suspect in a murder – two, if you believe the internet – but his wife, whoever the hell she is, can't be compelled to testify against him. *That's* what they'll be saying, Dad – that he's got something to hide.'

After I've calmed down, Dad tries to reassure me – this isn't what I think it is. Garrett, perpetually-single-changes-his-girlfriends-like-most-people-change-their-underwear Garrett, at the grand old age of twenty-seven, has simply decided to settle down. Then, as if that revelation doesn't stun me enough, Dad drops another bomb: I've met Garrett's wife.

'She's called Taylor,' he says. 'Sweet girl.'

'Is she on the run with him?'

'No,' Dad says. 'And your brother's not on the run.'

Until earlier today, I didn't think he was on the run either. In my mind, I made excuses for him, even voiced them to Lucky. Now, I feel stupid.

It takes fifteen more minutes to dissuade Dad from getting in his car and driving all the way up here. Somehow I manage it, and after we hang up, I start the engine, fully intending to head back to the cabin. But at the gas station exit I hesitate, and before I know it, I've put my blinker on and pulled out onto the highway again, though I'm not headed back to the cabin.

As I pull into Buddy's parking lot, it appears the bar is open, though it isn't exactly jumping: there are only two other cars. I climb from Jenna's Bug and pick my way carefully over the uneven snow-covered ground that no one's bothered to clear. The first thing that strikes me is that Buddy's seems a weird place for Garrett to patronise. The second thing that strikes me is that this is exactly the type of place

Garrett would go when he wants to be big man on campus – throw his money around, act like an entitled ass. Outside, along the front of the porch, sits a row of grubby-looking snow-covered tables and chairs. A single table's been cleared, an ashtray full of freshly stubbed-out cigarette butts on it. I climb the porch steps, which look like they'd be hazardous for patrons even without snow, and open the front door.

It takes a moment for my eyes to adjust to the bar's dim light; when they do, I see the interior is exactly what I expected from the outside: small, low-ceilinged, everything sticky-toffee brown – sticky floors and bar top too, no doubt – a pool table over one side, jukebox the other. The floor's split level, a wooden balustrade – moulded spindles that look like they've been torn from someone's home staircase – providing a barrier between the two levels, punctuated in the middle by yet more steps, which I descend to get to the bar.

There's no one around but an old man the far side of the room nursing a drink. Behind the bar is the usual array of liquor bottles, fridges full of beers and soft drinks. Above it hangs a sign:

> We don't serve women
> Bring your own

Classy joint, I think with a wry smile. Maybe this *is* Garrett's kind of place after all.

It's warm, and I instinctively go to remove my *Heartsick Stole My Heart!* beanie – which I'm wearing inside out – then think better of it, take my coat off instead.

I'm climbing onto a bar stool when my phone pings: Lucky.

God Steppy I'm so sorry. I didn't realise you didn't know.

Apparently I did, I text back. *Just didn't remember. Not your fault.*

I'm putting my phone away when a door behind the bar opens and a man appears. He's small and wiry but muscular – the kind of guy you'd put money on in a bar fight – wearing a shirt with sleeves rolled up to his elbows, revealing tattoos covering both arms, and a tweed vest. His hair is dark, and he has both an undercut and a topknot, a vibe somewhere between hipster and parkour athlete.

'Help you?' he asks, like he knows I'm not here for a drink. I wonder if he thinks I'm a reporter.

'You Evan? Evan Coombs?'

He narrows his eyes at me. 'Depends who's asking.'

'I'm Steppy,' I tell him. 'Jesse – at the gas station along the highway? – he gave me your name. Said you might have some information about Casey Carter. Her disappearance?'

At the mention of Jesse's name, the man, Evan, smiles. 'He did, huh?' He begins reaching glasses down from a shelf, polishing them with a chequered cloth from over his shoulder.

'I know this might be a weird question,' I say, 'but have we met before? Did I come here, ask you questions?'

'You for real?'

'I've been in an accident' – I pull off my beanie, show him my head, but he doesn't flinch, has probably seen much worse working here – 'can't remember anything that happened over the last . . .' I stop, consider. 'Well, I'm not quite sure how long, but the couple weeks before my accident, at least.'

'Who'd you say you are?'

'Steppy. Steppy Corner? My brother's Garrett.'

Evan makes the kind of face most people do when they find out Garrett and I are related, one that says they don't see it.

'Jesse said you told him,' I go on, 'or maybe you told his girlfriend, or his girlfriend's sister' – at this, a flicker of amusement crosses Evan's face – 'that *you* said it wasn't my brother the cops should be looking at?' Then I add, 'For Casey's disappearance.'

'I did?' He twists his mouth. 'Does it really matter now? I mean, the cops cleared your brother in relation to Casey. You know that, right?'

'I know,' I say, 'but people – the internet – still think he had something to do with it. So if you know anything that might help find her . . .'

Evan puts down the glass he's polishing, plants his hands squarely on the bar. 'Okay,' he says, 'but before I tell you this, I have to qualify it by saying I don't like your brother. He's a real dick.'

'Agreed,' I say. 'He comes here a lot?'

'Enough for my liking.'

'Do you know if he knew Casey? Like, if he'd met her before that night?'

'Not that I know of,' Evan says. 'I'd never seen her before that night either.'

'So who is it you think the police should be looking at?'

'Well,' he says, 'Halloween, Casey was here with a bunch of girl-friends. But there was one of 'em that . . . well, Casey and this girl, they really got into it.'

'They fought?'

'Not physically. Looked like it might come to that, though.'

'Do you know what they were fighting about?'

Evan twists his mouth again, shakes his head. 'So, like, before your brother gets chatting with Casey, I see this girl she arrived with – her friend – with your brother. Like, *all* over him. And I can tell your brother's not into her, is trying to give her the brush-off. But she's real persistent, this chick. And then along comes Casey, and it's game over for the friend.'

'How'd you mean?'

'I mean, your brother, beautiful girl.'

'So you think Casey's friend was jealous 'cos she liked my brother? She and Casey were fighting over him?'

Evan raises an eyebrow. 'Wouldn't be the first time.'

I'm not sure whether he means the first time two girls fought over my brother, or the first two girls fought over a guy in general. Either way, he's right. And Garrett, I'm sure, would have loved every minute of it.

'And after Casey went missing, did you speak to the police?'

'Sure.' Evan shrugs. 'Told 'em everything. But at that point, they were focusing on your brother. I heard through the grapevine they cleared him, but no one ever came back to tell me, or ask me anything else. I mean, I offered to show them the surveillance footage when they were here—'

'Back up,' I say. 'You've got it on tape?'

'We usually delete all footage after a week,' Evan says.

We're in the bar's tiny back office, leaning over a laptop on a cluttered desk. Evan sweeps stuff from in front of it – stapler, calculator, pile of invoices – and boots it up.

'Something told me I should hang onto this, though.' He opens a file on the desktop, presses play. 'There's no audio, but you can see what's going on.'

He steps back and I take his place, lean in.

The screen is split in two, each half showing footage of the bar from a different angle. It takes me a second to work out what I'm looking at, but one of the cameras is clearly positioned right above the bar, looking outward; the other above the front door, capturing punters coming and going. Although, as Evan says, there's no sound, the quality of the footage is clear; the date and time on the bottom of the screen reads: 10.31.16, 10.47 p.m.

'Keep your eye on this one.' Evan points at the left-hand side of the screen.

This half of the footage shows a sea of bodies, all in Halloween costume apart from my brother, whose only nod to the occasion is a cheap-looking plastic kids' mask, perched like a hat on the top of his head. He's talking to a girl with her back to the camera, and though they're some distance away, I can see from her body language that she's flirting. She's leaning in, standing on tiptoe to whisper in his ear – or shout; it would've been pretty loud that night – constantly touching her hair, tipping her head back, touching Garrett's arm. Even though I can't see her face, I know she's laughing at my brother's jokes. I roll my eyes.

Evan leans in, moves the footage on. 'So your brother and this girl are talking,' he says. 'Then nothing much happens for another few minutes.' He presses play again. 'Till this.'

My brother and the mystery girl have been joined by a third person I recognise as Casey. She's facing the camera and looks as beautiful in the video footage as she does in the photos I've seen of her. The three chat for a minute, then my brother ducks out, stands a step or so back, half talking to someone else behind him. Meanwhile Casey and the other girl appear to be having an animated conversation. The girl with her back to the camera is throwing her hands up. Casey seems to be trying to calm her down, though she looks exasperated at the same time, like she can't get a word in edgewise. The conversation – if you can call it that – continues for more than a couple of minutes, before the girl with her back to the camera grabs Casey's arm. Casey pulls away, almost spilling her drink, and my brother steps back in, apparently trying to defuse the situation. The other girl turns and storms off.

Evan leans in again. 'There she goes.' He points to the right-hand side, the footage from the camera above the entrance, and my eyes flick to the other half of the screen.

Sure enough, seconds later, a girl flies towards the front door, passes beneath the camera and disappears. Were it not for the fact that Evan rewinds the footage, presses pause before she exits, I don't think I'd have had time to recognise her. She's too fast. But as the screen freezes, I get a good look at her face for the first time. It's contorted in anger, framed by long brown hair, and though she's a chunkier build than Casey, the two girls might be mistaken for sisters. They even have matching outfits, though this girl's half-skeleton face is tear-streaked, and she pulls her flower crown from her head as she flees. Still, I recognise her. The second name on my list. The one I appear to have crossed out. Casey Carter's self-proclaimed bestie; founder of the Find Casey Carter Facebook group.

And now, in my mind, a suspect in the disappearance of her best friend.

Brooke Morgenstern.

14

Then

After Garrett's marriage bombshell, the rest of Thanksgiving dinner was strained to say the least, and by the end of the main course, I was wondering how much more I could endure.

When my cell phone started buzzing as the plates were being cleared, I slipped it from my pocket beneath the table, intending to silence it, before glimpsing the name lit up on the screen. My heart skipped a beat.

'Sorry,' I said to everyone, 'I have to take this.'

Dad gave a thumbs-up. 'Go for it.'

'Really, Stephanie? At dinner?' Mum said, tutting, despite the fact she'd hardly said two words to me all evening, despite the fact that I was not the one who'd made an already awkward night into a complete shit show.

I pretended not to hear her and hastily left the room, made sure I was far enough down the hallway before I answered.

'Paige?' I said, breathless.

There was silence, then a voice said, 'No, Steppy.'

'Travis?' My heart almost stopped.

'You've been calling her again,' Travis said.

'Like, two, three times, tops.'

'Six.'

'Who's counting?' I laughed nervously, felt myself redden. 'You screening Paige's calls now?'

He ignored me. 'It needs to stop.'

'I need to speak with her.'

'Paige doesn't need to speak with you.'

'She can tell me that herself.'

There was a pause, then Travis said, 'What do you not get, Steppy? After what your brother did, Paige doesn't want anything to do with your family.'

'After what my *brother* did? *You* slept with my best friend, Travis.'

'Steppy,' he hissed, 'get real,' and I wondered where he was, wondered if Paige was standing behind him, listening in. 'Things had been over between us for months.'

'Are you fucking serious?!' I shouted. 'We were still living together, Travis, still sleeping in the same fucking bed.'

Further down the hall, Dad's head popped round the door. 'Uh, everything okay?'

I covered the phone with my hand, forced a smile. 'Fine, yeah. Sorry, Dad. Work stuff.'

He hesitated, clearly concerned, then said, 'If you say so,' disappeared back into the dining room.

I waited till he'd gone, then turned, headed down the stairs to get more privacy. 'It would've been nice,' I hissed, without bothering to check Travis was still there, 'if I'd actually got that memo.'

There was silence again, then Travis, sighing. 'You'd completely checked out of our relationship.' He sounded weary.

'That's so not true,' I said. 'It's also not fair.'

'Come on, Steppy.' I imagined him the other end of the line, throwing up his hands. 'I barely saw you. And when I did, all you ever talked about was *Dark* fucking *Corners*.'

The venom in those last three words threw me for a loop. Travis was one of the calmest people I knew. Even when things angered him, he rarely lost his temper, barely ever swore – that was one of the things that had attracted me to him; that and the fact that, unlike previous boyfriends, he'd never sought any kind of bromance with my brother; had not, in fact, liked Garrett since the start. Not even during our long-drawn-out break-up, with its excruciating silences, its awkwardly polite, stilted conversations, did I ever see him lose it. The last time that had happened had been the start of the year, when Garrett returned from Thailand, was staying at our apartment. On the Garrett scale of fuck-ups it had been minor, really. He'd borrowed (i.e. without asking) a favourite sweater of Trav's, had worn it on a night out, come home next morning looking like he'd spent the night in a sewer.

'Jeez, bud, I'm sorry,' he'd said, when Travis remonstrated with him over it. 'Don't have a fucking stroke.'

We'd been crammed into the kitchen – me, Travis, Paige and Garrett. 'I've just got back from, like, three months in Thailand,' said Garrett, in a tone that said he couldn't see why Travis was making such a big deal. 'I haven't got any clean clothes, dude. What am I supposed to do?'

'Go to a laundromat, like any normal fucking adult human being,' Travis had said.

Paige, who by that time hadn't learned the hard way, still thought Garrett was pretty cute, stifled a giggle. He'd winked at her and she'd blushed, giggled some more. 'Laundromats are for fuckin' chumps,' he said – he'd never able been able to resist playing to the crowd – and Travis had rolled his eyes, said, 'Jesus Christ,' through gritted teeth.

An almighty row had ensued – so bad, Travis stormed out – and, having phoned Mum, given her some sob story about how Travis and I were treating him, my brother was gone by the afternoon, had checked into the nearest five-star hotel on Mum's advice, charged it to her credit card.

'Steppy? You still there?' Travis again.

I opened my mouth to speak, but couldn't; gulped down the lump in my throat. Though he'd never actually voiced it, I'd always felt that secretly Travis resented *Dark Corners*, specifically its – *my* – success. I suppose I thought he'd get over it, that when the hype died down, things would go back to normal. Until it did, he'd have to deal with it in the same way I dealt with the fact that although I'd wanted to stay in the UK after we graduated, we'd moved to New York, because it was what *Travis* wanted, where *Travis* was from, because *Travis* already had a job lined up, working at his dad's company. We *all* have to make sacrifices.

'I barely saw you,' he went on. He was calmer now, but that almost made it hurt more. 'You were so caught up in solving a bunch of strangers' problems, you couldn't see what was right in front of you.'

'What?' I managed a bitter laugh. 'My boyfriend and best friend hooking up behind my back?'

'No,' he said. 'That our relationship was falling apart.' He paused. 'That your brother raped Paige.'

Your brother raped Paige. The moment he said it, I felt like all the air had been sucked out of me. There was a ringing in my ears that filled my head, like the aftermath of a bomb going off. It had, in a way. I wanted desperately to unhear those words, unpick them like errant stitching, un-know what, deep down, I think I'd always known, though not even Paige had said it. I'd tried so many times to elicit the truth from her in the days, weeks, months after it all happened; had begged her to tell me. I'd left messages, sent texts and emails, but on the rare occasion I'd managed to get hold of her, the most she'd ever say was: *Something happened that night. Something bad . . .*

'Trav . . .' I started to say, before I realised he wasn't there any more.

I looked desperately at my phone screen – had he hung up? – realised my battery had finally died. *Shit.* Travis would no doubt think *I'd* hung up on *him*, would probably be saying to Paige right now, 'Told you so.'

Suddenly I felt like I was going to be sick. I lurched down the hallway intending to use the guest bathroom at the far end, realised halfway there I wouldn't make it in time, so pushed my way through the nearest door instead – Garrett's bedroom (he had his own room here, unlike me). I rushed into the en suite, where I fell to my knees, promptly puked up my Thanksgiving dinner into the toilet. Though it seemed kind of petty, the fact that it was Garrett's bathroom felt like poetic justice.

I must have sat with my head over the toilet bowl for five minutes, but when at last I stopped being sick, I felt better. I cleaned up as best I could, then drank some water from the tap, splashed some on my face – deathly pale in the mirror – and looked around. The bathroom was spotlessly clean, like a hotel bathroom awaiting guests, only a toothbrush, toothpaste and razor lying out on the sink. I turned off the light and headed back into the bedroom, realising as I did how alien the house felt, like a stranger's home. I opened the walk-in closet and switched on the light. It was empty, mostly, just a handful of clothes filling a fraction of the hanging space, a solitary pair of sneakers on the floor. Back out in the room, I marvelled at how tasteful it was: pale-coloured walls, bed linen in neutral shades and natural textures. It was a far cry from Garrett's teenage bedroom, with its unwashed clothes and dirty dishes, its posters of girls on the walls, its rumpled bed, stash of weed (and probably porn), under it. *This* decor had Mum's name all over it.

I don't know why I lingered. Maybe it was because I was reluctant to rejoin my family upstairs. Maybe it was simply curiosity, born of the fact that Garrett had apparently spent the night here after dropping Casey Carter home on Halloween. Maybe I was hoping to find something, some sort of clue – which, admittedly, seemed a long shot: the place was clean and empty. Maybe, though, all I really wanted, as ridiculous as it sounded, was to see for myself that Casey Carter wasn't here, like her absence somehow proved Garret wasn't involved in her disappearance – like he'd have been dumb enough to bring her here, stash her in his closet or under the bed.

But still, I breathed a sigh of relief: no Casey Carter, nor any trace of her either.

The room was dark, illuminated only by moonlight, a thin silvery strip falling across the room from the patio doors. As I'd rushed through to get to the toilet, I hadn't switched the light on, and I wondered what self-respecting detective (even an armchair one) would conduct a search in the dark. On the other side of Garrett's bed was a nightstand; on the nightstand a bedside lamp. I really needed to get back upstairs – they'd no doubt be wondering where I was – but still, I crossed to the nightstand and switched the lamp on, saw, now that I was closer, that the drawer was ever-so-slightly open. I slid it fully open and surveyed the sparse array of contents: an old watch, a packet of gum, a lighter, a couple of old pens, a phone charger, a tangle of USB cables . . . And something else. A slip of card. I picked it up – a matchbook – turned it over in my fingers. On the back was an ad for a tattoo studio; across the front, *Buddy's* was printed in olde-worlde font.

I gasped: *Buddy's*. The bar Casey was last seen at. If the matchbook was from Halloween, I realised, it could, sort of, back Garrett's story that he'd come here after dropping Casey home, spent the night. But that was the problem: I'd no idea how long the matchbook *had* been here. If Garrett had been to Buddy's before, he could have left it here any time before or since. I sighed, about to put it back, when I caught sight of something inside. A smudge of ink. Carefully I opened it up. Twenty pristine, papery matches, like tiny piano keys, and there, on the underside of the cardboard flap, a string of handwritten numbers.

03270929121501096

What on earth . . .? I held it beneath the lamp, as if that would literally shed some light on it. It didn't, not really, but there *was* something that struck me, something about the writing, something—

The whole room illuminated and I jumped, whirled round to see Mum standing in the doorway, her hand on the light switch.

'God, you scared me.' I put a hand to my chest, palmed the matchbook simultaneously, then slipped it into my back pocket without looking down.

'Can I help you with something?' Mum asked.

I held up my dead cell phone, gestured at the open nightstand drawer. 'My phone died in the middle of a call, can you believe?' I pulled a face: *What am I like?* 'I was looking for a charger.'

'You might have just asked,' Mum said. 'We have the same cell phone.'

'Right,' I replied. 'Guess I wasn't really thinking.'

She waited, watched me as I slid the drawer shut and switched off the lamp. I took my time doing it, tried my best to look like someone who was there for entirely innocent reasons, who hadn't just been caught snooping. As I passed inches from Mum and she flicked out the light, closed the door behind us, I could have sworn I felt the matchbook in my pocket, could have sworn the ink was radiating from it, pulsing like a vein. I could only pray I didn't look as guilty as I felt, that Mum couldn't tell I was hiding something.

For that was the odd thing about the matchbook, I realised: the writing. It wasn't some unknown stranger's. It wasn't even Garrett's. But I did recognise it.

And though a matchbook from a dive bar was not something I'd ever associate with my mother, the string of numbers staring up at me moments before had, I was quite sure, been written by her.

15

Now

There's not much more to be gleaned from the rest of the footage, but Evan plays it anyway. Cut back to Casey and my brother on the other half of the screen, and Casey looks a little shell-shocked, while my brother, true to form, appears to laugh the whole thing off. They chat a bit longer while they finish their drinks, their body language comfortable, flirtatious, before – fast-forward twenty minutes or so – leaving their empty bottles on a nearby table and heading through the crowded bar to the door. My tired eyes flick once again to the other half of the screen and I watch them leave together, Casey, smiling, a step ahead of Garrett, looking back at him every now and then like they're chatting, my brother's hand at the small of her back, guiding her gently. Nothing unusual, just a good-looking couple most people would probably assume were boyfriend and girlfriend leaving a bar. Then they're gone. The time stamp reads 11.39 p.m.

'And that' – Evan pauses the footage again – 'is the last official sighting of Casey Carter.'

My eyes ache from watching it so intently. 'Did the other girl come back?' I lean my head on one hand, massage my temple with the other.

'Not that I saw. Not that the camera picked up either.'

'But she could've hung around outside,' I say. 'Waited for Garrett and Casey to leave.'

'Coulda.' Evan shrugs. 'We gotta camera outside too, but it's not working.'

Back out in the bar, I've thanked Evan, am about to leave, when I think of something.

'I don't suppose you know what this means?' I take the Buddy's matchbook with the writing from my pocket, hand it to him.

'It's one of ours all right,' he confirms, nods at a container of matchbooks the other end of the bar.

'I'd figured as much,' I tell him. 'But look inside.'

He opens the matchbook, squints closer. 'That blood?' He raises an eyebrow, doesn't wait for an answer. 'What do the numbers mean?'

'I was hoping you could tell me.'

'Dunno. Phone number, maybe?' He rubs his chin. 'A foreign one? Seems kinda long, though.' He looks up. 'Where'd you get it?'

'I don't know,' I admit. 'I mean, obviously it came from here, but I've no idea how I ended up with it. Seems it was on me the night of my car accident, though: I found it in the jeans I'd been wearing.'

'This not your writing?' He hands the matchbook back.

I shake my head, decide not to mention I knew it was my mum's the moment I laid eyes on it at the cabin. That would only complicate things. 'I was wondering if I might have been here before, spoken to you, picked it up then, but you said I hadn't . . .'

'Right,' Evan says. 'I'm here most days, but even if I hadn't been and you'd stopped by, whoever was would've told me.'

'I'm only assuming it's significant because it was on me the night of my accident, but it might be years old, a total red herring.'

'Hey,' he reaches back out, 'let me see it again.'

I hand the matchbook back, watch him turn it over.

'Well,' he says, straightening up, 'the one thing I can be sure of is, whoever it belonged to, they got it no earlier than Halloween.'

'How come?'

'Our old matchbooks were only printed on one side,' he explains. 'This one?' He holds it out, shows me the back. 'It's got the ad for Heartsick Ink. We only started giving these ones out on Halloween.'

'For sure?'

He nods. 'Hundred per cent. I remember 'cos we'd run out of the old ones a couple weeks before. These new ones came in on Hallow-een. I was the unlucky sucker had to unpack 'em all, like I didn't already have enough to do getting ready for that night.' He looks at the ad again, then says, 'Hey, speaking of Heartsick Ink, how's Taylor holding up?'

It takes me a second to place the name, then suddenly I remember: Dad said Garrett's new wife was called Taylor. 'You know her?' I don't mention the word *wife*, am hoping it's not common knowledge yet.

'Sorta,' he says, 'through a friend of a friend. Nice gal.' He nods at the matchbook. 'The tattoo studio's below her apartment.'

The next morning, I arrive at the apartment Garrett and Taylor apparently now call home, in what can only be described as the more free-spirited side of town. In addition to the tattoo studio, there's an alternative therapies store, a shop that looks like it sells nothing but crystals and dream catchers, a whole-foods store and a marijuana dispensary. Right up Garrett's alley, I think, as I squeeze Jenna's Bug into the last remaining spot and walk the few yards down. There's a big red truck with Florida plates parked out front of the tattoo parlour, and as I pass on the sidewalk, I notice a man behind the wheel, looks to be asleep, his seat semi-reclined, cap pulled down so his face isn't visible.

Taylor looks as alarmed to see me as I was to learn of her.

She opens the apartment door a crack, says, 'Oh, it's you,' peers past me into the small landing at the top of the flight of stairs I've just ascended, and I wonder for a second if Garrett's hiding inside. But then she says, 'Thought you might be the cops. Or a reporter,' opens the door fully, gestures for me to come inside. 'They've been hanging around like flies on shit.'

'So, um, I've been told we've already met,' I say, following her down a short shabby hallway.

She casts a look over her shoulder, like, *Uh, okay* . . . as we enter an untidy but sparsely furnished living room. 'Sorry about the mess,' she says. Even though it's daytime, the blinds are shut. She crosses to an old leather couch and sits down, checks her phone. 'We just moved in, like, three weeks ago.'

Though there are packing boxes dotted about, it's the trash – old chip packets, overflowing ashtrays, empty energy drink cans – that seems to be the main cause of the problem.

Still, I try not to judge. 'Hey, that's okay. Guess you've been going through a pretty rough time.'

Taylor shrugs, moves a mug with what looks like the dregs of a milky coffee from the floor at her feet, slips a bright yellow Splenda dispenser lying next to it into the pocket of her hoodie. Something shifts in my memory, makes me think I already know this detail about her – *Taylor takes Splenda in her coffee* – and I wonder why, if I can remember random shit like that, I can't recall the things that actually matter.

'Not as rough as you,' she says, 'but yeah. Sorry about your mom. She was . . .' She stops. 'Guess I didn't know her all that well.'

I take a seat on a single dining chair, right as Taylor gets up, crosses to the window overlooking the street. She's pretty but too thin, with long brown hair, and wears an oversized sweatshirt and shorts, legs like toothpicks hanging from them, a pair of ratty-looking slipper socks on her feet. She parts the blinds, peers between the slats, lets them ping back into place, and I think about the guy in the truck outside, wonder if he's a journalist looking for a scoop.

'So,' I begin, 'when did you and Garrett . . . uh, tie the knot?'

I notice she wears rings on every finger, though none are particularly wedding-y. If Lucky and Dad hadn't both confirmed it, I'd wonder if my original source, Jesse, was mistaken.

'Right before Thanksgiving.' She pulls up the right-hand sleeve of her sweatshirt, holds the inside of her wrist out to me. It's bound with Saran wrap, through which I can just make out a date, tattooed in cursive script: *11.17.16.* Black ink bleeding into red skin tells me it's fresh.

'Huh. You just get that done?'

She nods. 'I don't go out much right now, but the guy downstairs did it for me, no charge. Thought it'd be a nice surprise for Garrett when he, you know, comes home.'

If he comes home. 'You heard from him?' I ask.

'Nuh-uh.' She shakes her head, crosses back to the couch and sits down again, draws her long legs up under her.

'And the last time you saw him?'

'Sunday before last, day of your accident and your mom's . . .' She stops herself. 'I wanted to reach out after it all went down,' she goes on, 'when you were in hospital. Just didn't know what to say. I mean' – she stuffs her hands into the pocket of her hoodie – 'guess I wanted to say sorry, too. About what happened that day at the cabin?'

'You're going to have to remind me.' I point at my head, without removing my hat. 'I can't remember.'

'You called me earlier that day. Wanted to talk?'

'I did, huh?'

'Yeah. But Garrett overheard you on the phone, got real mad. He was pretty paranoid, like, it wasn't his fault – I mean, you can understand with everything going on with that Casey girl – but he thought me and you were talking shit about him behind his back. So he drove us to your cabin.'

'You know what we talked about?'

'Me and you?' She shakes her head. '*We* didn't talk about anything. I waited in the car while he went inside. No idea what you and your brother were talking about but I was worried – he'd been in there a while – so I started beeping the horn and he came back out, like, totally pissed. We got into it right there – he was shouting, even fuckin' punched the Jeep – then he went back in, spoke to you again real quick, came back out, still mad as hell, and we left.'

'Where'd you go after that?'

'We stopped at the store, then Garrett dropped me home and left again. Dunno where he went. If I had to guess, I'd say he drove around to clear his head. He does that sometimes when we fight.'

Or drove to our parents' house in a rage, I think, killed Mum, but I quickly try and banish that thought. 'And after everything went down? Did you see him?'

'He came back here that night,' she admits. 'Musta been, like, sometime after nine, before ten?' She scoops her hair up into a messy bun, secures it with an elastic from her wrist. As she does, her left sweatshirt sleeve rides up and I see on her forearm a bunch of scars, a mix of fresh red and faded white. 'He was in a real bad way.'

'Did he say what happened?'

'He said your mom was already dead when he got there, but she was still warm – he thought she was still alive – so he tried to help her.'

For the first time it occurs to me that if I'd made it to the house after Garrett's call, hadn't crashed en route, then perhaps *I'd* have been able to help. Maybe, just maybe, I could have saved Mum's life. I swallow the guilty lump in my throat, ask, 'And after he came back here?'

'I helped clean up,' she says matter-of-factly. 'I mean, his knuckles were scuffed up real bad, his clothes all bloodied and dirty.'

'His knuckles were scuffed up? His clothes had blood on them?'

'He punched the Jeep, remember,' she says defensively. 'And he got the blood on his clothes when he tried to help your mom, plus he stopped to help you. He stank of gasoline.'

'Taylor, there was cash missing from the house, Mum's cell phone was gone. The cops mentioned something about a drug debt – that Garrett might've owed money? If he was the one who took those things—'

'He didn't kill your mom,' she says firmly. 'I know it doesn't look good, but he told me he didn't and I believe him.'

'Why'd he run then?'

'Are you kidding? After the whole Casey thing? He fuckin' told me the cops would try and pin his mom's murder on him, just like they tried to pin Casey on him. He was right.'

'The cops *didn't* pin Casey on him,' I say. 'They cleared him.'

'Okay,' she agrees, 'but only 'cos they had to – only 'cos his cell phone *proved* he had nothing to do with it. Didn't stop them hauling him in for questioning again after the gas station footage, though, did it?'

'Gas station footage?'

She stops, looks confused. 'You don't remember?'

I shake my head.

'That's what you were asking about when you phoned me the day of your accident,' she says. 'You know Garrett gave this girl Casey a ride home that night, from Buddy's?'

I nod. 'You were okay with that?'

'Course,' she says, though her face says otherwise. 'I mean, me and Garrett were supposed to go out for Halloween together, but we'd gotten in a fight, so I stayed home. He gave Casey a ride, sure, but only 'cos *she'd* gotten in a fight with her friend.'

I think of Brooke, the Buddy's video footage Evan showed me.

'Garrett said Casey's friend was supposed to be the designated driver that night,' she goes on, 'but she'd had a shit-load to drink. That's why he offered Casey a ride home. He's sober, see? We both are. Almost five months.'

I smile at her – *good for you* – but inside I'm thinking of the Buddy's video footage again, the beer in Garrett's hand . . .

'So he was just trying to be nice.' She rolls her eyes, like she's sick of having to explain it. 'I mean, he told me the next day what happened. We've got no secrets from each other, see?'

I don't. Garrett and the word 'nice' don't usually appear in the same sentence. I learned long ago that my brother doesn't do anything for anyone, not without there being something in it for him. And whilst, when it comes to secrets, I believe Taylor's been transparent with Garrett, I'm sure my brother has a whole closet-full of skeletons waiting for her to uncover.

'So,' I say, realising we've got off-topic. 'This gas station footage.'

'Oh, right, yeah. So, Garrett told the cops he dropped Casey home, went straight to your parents', right?'

'His phone data cleared him,' I agree.

'Exactly,' she says. 'But I guess when the cops checked, they found he stopped off en route at a gas station, used the payphone to call me, forgot to tell them. And I guess this made them feel like maybe he'd lied to them – deliberately left it out – so, like I say, they hauled him in for questioning again, but the fact that he stopped at the gas station really didn't change anything, so they let him go.'

'That's it?'

'Yeah. I mean, like, the cops found out about it ages ago, before Thanksgiving – even they're over it by now – but some douche leaked the footage a couple days ago and it's all over the internet: people are losing their shit, saying Garrett's a liar, that it proves he's guilty.'

It does seem like something of an overreaction. 'Why'd he call you?'

'From the gas station? Wanted to know if he could crash at mine. It was before we moved here,' she explains. 'I had my own apartment back then, closer to Buddy's.'

'And did you?'

'Did I what?'

'Let him crash?'

'Obviously not.' She frowns. 'I told him no way – was still pissed at him after we argued earlier – so he got back in his car, continued on his way to your parents'.'

'But why'd he call you from a payphone at all? Why not use his cell phone?'

''Cos he knew when I saw his name on caller ID I wouldn't pick up –'specially that late at night, after we'd argued. Not that it matters to all those frickin' armchair detectives out there. Doesn't help I switched my phone off after he called, either. People are saying it's 'cos I didn't want my cell phone traced, like somehow I was involved. But I only switched it off so Garrett couldn't call me again. It was after midnight. I wanted to get to sleep.'

'Do you have this gas station footage?'

'Don't *have* it,' she says, 'but I can find it.' She grabs her phone from the arm of her chair, types something. 'Here.' She hands it to me.

It's a video, stilled, of what looks like a gas station forecourt, a Jeep – my brother's, I assume – parked half in shot. Though it's night-time – the time stamp in the bottom right corner reads 12.15 a.m. – the place is well lit, the video quality good, so I recognise the figure in the foreground straight away: Garrett. I press play, watch my brother cross the forecourt, head round the side of the gas station, disappear out of sight. I wait. Seconds later, a middle-aged woman exits the gas station store, crosses the forecourt, and a few seconds after that, a car that must have been parked out of shot drives across the screen and exits. A minute or so passes – no sign of Garrett still – and a truck pulls in, parks right beneath the camera, blocking half the screen, so close I can see that the windshield's cracked. A man in a baseball cap gets out, looks around, crosses the forecourt and enters the store. Then nothing. I skip forward, see, what would have been a couple of minutes later real time, the male exiting the store and climbing back into his truck. He leaves, then a minute or so later, Garrett reappears from around the corner, crosses the forecourt, climbs back into his Jeep. He's shaking his head, looks annoyed.

The time stamp reads 12.22 a.m.

I look up at Taylor. 'That it?'

'Told ya. Nothing, right?'

I have to agree with her. It seems pretty unshady, though I avoid the comments beneath, don't want to know what the internet thinks.

'And you didn't speak to my brother again that night?'

'Like I say, I switched my phone off.' She tugs at the neck of her sweatshirt, and I catch a glimpse of a mark above her collarbone, the ghost of a bruise. For some reason I think of Paige. 'It's crazy the amount of hate Garrett's getting online,' she's saying. 'I try not to read it – they're just shit-for-brains – but if you ask me, it's Casey's friend they oughtta be looking at. I've been saying so since the start.'

'The girl she was fighting with that night?' *Brooke.*

Casey nods. 'There's something off with her.'

'You mean because she and Casey argued on Halloween?'

'Yeah.' Taylor nods, picks at her fingernails. 'But, like, it's not just that. She's been desperate to pin Casey's disappearance on Garrett from the start, even though the cops've cleared him. *And* she's fuckin' *obsessed* with Casey, like weird, fuckin' creepy obsessed.'

'You mean the Find Casey Facebook page?' I ask, though I'm not sure that counts. 'Because of all the photos she posts of them together?'

'I guess,' Taylor says. 'That and the fact she's moved herself into Casey's condo, like single fuckin' white female.'

16

Then

I'd tried shooing the cat out before I left for Thanksgiving dinner, but it had opened a lazy eye, surveyed me with a look that said, *Try it*. Still, I'd half expected it to be gone by the time I returned – possibly having shredded the contents of the cabin first – but it was exactly where I'd left it, fast asleep on the couch. In all honesty, I was glad. It was comforting to have someone – even a cat-shaped someone – to come home to, and although it hadn't exactly rushed to greet me, had only opened its eyes, yawned, stretched, purred loudly, begun butting its head against my legs, that was enough for me.

I fed it, then spent the next ten minutes looking for something I could use as a litter tray before setting it up in a discreet corner of the porch. After that, I settled myself on the couch, cat at my side, took out the piece of paper on which Jesse, the gas station guy, had written the bartender's name, and laid it on the coffee table in front of me. I hesitated. Since a list was how it had all started with Shaunee Hughes, I was somewhat reluctant to make one. However short, it felt like a commitment to something I might regret, something there could be no going back from. Nevertheless, against my better judgement, I picked up a pen, wrote *Brooke Morgenstern* beneath Evan's name. Brooke seemed like the logical place to start, and because, albeit unplanned, I'd already spoken to her, and because speaking to her had made me feel like I'd at least made *some* headway, I immediately crossed her name out.

I exhaled, looked at the cat. 'No going back now,' I told it.

Next, beneath Brooke's name, I added the obvious: *Loreen Skinner*. Uncomfortable though it might be, speaking with the missing girl's family, her mother especially, was a must. Brooke said Casey's mom had left town, so assuming she'd agree to speak with me at all, I guessed it might have to be by phone. I'd look into how to do that later.

Beneath Loreen's name I wrote *Rebecca Johnson*, perhaps my most reluctant addition. After reading the newspaper articles on her sister's disappearance, I still wasn't convinced I needed to speak to her at all, despite what Brooke seemed to think. Someone had been arrested and charged with Amy's murder. Why muddy the waters by throwing a second girl's disappearance into the mix if that case was already solved? Still, it couldn't hurt to add Rebecca's name until I'd dug a little deeper, could it?

Finally, almost an afterthought, I added *Luke* – a question mark in lieu of his surname – Casey's ex-boyfriend, who my brother had mentioned earlier that evening.

I sat back and surveyed the list. Not much to go on, but a start. Investigating seemed like too strong a word – *looking into* felt more appropriate – but I realised I'd been foolish to think I could come all this way and not at least do some digging. Plus, after Thanksgiving dinner, I could use the distraction. I felt shell-shocked. The call from Travis; the revelation that Garrett had a wife. Even if the marriage was completely innocent, with everything going on, at best the timing appeared more than a little tone deaf, and although I was trying not to read too much into it, it was hard not to. Twenty-seven wasn't all that young to tie the knot, but Garrett's childhood pet hamster had lived longer than most of his relationships combined, so whichever way I tried to slice it, it was weird. I couldn't help but wonder what was in it for my brother; couldn't help but wonder what the internet would make of it when they found out. But what did it matter? Garrett had nothing to do with Casey's disappearance. Just because the internet *thought* he did didn't make it true.

Because Garrett had been cleared by the police.

And now I knew why.

After I'd discovered the matchbook, right before Mum found me in Garrett's room, I'd followed her downstairs to her basement office, like a kid being led to the school principal. Luckily for me, my phone battery really was dead, so I'd waited patiently while she dug through drawers, looking for a spare charger, relieved I wasn't going to be caught out.

Despite my parents having lived there for years, I could only remember being in Mum's office once before, shortly after they moved in. A basement office sounds rather basic, but this was anything but. When I was in Murdoch making *Dark Corners*, my office had been diners or people's front rooms, local parks or, usually, my motel room. I'd made a makeshift workspace, moving the desk – at least I had a desk – to the least dingy corner, had hung the ubiquitous corkboard above, its equally ubiquitous and painstakingly pieced-together patchwork of photos, timelines and sticky notes held together with push pins and connected by red string. Once I returned to New York, my office space was a hastily purchased IKEA desk, which Travis grudgingly agreed I could squeeze into our bedroom, my 'office window' overlooking an ugly old air-conditioning unit; a brick wall beyond that.

The only thing I'd had in all my offices that Mum didn't was windows. But what Mum's office lacked in natural light, it made up for in, well, everything else. It was expensive-looking and formal, the ceiling dotted with chrome-mounted spotlights, walls hung with prints of her book covers from the Morningside Therapy series – the most famous of which, *Be More Owl*, a title that still made me guffaw (people actually bought into that?!), was front and centre – and framed magazine articles – *Secrets from the Morningside Therapist's Couch!* the headlines yelled; or *We Get the Morningside Therapist's Tips On* (enter any of the following) *A Happy Life!*; *A Happy Wife!*; *A Happy Marriage!*; *Success!* Ironic, that not one of them contained tips on how not to raise a fuck-up of a son.

Mum no longer had her therapy practice – the mountains outside Heartsick had proved too much of a schlep for even the most committed of patients – instead devoting her time to writing, but her office still housed a well-worn leather therapist's chair and couch, and a Victorian mahogany desk – another piece she'd gone to the trouble of shipping from the UK.

That desk, through which she was now rummaging, was where she did the aforementioned writing, so on its surface were arranged all the usual things: laptop, stacks of printed drafts and paperwork, pen pots filled with expensive pens, an equally expensive but unused leather ink blotter, and, standing on one corner like a desk-sized totem, a carved wooden owl – a gift from Dad when they first met all those years ago. Mum liked to tell people Dad bought her it because it reminded him of her – beautiful and wise – but Dad told me once that after they started dating, Mum chose her own gifts, had picked the owl out herself, instructed him to buy it. Mum also liked to tell people how owls not only represented wisdom but were a symbol of transformation, luck and self-actualisation, hence the bestselling *Be More Owl*. So it tickled me that the sum of her precious wooden owl's potential was to be used as a paperweight, an inadequate one at that: although weighty, it wasn't quite squat enough, so was suitable for no more than a few loose sheets. It wasn't particularly tall either – maybe eight inches – but it was, unmistakably, an owl, though more the suggestion of one than a realistic representation. It was completely smooth, carved from a single, solid piece of oak, the only angular feature the integrated base, which tapered slightly, wider at the bottom, with four sharp edges. On one of those edges was a small scrape, not noticeable on first glance – not at all, probably, if you didn't know about it – but on close inspection you could see the paler, yellowish wood beneath. Like fresh pink skin beneath a scab.

By the time Mum and I returned upstairs, me with charger in hand, I was relieved to find Dad, Garrett and Taylor part way through dessert. I plugged my phone in to charge nearby; at one point later caught Mum trying to take a sneaky look at it, see whose call I'd so urgently had to take during dinner. When I asked pointedly what she was doing – just as she had when I was snooping in Garrett's room – she claimed she'd mistaken my phone for hers, even though we both knew she hadn't.

Thankfully, though, the overall atmosphere did seem to have thawed. I managed to avoid Garrett, and Mum seemed to be making an effort with Taylor, even made her a coffee – something I'd never seen her do for any of Garrett's other girlfriends – adding almond milk and Splenda with more care than she'd ever shown me.

Even I felt more relaxed, which was why, when at last I took my cue to leave, I was caught off guard when Garrett said he'd walk me out.

'So,' I said, 'Casey Carter.'

We were standing at my car, in the freezing cold.

'Jesus, Step. Not this again. You're not Nancy fuckin' Drew, and I'm not a suspect in your shitty little podcast.'

'I'm flattered,' I said. 'Didn't think you listened to it.'

'I haven't,' he shot back, and immediately I scolded myself for taking the bait: though we didn't speak much, in the year since *Dark Corners* had aired, my brother had taken every opportunity to remind me he didn't think much of it; that he hadn't listened to a single episode; that despite its success, he didn't think podcasting was a real job. This from a man who spent last summer being paid less than nine dollars an hour to wash golf carts at a local resort.

'Did you come forward?' I asked. 'Or did the cops find you?'

'I came forward,' he said, 'like the good citizen I am.'

'And they cleared you, just like that?'

'Pretty much.'

'How?'

'If you must know,' he sighed, 'cell phone evidence.'

'You gave the cops your phone?' I couldn't hide my surprise.

'Didn't have to.' He shrugged. 'They asked if they could access my cell phone data, I told them, "Sure, do whatever the fuck you want." I've nothing to hide, Step; my phone proves it – shows I was where I said I was, when I said I was.'

'So you dropped Casey home, came straight here?'

'Yeah. We chatted in the car a few minutes outside her place, but apart from that . . .'

'You didn't go inside?'

'Nope. I mean, sure, I was *hoping* she'd invite me in – she was hot – but she didn't, so I left.'

I stifled an eye roll. 'Do you know Casey?' I asked. 'Had you met her before Halloween?' Brooke had said not.

Garrett shook his head.

'And Buddy's. You been there before?'

He nodded. 'Loadsa times. So it'd be pretty dumb of me to abduct some girl and hope I could get away with it, don't you think?'

I couldn't disagree. 'So you honestly don't know what happened to her? Like, if something went wrong, things got out of hand . . .'

'Fuck, Step, seriously? It's not enough that everyone round town thinks I did it. Like, the cops clear me, but all those fuckin' armchair detectives out there in internet land haven't got the memo. I can cope with that. But my own sister?' He looked genuinely upset. 'That fuckin' takes the cake, dude.'

'Look' – I glanced up at the house, caught sight of a movement in the huge apex window, a figure – Mum? – watching us; lowered my voice, though I knew whoever it was couldn't hear us – 'I don't think you had anything to do with it. Not really.' I forced a laugh. 'You can be pretty dumb, Garrett, but you're not that dumb.' As soon as I said it, doubt crept in. I thought of Paige, of Brooke – her conviction about Garrett being the last person seen with *another* missing girl. 'Casey didn't just vanish into thin air, though. Don't you wonder about what happened?'

Garrett kicked the tyre of my rental car. 'You know she has a jealous ex?'

My face said I didn't.

'Well,' he said, 'from what I heard, they had a pretty bad break-up. Happened months ago, but like a day or two after Casey vanishes, the guy shows up in town. Fuckin' suspicious, if you ask me.'

'Know his name?' I asked.

'Luke something.' He shrugged, and I felt a prickle of annoyance, wondered if he was being deliberately obstructive. 'Look, I'm not saying the dude had anything to do with it. All I'm saying is, all those fuckin' petty-minded internet sleuths so focused on me? There are plenty other suspects.'

'Plenty?'

'Okay, maybe not *plenty*, but more fuckin' viable ones. I mean, that's why they always start with the boyfriend, the ex, the spouse . . .'

'Speaking of,' I said, 'where does Taylor figure in all this? I mean, don't tell me you don't see how marrying her looks? You know what they're going to be saying online.'

'Oh,' Garrett said, a slow smile spreading across his face. 'I see what this is about. You and Travis. Well, I'm sorry you broke up and all, that you're bitter and single, that you can't be happy for me and Tay.'

I ignored him. 'Where'd you two lovebirds meet?'

'AA meeting,' he said, like they'd met in line at the grocery store.

'That even allowed?'

'*You're sober, Garrett? That's fuckin' great,*' he said, mimicking my voice. '*Congrats.*'

'You *are* sober?' My first thought was that that explained him and Taylor not drinking at dinner. My second was to wonder how long it would last.

'California sober. Over four months, if you must know.'

California sober. I might've guessed. California sober was better than nothing, though, and four months alcohol-free meant he hadn't been drinking on Halloween, a relief because in my experience bad things happened when Garrett was drinking. Dark things.

'You reach the apology stage yet?' I couldn't help myself.

Garrett only laughed, said, 'Think I missed that meeting.'

'And Taylor?'

'What about her?'

'What does she make of this whole Casey thing?'

'Step, come on.' He puffed out his cheeks. 'I see what you're trying to do. But me and Tay, we don't have secrets, and besides, nothing *happened* with me and Casey . . .'

'It would've done if Casey had let it.'

'Like Paige did?'

For a moment I couldn't speak. But as blindsided as I was that my brother had brought Paige up, there was part of me that felt relieved that he had, that I didn't have to.

'What happened that night in New York?' I asked. 'I need the truth.'

'Truth is, I was hammered, but so was Paige. I mean, you saw her.' He smirked. 'Want me to draw you a diagram? She was all over me.'

'Fuck you, Garrett.'

I opened the car and climbed in, but Garrett put a foot against the door, stopped me closing it. 'Look' – he held his hands up – 'okay, okay. I don't know what you're trying to accuse me of with Paige, but I did nothing wrong. Sure, I'm guilty of not being a gentleman, may have said I'd call her and didn't. I know that makes girls mad. But Paige wasn't exactly a lady either, if you know what I mean.' He winked at me. 'She's a sloppy drunk.'

I felt sick, wanted out of there so badly, but when I tried to shut the door again, Garrett was still blocking it. I put one foot back outside. 'Let go of the door, Garrett.'

He slammed it with such force, I only just had enough time to snatch my foot inside. Then he turned, walked away, flipping me the bird over his shoulder.

'Drive safe,' I heard him call.

I pressed the central locking button, watched in the mirror till he disappeared, swallowed up by the shadow of the house, my hands shaking, not from cold, or fear, but because I knew my brother was lying. Because I knew my brother and I knew he had a tell. A tiny muscle in the outer corner of his right eye that ticked when he was stressed.

If you didn't know about it, you wouldn't even notice it.

But I did, and I'd seen it, ticking like mad, when I asked about Paige.

17

Now

It's dusk as I draw up outside the condo, a two-storey brick and wood building on a quiet suburban street. According to Taylor, Casey's apartment is on the ground floor. There's a car in the driveway and light escaping from a downstairs window, though the apartment above is in darkness, so it doesn't look like her upstairs neighbour is home. I double-check the address. If Taylor's right and Brooke has moved in, the car most likely belongs to her.

I crunch up the driveway over frozen snow and knock at the door. There's no answer, so I step off the porch and look at the house, see a chink of light as a blind in the nearest window twitches. A few seconds later, the porch light comes on and the door's opened by a girl in a T-shirt with a photo of Casey on it, *#FindCaseyCarter* emblazoned above it. I recognise the girl as Brooke, Casey's 'bestie', not only from all the Facebook photos but now also from the Buddy's surveillance footage.

Her mouth drops open at the sight of me. 'Guess you better come in.'

Like Taylor, she casts an uneasy glance over my shoulder into the darkening street, as if maybe she's expecting someone else, or I've not come alone.

I follow her into the kitchen at the back of the apartment. A window above the sink looks out back, but all I can see is trees silhouetted in the fast-fading light.

Brooke draws the blind, turns. 'You okay?' she asks, a mix of wary and concerned. 'You look kinda pale.'

The kitchen's bright, too bright. I lean heavily on the counter top, realise I haven't eaten in a while. My head's splitting.

'Here.' She helps me to a stool at a breakfast bar, then fetches me a water.

I take a rattling meds bottle from my pocket, fumble with the childproof cap, then pop a couple of pills, while Brooke, over the other side of the kitchen, appears to be making a sandwich. When she's done, she takes a seat opposite me and slides the sandwich across.

'You look like you need to eat,' she says. 'PBJ okay?'

I'm not a fan of peanut butter, but I nod feebly through the pain.

We don't talk while I eat – I couldn't even if I wanted to – though Brooke seems content to watch me. I don't know how long we sit like that, but when at last I finish the sandwich, baby bites, the pain meds have started to kick in, or at least have taken the edge off my crashing headache.

I push the plate away – 'Thanks' – look around. 'You looking after the place?'

'Casey's mom asked me to, till Casey gets back.'

I blink in the harsh light, not sure this is what Casey's mom would have in mind: there's a wall calendar, still on October, with its picture of fall leaves, like time has stopped; dead house plants on the windowsill, takeout cartons everywhere, dirty dishes overflowing in the sink and piles of mail on the counter top. My eyes wander over the mess to the fridge door, stuck with a guddle of photos, lists and post-cards. Front and centre is a picture frame, the words *If friends were flowers I'd pick you* painted around it; in it, a photo of a high-school-aged Brooke and Casey, arms round each other, grinning goofily at the camera.

Brooke follows my gaze. 'I got Casey that for her birthday.'

I look at her properly for the first time, and it strikes me that, sans make-up and photo filters, real-world Brooke looks less Casey-like than I thought.

'Nice necklace,' I say, pointing at the silver half-heart pendant round her neck. I think I recognise it from the Halloween selfie, the opposite half of the one Casey's wearing in the photo.

She shoots me a weird look, says, 'Uh, thanks.'

'It's a friendship necklace, isn't it?'

She nods, 'Yeah,' and something about the whole exchange gives me déjà vu, makes me think of the list of names, Brooke's crossed out.

'We've met before,' I blurt out, even though I can't be sure.

She looks at me weird again. 'That accident did a real number on you, huh?'

So she knows. I guess everyone in town does. 'My memory's defin-itely a little hazy,' I agree, understatement of the century, but something tells me admitting I have zero memory of any earlier meeting would be a mistake.

'Look,' Brooke sighs, 'I know we didn't get off to the best start, but I am sorry. About your mom.'

At the mention of Mum, I feel myself sway. *Keep it together, Steppy.* 'Speaking of,' I say, 'where were you the night of the twenty-seventh?'

'Twenty-seventh of what?'

'November. Day of my accident? The day my mum was . . .' I stop, still unable to say it.

'Are you for real? You think *I* had something to do with your mom's murder? I've never even met her. Why would I want her dead?'

'I don't know,' I say. 'But your best friend's missing. Maybe you went to the house to speak to my brother about Casey – confront him, whatever – but he wasn't there, you got into an argument with my mum instead, the whole thing got out of hand . . .'

'You know the cops are looking at your brother for your mom's murder?' she says. 'I mean, no offence, but it's obvious he did it – he was practically caught red-handed.'

'Brooke,' I say gently. I remove my Heartsick beanie, place it on the counter between us, and her eyes widen at the sight of my scar. 'I know you and Casey argued that night, at Buddy's.'

This is my second theory: that Brooke killed Casey after they argued on Halloween, hoped the cops would pin it on Garrett, the last person seen with her. Then, when they didn't – thanks to Garrett's cell phone data – she killed Mum to take the heat off the Casey case, frame Garrett for his own mother's murder. It *sounds* far-fetched, but judging from the look on Brooke's face when I mention the fight, not wholly implausible.

'How'd you know?' she asks.

'I saw for myself.'

She looks confused.

'Buddy's,' I say. 'The surveillance footage from Halloween.'

She bites her lip, looks down at the table.

'What were you and Casey fighting about?'

She shrugs. 'Don't remember.'

'Maybe I can refresh your memory.' I realise the irony of that state-ment even as I say it. 'You were supposed to be the designated driver that night, but you'd been drinking.' I don't add what Evan told me – that she and Casey were fighting over my brother.

'Who told you that?' Brooke asks poutily, then, without waiting for an answer, 'Okay, yeah, that was a part of it.'

'There was more?'

She looks up suddenly, right at me. 'You know how hard it is to be best friends with someone like Casey? Like, we've known each other since kindergarten. All my life I've been the less pretty one, less popular, less smart. People think I don't know, but I do.'

'It can't have been that bad,' I say. I remember something Lucky said – or was it the TV news report? – about Casey being from Florida. 'I mean, you must've moved here to be with her.'

'Huh,' she scoffs. 'Casey moved here and didn't even tell me, that's how much she values our friendship. Her mom said it was because she needed to make a clean break, didn't want her ex finding out where she was . . .'

That ex again. 'Doesn't sound unreasonable.'

'Really?' she snaps. 'Would you leave town, the place you grew up, lived all your life, not even tell your best friend, just fucking ghost her?'

I think of Paige, how inseparable we are – *were*. 'Guess not.'

'Then,' she goes on, 'when she *eventually* contacts me to let me know where she is, and I give up my life, move halfway across the country just to fucking be with her, it's like I'm chopped liver. Like, she said she'd get me a job at the restaurant she was a server at – just bussing tables, but it would've been a start . . .'

'She didn't?'

'Nope.' Brooke shakes her head. 'When I got here, she's all like, sorry, I asked my boss, we've got no vacancies. Then, later, I find out they were hiring for two weeks, right after I moved to town. Casey lied. It's like, we've been friends all our lives – besties – and now you're too fucking good for me? You know, before I came, we talked about getting a place together, but this' – she throws up her hands – 'it's a one-bed, and once I got here, every time I brought it up, she made excuses, like' – she puts on a whiny voice – '*I have to see my lease out*; *I don't have the money to move right now*. Total. Fucking. Bullshit.'

'So things came to a head on Halloween?'

'Sorta,' Brooke says. 'It started the weekend before. We'd been out, and I'd posted a photo of us on Facebook. It was real cute – we both looked hot – but I fucked up, tagged Casey and our location.'

I think back to my library visit, remember how Casey hadn't posted on Facebook in the best part of a year. Guess now I know why. 'This ex have a name?'

'What's it to you?'

'Nothing,' I say quickly. 'But Casey was concerned enough about him that she didn't want him knowing where she was.'

'Right,' Brooke says guiltily. 'Me tagging her was a total accident – I untagged her and the location next day. But she was so mad, made such a big frickin' deal of it. I mean, the photo was up there for, like, not even twenty-four hours, but she acted like I'd just signed her death warrant or something.'

'You must've made up again by Halloween,' I say. 'You looked good in the photo.'

'I guess.' Brooke fiddles with the necklace. 'But things were still pretty tense. Like, you know when there's beef but neither of you will say anything? That was us. I mean, I'd apologised, like, fifty thousand times, even offered to be the designated driver that night to make up for it. But nothing was ever enough.'

'So what happened when you got to Buddy's?'

'It was okay at first. We kind of just did our own thing, ignored each other. We both get talking to people and I meet this cute guy, your brother' – she rolls her eyes – 'and he's acting like he's all into me, then boom, along comes Casey, and it's like I don't exist.'

I feel bad for her, know Garrett would never have been interested in her anyway. 'And after that?'

'After that, I started drinking. I mean, okay' – she rolls her eyes again – 'I'd had a couple beers before that . . . I know it was stupid. But I was pissed about the whole situation. Like, I don't think Casey gave a shit about me. Everything was about her. I could've disappeared off the face of the earth and she wouldn't've noticed—' She clamps a hand over her mouth. 'God. I didn't mean it like that.' She begins to cry.

'I get it,' I say. 'It's not easy. But all friendships have their ups and downs.' I know this better than anyone. 'I'm sure you'd have worked it out.' Would they have, though? Because I know, deep down, that some things aren't fixable.

Brooke doesn't reply, buries her face in her hands.

'So after you left Buddy's,' I say, trying to sound casual and sympathetic all at once, 'did you go straight home?'

She sniffs, nods.

'Alone?'

She nods again.

'So you didn't see Casey again that night?'

She looks up, wide-eyed. 'Jesus Christ. First it's your mom, now you think I had something to do with whatever happened to Casey?'

'I don't think anything,' I tell her. 'Just that it would've been understandable if, after you left Buddy's, you'd – you know – hung around for a while outside. Maybe you wanted to confront Casey about how she treated you?'

Brooke hops from her stool, plucks a tissue from a nearby box. 'I wish I had,' she says, climbing back up, 'then she might still be here.' She blows her nose loudly, looks at me through tear-filled eyes. 'When we first met,' she says, 'you asked me if I called the cops about Casey the next day.'

I did? I catch myself, say confidently, 'I did.'

'I should've done' – she hiccoughs – 'just like I shoulda gone inside when Casey's mom asked me to check on her that morning. But like I told you, I didn't have a key, and I guess I was still so mad at her.' Her face crumples and she dissolves into tears again.

'It wasn't your fault,' I tell her. 'How could you know what would happen?' I give her a moment to collect herself. 'Look, I know this is hard, but what do you think happened to Casey?'

She looks at me funny again. 'Well, I know the cops cleared your brother . . .'

'I'm sensing a *but*.' I guess I shouldn't be surprised. Taylor warned me Brooke was intent on pinning Casey's disappearance on Garrett, despite the evidence.

'I found something out the other day. You know when the cops spoke to your brother, after Casey was officially reported missing?' She doesn't wait for me to reply. 'Well, apparently he had scratches. On his face, wrists. He told the cops he had a fight with his girlfriend, that she scratched him up pretty bad.'

'He did,' I say. 'His' – I stop myself just in time from saying *wife* – 'his girlfriend told me. They fought earlier that day.' Did Taylor say it got physical?

'His face wasn't all scratched up that night at Buddy's,' Brooke says triumphantly, like she's read my mind.

'You sure about that?'

'Sure I'd remember if it was.'

'Really? Because it probably wouldn't've stood out – everyone was in costume . . .'

'I get it.' She shrugs. 'You wanna believe your brother's innocent. Plus I lied to you about the vigil, so you don't believe me about anything now. But I gave you Rebecca Johnson's email address – why would I have done that if—'

'Rebecca Johnson?' It's a name I've not heard before, yet somehow it's familiar. Then I realise: the fourth name on my list, the only name that rang a vague bell. And now I also realise why: *my emails!*

'Yeah.' Brooke gives me one of those looks again. 'You email her?'

I ignore the question. 'Why'd you lie to me about the vigil?' I ask instead, though I've no idea what vigil she's even talking about.

'I don't know,' she says in a small voice. 'You wanted to talk to Loreen, Casey's mom, and I guess I just wanted to protect her, you know? I'd already told you Loreen had left town, so when you asked about the vigil and I knew she'd be there, I told you the wrong time on purpose. I mean, I've felt real bad about it ever since. I want to find Casey more than anything. So if you meant what you said – that you just want to get to the truth – and you think speaking to her mom will help, I can make it happen. Besides,' she adds, and I can't help but wonder if this is the real reason she's willing to connect us, 'she can vouch for me.'

'Huh?'

'You asked me where I was the twenty-seventh, the night your mom was killed? Well, I have an alibi. I spent that whole evening with Casey's mom and half-brother at their motel. We had a movie night, watched Casey's favourite Disney DVDs together. Ask them. I was there till like one in the morning.'

18

Then

Watson Street was on the outskirts of town, a cul-de-sac on a dead end street, not far from Buddy's Bar. Out front, each condo had a shared yard and driveway; out back, another smaller yard giving way to trees, forest and, beyond that, mountains.

It was dark. I parked up under one of the few street lights and double-checked the sat nav. I was certain I was at the right address, but the street was completely deserted. I sighed and massaged my temples, wishing I'd just stayed home. I'd barely slept last night after Thanksgiving dinner. It wasn't like I hadn't known all these months that something bad had happened between my brother and Paige, but Paige's refusal to tell me what made it easier to ignore, convince myself I was catastrophising. But hearing those words, that my brother had raped my best friend, had brought it all home. I could ignore it no longer, felt sick at what Paige must have been going through, was angry at Garrett, ashamed of myself for being too much of a coward to come right out with it when he brought Paige up, confront him about what he'd done. I also, selfishly, felt hurt. Hurt that Paige had chosen to confide in Travis, not me, though I knew I had no right to be, was filled with self-loathing for even thinking it.

My phone pinged, interrupting my thoughts: the cabin owner, replying to my previous day's cat-related text.

Hey Steppy, sorry I'm just getting back to you. Was with family for Thanksgiving all day yesterday (belated Happy Thanksgiving BTW!). A cat? No. Why?

Happy Thanksgiving! I texted back. *No worries. A cat turned up at the cabin, that's all. No collar. Kinda skinny. Not sure what to do with it!*

She texted straight back.

There's a good veterinarian in town. You could take it there, see if it's chipped? Should be an old cat carrier round back. You're welcome to use it.

I shoved my phone into the cup holder and climbed out the car. The street was poorly lit, but out of the corner of my eye I spotted a figure – a man, a couple of houses down the other side, collecting his mail.

'Excuse me?' I called, crossing the empty street, but he didn't seem to hear. The houses were set far enough apart that to catch up to him I had to break into a jog. 'Excuse me!' I called again, louder this time. 'Is this Casey Carter's street?'

The man turned, squinting at me through the darkness. He was small and elderly, bulked out by a heavy plaid jacket, with fluffy white hair and glasses. He clutched his mail to him with one hand, steadied himself on the mailbox with the other.

'You a reporter?' His breath clouded the air.

I made a split-second decision, decided to be upfront. 'Podcaster,' I told him.

'A what now?' He chuckled, clearly tickled by the term.

'I make podcasts?' He looked blank. 'They're like radio shows, but you get them online.' He nodded, but I could tell he didn't get it. 'I'm here for the vigil?'

'Well bless your soul, you're three hours too late.'

I looked at my watch. Five past nine. 'Too late? I was told nine p.m.' At least I could have sworn Brooke said nine.

'Well, um . . .?' the man said, and I could see he was searching for a name. He gave off befuddled old grandad vibes, but something told me he was sharp as a tack.

'Steppy,' I told him, then, seeing the look on his face, 'short for Stephanie.'

He looked tickled again. 'Well, Steppy – I'm Hank, by the way – I'm afraid whoever told you nine was wrong. It was six. Good turnout, too.'

'Shoot,' I said. 'I wanted to come along, show my support.'

'You know Casey?'

'No,' I admitted. 'Do you?'

'Just to say hello, but she's a friendly gal. It's mostly old-timers in this street' – he nodded at the other properties – 'but she fit right in. Quiet. No trouble.'

'Which one's her place?'

He pointed his bundle of mail in the direction of the condo across the street, one down from where I'd parked. 'That one there.'

'First or second floor?'

'First.'

'She got an upstairs neighbour?' Despite the relatively late hour, there were no lights on in either apartment.

'Marsha,' the man said. 'Lives alone, but she's outta town. Been gone a couple months, visiting with her mother. She's sick – Marsha's mom, not Marsha.'

'I don't suppose anyone in the street's got, like, a surveillance camera?' Hank just laughed.

'Do you remember the last time you saw Casey?' I asked him.

'Sure do. The night she vanished. Halloween. There aren't any kids on the street and most trick-or-treaters don't venture this far down, but there were a couple early on. I was out getting my mail and I saw her at her door, giving out candy.'

'And later that night? Much later. You didn't hear or see anything?'

He pointed to his ears: hearing aids. 'Wish I did,' he said apologetically, 'but I'm an early-nighter. Switch 'em off when I go to bed.'

A car pulled out of a driveway further down the street. As its headlights swept past, it honked its horn and Hank waved. It struck me once more, this time with a chill, how poorly lit the street was. It also struck me, with even more of a chill, that if you were going to kidnap someone, a quiet, badly lit street full of old people would be a pretty good place to do it.

I turned my attention back to Hank. 'Ever have any problems with break-ins, prowlers?'

He raised his eyebrows. 'Like I say, it's pretty quiet.' He considered. 'Was one guy, though, right after Casey vanished.'

'Oh?'

'Yeah. Drove a big red truck, cracked windshield, out-of-state licence plates. I'll be darned if I can remember which state, though.'

'Could it have been a reporter?'

'Didn't look like one. Didn't act like one, either. Plus, it was after Casey disappeared but before the press got a hold of the story.'

'Did you tell the police?'

He nodded. 'Surely did. They knocked on my door a couple days later.'

'What did he look like, this man in the truck?'

'Didn't get a good look at his face, but he was tall.'

For a moment my heart almost stopped, but then I remembered the red truck – hard to confuse with Garrett's khaki-coloured Jeep – the out-of-state licence plate.

'Wore a baseball cap,' he went on. 'Dark-haired, too.'

I breathed a sigh of relief. Definitely not Garrett. 'What was he doing?'

'He parks up at Casey's – right out front – gets out, goes to the front door, knocks – no answer – tries the handle. I'm watching all the while from my window, and then – then I see him going round the side. He's peering in the windows, and I'm thinking, oh Lord, this ain't right, so I rush outside – fast as I can rush anywhere these days – get halfway down the driveway and he's disappeared round back, so I holler 'cross the street, hey, what do you think you're doing? Well, he must have heard me, 'cos before you can say Jiminy Cricket, he appears again, back up that drive fast as you like, climbs into his truck and drives off.'

'You think he had something to do with Casey's disappearance?' It seemed kind of a dumb question.

Hank didn't seem to think so, though, considered again. 'Could be,' he said. 'I mean, I feel bad I didn't do more, but for what it's worth, I didn't *know* Casey was missing at that point. I mean, I'd seen her friend a little earlier the same day, looking for her.'

'Brooke?'

Hank shook his head. 'Don't know her name. All I know is she was here November first – I know because it's my late wife's birthday. She didn't seem too alarmed, though, whoever she was, so I wasn't either. Guess I thought nothing more of it. Not till the police came knocking on the third, said she'd not been seen in two days.'

'So,' I said, 'if you had to hazard a guess about what happened to Casey . . .'

'I'll be darned if I know.' He frowned. 'I just pray they find her. There's a guy in town, though. Garth. Gareth?'

My heart began to race. 'Garrett?'

Hank's eyes lit up in recognition. 'Garrett! That's the one.'

I felt a knot in my stomach. 'What about him?'

'He was the last person seen with Casey, so everyone thinks it was him did something to her.'

The knot tightens. 'You think so too?'

He pointed across the street with his bundle of mail again. 'Not according to that porch light.'

'Porch light?' I followed the direction he was pointing in, but there was no porch light to be seen.

Hank nodded sagely. 'Porch light was out. Casey left it on every night. Switched it on early evening, only turned it out when she went to bed.'

'But if you're an early-nighter,' I said, 'how do you know she turned it out that night?'

'Because it was off next day, when I took my morning walk. I don't know if Casey's friend had a key, but she didn't come by till after I'd been on my walk, so even if she did, *she* can't have switched it off. And,' he added, 'case you're wondering, it was definitely on the evening before: it was already dark when I saw Casey giving the kids candy on Halloween, and it was on then – wouldn't've been able to see her otherwise.'

'So, what?' I asked. 'You think that Casey got home safe – that this Garrett' – I said my brother's name like I didn't know him – 'dropped her home, then left, and she switched off the porch light, went to bed?'

Hank nodded again. 'If you ask me, whatever happened to poor Casey happened sometime after she came home that night, after she went to bed but before her friend came by next day.'

'But someone else could have switched off the light,' I posit, 'to make it *look* like Casey got safely to bed.'

'Could've,' Hank said. 'But that's the point: if someone did, they would've had to know that's what she did – know her well enough to know her routine.'

'And this Garrett guy,' I filled in, 'only met Casey for the first time that night.'

'Right!' he said triumphantly. 'That's what I heard, too. So *he* couldn't've known.'

'So,' I said, 'what you're saying is . . .'

'What I'm saying is,' he finished for me, 'if it's true this Garrett guy dropped Casey off, drove straight to his parents', then the cops are right – poor guy had nothing to do with it.'

19

Now

I have a laptop. I messaged Dad yesterday, told him mine wasn't working, and he got his secretary, Betsey, to FedEx me an old one of his. I arrive back at the cabin to find it on the porch.

I carry it inside and unpack it, though I'm completely drained. Not only do I have everything I learned from Brooke to consider, as I was leaving Casey's condo I ran into a neighbour of hers, Hank, another person I've apparently met before but have no memory of.

Hank said that when we met before my accident, he told me something about Casey's porch light – that she always switched it off last thing at night; how it was off the morning of November 1, suggesting she got to bed safe. I can't help but wonder if he's the independent witness Lucky talked about; whether the porch light nugget is the piece of information he couldn't disclose. But it's not just the porch light – I fire up my new laptop – there's what Hank told me about the truck, the red one with a cracked windshield and out-of-state plates, a driver who wasn't Garrett.

But – I connect to the Wi-Fi, open the internet browser – Hank told me something else too: last weekend, he saw the same red truck outside Casey's place – same guy, too – except this time, no cracked windshield. He said it drove off pretty quickly – probably because Brooke's car was in Casey's driveway – but not before he glimpsed the licence plate. The truck was from Florida.

And all the while he was telling me this, something in my memory was stirring, knotted threads slowly untangling themselves.

The gas station footage Taylor showed me earlier today is easy enough to find online – it's doing the rounds on social media. I open it on Twitter and press play, pause it at the point a red truck heaves into sight and a man in a baseball cap gets out. The truck's parked right beneath the camera, the bottom portion – the front bumper and grille, licence plate – out of shot, so I can't confirm it's got Florida plates, but – I peer closer at the screen – sure enough, a vertical line runs up the passenger side of the windshield, bottom to top. *Bingo!* Okay, so red trucks are a dime a dozen, cracked windshields too – *and* men in baseball caps. But there has to be a chance it's the same truck Hank saw and, come to think of it, the same truck *I* saw parked outside Taylor and Garrett's apartment earlier today – the one with the guy asleep behind the wheel. I didn't think much of it then – assumed it was a reporter – but that truck had Florida plates. It didn't have a cracked windshield, though, but that would fit with Hank's most recent sighting: it'd been over a month since he first saw the truck; over a month since the gas station footage. Guy must've had his windshield fixed.

I flop back on the couch, exhausted but exhilarated. Whoever the truck belongs to could be a vital witness. Suspect, even. He was in town the night of Casey's disappearance, appears to have hung around since. He's also, if the licence plate's anything to go by, from the same state as Casey.

I have to find that truck.

But that's not the only thing I need to find, because it wasn't only my conversation with Hank that was illuminating. My conversation with Brooke was useful too. And though I still don't know who Rebecca Johnson is, I'm pretty sure we've been in touch.

I sit up, head pounding, hunch over my laptop again, breathe deeply as I log into my emails, scroll through the hundreds of unopened ones until I find the one I'm looking for. It's right back close to the start of them, because it was received the night of my accident. When I checked my emails at the library, I noticed it because its subject line stood out among all the *get well soon*s, the *sorry your mum died*s and the *what the hell happened*s. I don't recognise the sender's name, though. Or to be precise, I recognise the name because Brooke mentioned it earlier, I've just no memory of knowing it. Now I get chills even looking at it; the subject line even more so: *Your sister, Amy*

Since Brooke told me she'd given me Rebecca Johnson's email address, I'd put money on this email being a response to one I sent, so I flick to my outbox, and sure enough, there it is: an email to Rebecca Johnson on November 27.

I open it.

Dear Rebecca,

My name's Steppy and I'm a podcaster from the US. I was given your name and email address by Brooke Morgenstern, because I'm looking into the disappearance of Casey Carter. Brooke told me you reached out to her recently about the circumstances surrounding the death of your sister in Thailand last year.

So before I go any further, full disclosure, I should tell you that as well as being a podcaster, I'm also Garrett Corner's sister. I'm guessing Garrett's name is familiar to you, as although Brooke didn't tell me too much - she said I should let you fill me in - she did say my brother was the last person seen with your sister before she disappeared; also, though she didn't say so explicitly, she implied that you think he had something to do with what happened to your sister. You probably already know this - from what I gathered from Brooke it's what prompted you to contact her in the first place - but my brother has also been linked to the disappearance of another girl, in Heartsick, CO, USA. I know you'll think I'm trying to exonerate my brother, and I guess, if I'm being completely honest, I probably am. But also what I want more than anything is to get to the truth, to run every lead down whether or not I like what I uncover. I should say, though, that at this point, police have cleared my brother of any involvement in Casey's disappearance (cell phone data, so pretty concrete), and as yet she's not been found, so it's not even known she's come to any harm.

Regarding your sister's case, my brother returned from Thailand in January this year, and though he mentioned a girl who'd died while he was out there, he said he didn't know her. I've read a lot of online news articles on Amy and seen that a local man was convicted of her murder - one of the reasons I've been torn about contacting you, as I don't want to needlessly open old wounds. But the whole *thing's been preying on my mind, so I was wondering if you could shed any further light on the little I know.*

With thanks for your time.
Yours sincerely,
Steppy Corner

Holy shit. I sit back. Garrett potentially linked to another missing girl? Brooke told me this the first time we met?

Hands shaking, I return to my inbox, open Rebecca Johnson's reply.

Hi Steppy,

Thanks for your email and your honesty. I don't really know where to start. My sister, Amy, was backpacking round Thailand with friends in late 2015 on her gap year. You're right, the police arrested a local man, but my family and I (and locals on the island of Koh Tao, where she'd been staying) never believed he was guilty. We heard there was pressure on the police to make an arrest (bad press affects tourism), so we don't blame them, but have always suspected he was framed. That's why we didn't attend the trial - why we haven't been back to Thailand at all since we had Amy's body flown home.

It's true I contacted Brooke Morgenstern through Facebook after reading about Casey Carter's disappearance online. You ask if I can shed any light on the matter. Truth is, I'm not sure I can, though I'm happy to tell you the little I know, and while I think Brooke might have overstated the link between Amy and your brother (I understand she's not your bro's biggest fan!), I do have my suspicions about his involvement, although no concrete evidence. As for your brother being the last person seen with Amy, I don't know that's true for a fact, but I do know they knew each other. When Amy Skyped home right before Christmas, she mentioned this guy she'd been hanging out with. She didn't say much, other than that he was American, a few years older than her, 'really fit', and super fun. She didn't say they were dating or anything, but it was obvious she liked him, and while she didn't have any photos of him - I asked her - she was friends with him on Facebook, made me look up him up then and there.

Amy went missing on 28.12.15. At the time, I didn't think anything of the American guy she said she'd met. I didn't think much of it after she was found either, over two weeks later - my parents and I were too devastated, and the police in Koh Tao made the arrest soon after. But a few weeks later, another girl - I think from the Netherlands - messaged me through Facebook, said that even though someone had been arrested, she thought she should let me know that she'd seen Amy on the ferry to Koh Tao the day she was known to have travelled there, and that she'd been with 'some guy'. Until then, my parents and I had been under the impression she'd travelled to Koh Tao alone, as that's what police told us, based on what her friends told them. The girl who saw Amy knew her as they'd been staying at the same hostel on Ko Pha-Ngan for a couple of weeks. She recognised the guy she was with - said he'd been staying at the hostel too - and although she didn't know him well, she knew he was American, described him as tall and Scandi-looking, and said he went by the name Garrett. After that, I went back to Facebook and searched your brother's friends. My sister was no longer among them. I can't be sure, but the only explanation I can think of is that he unfriended her in the aftermath of what happened, and the only reason I can think of for that is that he wanted to wipe any connection to her.

I know this isn't proof of anything, but it always struck me as strange that your brother didn't stick around after my sister vanished. The Dutch girl who said she saw Amy and Garrett on the ferry that day said she told the local police, but they weren't interested. That's why she contacted me. Then, when I read about Casey Carter online, saw your brother's name and realised it was the same person, well . . . I'll leave you to make your own mind up about whether it's all one big coincidence.

Anyway, I'm sorry if that leaves you with more questions than answers, but that's really everything I know.

Best,
Becky

I'm stunned. Beside me, the cat's sleeping soundly, oblivious to what I've uncovered. Two missing girls, on opposite sides of the world. One dead. Nothing obvious linking them. Nothing obvious except my brother. It *could* just be coincidence, but I'm not convinced. I recall something one of the retired cops who worked the

Shaunée Hughes investigation told me: *there* are *no coincidences in these types of case.*

Any exhilaration I felt at my earlier truck discovery has evaporated. My head's pounding, my scar feels like it's on fire. I log out of my emails, pop a couple of pain pills, then return to my laptop, read everything I can find on Amy Johnson.

It's a weird feeling, because according to my email to Rebecca, I've already read most of it, yet I remember nothing.

In the email I sent Rebecca on November 27, I told her that I thought Garrett had mentioned Amy in passing when he returned from Thailand.

'Some girl died,' he said like it was nothing, fiddling with those stupid leather bracelets of his. 'British chick.'

Assuming he was referring to Amy, though (I do another quick internet search: no other British girls were murdered on or near the island around the same time), I realise something doesn't add up. Garrett told me about the girl who died on January 5, the first night he stayed at mine and Trav's. I know because I remember where I was when he told me: rolling out the futon on the bedroom floor. I know it was the fifth, and no later, because a good friend's birthday was on the fourth; Travis, Paige and I were going out for it, and Trav was pissed that Garrett had asked us to pick him up from the airport early the next morning.

But – and here I double-check, bring up some of the other news articles – although Amy Johnson went missing on December 28, according to the papers her body wasn't found until January 12. So how could Garrett know she was dead a whole week before everyone else did?

A whole week before her body was found.

Feeling sick, I log into Facebook, begin frantically trawling Garrett's photos, ignoring the comments about Casey that pepper them. Though

Garrett told me that night in New York that he didn't know the dead girl, Amy's sister said he did – that he and Amy had been Facebook friends. She also said she suspected Garrett bumped Amy from his friend list, but if I could find a photo of them together, it would prove he lied about not knowing her.

But Garrett doesn't take photos or post them. When you have as many friends as he does, you don't need to: people take photos and tag you. There are thousands of photos on his Facebook: nights out, parties, holidays, road trips. I scroll far enough back until I hit the end of last year. Then I stop. Begin clicking on photos. I'm around the right time, yet there seems to be a gap of at least three months. Because there are so many photos, it's not really noticeable – not unless you're checking – but I realise now there are zero photos of Garrett in Thailand.

Weird.

I go through his friend list next, till I find one of his buddies I know was in Thailand with him, begin trawling through *his* photos. There are hundreds of Thailand – cityscapes, beaches, parties, group photos, selfies – my brother in many of them, acting the clown, pull- ing over-the-top catalogue-model poses, cheers-ing the camera with bottles of beer or flipping it the bird. I know what Amy looks like – I've seen photos of her online – and I certainly can't *see* her in any of the images Garrett's friend has posted . . .

It feels like I spend hours going through Garrett's friends' photos before I give up. But while I don't find any trace of Amy Johnson, there is something I notice that explains why none of the photos Garrett's in are visible on his own Facebook: while all his other friends are tagged in them, Garrett isn't.

Beside me, the cat's woken up, is watching sleepily.

'Why would my brother go to the trouble of untagging himself?' I ask it, for I'm certain that's what he's done. In every single one.

In a last-ditch attempt, I return to my Amy Johnson internet search, and a blog she'd been keeping called *Not the Flying Amy Johnson!* The last entry's dated December 25, 2015. I skim-read it – no mention of Garrett – am about to close the window when I see a link to an image gallery, click it. The page fills with rows of thumbnails. I scroll through. There are photos of beaches with golden sands, azure seas and lush green foliage. There are pictures of waterfalls and boats and cocktails and beetles. There are cityscapes, shots of markets and temples. And dotted among them, photos of Amy: mid star jump on the beach; cross-legged on the sand, looking out to sea; giving a peace sign in a bikini and Christmas deely boppers. One of the last photos I come to shows a large group of people in a bar, male and female, young, gorgeous and tanned. Some have their arms round each other, smiling at the camera, others look more natural, caught unawares, mid conversation. I scan every face, recognise no one except, at the very centre of the group, Amy, hair down, wearing a crocheted halter top and skirt. The caption beneath the photo reads: *Friends old and new!* and I find myself smiling – she looks so happy. But my smile dies when I catch sight of something – well, someone – at the edge of the photo, almost out of shot. It's a man, for sure, and while it's impossible to know for certain, he looks tall. A sliver of his left-hand side is visible, but his head is turned from the camera so his face can't be seen, and he's wearing a hat. One of those bucket types that haven't been in vogue since the nineties. His left arm is just in shot, too, long and tanned, one hand resting on the shoulder of a girl in the foreground of the picture.

And on his wrist, those stupid leather bracelets.

My brother's bracelets.

20

Then

The next morning, I headed back into town, the cat in the carrier I'd found round the back of the cabin on the passenger seat beside me.

After what I'd learned from Hank, Casey's elderly neighbour, I felt lighter, though I wasn't sure why: I already knew, albeit from Garrett, that the police had cleared him. I already knew, thanks to his cell phone, that the evidence was indisputable. I suppose the porch light titbit was just one more piece of the puzzle, an extra bit of exculpatory evidence – the cherry on the cake, if you will – because coming from Hank, who didn't know Garrett so had no dog in the fight, it was completely object-ive. So while my brother may have been many things – a rapist, a liar, a cheat and a sociopath – he was not, it turned out, Casey's abductor.

The internet community had yet to get that memo, though – or if they had, they were choosing to ignore it – and were still very much gunning for Garrett. Which was why, that morning, instead of wasting more hours online reading the baseless opinions of people not in possession of all the facts, I'd decided to take the cat to the vet.

The Heartsick Animal Hospital was a compact but swish new-build in an area of town I didn't know well.

'I called earlier, about my cat,' I told the receptionist when I arrived.

'Name?'

'Stephanie.'

'How old is Stephanie?'

'Oh.' I laughed. 'I'm Stephanie. This is . . .'

I stopped, remembering that of course the cat didn't have a name. It was just *the cat*.

On the drive over, I'd switched on the radio and Bruce Springsteen had been playing, but it was something upbeat, which felt somehow inappropriate, so I'd switched it off again. The cat had howled in protest.

'You like a bit of Springsteen, huh?' I'd glanced down at the carrier on the passenger seat.

The cat made a noise – *peep!* – so I switched the radio back on, and it began purring so loudly I could hear it above the sound of the music, above the sound of the car engine, even.

I realised the veterinary receptionist was staring at me, snapped out of my reverie.

'Bruce,' I told her, though I didn't even know whether the cat was a he.

'Fill this in, please.' She handed me a form.

While I wrote, I asked her whether there'd been any reports of missing cats matching Bruce's description.

'You can check the notice board,' she said, 'but it's most likely a stray. We get a lot of seasonal workers, kids from outta town. They get a cat for company while they're here, then, when end of season rolls around, they move on, abandon it.'

I checked the notice board – no missing cats – then took a seat in the brightly lit waiting area, a prominently placed Casey Carter poster on the wall opposite. A combination of the weight of Casey's stare and a girl a couple of seats down who'd begun side-eyeing me, nudging her mother, who was sitting next to her, made me squirm. I stood, began perusing a nearby display of pet stuff, picked out some toys – brightly coloured plastic balls with bells inside; a pack of catnip mice; a colourful felt fish adorned with feathers, dangling from the end of a plastic fishing rod – held them out for Bruce to approve through the bars of his carrier, along with a glittery red collar that reminded me of Dorothy's ruby slippers, with a funny little silver bell.

Fortunately, we didn't have long to wait, and once in the consulting room, the diagnosis was a simple one: Bruce was indeed a he, a young neutered male with no identity chip and in need of de-worming, de-flea-ing and a good groom. The vet, a middle-aged woman, friendly and thorough, thankfully gave no sign she recognised me, either as Garrett's sister or the voice of *Dark Corners*. The vet nurse, however – a heavily pregnant brunette – was a different story. Though quiet and polite, there was an intensity about her, a way she watched me that made me think she knew me; and though I couldn't quite place her, put it down to the hundreds of photos of good-looking brunettes I'd seen online recently, I could have sworn I recognised her too.

Consultation over, it was almost a relief when the nurse walked me back round to reception, but any relief was short-lived when I saw the line that had built up at the desk. As I approached, a couple of people turned to stare, and I could have sworn one snapped a picture on her phone.

The vet nurse, still at my side, took my elbow, whispered, 'How about I let you pay in the office, Steppy?' and before I had time to respond, she'd steered me gently to a side room.

'How'd you know I go by Steppy?' I asked as she closed the door. I'd registered under my Sunday name.

'Ah.' She smiled, and there was something familiar in it, something from a long time ago. 'You won't remember me, I'm sure,' she said. 'In fact – this is kind of awkward – I used to date your brother.'

'Jenna?' I'd only met her a handful of times, but she and my brother had gone steady for a while back in high school. 'Of course I remember you. God. How long's it been?'

'Too long.' She stroked her baby bump absently. 'But I heard you were in town.' News travelled fast in Heartsick. 'Are you looking into Casey Carter's disappearance?'

So she knew about the podcast. 'I'm home for Thanksgiving,' I said, a little too defensively.

'Sorry. I didn't mean to . . .' She busied herself, grabbed the card machine from the desk.

'You forgot those.' I pointed to my haul of cat toys, Bruce's sparkly new collar.

'It's fine.' She waved me away and I tapped my card.

'Thanks,' I said, 'and congratulations.' I pointed lamely at her bump. 'How'd you end up in Heartsick?'

'Oh, you know,' she said. 'Got married. Small-town life appealed. Plus my mother-in-law lives the next town over.' She stopped. 'And Garrett?' I felt myself tense. 'How's he holding up?'

'You know Garrett,' I told her.

She didn't reply, picked up the glittery red collar, addressed Bruce. 'How about we get this on you, little guy?'

Bruce regarded her with suspicion as she opened his carrier, began fastening the collar round his neck.

'Hey, Jenna. Can I ask you something?'

'Sure,' she said, her back to me.

'You and Garrett. You were together a while. What was he like? I mean, as a boyfriend?'

'At the start?' She said it like a question. 'At the start he was great – funny, generous. And he was so good-looking. All the girls had a crush on him. But after a while . . .' She stopped.

'After a while . . .?'

'Well, I guess it was like he changed, you know? He could still be lovely, but he had this real mean streak, a dark side. He'd say things to me – call me stupid, tell me what I could and couldn't do, say I dressed like a slut.'

'Jesus, Jenna. I'd no idea.'

'He was so jealous, Steppy. Like, I couldn't talk to anyone – not just other guys. He didn't like my girlfriends, thought they were turning me against him, trying to get me to break up with him. Which was true,' she admitted, 'they were.'

'And did you break up with him?'

She gave a small nod. 'More than once. It was hard, though, you know. Like, he'd try to win me back, promise he'd change. I was sixteen, seventeen. Garrett was my first real boyfriend. I guess I thought that was what love was.'

'So when did you realise it wasn't?'

'Hey,' she said suddenly. She tapped the little silver bell on Bruce's collar. 'You know this is an ID capsule, right?'

'I didn't,' I admitted, thrown. 'But Garrett. What made you realise?'

She hesitated. 'He got physical.'

'He hit you?'

'No. He didn't hit me. But we were at your house one evening and we got into it. I can't remember what about. Something dumb. Next thing I know, I'm on the floor, no idea where I am. He'd put his hands round my throat. Choked me out.'

'You lost consciousness?'

She didn't reply, fastened the door of Bruce's carrier. 'Since this whole Casey thing?' She turned, and my eyes flicked instinctively to her neck, like I might see a sign of what my brother did to her, a remnant from all those years ago. But of course there was nothing. 'Other girls have reached out to me, Steppy. Told me Garrett did the same to them.'

21

Now

As I was leaving Casey's condo yesterday, Brooke and I exchanged phone numbers, and this morning she texts me to say that Casey's mom and half-brother, Cody, are open to meeting me.

Before that, I search out local auto repair shops online, drive round in a bid to establish if anyone's had a windshield repaired on a red truck.

'Nope,' the first man tells me, wiping his hands on a grease-stained rag before retrieving his glasses from his overall pocket, peering through them at my phone screen. The cell phone Dad gave me as a stopgap is too old for the internet, so before I left the cabin, I took a photo of the red truck in the gas station footage with it instead – not ideal, but the best I can do. 'Ain't had no truck with a windshield like that in the last few weeks.'

The second repair shop is a similar story. 'If I did replace it,' the guy says, through a background noise of whirring machinery and the clink of tools, 'I wouldn't be able to tell ya.' He must see the disappointment on my face, because then he winks at me, says, 'But I can tell you I didn't.'

There are only two auto shops in Heartsick itself, but I have time to kill before my meeting with Casey's mom and brother, so on a whim, I try one last place outside town. Something tells me it's worth a shot: maybe, if the owner of the red truck does have a connection to Casey, he'll want to fly under the radar.

Unlike the other two garages, this place appears to be a one-man business, and is definitely more isolated. Accessed via a rutted track, it's situated in what looks like an old lumber yard. As I climb from Jenna's Bug, dart through the now fast-falling snow, the owner stands at the open doors, watching me approach. He has a mug of something in one hand, which he sets down next to him on an upturned metal trash can.

'Help ya?' he asks, though he doesn't move, meaning that while he's relatively sheltered, I'm left standing outside.

'I hope so.' I smile, but he doesn't smile back. My fingers are so cold I fumble with my phone, almost drop it. 'I was wondering if you've replaced a windshield on a truck like this in the last few weeks?'

I hold my phone out, image of the truck on screen, and the man takes it, barely glances at it before handing it back.

'Naw,' he says, but I think he's lying. The corrugated-metal building rattles in the wind.

'You need a closer look?' I hold the phone out again, but he waves it away.

'Told ya,' he says. 'Never seen it.'

And if the first time I think he's lying, this time I'm sure, though something tells me it would be a mistake to push.

I thank him anyway, leave him my number just in case, then beat a hasty retreat. As I begin to putter my way back down the frozen track in Jenna's Bug, I glance in the mirror, see the man still in the doorway, watching me leave, slipping his phone from his pocket as he does.

*

It turns out that the motel Loreen Skinner and Casey's half-brother are staying at – the Mountain Gateway Motel – is on the adjoining site to Buddy's Bar. As I cross the gravelly parking lot, I can't help but wonder how Casey's mom feels staying so close to the last place her daughter was seen.

Brooke's given me the room number, but says I won't need it – it's the endmost corner room, ground level. I step up onto the veranda that runs the length of the building and knock, the door answered almost immediately by a guy I guess must be Casey's brother, closely followed by a large German shepherd.

'Hey,' he says, 'I'm Cody.' We don't shake hands. 'Come in.'

The motel room's as shabby on the inside as it is outside. It's the kind of place seasonal workers stay, not affluent out-of-towners coming for hiking weekends in summer or ski season in winter; reminds me, with a strange mix of despair and nostalgia, of the room I rented in Murdoch when I was making *Dark Corners*.

A wood veneer nightstand that's seen better days separates twin beds with matching pink counterpanes, wall-mounted lamps either side. The frosted glass shades are nicotine-stained and the room is stuffy, smells of stale tobacco, despite the sign on the back of the door reminding guests not to smoke.

The dog prods my hand with its long nose until I pat it – 'He's fine,' Cody tells me, 'a big ol' softie' – before padding over to a woman seated on the end of one of the beds, where it settles beside her.

'Steppy?' Casey's mom asks. Both she and her son are wearing *Find Casey* T-shirts, same as Brooke's.

'Thank you for seeing me, Mrs Skinner,' I say. She doesn't get up, though I offer my hand and she takes it.

'It's not Mrs,' she says. 'And Loreen, please.'

A truck thunders past outside, and though there's a parking lot between highway and motel, the walls shake like they're made of cardboard, faded prints rattling in fancy gilt frames. The dog lifts its head, whines softly.

'I'm so sorry about your mom, hon,' Loreen says, as the rumbling subsides.

'Thanks,' I tell her, though I can barely meet her eye. I'm flooded with guilt that at a time like this, she's the one offering condolences.

I take a step back, feel myself wobble, put a hand out to steady myself.

'You okay?' Loreen jumps up, and I open my mouth, can't reply. 'Cody,' she instructs, 'get Steppy a seat. Here . . .' She fetches me a can of room-temperature soda, which I accept gratefully, while Cody grabs a chair. 'Take your time.' Loreen guides me to the seat and I sink into it, take a drink of soda.

Loreen returns to the bed, watching me with hawk-like concern. If Brooke looks like Casey in a wannabe way, a less good-looking younger sister, Casey's mom resembles her more effortlessly, like an older one. She's younger than she looks in the photos I've seen of her, though, and while her resemblance to Casey is striking, it's as if someone's drained all the life from her.

Cody perches awkwardly on the end of the other bed, while I take my time sipping my soda and survey the room. Apart from the beds, nightstand and chair that I'm sitting on, the only piece of furniture is an old desk, a map spread out on its surface, so large it overhangs on three sides. But what the room lacks in furniture it makes up for in clutter: the dog's food and water bowls and a huge sack of kibble, overflowing suitcases, newspapers everywhere, an open laptop on Cody's bed . . .

'We've had reporters hounding us for weeks.' I look up at Cody's voice, see he's moved to the window, is peering beneath the net curtain.

Cody looks nothing like his mom or Casey; he's fair for starters, with a skinhead cut, tattoos over his knuckles and neck (not the hipster kind), a couple even creeping onto his face.

'I get it,' I say. 'But if you don't mind me asking, Mrs Skinner – Loreen – why did you agree to talk to me? I mean, you know Garrett Corner's my brother?'

Loreen and her son exchange glances as Cody sits back down.

'We know,' Loreen says. 'And we also know the cops have cleared him' – she looks a little embarrassed – 'when it comes to Casey, anyhow.'

'If the cops are right,' Cody jumps in, 'then someone else took Casey. An' all that internet shit's just a distraction.'

'We know you helped solve the Shaunee Hughes case,' Loreen adds, 'and we want to find Casey. *That's* why we're willing to talk. So what can we tell you?'

'I guess to start, just tell me about Casey. If it's not too painful.'

'She's my best friend.' Loreen wrings her hands. 'I was young when I had her – real young. Her dad wasn't around, so for the first four years it was just me and her. That's not to say that when Cody come along she wasn't happy. No, she dotes on him' – Loreen looks at her son – 'isn't that right, Code?'

Cody clears his throat.

'Like a second mom to him, even at that age,' Loreen continues. 'Gave me no hint of trouble' – she jerks a thumb in Cody's direction – 'not like this one.' Though she doesn't say it unkindly, Cody hangs his head, and I can't help but wonder what kind of trouble he gets into.

'Did Casey go to college?'

Loreen gives a shake of her head. 'Shoulda done. She was on the honour roll in high school. But she started dating Luke – her ex? – senior year of high school.'

Luke – the ex Lucky and Brooke mentioned, the fifth name on my list.

'He was older than her,' she goes on, oblivious, 'already had a job. Casey thought he was the bee's knees. She coulda gone to any college she wanted, but there was no reasoning with her after that. Luke didn't want her to leave, and she didn't want to leave him. That was that. She got a job at Applebee's, waiting tables.'

'But she wasn't with Luke when she moved to Heartsick? I heard they broke up, that she came here to escape him?'

Cody cracks his knuckles.

'You know what Casey's short for?' Loreen asks suddenly.

I could hazard a guess, but I shake my head.

'Cassandra,' she answers. 'And you know the meaning of Cassandra?'

'I don't,' I admit. 'Can't even hazard a guess.

'Means "one who excels over men".' Loreen scoffs. 'I gave her that name after her daddy skipped out on us when I was five months pregnant. Swore my little girl wouldn't be someone who let a man control her, tell her what to do. Look what happened.'

'She seemed to be doing well, though,' I say. 'She'd made a clean break of it, lived independently, held down two jobs. Brooke said—'

At the mention of Brooke, Cody snorts.

'Cody,' his mom warns. She addresses me. 'Look, Brooke's okay, means well, but whatever she's told you, you should take it with a grain of salt.'

'Whole fuckin' mountain, more like.' Cody snorts again. 'That girl wouldn't know the truth if it bit her in the ass.'

'So they weren't best friends?' I ask. 'Brooke told me they knew each other since kindergarten?'

'That much is true,' Loreen says. 'It's more just . . . well, I guess

Brooke's heart is in the right place. But she can be . . . I don't know. Needy.'

'Fuckin' desperate is what she is,' Cody says.

'*Cody,*' his mom admonishes him, sharper this time.

'Sorry, Mom' – he holds up his hands – 'but it's true. Like, she wants to *be* Casey or something. It's fuckin' tragic.'

'Enough, Code,' his mom tells him. 'Look,' she turns to me, 'when Casey moved here to get away from Luke, it was a clean break. From everything. And I guess you could say, sad as it is, that included Brooke. Their lives had been going different directions for a while. Like I say, Brooke means well, but she's kind of young-acting for her age. She loves Casey, sure, but a bit too much. Like, she would copy her, buy the same clothes, same perfume, make-up. Casey would get her hair cut a certain way, Brooke would get hers cut too, exactly the same, very next day. She always had to know where Casey was, didn't like her spending time with anyone else – and I don't just mean Luke, I mean her family – me and Cody – other friends.'

'She'd started stealin' shit from her too,' Cody adds.

I look to Casey's mom for confirmation. Outside, another truck thunders past, sends the pictures rattling once more, the ceiling light flickering. I look up, see dead flies silhouetted in the frosted shade.

'Casey *suspected* she was,' she says once it's passed. 'Didn't know for sure.'

'What kind of stuff?'

'Stupid stuff, mostly – clothes, make-up, jewellery. Nothing valuable. It'd go missing, then Casey would see Brooke with it, but if Casey said anything, Brooke would just deny it, say she'd bought the exact same thing, that it was coincidence.'

'Brooke told me she didn't move to Heartsick right away – that she didn't know where Casey had gone at first. But when she found out, she moved here too?'

Loreen sighs. 'Within a week of discovering where Casey was, Brooke had rented a U-Haul, drove across seven states to get here.'

'She said they were planning to rent a place together?'

Cody tips back his head. 'Un-fucking-believable.'

His mom ignores him. 'Brooke wanted to get a place with Casey, for the two of them to move in together. Casey didn't want to, but she was too nice to tell Brooke that. I mean, luckily she had her own place already. It was only one-bed, so she just kept making excuses.'

'That's where I spoke to Brooke,' I tell her. 'Casey's condo? She said you'd asked her to look after the place.'

Cody looks like he's about to pop a blood vessel. 'Jesus fuckin' Christ . . .'

Loreen puts out a hand, stills her son. 'It was Brooke suggested it,' she says. 'To be honest, I agreed, told her she could, just till . . . well' – she looks at Cody again – 'till Casey comes home. I mean, the plants need watering, the mail needs taking in . . .'

'What Mom's not telling you,' Cody says, 'is that Brooke was hanging around here at the motel so much, we couldn't take it no longer.'

'Don't get me wrong,' Loreen says quickly, 'we've been grateful for her support.' I glance at Cody's face; it says he disagrees. 'I mean, she set up the Find Casey Facebook page, organised searches, a real nice vigil . . .'

I think of Larry Polk. He organised searches and a vigil for Shaunee Hughes.

'Brooke wants to find Casey as much as we do, doesn't she Code?'

Cody makes a non-committal noise. 'She's organised a second vigil tonight. You know that?'

I shake my head. I only knew there'd been a first because Brooke mentioned it. 'Will you be going?'

He shakes his head. 'First one was outside Casey's condo. This one's at the park.'

'We went to the first,' Loreen tells me. 'And it's not that I don't want to go to tonight's. But it's hard, you know? I mean, we appreciate everyone coming out in support of Casey—'

'Fuckin' grief tourists,' Cody interrupts.

'Cody!' his mom says. 'People just want to find her.'

'People need to be out there lookin' for her is what they need to be doing, not holding vigils.' He stands, crosses to the window again.

'You been on any of the searches?' I ask.

'A few,' says Cody, ''cluding the one when they found her car.'

'That's why we brought Rocky,' Loreen says. At the sound of his name, the dog's ears prick up. 'He's Casey's dog, really. She got him as a pup, rescued him from a puppy mill. We hoped he might be able to track her scent or something, have some kind of instinct for where she is.'

'Problem is,' Cody says, 'we don't know exactly where she went missing from, only when.'

'Did you know Casey and Brooke argued on Halloween?' I ask.

Cody stuffs his hands in his pockets, mumbles, 'Doesn't fuckin' surprise me.'

'We didn't know,' Loreen admits, 'but, like Code says, it's not surprising. They didn't argue all that often—'

'Oh, *come on*,' says Cody.

'No, Cody,' his mom tells him. 'Casey wasn't confrontational.'

'True,' he concedes, leans against the windowsill.

'She'd bottle it all up instead,' his mom explains, 'complain to me on the phone – we spoke every day – but I do know that a few days before she disappeared, her and Brooke had a real doozy.'

Assuming Brooke told me the truth, I guess this was the argument she mentioned, the one that precipitated things coming to a head on Halloween. 'You mean because Brooke tagged Casey by accident on Facebook?'

'Weren't no accident,' Cody says under his breath.

'We don't know that, Cody,' Loreen tells him. She turns to me. 'Not even Casey thought it was deliberate. It was just Brooke being Brooke. She could be careless like that. And she deleted it soon as Casey told her to.'

'It was too late by then, Mom.' Cody crosses his arms. 'Luke, her ex, he was on his way to Heartsick soon as he saw that post.'

'I heard he turned up in town after she disappeared,' I say. 'But I also heard police spoke with him, ruled him out.'

'Right,' Loreen says. 'Apparently he was in Colorado Springs when Casey vanished.'

'Does this Luke have a surname?' I ask.

'Fisher,' Cody says.

I make a mental note, hope my memory will hold up. 'You don't happen to know what vehicle he drives?'

'Cody?' his mom asks.

'Used to be a pickup,' Cody says, and my heart skips a beat. 'Toyota Tacoma, I think. Silver. Last time I seen him in it was over a year ago, though.'

Not a red truck, then. Still, if Cody hasn't seen him in it for some time, he could have changed it. 'If you don't mind me asking,' I say to Loreen, 'I heard you got a text from Casey's phone, early hours of November first?'

Loreen looks upset.

'Can I ask what it said?'

She takes out her phone, scrolls through it, hands it to me.

Hi mom going to take off for a few days need some space to clear my head. Casey

I look up at her. 'You don't think Casey wrote this?'

Loreen shakes her head. 'She'd never send me something like that, period, let alone at one forty in the morning. She'd also never take off without letting one of us know where she was going – me and Codes were the only ones she told about coming here – so I knew, soon as I got it, something was wrong.'

'Plus she doesn't write like that,' Cody says. 'One long sentence. Doesn't even sound like her. And why the fuck would she sign it Casey? Like her own mom don't know who she is?'

It does seem weird, makes me think about the porch light thing again – how someone who knew Casey, her routine, could have switched it off that night. It seems entirely possible the text message is something similar, a crude attempt to make people think she left town of her own accord.

'I know this might be a difficult question,' I say, 'but do you have any theories about what might have happened to Casey?'

'It's gotta be a stranger,' Loreen says quickly, and I wonder whether that's based on anything other than not being able to come to terms with the thought of her daughter being harmed by someone she knows.

'Cody?' I look over to the window. Darkness has fallen. Behind him, I can see the flicker of the neon motel sign through the nets.

He nods in reluctant agreement. 'My feelings for Brooke aside' – he says it in a tone that makes it sound like he has a hard time parking those feelings – 'Mom's right. Has to be a stranger. My money *was* on Luke, but when the cops said there's no way he done it . . . Same with your brother,' he adds. 'No offence, but we obviously had to consider him.'

'None taken,' I assure him. If Cody knew Garrett like I did, I doubt he'd be apologising.

'Speaking of your brother,' he says, 'they found him yet?'

'Not as far as I know,' I tell him. 'But while we're on the subject, do you remember if you saw Brooke on November twenty-seventh?' I'm reluctant to ask a leading question, but I also don't want to sound accusatory by asking Loreen and Cody what their alibi is for the night Mum was killed.

'The twenty-seventh?' Loreen repeats. She and Cody look at each other.

'Guess we coulda,' Cody says. 'All the days pretty much blend into one right now.'

'We seen a lot of her,' his mom adds.

'More than we'd like.' Cody again.

'It was the night of my accident,' I tell them. Loreen makes a small O shape with her mouth. 'The night my mum was . . .' I don't have to finish.

'Sunday,' Cody says. 'Yeah, we did see Brooke.'

'She was here all night watching movies,' his mom agrees. 'Brought round a whole loada Disney DVDs – Casey loves Disney.'

'And you know for sure it was the twenty-seventh?'

'Yeah,' Cody says. 'Now that we know it was the day of your accident. See, we heard all the cop cars flying by, sirens blaring. Knew something was up. I mean, obviously, after, we found out what had happened. But at the time we thought it might've been to do with Casey – like maybe they'd found her? So Mom called Officer Melville to check.'

I'm back out in the car, the flickering motel sign reflected in the misted interior mirror not helping my migraine, which has been getting worse all evening. My scar's nipping more than usual and I wonder if something's wrong with it, wonder if I shouldn't be wearing this stupid hat so much. I pull the beanie gently from my head, use it to wipe the mirror, then survey myself, face lit up in neon pink and blue, am surprised to see my scar looks okay – as okay as something like that can ever look. Rest of me's a different story, though. The little make-up I applied this morning has worn off and my skin looks sallow: yellow where the bruising's fading, dark purple under my eyes. Even with a hat on, I must look alarming. Without it, God knows.

I don't know what makes me think of it at that moment – my own reflection; all the online photos I've been looking at – but I remember something I read a while ago, something about how it's only other people who see us as we truly appear: when we see ourselves, it's generally in mirrors, an inverted reality. But I also remember thinking that that's no longer the case – not these days, not with social media, the amount of selfies people take. And that's when it hits me: *a mirror image!*

My new laptop's in the footwell, so I grab it, boot it up, and though the signal's weak, I manage to connect to the motel's Wi-Fi and log into Facebook, find the photo. And there it is. The Brooke and Casey selfie. The one from Halloween.

And in it – I peer closer at the screen, at the silver pendant round Casey's neck – proof that Brooke's been lying.

22

Then

I'd always wondered how families could be so blind, wondered how, for some, blood was always thicker than water. I thought foolish those who no matter the evidence before them refused to see it, refused to believe their family member capable of whatever terrible crime they'd been accused of. Like Larry Polk's family. Larry was a loving husband, father, brother, son and uncle. He'd been married almost forty years to his high school sweetheart. He was generous, everyone said, would do anything for anyone. He held down a job, had worked for the same family-owned manufacturing firm the last twenty-something years. His boss described him as a good worker, reliable. He'd give a stranger the shirt off his back, his co-workers told me; was a Little League baseball coach, for Christ's sakes. No, Larry wasn't capable of murder.

Only his eldest daughter, Kara, Shaunee's best friend, seemed to think otherwise. She'd messaged me after *Dark Corners* aired, told me that whilst all these years she'd genuinely never suspected her father had anything to do with Shaunee's disappearance, after he was arrested, after she *really* thought about it, she reached the conclusion that he was, in fact, quite capable. The signs had always been there.

I'd met Kara for coffee a two-hour drive from her home, somewhere neither of us would be recognised, after all the media attention had finally begun to die down.

'He's definitely got a dark side,' she told me, hands wrapped tight around her coffee mug, though the day was warm. 'He can be charming, sure. He can be funny, kind. He was protective of us, me and my siblings' – *Aren't all dads?* she'd later asked – 'but I guess we put it down to what happened with Shaunee, you know? Like, parents in Murdoch didn't give their kids the same freedom after that. Who could blame 'em? But when I think about it now – about Dad – it was more than that. There was other stuff, I mean, like his temper. It could turn on a dime. You know when people describe a switch flipping? Well, that was Dad.'

'When did you know,' I'd asked her. 'For sure?'

'That my dad was a monster?' She'd sipped her coffee, considered. 'I think I always knew. That he murdered Shaunee?' She thought some more, put her coffee down. 'It's hard to explain, but I guess it was more a gradual thing. I mean, it wasn't like an epiphany – I didn't wake up one morning, know for sure he was a killer. In the end, it just added up. Everything I heard in the podcast made sense.'

I'd thought a lot about Kara in the months since, the courage it took to admit that your life as you knew it had been built on lies.

'I can't trust my memories any longer,' she'd told me. 'Like, the happy times' – and there had, she told me, been happy times – 'I don't know if they were for real, or if my dad was pretending that whole time.'

I wondered how it would feel to realise that the dad you'd looked up to your whole life, the son you'd raised or the man you'd chosen to father your kids was not who you thought he was. Kara had been the only one in her family willing to speak out, and I'd admired her for it; hoped that, given similar circumstances, I'd be a Kara too, brave enough to speak up. But after what Garrett had done to Paige, after what Jenna told me, I had to face facts: was I really a Kara, or had I been blind to Garrett's behaviour, not because I didn't recognise it, but because I simply refused to see what I didn't want to? I liked to think I wasn't blind when it came to my brother's faults, or the fact that my parents spent their life making excuses for him – protecting him, even. For me, unlike my parents, thinking the worst of Garrett didn't seem much of a stretch. So what I'd learned about him these past few days shouldn't have come as a surprise.

But although Garrett having nothing to do with Casey's disappearance was a demonstrable fact, what I couldn't shake, what made me feel so uncomfortable, was having to admit to myself that I'd always known he was capable of it. That whatever happened to Casey – assuming she had been abducted – had not been at the hands of some monster, but a seemingly ordinary, everyday guy, someone like Larry Polk or Garrett. Someone with a dark side, hidden beneath a veneer of respectability and charm.

After loading Bruce into the car round the back of the vet's, I headed out to the main street again in a bid to find the pet store Jenna had said was half a block down. It was definitely a day of firsts, I thought, as I pushed through the door, past yet another Casey Carter poster: I'd never been in a pet store.

The place was quiet and dark, the only sound trickling water and the hum of fish tanks coming from a wall of aquariums, lit up at the back of the store like a bank of flat-screen TVs.

There was no sign of anyone, neither owner nor customer, and it wasn't until I turned down the nearest aisle, dusty shelves crammed with supplies for small furries, that a voice made me jump. 'Help you, there?'

I followed the aisle as far as the fish tanks and found a cash desk, a man seated at it who resembled a walrus, with a beard crows could nest in.

'I'm looking for a kitty litter tray,' I said.

'You're in the right place.' He rose with some difficulty and lumbered off down the nearest aisle. I followed. About halfway along, he stopped, turned. 'Say, don't I know you from somewhere?'

'I don't think so,' I said. 'Guess I've just got one of those faces.'

'It's the voice.' He started down the aisle again. 'You on TV?'

'You listen to podcasts?'

'You're shitting me! *Dark Corners*! That's you! Man, I love that show. You gonna do a second season?' Before I could answer, he stopped, pointed to a selection of plastic trays. 'We got three types. Take your pick.'

Just then the store door opened and a young man, late teens, entered. He was fair, with a skinhead and tattoos all over his hands and neck. He looked pretty downcast.

'Hey, man, you got—' he called, stopped when he saw me. 'Oh, hey, sorry.'

'It's fine,' I told him. 'I'm still browsing.' I turned to the store owner. 'Go ahead.'

The owner lumbered off again and I returned to the display, pretended to be weighing up litter trays.

'How you holding up?' I heard him say. The customer said something in reply I didn't catch, and I heard the store owner ask, 'And your mom?'

I picked out a middle-price litter tray, then continued to fake-browse for a couple more minutes, watched from a discreet distance as the customer took out his wallet and the store owner stopped him. 'On the house, bud,' he said. 'I can drop it off tonight, after we close.'

The customer nodded, though he looked uncomfortable. 'Appreciate it.'

Once he'd left, I approached the counter, where the store owner had a ledger open, was writing something down. When he saw me, he put down his pen, grabbed the litter tray. 'Sorry about that,' he said. His eyes kept flicking to the store door. I got the impression he was itching to tell me something. 'Say,' he began, 'you heard about that girl? One who's missing?'

'Casey Carter?' I nodded.

'That guy, bought the dog food? That's her brother — well, half-brother.'

'The one who just left?' I turned quickly, though I knew it was too late. *Dammit.*

'Yeah.' The man nodded. 'Him and his mom, they got a German shepherd, order its kibble here. I gotta deliver it.'

'They're staying in town?'

'Uh-huh.' He scratched his beard. 'Musta been over three weeks now.'

Weird. Brooke said they'd left. 'Where?'

'Look . . .' The man sounded torn. 'I'd love to help, but . . .'

'Oh,' I said. 'Totally understand. Wouldn't want you getting in any trouble.'

There was an awkward pause, broken by the sound of a phone ringing from somewhere out back.

The man glanced in its direction. 'Hey, sorry, mind if I . . .?'

'Go for it,' I told him.

He lumbered through a door into a back room, and I heard him answer the phone. 'Heartsick Pets, Marty speaking.'

My eyes wandered over the counter to the open ledger. I felt guilty – I wouldn't usually resort to such tactics – but before I knew it, I'd reached out and spun it round, slid it across the counter. It appeared to be an order book, page after lined page filled with dates, names, phone numbers, dollar amounts. And addresses.

I drew my finger down the open page until I hit the last entry: *Cody Skinner.*

Skinner. Casey's mom, Loreen – her surname was Skinner. Cody had to be her son.

But it wasn't until I saw the delivery address that my mouth dropped open, and I was still staring at it when I heard the man's voice again from out back – sounded like he was wrapping up the call. I just had time to turn the ledger round, slide it back across the counter.

'*Phew.* Sorry about that,' he apologised as he reappeared, out of breath. 'Been non-stop today.'

'No worries,' I told him, paying for my litter tray.

'Hey,' he said, and I saw his eyes flick to the open ledger. I held my breath. 'You need a hand with that?' He nodded at the tray.

'I'm good, thanks.'

He followed me to the door, held it open for me. 'You should think about it,' he said.

'Sorry?'

'The Casey Carter case. It'd make a great second season.'

'I will,' I told him over my shoulder, though I was lying.

What I was really thinking about as I stepped out onto the cold street was why Brooke had told me Casey's mom and brother were no longer in town. Especially since it appeared they were staying at the Mountain Gateway Motel. The very same motel on the next-door lot to Buddy's where I'd bumped into Brooke on Thanksgiving. Brooke and a large dog: a German shepherd.

A German shepherd that I was now sure belonged to Casey's mom and brother.

And I'd bet money I knew which room they were staying in.

23

Now

According to Cody, Brooke's organised another vigil at the park this evening, which seems as good a place as any to confront her about the necklace. But while I know she's lied about that, it looks like she was telling the truth about her alibi for the night Mum was killed, unless Casey's mum and brother are covering for her and they're in it together, all alibi-ing each other. If they are, I think, I'm screwed, but somehow I can't see it, especially with Cody. He hates Brooke.

I'm early for the vigil and haven't eaten in hours, so back on the road, I stop at the first diner I come to, take my laptop in with me. While I eat, I pop a couple more pain pills, search for anything I can find on Luke Fisher. But while there are plenty results on both Google and Facebook – Luke Fisher's a common enough name – none have any obvious link to Casey.

It's starting to snow again as I pull up at the park, so I'm surprised to see quite a crowd. Someone's handing out candles at the entrance and I take one, make a beeline to where most of the people are gathered, but I spent longer than intended at the diner and have

arrived somewhat late. As I get closer, it looks like the vigil's drawing to an end.

The crowd shuffle in the snow to keep warm, their collective breath
clouding the air, candles clasped in their hands. More candles, this
time in jars, punctuate the snow-covered ground. As I weave my way
through the tight-knit group, I recognise a figure, the only person
facing outward, beside a blown-up photo of Casey.

'. . . She was special to each and every one of us.' Brooke is addressing the crowd. 'Whether you knew her or not. I wanna thank you all
again for showing up tonight.'

There's a moment's silence – people not quite knowing what to do –
then a smattering of applause before the gathering begins to disperse.
Like a salmon swimming upstream, I battle my way against the flow,
and when I emerge the other side, Brooke, turned away from me now,
is collecting her things. Amid the glowing candles around Casey's
photo, people have laid flowers.

'White lilies, Casey's favourite,' I hear Brooke tell a girl standing
next to her, and I find myself wondering if it's true.

I put my hand out, touch her lightly on the shoulder. 'Brooke?'

She stops, turns, doesn't look thrilled to see me.

Clearly sensing tension, the girl she was talking to takes her cue to
leave, hugs Brooke and exits.

'Nice turn-out,' I say.

'A lotta people love Casey,' Brooke says.

Or are just rubbernecking, I think. Though isn't that what I'm
doing? 'I thought I'd stop by, say thanks for putting me in touch with
Casey's mom and brother.'

'Half-brother,' Brooke corrects me.

'Half-brother,' I repeat.

She stares at me a moment. 'Something else?'

'Actually, there is. I wanted to ask you about the necklace you were wearing when I came to see you at Casey's – the half-heart one.' She probably has it on right now, I think, hidden by her coat.

'What about it?'

'It's a friendship necklace, right? You've got one half' – I lean down, light my candle using someone else's, place it in one of the few remaining empty jars – 'Casey's got the other.'

'That's kind of the point,' she replies snarkily.

'Right,' I say. 'So how come, when I saw you yesterday, you were wearing the exact same half as Casey is in that photo?' I point at the blown-up picture behind her. Having been reproduced many times larger than the original, up close it's pretty pixely. Still, Casey's necklace is clear enough to see.

'Dunno what you mean,' Brooke says. 'Look' – she points at the photo, at Casey's décolletage – 'Casey's wearing the other half – her half.'

'That's what I thought,' I say, 'at first. You see, I assumed you and Casey each had a pendant. They're two halves of a broken heart, fit perfectly together to make a whole. That photo' – it's my turn to point – 'was taken in a bathroom mirror. Everything's inverted, meaning the necklace Casey's wearing here is shown in mirror image.'

'I know what inverted means,' Brooke snaps, and I can tell she's rattled, is trying to work out where I'm going with this.

'Well if you know what that means, you'll also know it makes that necklace – the one Casey's wearing in the photo – exactly the same as the one I saw you wearing. *Not* the other half. What I haven't quite worked out is why. Why would you and Casey have the *exact* same half of a friendship necklace? It doesn't make sense.'

Brooke shushes me. She looks around, presumably to ensure no one's listening, but most of the crowd have already left and the few remaining stragglers are far enough away.

'I lost my half,' she says, 'okay? Casey felt bad, gave me hers to replace it, right after that last photo was taken.'

'But you'd argued a few days before. You said there was tension between you on Halloween – that you argued again later. So why would Casey give you her necklace?'

Brooke lowers her voice, says, 'We were like sisters,' and I can't help but notice she uses the past tense. 'Sisters fight,' she goes on, 'but we made up before we went out that evening, and Casey knew how upset I was to lose my half. I didn't want to take it, but she insisted.'

I wonder if I'm being played, if Brooke's lying – again – but she does sound convincing. Then I think of Cody. *That girl wouldn't know the truth if it bit her in the ass . . .*

'Look,' she says, and her tone's conciliatory, which is why what she says next comes as a surprise. 'Like I say, I'm sorry about your mom and your accident. I know you're going through a lot, which is why I didn't say anything last time we met, but if you're gonna keep going round accusing innocent people—'

'I'm not accusing anyone of anything,' I reply.

'Making me look' – she ignores me, carries on – 'like *I'm* the one doing something shady. But you're focusing on the wrong person.'

'Who *should* I be focusing on?' I ask, have a feeling I already know.

'Your brother.'

There's a peal of laughter from the other side of the park, car doors slamming.

'We've been through this, Brooke,' I say. At least I think we have. My head's throbbing again. Any renewed energy I had has deserted me, and I'm beginning to doubt myself.

'I know, I know.' She flicks a gloved hand. 'The police cleared him, yada yada . . .'

'They have,' I tell her. I'm not sure where's she's going with this, but I feel she's clutching at straws.

'Well I hate to burst your bubble, but a couple showed up in town. They heard about Casey.'

'And?'

'And they're saying,' Brooke says slowly, savouring the words, 'that a few years ago, at college, Garrett raped their daughter.'

'What?'

My brain struggles to compute what I've just heard, scrambles to remember. Garrett dropped out of so many colleges, I lost count. Though I always had the impression he'd been asked to leave more courses than he quit of his own volition, I never enquired, never sought detail, and no one ever told me. If it did come up, Dad would just sigh, Mum make excuses. *It wasn't the right fit*, she'd say.

'You're sure?' I ask at last.

'I've spoken with them.' There's a glint in Brooke's eye. 'Jerry and Lois McKinley.'

Somewhere in the back of my battered, worn-out brain a faint bell rings. *The McKinleys.*

'They were at the first vigil,' Brooke goes on. 'I spoke with them. Their daughter—'

'Wait – McKinley?'

'Yeah,' she says cautiously, like she thinks she's missing something. Because she is. 'Why?'

I don't answer. I'm thinking back to my conversation with Lucky. We're in his car, the day after I was discharged from hospital, and he's telling me about the couple who stopped to help me after my car accident.

Lord knows what would've happened if the McKinleys hadn't come along, he said.

Can it really be, I wonder, that the couple who saved my life are the same couple who, according to Brooke, claim Garrett raped their daughter?

24

Then

I arrived back at the cabin to find Garrett's Jeep parked outside, Garrett waiting on the porch.

'Well, hey,' he called as I climbed from the car. 'Who's this?' He nodded at Bruce.

The last person I wanted to speak to right now was Garrett, especially after my conversation with Jenna, so I pushed past him up the steps, asked, 'You reach that apology stage yet?'

'About that. Yeah.' He took the cat carrier from me while I fumbled with my keys. 'Look. I know I was a dick at Thanksgiving. It's been a difficult few weeks, what with everyone thinking I'm a killer and all.'

Classic Garrett. An apology that didn't involve the words *I'm sorry*. Making light of stuff that wasn't funny. Like a missing girl.

I opened the cabin door a crack, let Bruce dart inside. Garrett went to follow, but I put out a hand. 'Let's talk out here,' I said, even though it was freezing. I had no desire to be in an enclosed space with my brother.

'Whatever.' He shrugged, turned, leaned on the porch rail, stared off into the trees like a catalogue model.

Darkness was growing, and the forest felt like it was closing in on us. I shuddered.

'Remember what you told me,' I asked, joining him at the rail, 'in New York?' Just saying the words filled me with anxiety, but I needed to know.

'About Mum and Dad?'

His answer took me by surprise, because that wasn't what I meant. *That* was a conversation I'd been trying to forget, but now I was back there, I couldn't escape.

'You know the real reason we moved to the UK in '91 wasn't anything to do with Shaunee Hughes disappearing?' Garrett, in the back of the car we'd borrowed from a friend to pick him up from the airport, had leaned forward between the seats.

My stomach had sunk. I should have known this was his game, could sense he'd been itching to tell me something ever since he'd rocked up in arrivals looking like he hadn't slept in days, tanned, unshaven, in need of a haircut and wearing a one of those goofy bucket hats – the type that hadn't been in since the nineties – yet still somehow ridiculously handsome.

Though Mum and Dad had never told me explicitly that Shaunee Hughes's disappearance was the catalyst for our move, they hadn't *not* told me either. So that was what I told journalists when they asked. Maybe I was stretching the truth, but it wasn't like my parents hadn't read all the interviews, and they certainly hadn't disabused me of the notion, so I simply kept the narrative up. Over time, it evolved from *I guess my family left because of it . . .* to *My family left because of it.* I said it so many times, it sort of morphed into the truth.

'Dad had an affair.'

Travis, behind the wheel in bumper-to-bumper traffic, almost ran into the car in front.

'Fuck's sakes, Garrett.' I shot him a look in the mirror. 'That's not funny.'

'It's not meant to be. It's true. Mum told me recently, I guess after you'd been going round saying in all those interviews that Shaunee's disappearance was the reason we left.'

'Why would Mum tell you?' *You, of all people*, I meant.

'Dunno,' he said. 'Guess she was in a sharing mood. All I know is Dad was cheating with someone at the hospital and she gave him an ultimatum: move to the UK, fresh start and all that shit, or she'd leave without him, take us with her.'

After I'd got over the shock of finding out Dad had cheated – I never spoke of it again, not even with Travis – I'd wondered: did it really matter that Shaunee Hughes wasn't the real reason we'd left Murdoch? Maybe, I thought, inasmuch as the narrative I'd been ped-dling all those months wasn't true, but it wasn't like I'd deliberately lied. Really, it was Mum and Dad who hadn't been honest. But then why would they be? Appearances were everything to the Corner family, especially Mum. Dr Jayne Corner, self-titled Morningside Therapist, a woman who, in every interview she'd ever done, called Edinburgh her hometown, when in actual fact she'd grown up just outside Glasgow, fought her way to university, spent years cultivating a refined Edinburgh accent. Even the 'Y' in her name was a later addition, to make her appear more interesting. Truth was, Mum was born plain old Jane, but to admit that truth would ruin her carefully created construct of the perfect family.

'Step?' Garrett sounded impatient. 'Do I remember what?'

I shook myself back to the present. 'That first night in New York, when I asked why you came home early from Thailand?'

'What about it?'

'You mentioned something about a girl dying while you were out there.' With everything else going on, other than my initial internet search, I'd given little more thought to what Brooke had told me, about Garrett's supposed link to another missing girl. Brooke, after all, was a proven liar. But just because she'd lied about Casey's mom being in town didn't mean she'd lied about the girl in Thailand. And after my earlier discussion with Jenna about the *other girls*, something about the whole Thailand story, I wasn't quite sure what, was niggling at me. 'Did you know her?'

'The girl who died? No, I didn't know her. I told you. I mean, like, our paths *might've* crossed at some point – I dunno. This about Casey?'

'It's about the way you treat women, Garrett.'

He pounded his hands on the porch rail. 'Oh come on . . .'

'I ran into Jenna today.'

Garrett stared straight ahead, tried not to look rattled, but I could see the muscles in his jaw tensing, his hands clenching and unclenching on the porch rail.

'She told me why she dumped you.'

'Funny' – he laughed – '*I* remember dumping *her* ass 'cos she was a cheating skank.'

'Jesus, Garrett, what the fuck's wrong with you?'

'What the fuck's wrong with *me*? She was my high school girlfriend from, like, ten fuckin' years ago. I mean, you know she hooked up with Lucky after we broke up?'

'What? *That's* why you and Lucky fell out?' I'd always known there had to be something. Lucky had just stopped being a part of Garrett's life. 'Lucky and Jenna got together?'

'They're still together,' he said, and I thought of Jenna's baby bump, wondered if it was weird she hadn't mentioned it. 'My best bud and my girlfriend. Can you imagine? Oh, wait' – a slow smile crept across his face – 'course you can.'

I chose to ignore that last comment, said instead, 'I'd no idea.'

'Well, maybe you also don't know Lucky's a cop,' he went on. 'That him and Jenna moved to Heartsick last year. You think it's coincidence that of all the small towns in Colorado, some hotshot big-city detective like Lucky ends up here? Then some girl goes missing, I'm the last person to see her, and suddenly Detective Luck's on the case and *I'm* the prime suspect?'

'Except you aren't,' I said wearily. 'Those same cops you seem to think are out to get you cleared you.'

'Fuck, Steppy.' He grew animated. 'Don't you see? The cops only cleared me 'cos they didn't have a choice. And anyway, everyone online still thinks I did it.'

'Can you blame them?' I asked, incredulous. 'I mean, don't you think the fact you've been cleared yet people still think you're somehow involved says more about you – the way you behave – than them?'

'Are you for fuckin' real?' Garrett started to pace. 'Like you'd rather take the word of complete strangers over your own brother? Dammit, Steppy' – and with a suddenness that seemed to take even him by surprise, he kicked the porch rail so hard it splintered – 'does family mean nothing to you?!'

'Look,' I said, suddenly conscious of how dark it was growing, that we were out here all alone. 'It doesn't matter what I think. Or anyone else. The cell phone evidence doesn't lie.'

'Right,' he said. 'Right. The cell phone evidence *doesn't* lie.' He took a step towards me, towering over me. 'Just promise' – he took hold of my shoulders, was so close I could smell alcohol on his breath – '*promise* you'll stop digging for shit on me.'

Only if you'll look me in the eye and promise me *you didn't lay a finger on those girls. On Casey and Amy and Jenna and Paige.* That was what Steppy the podcaster wanted to say. Impartial, objective, rational.

Brave. But instead I heard Garrett's sister Steppy say in a whisper, 'I'll stop digging. Promise.'

'See?' He smiled, let go of my shoulders. 'That wasn't so hard.' And with that he was off, jogging down the porch steps, and I could finally breathe.

As I watched my brother climb into his car, something brushed against my leg, made me jump. I looked down. Bruce had appeared from the house, was standing next to me at the top of the steps. Together we watched Garrett go.

But not until I saw his tail lights disappear into the trees, swallowed up by the night, did I remove my tightly crossed fingers from behind my back.

25

Now

Last night, when I returned from the vigil at the park, I called Lucky.

'McKinley,' I said when he picked up.

I hadn't even taken off my coat. The cat was winding its way round my legs, purring.

'Excuse me?'

'Mr and Mrs McKinley.'

There was a pause, and I could tell the penny had dropped. 'How'd you find out?'

'It doesn't matter,' I told him. 'Just tell me the couple at the crash site the night of my accident aren't the same couple who've been in town accusing my brother of rape.' There was silence on the line. 'Lucky?'

'I'm here,' he said. 'And yes, the couple who helped you – saved your life – have also accused Garrett of raping their daughter.'

'You didn't think to tell me this?'

'It's not your business,' he said bluntly. 'Besides, what difference would it have made?'

'To me, not much. To Mum's case?' I made a face, even though Lucky couldn't see me. 'Uh, I don't know. You've got two people, presumably harbouring a pretty big grudge against my brother, who happen to be on a remote mountain road that leads to my parents' house, driving *away* from it right around the time my mum's murdered.'

'Look,' Lucky said, 'I've been completely upfront with you, already told you more than I should have. But the McKinleys aren't involved in your mom's death. That's all you need to know.'

'Are they still in town?'

'You know I can't tell you that.'

'That means they are.'

'Look, Steppy—'

I hung up. Lucky tried calling back a few times, but I let it go to voicemail while I fed the cat, and he eventually gave up.

I spent most of the night thinking about the McKinleys, the information Brooke had shared with me. It had been designed to hurt, to blindside me, I was sure – Garrett, implicated in a rape – maybe even make me think my brother capable of being involved in Casey's disappearance. But the more I thought about it, the more I realised Brooke had actually scored something of an own goal. Because whilst I was sure Garrett couldn't have been involved in Casey's disappearance, I'd so far been unable to rule him out when it came to Mum. Now, though, it seemed he wasn't the only person with motive, means and opportunity. And whilst I could believe my brother capable of a lot of things, killing his own mother when she'd always protected him, would have travelled to the ends of the earth to do so, would have been akin to killing the goose that laid the golden egg. And precisely because Mum would have done anything to protect Garrett, I also knew she wouldn't have taken kindly to the McKinleys. All of which made Garrett's story about stumbling upon the crime scene that night, finding Mum dead, more plausible. Perhaps the McKinleys had gone to the house to confront Garrett but had met with Mum instead. Maybe they'd told her a few home truths and things had got out of hand . . .

Which is why I need to speak to them.

Making sure I withhold my number, I spend the best part of the next morning phoning nearby hotels and ski resorts. I know that none of them will tell me whether the McKinleys are guests – I'm not stupid – so when reception picks up, I say in my most confident voice, 'Hi, yes. Can I leave a message, please, for Mr and Mrs McKinley?'

The first few places I call give me the same response: a pause on the line, the clack of a keyboard, then, 'I'm sorry, but we don't appear to have any guests by that name.'

I'm into double digits when I finally hit it lucky and, after the usual pause, the receptionist says, 'Certainly, madam. What would you like the message to say?'

I hang up, heart almost beating out of my chest, then take extra care over my appearance as I get ready, before pulling on my inside-out beanie. I'm quite sure I won't make it through the lobby of a five-star hotel with my stapled-together head wound on show.

When I arrive at the hotel – an expensive ski resort some way outside town – I find it bustling. I begin by approaching the front desk and asking for the McKinleys. The receptionist gives me a doubtful look, one that says she's got security on speed dial, but tries their room anyway.

'They don't appear to be in,' she says as she hangs up the phone. 'May I take a message?'

'Can you give them this, please?' I hand her an envelope.

'Certainly.' She places it into a pigeonhole and turns to the next guest, while I take a seat in the furthest possible corner of the busy lobby and wait.

About twenty minutes later, a couple appear. They're walking quickly, expressions glum, are almost past the front desk when the receptionist sees them, leans over it, calls discreetly, 'Mr and Mrs McKinley?' In her hand she waves my envelope.

Mr McKinley leaves his wife's side to collect it, opening it as he makes his way back to join her, a look of puzzlement spreading across his face.

'What is it?' I'm pretty sure his wife asks, her voice almost swallowed by the hubbub of the lobby.

Her husband glances back towards the desk, but the receptionist is already busy checking in another guest. 'I'm not sure,' I think he replies.

I bide my time until they've almost disappeared, then spring from my seat, catch them at the elevators out of sight of the lobby. The short dash has left me breathless.

'It's empty,' I say. 'The envelope.'

They turn simultaneously, the puzzlement on their faces turning to alarm. Mrs McKinley jabs at the elevator button.

'There's nothing in it,' I say again. 'I'm sorry. I didn't know what you looked like, and the police wouldn't tell me where you were staying. The hotel wouldn't have either, except . . .' They're still staring at me, clearly wondering what to do. 'I'm Steppy,' I say. 'I don't know if you remember me.' Their expressions tell me they know exactly who I am.

'We're glad you're okay,' Mr McKinley says, taking his wife's hand, pulling her closer to the elevator as it pings and the doors open. He's about to step in, but there are people getting out, lots of them. He steps back, waits. 'But we've nothing to say to you.'

'You saved my life,' I say. 'I wanted to thank you.'

Mrs McKinley hesitates, looks at her husband. 'Jerry?'

'Really,' I say. 'And, well, also, I wanted to talk to you about your daughter.'

The McKinleys' hotel suite is the polar opposite of the Skinners' motel room, the type of place my brother charges to our parents' credit card without a second thought. It's spotless but for a couple of open cases, clothes folded neatly in them or nearby. Looks like they're getting ready to leave.

I'm already carrying my coat, but the room's warm and I'm not feeling great after my long drive, the adrenaline rush of executing my cunning plan now wearing off, so I remove my beanie, self-consciously rake a hand through my hair – what's left of it – careful to avoid my scar. Mrs McKinley flinches, though makes no comment, and I wonder about the scene she and her husband were faced with when they stopped that night; wonder how much worse I looked then.

She pours herself a water, offers me one.

'Please,' I say. My mouth's bone dry.

'Madison,' she says, handing me a glass.

'Excuse me?'

'Our daughter's name is Madison. But maybe you already know that.'

I don't, had avoided googling the McKinleys and their daughter for fear of what I might find, preferred instead to hear it from the horse's mouth. 'I guess you already know who my brother is,' I say.

The McKinleys look at each other, and something tells me this exchange isn't going to go as smoothly as my meeting with Loreen and Cody.

'We're sorry about your mom,' Mrs McKinley says. 'Truly.'

I put my water down. 'Actually, that's kind of what I wanted to talk to you about.'

Mr McKinley looks displeased. 'I thought you said you were here to talk about Madi?'

'It's sort of all connected,' I say. 'You know the police are looking for my brother in connection with my mum's death?'

They nod in tandem.

'Well, I wondered what you can tell me about that night. I mean, you were there. You must have been among the last people to see Garrett.'

'We'd no idea it was him,' Mr McKinley says. 'Not till the police told us after.'

'It was dark,' his wife explains. 'We'd only seen your brother before in photos. Didn't recognise him.'

'Lucky for you,' Mr McKinley mutters, and I see his wife squeeze his hand, a gentle reminder. 'No, Lois.' He turns to her. 'I'm gonna be honest here.' He looks right at me. 'If I'd known that was your brother that night? So help me God, I swear I'd have killed him for what he did to Madi. I'd have killed him, and you'd have died in that car, 'cos it would've gone up in flames, you still inside.'

'Jerry,' Mrs McKinley says, and I wonder if he was this honest with the cops, wonder if his wife's worried I'll rat him out.

But so what if I do? It's no crime to fantasise about killing my brother. If it was, half the state would be locked up. My mum's actual murder, on the other hand . . .

'Can I ask what you were doing in town in the first place? I mean, you're not from Heartsick, are you?'

Mr McKinley puffs out his cheeks. 'We already told the police all this.'

'*Jerry*,' Mrs McKinley scolds again, and I get the feeling this is something she's used to. She looks guiltily at me. 'Truthfully? We were hoping to speak with your parents. You see, we'd seen about the missing girl, Casey, read stuff online – people saying your brother had something to do with it.'

'I'm guessing you also know the police cleared him?'

'Nonetheless,' she says, 'things had already started to snowball. Seems like someone tipped the press off about Madi's story and they started contacting us. They said if we spoke to them, we could get it out there. They said people should know.'

'You've spoken to the press?'

'Not yet,' she admits. 'We didn't like most of them. They were kind of pushy. Except Keith Morrison,' she adds. '*Dateline* have offered to do a sit-down interview with us.'

I know it's ridiculous, but I feel a pang of betrayal. Keith Morrison interviewed me for a follow-up *Dateline* episode on Shaunee Hughes, having originally covered the case in the mid nineties. I really liked him, felt we had a good rapport.

'We haven't said yes,' she goes on, 'but we haven't exactly said no, either. Keith's on standby, says once we're ready, he'll fly out to wherever we are, do the interview.'

'And the night of my accident,' I say, keen to change the subject, 'the night my mum died. Why were you on that road?' It's remote, after all, leads to none of the local ski resorts.

'We . . .' Mrs McKinley hesitates, and I glance at her husband. He's staring down, stony-faced. 'We were going to confront your parents,' she admits, 'tell them what your brother did to Madi.'

'My mum was home alone that night,' I say. 'Dad was in the city.'

'We didn't know that,' she says. 'Not till after.'

'So what did Mum say when you confronted her?'

'That's just it,' she replies. 'We didn't go through with it.'

Oh, give me a break, I want to tell her. Instead I say, 'But you were on the road to their house, were going the opposite direction to me when you saw my car go off the road. I was headed *up* the mountain, towards my parents' house. You were coming *down*, driving away from it.'

'Right,' Mrs McKinley agrees. 'We set out to your parents' place from here, so we came at it from the other side of the mountain, the other road. But when we got there, we changed our minds.'

'You didn't go up to the house?'

'No,' Mr McKinley says firmly, the first time he's spoken in a while. 'Closest we got was the end of the driveway. We sat idling a couple minutes, then drove on.'

'We were arguing,' Mrs McKinley admits. 'Truth is, I was never completely sold on the idea of confronting your parents. Jerry, well' – she pats her husband's hand – 'Jerry wanted to.'

'So if you changed your minds,' I say, 'why not turn round when you hit the driveway, go back down the route you came?'

Even as I ask it, I'm acutely aware of the fact that had they done this, our paths wouldn't have crossed that night and I probably wouldn't be sitting here. *If the couple driving in the other direction hadn't seen you go off the road . . .*

Mrs McKinley gives a half-hearted shrug. 'We just kept driving, I guess.'

'We decided to get a bite to eat in town,' Mr McKinley adds quickly. 'That other road's the quickest route into Heartsick.'

That much was true. My parents' house can be accessed from either end of a road that arcs up through the mountain. You only have to keep on driving and you'll pass it, come right back down the other side. But would you really psych yourself up to confront the parents of the guy you say raped your daughter, I wonder, only to get cold feet, grab a burger instead?

'Look,' Mr McKinley says, like he senses my scepticism. He lets go his wife's hand. 'I know what you're thinking, but we didn't have anything to do with your mom's death. We wanted to talk to your parents, sure, but we weren't angry with *them*.'

I want to believe him, don't want to think I'm sitting across from my mum's killers, but he seems pretty angry to me.

'We get it doesn't look great,' he goes on, 'but it doesn't really matter: the police have cleared us. We're free to go.'

'And my brother?' I ask, sensing it's best to move on.

'What about him?'

'How did he seem that night?'

'It was dark, chaotic,' Mrs McKinley says. 'Jerry was with your brother, trying to get you out of the car. I'd gone back up to the road to call for help, so I don't really know. Jerry?' She looks to her husband.

'It was pretty intense,' he admits, 'so I guess I wasn't paying too much attention to anything other than getting you out of that car.'

'My brother didn't say anything?'

'Not that I recall. I mean, I guess we discussed how best to free you; I gave him some instructions, but like Lois says, it was pretty chaotic. Once we'd gotten you out, he left the scene right away.'

'We didn't realise he'd gone,' Mrs McKinley adds. 'Not until the EMTs came, the police. They ask us what happened, and when Jerry looks round for your brother, he's already left.'

'Did you notice anything about him – his clothing?'

'You mean like blood?'

I nod. That's exactly what I mean. If he *had* just killed Mum . . .

Mrs McKinley defers to her husband again.

He sighs irritably. 'Again, not that I recall. But it was dark. Only light we had was the flashlight on my cell phone.'

I wonder for a moment why they wouldn't have used Garrett's cell phone flashlight too. Then I remember: Lucky said Garrett and Mum's phones were switched off around the time they reckon Garrett left our parents', the implication being so he couldn't be traced.

'Plus,' Mr McKinley goes on, '*all* our clothes were pretty messed up. I was covered in mud and blood, Lois too. You were bleeding pretty bad when we got you out, so I guess we wouldn't have thought anything of it if your brother's clothes were stained.'

I had to admit that in the dark it probably would have been pretty easy to mistake any bloodstains already on Garrett's clothing for mud and dirt, or pass them off as my blood. But a convenient cover-up like that could work both ways: if one or both McKinleys had killed Mum, any blood on *their* clothing would have been disguised too.

'And your daughter,' I say. 'Madison. I know I'm probably the last person you want to discuss this with, but can you tell me what she accused my brother of?'

'What he did to her, you mean,' Mr McKinley says, through gritted teeth.

'Madison and Garrett were at the same college,' Mrs McKinley explains. 'They didn't know each other. Madi said they met for the first time at a party that night – the night he . . .' She stops.

'She'd been out with a group of friends,' her husband takes over, 'but they'd gotten separated. She'd been chatting with your brother at a bar. It was late. They'd been drinking.'

'Madi wasn't drunk,' Mrs McKinley cuts back in, 'just a little buzzed – so was your brother. But she said he seemed nice, acted like a gentleman, offered to walk her to her dorm, so she accepted.'

It's a sad fact of life that beautiful people appear more trustworthy. Garrett harnesses his looks like a superpower.

'When they got there,' she continues, 'there was no one else around.

Madi said it was clear Garrett wanted to be invited in, said she started to feel uncomfortable, that everything happened so quickly after that. Basically, your brother forced his way into her dorm room, choked her out' – she puts a hand to her mouth, squeezes her eyes shut – 'then raped her.'

I feel sick. My head starts to pound. 'I'm so sorry,' I say. It sounds so lame. 'Did Madison go to the police?'

'Campus police, yes, a couple days later,' Mrs McKinley says. 'But they didn't do anything, and Jerry and I didn't find out what happened for two months, not till one of her friends called us at three in the morning, said Madi had had some kind of breakdown. Her friend wouldn't tell us what had happened – not exactly – but we knew it was something bad. We drove through the night to get there, picked Madi up, brought her home.'

'That's when she told us,' Mr McKinley says, hands balled into fists.

'We phoned the college immediately,' says Mrs McKinley. 'They launched an investigation, but campus police hadn't even logged the report Madi made, and after that, they pretty much said it was her word against your brother's. Some of the students protested, made Garrett's life pretty hard. We heard he dropped out in the end, but it didn't matter. Madi couldn't go back.'

'When did this happen?' I ask. Garrett hasn't been in college for years, so I know not recently.

'Two thousand and nine,' says Mrs McKinley. 'Madi was nineteen.'

I think back. That was the year I graduated from uni, I realise, so I wasn't even in the country. Whatever fuss might have followed Garrett dropping out of college, I would no doubt have been oblivious. Mum and Dad certainly wouldn't have said anything. It would have all been hushed up, never spoken of again.

'And Madi?' I ask. 'Is she here with you? I mean, you could go to the police. Now.'

Mrs McKinley looks alarmed. 'You don't know?'

I shake my head.

'Madi couldn't live with what your brother did to her,' Mr McKinley says, his face like thunder. 'She killed herself two years ago.'

26

Then

If Garrett was right and Dad had been the reason behind our move from the US to the UK in '91, then I was equally certain that Garrett was the reason behind our 2003 move back again. The reason my parents gave at the time was that Dad had received a job offer in Colorado too good to refuse. This was only partly true. Dad did receive a good offer, but only after applying for jobs in the US following a particularly fraught year caused by Garrett's behaviour, culminating in him being expelled for bringing a knife into school.

Mum, in typical Mum fashion, blew the whole thing off.

'It's not like he did anything with it,' I'd heard her telling Dad one night in the kitchen after they'd returned home from a meeting with Garrett's head teacher. 'The whole thing's been blown completely out of proportion.'

'Garrett's form teacher said Garrett threatened another boy,' Dad said.

'That boy threatened *him*,' Mum replied. 'Garrett wouldn't hurt a fly.'

Perhaps if the knife incident had been an isolated one, that would have been easier to believe. But every week there seemed to be something new with Garrett. His teachers struggled to control him, his peers were mostly afraid of him, and Mum and Dad let him get away with everything.

For a while after our return to the States, he adapted well to freshman life in high school. It appeared he'd turned over a new leaf.

'He's really flourishing,' Mum said.

All it had taken, she insisted, was a system – a school, teachers, classmates – that truly understood him.

But although things did seem to settle down, there were still flashes of the old Garrett, that dark side lurking beneath the surface: looking back, I don't think he'd changed at all. I think he just got smarter, better at hiding it. At not getting caught.

That night, after coming home to find Garrett on the porch, I dreamed Travis and I were still together, Paige was still my best friend. She and Garrett were staying with us, like they had in January. But Garrett hadn't just arrived home from Thailand; he was going there, had announced he was taking Paige with him.

When I woke the next morning, I took out my phone and stared at the email address Brooke had given me for Rebecca Johnson. Garrett had moved the conversation on from the subject of Thailand so quickly last night, I felt there had to be something in it, but did I really want to open that can of worms? I wasn't sure, so decided to hold off contacting Rebecca for now, see what I could learn from Heartsick PD instead.

If *Dark Corners* had taught me anything, it was that members of law enforcement generally fell into two camps: those more than happy for an outsider to take a fresh look at a case, who were generous with their time and information; and those who were sceptical, closed off and unwelcoming. I suspected that when it came to active cases, most cops would be the latter. The fact that I was a meddling podcaster, as well as the sister of someone who in many people's eyes was the main suspect, probably wouldn't help.

But I had an in at Heartsick PD, and when I asked if Detective Luck was available, explained that my brother had gone to high school with him, the detective who greeted me was friendly. 'No kidding,' she said. 'You're an old friend of Nate's?' Fortunately, she didn't seem to recognise me, and when she asked my name and I hesitated, smiled, said, 'Uh, how about I surprise him?' she wavered only a moment before returning my smile. 'Sure thing. I'll be right back.'

A short while later, Lucky appeared, looking all grown up in his suit, takeout coffee in hand, which he almost dropped when he saw me.

'Hey, Lucky, how's it going?'

He cast a glance at the detective who'd fetched him. She looked unsure, and for a second I was too, before Lucky made a beeline for me, folded me into a great big hug.

'Steppy Corner,' he said, shaking his head, laughing. 'How you been?'

At the mention of my name, the other detective did a double-take, looked from me to Lucky, said, 'I'll leave you guys to it,' and made herself scarce.

'Shit. I mean, *shit*.' Lucky held me at arm's length, looked me up and down. 'Steppy Corner,' he repeated, still shaking his head. 'My *favourite* Corner.'

'That's not saying much.' I laughed, and he smiled.

'How've *you* been?' I asked. 'I mean, it's been how long?'

'Good few years,' he said, then, 'Jeez, where're my manners? Get you a coffee?' He held out his, and I wasn't sure if he was offering me it or one like it.

'Thanks, I'm good. So' – I spread my arms wide – 'you always wanted to be a cop. Now look at you.' Lucky had taken a step back, was surveying me like I was surveying him. He was tall and handsome, looked older than his twenty-eight years, but in a good way – mature, clean-cut. He'd always been tall, but he'd filled out, lost that gangly teenage-boy look I remembered so many of my brother's friends having. 'Small world, hey?' I said. 'How'd you end up here?'

'My mom lives the next town over and her health's not so good. I applied for a transfer, somewhere closer, made the move last year.'

I smiled with relief – *of course you did* – couldn't believe that for even one second I'd let Garrett make me doubt him. *As if* Lucky had moved to Heartsick to pursue some vendetta against my brother.

'You look well,' I said, then, pointing at the gold band on his left ring finger, 'Something you want to tell me?'

'Oh, this?' He held up his hand, laughed (he had an infectious laugh), said, 'I hate to break it to you, Steppy – I know you always had a little crush on me' – he grinned – 'but I'm afraid I'm off limits now.'

'Congratulations, Lucky. I couldn't be happier for you.' His friendship with my brother notwithstanding, Lucky had always been one of the good ones. 'But I have to be honest. I already knew. See, I bumped into Jenna.'

'Ah.' He went all serious. 'And *I* have to be honest: she told me. Said she didn't tell you 'bout me and her, though.'

'*She* didn't.'

'Garrett,' Lucky said.

I nodded, right as the lobby door opened and a couple of cops walked by. 'Hey, Nate,' one of them called.

Lucky held up a couple of fingers, a half-hearted wave, then turned back to me. 'Look, uh, I think I know why you're here.' His face was tense. 'But you know I can't tell you anything, right? I mean, not about the case, your brother . . .'

'From what Garrett tells me, he's not even a suspect.'

'Right,' Lucky said.

'So really,' I went on, 'we'd just be two old buddies catching up. About my brother.' I pulled a face.

Lucky looked torn.

'Look,' I said, lowering my voice. 'I know you and Garrett don't speak any more. You don't owe him anything. But I'm not asking for him. I'm asking for me.' I knew it was unfair, that I'd no right to ask for either of us. 'I'm scared, Lucky.' My voice caught in my throat. 'Scared I've missed something. You know as well as I do what Garrett's like. But what if he's done something really bad this time? Something there's no going back from?'

'What exactly *are* you asking?'

I sighed. I wasn't even sure. 'I guess I'm just trying to figure out what the hell's happened,' I admitted. 'I mean, Garrett told me the police cleared him, but people keep saying . . .'

'People?'

'Internet mostly.'

'Come on now, Steppy.' Lucky gave a rueful smile. *That old chestnut.* 'You know the internet. All those armchair detectives.' He stopped, said quickly, 'God, sorry. I don't mean you,' looked genuinely worried he might have offended me.

'Wait,' I said. 'You're not a podcast fan, are you?'

'Don't flatter yourself, Corner.' He laughed. 'I haven't listened to a single episode of . . . what was it called?'

'*Oof.*' I clutched at my heart.

'My good lady wife, on the other hand . . .' He gave an exaggerated sigh, the air of a long-suffering husband twice his age. 'Well, I think the term they use is *super fan*.'

'I always knew you had great taste in women.'

He turned all serious again, lowered his voice. 'What *do* you know?'

'About the case? Casey Carter?'

He nodded, so I told him.

When I finished, he looked about him, then took me by the elbow, steered me from the reception. 'Come with me.'

I followed him down a hallway and past a few doors. He paused at one, listening – a sign on the door read *Vacant* – cracked it open, stuck his head inside. He swiped the sign to *Engaged*, held the door open for me. 'Wait here.' It swung shut behind him.

I found myself in a small interview room, plain white walls and sparse furnishing, no two-way mirror, though – just a table and three chairs, a camera mounted out of reach in one corner. Not knowing what I was supposed to do, I sat down in the chair with its back to the camera. A second later, Lucky reappeared carrying a laptop.

'*Is* Garrett a suspect?' I asked as he pulled out a chair, sat down opposite me. 'I mean, I know he's no angel' – said the mother of every serial killer ever; I cringed even as I said it – 'but you don't think he's capable of . . .?'

'You want the truth?'

I looked at him.

'Honestly?' Lucky leaned back in his seat. 'Some of the shit Garrett pulled in high school? It was fucked up, man. I mean, even before what happened between me and him, I knew I couldn't be around him much longer – just didn't know how to go about cutting ties.' He laughed coldly. 'Guess I should've thanked him for doing it for me.'

I wanted to ask him what he meant, but he was on a roll, so I let him talk.

'But look,' he went on, 'what I think about your brother doesn't really matter. The important thing for you to know is that when it comes to Casey Carter, Garrett's in the clear. He *was* a person of interest, but not any more. Cell phone evidence.'

I breathed a sigh of relief. So my brother had told me the truth. 'Cell tower pings?' Everyone knew about those.

Lucky shook his head. 'His Location History. He let us access it. Smart move, I guess, if you're innocent. Like having a GPS attached to your ass. Then there was the gas station footage.'

'Gas station footage?'

'Yeah. Garrett's cell phone data showed he stopped at a gas station along the highway after he dropped Casey off. We found out about it a while back, managed to get the surveillance footage, brought him back in for questioning. I mean, it didn't look great that he hadn't mentioned it, but he swore he'd just forgotten. Plus, gas station's en route to your parents'. If anything, it backs his story.'

'You were the one that interviewed him about it?'

'Not me. That'd be a conflict of interest, given our history.' He pulled the laptop towards him and opened it. It whirred to life. 'I could do with another one of these,' he said suddenly. He picked up his cardboard coffee cup, tapped it on the table. It made a hollow, empty sound. 'Get you that coffee now?'

Was he kidding? I screwed my face up at him, but he ignored me, left the room without another word, closing the door behind him. For a moment I didn't move. Was this a test? I turned in my seat, looked up at the camera. There was no blinking light. Did that mean it wasn't on? I reached out towards the laptop. Stopped. If I touched it, would a SWAT team burst through the door, arrest me? Arrest me for what? Fuck's sake, Steppy, I told myself. It's Lucky we're talking about here.

Cautiously I reached out, turned the laptop towards me, saw the stilled video image on the screen in front of me and hit play.

27

Now

'Jesus, Steppy,' Lucky says when he answers the door. 'I thought I made it clear you weren't to see them?'

'You said you couldn't tell me if the McKinleys were still in town,' I say, smile at him sweetly, hand him the bottle of wine, the flowers for Jenna. 'That's different.'

Lucky shakes his head and I can tell he's pissed off, but then Jenna appears. She still looks like Jenna, just older, though if I'd bumped into her in the street, I'm not sure I'd have recognised her, not least because she's heavily pregnant, looks ready to pop. She's wearing scrubs, a cardigan thrown over them, is smiling tiredly.

'Lucky,' she says to her husband. 'Where are your manners?' She turns to me. 'Steppy, welcome. I'm so sorry about your mom.'

'Thanks, Jenna.' There's an awkward silence before I point at the flowers Lucky's holding. 'These are for you,' I say. 'It's been a lifetime.'

She looks surprised, and I see Lucky trying to catch her eye, shooting her the kind of look I'm growing used to these days, one that tells me I'm missing something.

But Jenna bats it away. 'Come inside,' she tells me. 'You must be freezing.'

I was worried it was going to be awkward seeing Jenna after so long. I don't exactly stay in touch with my brother's exes – things rarely end amicably; I try not to get involved – but she's incredibly welcoming, the house is warm and something smells tasty.

Lucky's in charge of the cooking, and as I help Jenna lay the table, she asks, 'How's your cat?'

'I'm sorry?'

'The one at the cabin.'

My first instinct is to wonder if Lucky mentioned it, but I don't think I told him.

'You paid a visit to Jenna's workplace a couple weeks ago.' Lucky appears in the doorway, casserole dish between oven-gloved hands. 'She's a veterinary nurse.'

'You don't remember?' Jenna asks as we take our seats.

I shake my head, embarrassed.

'You brought him for a check-up. Said he turned up at the cabin in a bad state.'

'He's a he?'

'Sure is. We scanned him for a chip, but there wasn't one.'

'But he's wearing a collar,' I tell her, 'he must belong to someone.'

'A red collar?' Jenna asks. 'Glittery?'

I nod.

'You bought it for him when you brought him in. Some kitty toys, too. You named him, you know?'

'I did?'

'Bruce.'

'*Bruce?*'

She laughs. 'Yup.'

I can't quite believe what I'm hearing. These bits of my life, so recent, yet I've zero memory of them.

'You must think I'm crazy,' I say. 'It's like, there's before I came to Heartsick, then when I woke up in hospital. But in between?' I shake my head. 'No matter how hard I try, I can't remember.'

'Hey,' Lucky says, 'that's okay.'

'You'll remember,' Jenna agrees. She reaches out, touches my arm. 'When you're supposed to. To be honest' – she leans back in her chair, rubs her baby bump – 'I'm kind of glad you don't. The vet part, at least.'

'Oh?'

'Yeah.' She laughs. 'See, I know we hadn't seen each other in a while, but when you came in that day, I recognised you straight away. Not just as Garrett's sister. See, I'm obsessed with *Dark Corners*, so I tried to play it all cool, but I probably just came across like a total dork.'

Lucky rolls his eyes. 'Told you she's a fan.'

'Nathaniel Luck.' Jenna swats her husband playfully. 'He's not wrong, though.' she admits.

Dinner's good. No one mentions Mum or Garrett or Casey or the McKinleys, and for an hour or two, I can pretend the last few weeks don't exist. After we're done, Jenna excuses herself, leaves me and Lucky to talk over coffee.

'So,' Lucky asks, 'how are you feeling about tomorrow?'

'The funeral?' I haven't really thought about it – have been actively avoiding thinking about it, filed it away in a little box in my head, thrown away the key. 'In denial,' I tell him.

'That figures.' He nods. 'You heard anything from Garrett?'

'Nope.' Through in the kitchen, I can hear taps running, dishes clattering into the sink. Everything so normal. 'You come up with any other suspects?'

He raises an eyebrow. 'Working on it.'

'I've been meaning to ask,' I begin cautiously. 'In the car, the other day, when I was asking about Mum, Garrett's motive . . .'

'Uh-huh?'

'I said something about Dad not being a suspect, and you got all weird.'

'I did?'

'Dad's *not* a suspect?'

'He's not.'

'You cleared him.'

'In the end.'

'What the hell does that mean?'

'It means . . .' Lucky stops. 'Look. You want to know the truth?'

I nod, though I'm unsure.

'Your dad wasn't exactly honest with us at the start.'

'He lied to you?'

'You could say that.'

'About what?'

'It really doesn't matter. What matters is that he was in the city when it all went down – we know that for sure.'

'Phone evidence?'

'Phone evidence and witness corroboration.'

'What witnesses?' I find it surprising that on a Sunday evening Dad was anywhere but alone in his Springs apartment.

'Come on, Steppy,' Lucky says, though he looks torn. 'You know I can't tell you that. It's a conversation you should have with your dad.'

'And the McKinleys?'

He sighs: *this again*. 'What about them?'

'Do they count as suspects?' When I got back to the cabin earlier, I googled Madison, found her obituary. Though no hint of any motive behind her suicide was given online, it's clear from my meeting with her parents that they blame my brother. 'I mean, they were in the area at the time,' I say, 'and Mr McKinley sure has a temper. I'm not saying they planned it, but what if they went to confront Garrett, found Mum home alone . . .'

'The McKinleys cooperated fully,' Lucky says, 'which I'm guessing you'll already know if you've spoken to them. They gave us everything we asked for, and there's no trace of them at the scene – no fingerprints, DNA.'

'They could've worn gloves.'

'I thought you said they didn't plan it?' Lucky laughs, a tired, frustrated laugh. 'Whatever,' he says, 'it doesn't matter. We've got surveillance footage showing exactly what time they left their hotel that night. There's no way they had time to drive to your mom's, kill her, then get down the mountain to your accident site. You gotta give it up, Steppy. The McKinleys are in the clear.'

'I know.' I nod glumly. 'It's just you said it yourself: Mum's killing was brutal.' My eyes fill with tears. I look away, feel Lucky's hand on my shoulder. 'It was personal.'

'It was,' he says softly.

'You really think he did it.' It's not a question. *Garrett*.

'Look, Steppy. You've lost your mom. With everything that's happened, you've barely begun to process it, let alone grieve. But I feel like you want her killer not to be Garrett so badly it's clouding your judgement.'

'And I feel you want her killer to *be* Garrett so badly it's clouding yours,' I snap, immediately feel guilty.

But Lucky, good old Lucky, lets it slide, gets up from his seat and crosses the room, slips something from a briefcase.

'I'm going to show you something, Steppy,' he says. 'Okay?'

I don't answer, and he sits back down, slides what looks like an A4 photo across the table, face down. I go to turn it over, but he puts a hand out. 'Wait.'

I look up at him.

'You know where your mom was found, right?'

I open my mouth, close it again. Do I? I don't think that particular detail has been in any of the news reports, and if someone's told me, I can't remember.

'She was found in her office,' he says.

For some reason this throws me. I always thought it would be the kitchen. Or the lounge. Maybe even her bedroom. But her office, tucked away downstairs? Did someone get into the house somehow and find her there, or did she know her killer, invite them into her inner sanctum . . .?

'Did she . . . did she have defensive wounds?'

'A couple, maybe, but it looked like the attack took her by surprise. She didn't have much chance to fight back. Which would suggest . . .'

'She knew her attacker,' I finish. Swallow.

'Steppy, Garrett's DNA was all over your mom's office.'

'But he found her. According to Taylor, he tried to save her – he would've been covered in her blood.'

'Mm-hmm. Except we found traces of Garrett's blood mixed with your mom's in his bathroom sink. And that's not all,' he tells me, 'but before I go any further' – he nods at the piece of A4 – 'I should say that the only other person who's seen this photo outside of the police is your dad. We had to get him to identify it so we knew whether it came from the scene or if the killer brought it with them. Go ahead . . .'

I turn the photo over, though it takes me a second to realise what I'm looking at: a wooden owl. Not any wooden owl, but the one that's perched for years on Mum's desk, wherever in the world we've been living; the one Dad gave her when they were dating because – so Mum told everyone – he said it reminded him of her: beautiful. Wise.

But there's something different about how the owl looks in this photo, the reason I didn't recognise it straight away. It's the colouring. Instead of its rich uniform oak brown, the wood's splotchy: bleached-looking in some parts, stained dark – so dark it's almost black – in others.

'This, right here' – Lucky taps the photo – 'we're pretty sure this is the murder weapon. We found it in Garrett's sink. Someone had had a go at cleaning it with bathroom cleaner, didn't do a very good job.'

And suddenly it dawns on me what those dark splotches are.

'Now do you get why I think it's personal?' Lucky asks.

I don't answer, touch my collarbone, feel the tiny scar pulse, like it has a life all of its own.

But while the scar may be faded, the memory's still fresh, a memory from twenty years ago, and the only time in my life I truly lost it. I was nine and Garrett seven, and for no other reason than that we'd disagreed over something trivial, he picked up the owl and launched it at me. Its smooth head fitted perfectly into his small hand, and I ducked a second too late as it came flying towards me. Luckily, owing more to Garrett's aim than my ducking, it missed my head, though it still struck me just above my collarbone, the force of it enough to knock my feet from under me. Meanwhile, the owl continued its trajectory, hit the exposed stone wall – we lived in a barn conversion in Surrey – and fell to the floor with a thud. The owl left its mark on me, one that required two stitches; the stone its mark on the owl, shaving the tiny piece off one corner. Garrett stood and laughed and I let out a roar, charged at him and shoved him hard, sent him flying. There was a chair behind him and he fell over it, landed heavily the other side and broke his wrist.

There was a moment's silence while he assessed the situation, then he opened his mouth and wailed like a baby. Hearing the commotion, Mum rushed into the room, saw her wooden owl lying on the floor, saw me bleeding, Garrett howling, clutching his wrist.

'She . . . she . . . she pushed me,' he cried, red-faced and snotty, through ragged, babyish sobs, shooting me a simultaneous look that said, *You're for it now.*

'What were you thinking, Stephanie?' Mum demanded. 'Your brother's so much smaller than you.' (Which of course, back then, he was.)

'He started it.' I glared at Garrett, gritting my teeth through my own pain as the adrenaline wore off.

Garrett's arm was in a cast for a few weeks. I was grounded, even though in the UK grounding wasn't really a thing. My pocket money was also stopped. Garrett, on the other hand, was spoiled rotten by Mum. My wound was small but deep. I still bear the ghost of those stitches to this day, the little scar that reminds me of a pond skater above my left collarbone.

'Steppy?' It's Lucky. 'Now do you get why it's personal?' he repeats.

I nod glumly, because I do.

Because Garrett and that owl have form.

28

Then

The footage on the screen was clearly from an interview room similar to this one, if not this one itself. Shot from a wall-mounted camera like the one above me, the image was somewhat grainy, though I recognised my brother. A detective – female – sat opposite him.

'Hey, Garrett. All right if I call you Garrett?' As the video sprang to life, I recognised the voice, realised it was the detective I'd met in reception, though her back was to the camera. She had a blonde ponytail, and while my brother preferred brunettes, she was good-looking, just the right side of young enough to be of interest to him. I guessed the cops would be on to that, guessed it was the reason she'd been tasked with interviewing him in the first place.

'Sure.' On the other side of the table, Garrett sat back, completely relaxed.

'So . . .' the female cop said slowly, opening a folder in front of her, leafing through it. Garrett shifted in his seat, leaned forward ever so slightly. 'I've got your cell phone data here.'

He nodded.

'And you know —'cos we had a conversation before, right? – that the data doesn't lie?'

Garrett smiled. 'Lucky for me.'

'Right,' she said. 'Because it backs your story – you dropped Casey off, drove to your parents', were there the rest of the night.'

'Like I told you.'

'Almost,' the detective said. 'See, there's just one thing we need to clear up. Something else we learned from the data, why we asked you down here today.'

'What's that?'

'The gas station.'

My brother looked blank a second, then said, '*Shit*, yeah, I totally forgot.'

'You forgot you stopped for gas?'

He hesitated, like it was a test. 'Not for gas,' he said. 'I stopped to get a snack.'

The detective shook her head, disappointed. It had been a test. 'We got surveillance footage, Garrett. We know you didn't go into the gas station store. Try again.'

'Okay, Detective.' He held up his hands in mock surrender. 'Yeah, that's it. I was *gonna* get a snack, but I got kinda sidetracked, used the payphone.'

'Who'd you call?'

'My mum?'

'That a question?'

'No. I called my mum, let her know I was on my way over.'

'You're, what' – she looked at the paper in front of her – 'twenty-seven, and you still have to call Mommy, let her know you're on your way home?'

'You don't know my mum, Detective,' Garrett replied, with a

light-hearted look that said she didn't want to. 'And it's not my home. I don't *live* there, just crash there sometimes, when I need a place to stay.'

'After midnight?'

'Huh?'

'It's okay to call your mom after midnight? Wake her up?'

'My mum's a night owl, Detective.' The smile was gone. 'She writes at night.' Garrett was a consummate liar, but he wasn't used to being grilled. I could sense his patience wearing thin, his words becoming spiky. He didn't take kindly to people who figured him out.

'Okay.' The detective nodded coolly, as though what he'd said made complete sense. Like she believed him. 'But, see, problem is, Garrett – and I hope you won't take this the wrong way – I know you're lying.'

Garrett slouched in his chair, adopted the air of a drunk. 'About what exactly, *Ossifer*?' The smooth charmer hadn't worked. Now he'd play the clown.

The detective slapped a piece of paper down in front of him.

'What's this?' he asked.

'Payphone records. From the gas station.' She traced a line down the page with a pen, stopped. 'Recognise any of the numbers?'

Garrett pushed the paper away. 'Okay, you got me again. So, uh, now that I think about it, maybe I didn't call my mum. Maybe I called my girlfriend, Taylor. There's no law against that, is there?'

She held her hands up: *you got me this time.* 'Absolutely not,' she said. 'Lying to the police, on the other hand . . .'

'Oh come on.' He leaned forward, put his head in his hands, shook it slowly, more frustrated than worried or upset. 'So I called my girlfriend from a payphone. Big deal. I already told you the first time we talked, we'd gotten into a fight earlier that day.'

'So why did you call her?'

He lifted his head, looked right at the detective. 'So, uh, actually' – the charming smile had returned – 'this is a bit embarrassing . . .'

She didn't miss a beat. 'For you or me?'

Neither did he. 'Depends what kinda girl you are.'

The detective sighed. 'In this job, I've heard it all. Ain't nothing you can say'll embarrass me.'

'Good. Right. Okay. So I phoned my girlfriend 'cos I wanted to know if I could stop by her place. To, uh, you know . . .'

'A booty call, you mean.'

Garrett acted shocked. 'If you want to put it crudely, Detective, then yes.'

'But you'd been fighting earlier.'

'What can I say?' He shrugged. 'We fight hard, we love hard.'

'So, what, your girlfriend – uh, Taylor, is it? – she said you could come on over?'

'Well, obviously not. She was still mad. See, we were supposed to be going out together that night, for Halloween—'

'She turned you down,' the detective interrupted.

Garrett nodded, pouted.

'But you were on the phone . . . let's see' – she consulted the records – 'five, almost six minutes. If it was as simple as your girlfriend turning your ass down, why'd the call last that long?'

'What can I say?' Garrett said again. 'My girlfriend had a place in town. I thought it'd be easier to crash there for the night rather than go all the way to my parents'. She said no, I was trying to persuade her . . .'

The detective did that nodding thing again. Considered, thoughtful. 'Okay, Mr Corner' – it was Mr Corner now – 'I think that answers all our questions. For now.'

'I'm free to go?'

'You've always been free to go. Thank you for your time.'

Garrett didn't bother replying. The detective began gathering papers, but as my brother made to stand, she stopped. 'Oh, hey, one more thing. Why the payphone?'

''Scuse me?'

I held my breath.

'Why stop and use the payphone in the first place? Why not just call your girlfriend on your cell?'

Garrett turned back, thought a moment. 'Gee, Detective,' he said. 'Well, this is a little embarrassing too. But, see, sometimes when I call my girlfriend late at night for, like I said . . .'

'A booty call.' The policewoman sounded impatient. 'Got it.'

'So – and she'll tell you this herself – I can be pretty persistent. You know what guys can be like?' I could tell he was trying to make her feel uncomfortable, but the detective was unbowed, held his stare. Garrett wasn't used to this – I could see it threw him – but he pressed on. 'Sometimes, if I call her from my cell late at night, if she knows I've been out partying, she won't answer. I called her from a payphone so my name wouldn't come up on caller ID – so she wouldn't know it was me.'

The detective nodded. Entirely reasonable. 'So you didn't see her at all that night? Your girlfriend?'

'You already know I didn't. I went straight to my parents'.'

'Did you try calling her again?'

'Um. I don't think so. I mean, I might've *tried*, but she'd switched her phone off. She does that sometimes.'

'Right. Like, if you call her late and she doesn't want you calling back. You'd been fighting.' She nodded again. 'Makes sense.'

There was a pause, then Garrett said, 'Look, Detective, I've answered all your questions. I'd like to leave.'

'As I say, Mr Corner' – she began gathering her things again – 'you're free to go.' She stood. 'Thank you for your help. We'll be in touch if there's anything else.'

The video ended. I sat back in my chair, looked around. I'd been so engrossed in it, I'd barely noticed Lucky was still gone. That coffee was taking a long time.

I thought about what I'd just seen, whether it changed anything. Not really. Not in the sense that, like Garrett said, there was no crime in stopping at a gas station, using a payphone. But the more I uncovered, the more uncomfortable I felt. It wasn't Garrett's smart-alec attitude that bothered me – that was par for the course. Nor was it his explanation for calling Taylor that night. That was perfectly plausible; even the fact that he'd forgotten to mention his stop-off to police when they first spoke to him. No, it wasn't any of these things.

So what was it?

I glanced at the screen again, frozen in time, double-checked the date: 11.15.2016. November 15.

I thought back to Thanksgiving dinner. *Week ago today*, Garrett had said, when Mum asked him when the marriage had happened. *Drove there Wednesday, married Thursday* . . .

So, Garrett had spoken to the police on Tuesday, November 15. The following day, Wednesday, he and Taylor drove to Vegas. The next, they were married.

Two days after the police asked about a phone call he made to his girlfriend, Taylor, on the night Casey Carter disappeared, Garrett and Taylor tied the knot.

29

Now

It's late and I'm back at the cabin. I'm exhausted, my head's splitting, but I can't even think about going to sleep, so I'm doing the washing-up. As I load that morning's breakfast dishes into the sink, I wonder what Lucky meant when he said Dad lied to the police, wonder if I'm reading too much into the fact that Mum was killed with a wooden sculpture that Garrett used as a weapon against me some twenty years ago. After he'd shown me the photo, Lucky admitted that Dad told him about Garrett throwing the owl at me. But while I get where he's coming from – it does seem personal – it also seems a bit of a reach. Garrett was a child when he hit me with the wooden owl. Throwing an object at someone in a child-ish fit of anger is quite different from bludgeoning them to death with it.

Isn't it?

It's only because I glance at Bruce as I wait for the sink to fill that I know something's up. Over on the couch, washing his undercarriage, he freezes abruptly, sits up like a meerkat. I suddenly realise I'm hold-ing my hands under the running tap, that the water's scalding, snatch them from beneath it.

'What is it?' I ask him.

I shut off the tap, listen, hear the sound of a car engine, tyres crunching on snow.

For some reason, my first thought is that it's Lucky, that he's come to check I'm okay after all the information he sprang on me earlier. But I've not long come from his house, and besides, he'd always call before stopping by, especially in the middle of the night. Especially with a killer on the loose.

I dry my hands and rush to the nearest window, part the blinds and peek out, but all I can see is headlights, blinding me. As the lights cut out and the engine dies, I see a large vehicle, a flash of colour through the dark: a red truck. *Shit.* I let the blinds snap shut. My heart's hammering as I inch silently to the door, not knowing what to do. It's obvious I'm home: the cabin lights are on, Jenna's Bug's parked outside.

A car door closes quietly, more crunching snow, footsteps this time, heavy boots up onto the porch. Whoever it is pauses when they reach the door. Then they knock. I hold my breath, look at Bruce, signal to him to keep quiet. He stares at me, startled.

Whoever it is knocks again, calls out, 'Hey. I know you're in there.'

I look around for my phone – Dad's phone – can't see it, see a knife drying by the sink instead, dart across to the kitchen and slip it into the pocket of my hoodie before returning to the door and opening it. A man's standing there: Garrett's age – bit younger, maybe – and around the same height, but dark-haired, wearing a baseball cap. It takes me only a second to recognise him – the driver of the red truck from the gas station – though I've only seen the footage a couple of times.

'I'm Luke,' he says.

My mouth drops open. *Casey's ex.*

'Can I come in?' When I hesitate, he holds out his hands, shows me they're empty, like somehow that proves he's not a threat. 'I just want to talk.'

Reluctantly I stand aside and let him in. Bruce takes flight upstairs.

'Okay if I sit down?'

I fold my arms. 'Go ahead.'

Unlike Casey, Luke's not conventionally good-looking, but I can see him having a hold over her all the same. He takes a seat on the couch, the side that was, until moments before, occupied by Bruce.

'What do you want to talk about?' I ask.

I remain standing, try to keep as much space as possible between us, as little as possible between me and the door.

'You tell me.'

I stare at him blankly.

'You've been asking about me round town.'

I slip a hand into my pocket, feel my fingers close round smooth, cold steel. The knife's blunt as hell, though it's some comfort at least. 'You're right,' I admit. 'Where were you the night of the twenty-seventh?'

He looks confused. 'Twenty-seventh of what?'

'November,' I say. 'The night of my accident. The night my mum was killed. I'm sure you've heard.'

'Course I have, but . . . *Fuck*, what, you think *I* had something to do with it? Your mom's murder?'

'You tell me. Maybe you think my brother had something to do with Casey's disappearance, so you went looking for him at my parents' house, met my mum instead . . .'

'You know the cops think your brother killed your mom,' he says. 'Besides, I wasn't even here that day.'

'Really?'

'Straight up. I mean, I hung around for a bit after Casey disappeared, spoke to the cops, helped with some of the searches, but I drove back to Florida November fifteenth. My fuckin' boss threatened to fire me if I didn't.'

'Yet you're here now,' I say.

'Yeah. Came back last weekend, thought, fuck it, let the heartless fuckin' son-of-a-bitch fire me if he wants.'

Last weekend. My memory's not great, but I think it tallies: I'm sure that's when Casey's neighbour, Hank, said he saw Luke's truck for a second time. If Luke recently returned to town, it probably made sense that he'd swing by Casey's place, see what was going on.

'We done here?' he asks.

'Not quite,' I say. 'See, I know you lied.'

'Jesus. I already told you, I wasn't here the twenty-seventh. You can call my boss, check with the cops – I told them I was leaving town.'

'Not about that,' I tell him. 'About the night Casey disappeared. You lied, told the cops you were in Colorado Springs. But I know you weren't. You were here, in Heartsick.'

'No I wasn't,' he says quickly. 'I was headed here, sure, but that night? Halloween? I *was* in Colorado Springs. The cops know – my cell phone proves it, was pinging a tower right by the motel I was staying at.'

'You sure about that?'

'I didn't arrive in Heartsick till November first, day *after* Casey vanished. So if you're trying to pin *her* disappearance on me now—'

I don't bother to let him finish. 'I've got proof, Luke.' He opens his mouth to speak, but I hold up a hand. 'The video of my brother at the gas station the night Casey vanished? The one that's doing the rounds on the internet? It shows you at the same gas station. Same time.'

Luke starts to get up, and not sure if he's going to make a run for it – or something worse – I take a step back.

'Wait,' I say. 'Hear me out. I've not told the police. Yet. But if anything happens to me, they'll find out: I've instructed my lawyer to send them a letter.' I don't have a lawyer, nor have I instructed anyone to do anything, but it seems to work, because he sits back down.

'*Fuck.*' He sounds more defeated than angry. 'Okay, so I was in Heartsick that night. But I didn't do anything to Casey – you gotta believe me.'

'I want to, Luke, but you have to admit, it doesn't look good. I mean, your cell phone's pinging a tower in Colorado Springs while you're in Heartsick. Looks like an attempt to create a false alibi, if you ask me, which also makes the whole thing look premeditated.'

'There is no *thing*. I didn't even see Casey that night. Yeah, I was in Heartsick, and yeah, technically my cell phone was pinging in Colorado Springs—'

'Technically?'

'I left it at the motel that night. Not on purpose,' he adds. 'It was an accident – I leave my cell phone places all the time.'

'Did Casey know you were coming?'

'No,' he admits. 'We hadn't seen each other or spoken for months. I just wanted to talk.'

'That's a long way to come just to talk. Especially since it doesn't sound like Casey wanted to talk to you – doesn't sound like she wanted anything to do with you. How'd you even find her?' I ask; then, before he has time to answer, I say, 'Don't tell me. Facebook.'

He nods dejectedly. 'Her friend Brooke. She posted a photo of her and Casey a few days before. Tagged the bar they were at.'

The photo Brooke and Casey fell out over. Casey was worried about Luke finding her. She was right to be worried. By the time Brooke deleted the photo, Luke had already seen it, knew where they were. It was too late.

'You know Brooke?' he asks.

'Sort of.'

'Fuckin' hate that girl.' He's balling and unballing his fists. 'Always getting involved in other people's shit, 'specially Casey's. But I gotta give her credit. She did me a real favour that day. I'd been looking for Casey for months, and that fuckin' big-mouth goes posting where they are all over Facebook?'

'So you got in your truck and drove to Heartsick. And when you got here, you were going to – what? – find Casey, beg her to take you back?'

'Not that night, no. I planned to stay the night at the motel, drive the last leg of the journey to Heartsick the next day. But it was Halloween, Casey's favourite holiday. I guessed she'd be going out, so after I checked in, grabbed a bite to eat, I decided to jump back in the truck, drive to Heartsick, go round some of the bars, see if I could find her. By the time I realised I'd left my phone at the motel, it was too late to go back for it.'

'So what happened? You get to Heartsick, see Casey leave Buddy's with some guy – my brother – follow them home?'

'*No*,' he says. 'Look, I admit I drove round a few bars, but I realised pretty quick I'd never find her. It was busy. Everyone was in costume . . .'

'So, what? You went to her condo, waited there instead?'

'How could I when I didn't even know where she lived?'

'You must've found out,' I say. 'Casey's neighbour saw you.'

'Not till after she disappeared. That night – Halloween – I slept in my truck at a rest stop off the highway. You gotta believe me. I'd never have hurt Casey. I loved her.'

I notice he uses the past tense. 'She didn't love you,' I say. 'Not any more. She'd moved on.'

'That's not true!' He leaps up, thrusts a hand in his pocket, and I brace myself, tighten my grip on the knife handle, but what he pulls out is not the knife or gun I've conjured, but something tiny and silver, glinting in his hand. I feel myself relax.

'Here.' He passes it to me. 'If Casey didn't love me, why would she still wear it?'

I take it from him, turn my hand over and gasp. It's a chain with a silver heart pendant, not a whole heart but a half, a jagged line down one edge.

'I must've still meant something to her,' Luke goes on. 'That photo Brooke posted, the one where she tagged them at the bar? Casey's wearing her half of her necklace in it. *Our* necklace.'

'You gave her this?' It's exactly the same as the one Brooke has, the one she claims is a friendship necklace, the one she claims Casey gave her after she supposedly lost hers. Exactly the same but for one thing . . .

'Not this half,' Luke clarifies, unaware of the bomb he's just dropped. 'This half's mine. But they match, right? Casey's got the other half. The mirror image.'

30

Then

Back at the cabin, I tried calling Paige again. I hadn't been this desperate to speak to her in all the months I'd been calling her, even after everything went down in New York. I hadn't felt so in the dark about something since then, either.

Looking back, it had been the perfect storm and, as much as it pained me to admit it, Travis was right: there'd been problems between us for months, long before Paige and Garrett came to stay in January. The final nail in the coffin for our relationship had not been what happened between Paige and Travis, but the success of *Dark Corners* – Travis had admitted as much when he'd called me on Thanksgiving. Now I couldn't help wondering whether if *Dark Corners* hadn't come along (or come along but not been successful) we'd still be together. Not that Travis would have admitted it – I'm not even sure he realised – but I think he much preferred PA Steppy, the Steppy who hated her job but coasted along, the Steppy who was there when he got home in the evening, who shopped for groceries – or was at least around to order takeout – who listened to him complain about the pressures of his job, his co-workers, his dad. The Steppy he had no need to resent or envy.

I also wondered if we'd still be together had Garrett not announced he was coming home from Thailand early, hadn't asked to crash at our apartment for a few days. What would have happened if we'd just said no?

The whole thing had started to unravel a couple of days into Garrett's stay, when he and Travis fell out – the clothes-borrowing incident – and Garrett relocated to a nearby hotel. The following day, Paige, Travis and I had been due to go out for yet another birthday, and Garrett, still in the city, had invited himself along.

It was a nice enough evening. Paige alternated between talking to my brother and talking to me about my brother; Garrett alternated between talking to Paige and every other girl in the bar.

'Your brother's *so* funny,' Paige had said to me at one point in the evening, during a bathroom break. 'And he's sweet.'

I hadn't bothered disillusioning her. People either saw Garrett for what he was or they didn't. Most worked it out in their own time. If Paige hadn't by now, despite all the stories I'd told her, despite having lived under the same roof as him for two whole days, then that was on her.

When I look back, I wonder about that too: would things have been different if only I'd warned her?

A little after 2 a.m., Travis and I were ready to call it a night, so he called us an Uber. Though it was the weekend, he had an early work call Saturday morning – one of the downsides of working for his dad's company – and I was still working seven days doing promo stuff for *Dark Corners*. We'd assumed Paige would ride with us, but when we told Garrett we'd be heading home soon and he'd shouted, 'Fuck work!' (spoken like a man with no job) and announced his intention to take the party to a nearby club, I saw Paige waver: should she go with him or come with us?

A short time later, a bunch of us were out on the sidewalk, waiting for various cabs, and next thing we knew, Garrett and Paige had disappeared. Someone told us they saw a group of people, Paige and Garrett among them, hailing a yellow taxicab; someone else that the pair of them had left together alone on foot. Either way, though I wasn't quite sure why – Paige was an adult, after all – I felt uneasy. I tried calling her, but – typical Steppy – my battery died, so I switched to Travis's phone. But Paige wasn't picking up, so after a handful more calls, a few voicemails – 'It's me. Where'd you go?' – I began texting her.

You with Garrett?

My phone died. We're in an Uber.

Where are you?

Me and Trav back at ours. Let me know you're okay pls.

She didn't reply to any of them.

Late morning Saturday, with Travis finished work for the day and gone to the gym, I was lounging on the couch, surfing the net, when I heard the front door of our apartment go, called, 'Hey, Paige, that you?'

There was no reply, so I'd heaved myself up, gone through to the bedroom and found her. She had her back to me, was flinging clothes into a holdall, and I could see she was wearing the same outfit as the night before.

'Look what the cat dragged in!' I joked. 'Where did *you* get to last night?'

I kicked myself now for making light of it, felt so guilty, but for some reason it hadn't dawned on me right away that something was wrong. It hadn't occurred to me, though it should have, just how out-of-character this was for Paige: in all our years at uni, she'd been the sensible one, never drinking too much or staying out too late, the reliable friend, always looking out for others – the ones who got into scrapes.

She'd turned. Her eyes were puffy, her make-up smudged. Her hands were all scuffed up, I noticed, and she had a cut on her cheek, red marks on her wrists, arms . . .

'*Jesus*,' I said. 'Did you fall?' But that wouldn't have explained the marks on her neck.

She looked ashamed, turned away again, said only, 'Sorry I didn't text back,' continued packing.

I'd asked if I could do anything for her, get her anything – clean clothes, food, Advil – but she politely declined. After that, she'd cut her trip short, made some excuse about needing to get back to Connecticut, said she was starting her new job Monday, even though I knew she didn't start till a week Monday – she'd been due to stay with me and Travis till the following weekend.

When I tried calling her the next week, she didn't answer; nor the next, when I called to ask how her new job was going. When I sent her the usual *Hey friend!* text, to which she'd always reply, *Hey friend!*, that had gone unanswered too.

'I'm really worried about Paige,' I said to Travis one night a few weeks later, on a rare evening we were home together. I was watching TV, lying on the couch; Travis on the floor, leaning against it, watching Netflix on his laptop.

The past few months, with me away so much and Travis working more than ever, we'd been like ships in the night. But in the days after New Year's, when Paige and Garrett had been in town, we'd spent more time together than we had in ages. I'd hoped things were looking up for us, but since Garrett and Paige had left, Travis and I had seen less of each other than ever.

'Huh,' he said, not looking up.

'She's being weird. I never hear from her.'

Though Paige was now, technically, replying to my texts – just – we hadn't spoken at all; she kept making excuses not to take my calls: she was working; busy; tired.

Travis took out an earphone. 'I think she's gotta lot of stuff going on.'

'Really?' I sat up. 'You've spoken to her?'

Travis and Paige had always gotten along, but they weren't close. The three of us had met at uni in the UK, had bonded over being American (plus the fact that Travis and I each had one British parent), and had formed a tight group. After graduating, we'd all moved back to the States – Travis and me to New York, where we'd moved in together, Trav waltzing straight into a job with his dad's company; Paige to Connecticut, near to her parents. She'd come see us in New York; me and Trav would drive down to Connecticut, spend weekends with her and her family. Paige and I chatted by phone at least once a week, were always texting, even if it was just a *Hey friend!* But Travis and Paige? They had each other's numbers, sure, but they didn't speak by phone, rarely texted. They certainly didn't meet up without me – didn't do coffee or lunch dates, or go to the movies together. I was the glue that held us all together. Without me, I was quite sure, the two of them would have lost touch years ago.

Which was why it was so surprising when Travis replied casually, 'Just on the phone.'

I should have been suspicious right there, but I actually found it funny. 'You and Paige? You talked on the phone?'

It was only afterwards, as I lay in bed that night – Travis still watching Netflix in the lounge – that I began to feel uneasy. It wasn't that I didn't trust him and Paige. Not at all. It was just I'd had no idea that outside our friendship as a threesome they were even speaking. Especially when *I* couldn't get Paige to give me the time of day.

The next morning, me still in bed and Travis getting ready for work, I'd asked him. 'When you say you and Paige spoke by phone, you mean, like, once, right?'

He'd hesitated. With hindsight, I should have known then and there.

'She's going through a rough time,' he said, not meeting my eye, and I think I said, 'Huh.' There followed another pause before he added, 'I mean, you know about that night, right?'

'What night?' Though it seems silly now, I genuinely had no idea. Not then.

'Come on, Steppy,' Travis had said. 'That night we all went out? Josh's birthday? When we came home and Paige ended up back at your brother's hotel?'

I felt a strange prickling sensation all over. 'Paige went back with Garrett that night?' Deep down, I think I'd always suspected as much.

Travis looked at me funny. 'You didn't know?'

'No. Did they—'

'I'm running late.' He left the bedroom to grab his coffee from the kitchen.

I waited for him to come back, didn't realise our conversation was over until I heard the apartment door close.

After that, things between me and Travis and me and Paige became even more strained. Paige seemed to have stopped replying to my texts completely again (I'd wondered if Travis had spoken to her, told her about our conversation), so out of desperation, I'd texted Garrett, who'd also left New York the day I last saw Paige, without even saying goodbye.

What happened between you and Paige???

He didn't reply.

Meanwhile, Travis was working longer and longer hours and, having been more like roommates than boyfriend and girlfriend for weeks – okay, maybe months – now we felt like complete strangers. Then, a few weeks after the strained Paige conversation with Travis, I discovered she'd been in New York, not even called me. What was more, she and Travis had met up.

More than once.

'I don't understand what's happening,' I told him over takeout a few nights later. 'Why didn't Paige tell me she was in town? Why didn't *you?*'

'I think that's a conversation you need to have with her,' was all he said.

I tried, honestly I did, but she still wasn't taking my calls. She had started replying to my texts again – I think she realised I was suspicious, that I was trying to figure out what was going on – but only the bare minimum: a *Yes* or *No*, a *Thanks*; a *Sorry missed you in NY. Super busy with the new job! Hope we can catch up soon* when I asked why she hadn't let me know she was in the city. She didn't even sign off with a kiss.

One night, I'd had enough and demanded Travis tell me what was going on – *with* Paige, rather than *between* the two of them (it sounds naive, but I'd still no idea). He'd sighed heavily, told me yet again, 'Look, Steppy, that's a conversation you and Paige really need to have,' like he was some kind of high school counsellor, me and Paige fifteen-year-old besties who'd fallen out. I'd lost the plot, shouted, 'Fuck's sakes, Travis! I've tried so many fucking times but she doesn't respond!' To which he gave no reply – he never was one for confrontation – other than a slight raise of his eyebrows, so I'd taken a deep breath, pleaded with him. 'Just tell me what happened, Garrett,' I begged, realising too late that I'd called him by my brother's name, and Travis had given me this look like he hated me.

'You must know,' he said, 'deep down,' like this was some kind of Freudian shit. And in that moment, suddenly I think I did. But Travis was referring to what had happened between my brother and Paige, and what had dawned on me was the realisation of what was going on between my best friend and my boyfriend. 'What he did to her that night,' he'd gone on, 'it was bad.'

But at that point I was hung up on Travis and Paige, couldn't move past it. I'd felt sick, asked, 'You and Paige. What's going on between you?' Travis hadn't answered, again, and this time I'd seen what I was supposed to, his non-answer confirming it.

It was another three agonising weeks before we officially ended things. Ten long years and it was over. After that, Travis moved out, though it took him until mid November to collect the last of his shit, which, stupidly, I didn't mind, as it gave me hope, made me think – I didn't find out that he and Paige had actually moved in together until that last day I saw him – that things might somehow be repairable, when all it really did was prolong the pain. The only upside was that after the success of *Dark Corners*, I didn't have to worry about how I could afford the rent on my own.

Of course, both Travis and Paige *swore* nothing happened between them till after me and Travis were no longer together. We all knew it wasn't true, but even if it had been, the fact that they thought that made it acceptable – my best friend and newly ex-boyfriend getting together a hot minute after we broke up – was laughable.

And through it all – the break-up, the move out, the trying to move on – the Garrett thing remained, hung over all three of us like a cloud. I was still in the dark about exactly what had happened that night, despite beseeching Paige by text message numerous times – even after it was over between me and Travis, even after she and Travis were officially together – to tell me the truth, promising that whatever had happened, however bad things had become between us, I'd listen when she was ready to tell me. She never did. Travis told me afterwards, via one of his typically pragmatic (cold) emails, that he and Paige had been there for each other, and though he didn't say it as such, the implication was that I hadn't been.

When we were together, Travis and I weren't the type of couple who lived in each other's pockets, made grand declarations of love or public (i.e. on social media) gestures. Neither of us was particularly romantic. But we were solid – I'd thought so, at least. Never in a million years did I see us ending up like this (but then who does foresee their boyfriend leaving them for their best friend?). But while I'd been devastated at the breakdown of my relationship, what hurt more was the loss of my friendship with Paige. That had felt like a bereavement – still did – and in the weeks afterwards, I swung from hating Paige to hating Travis to feeling sorry for Paige to hating Travis again.

But most of all, I hated Garrett.

For Garrett – typical Garrett – had been the spark that lit the touch paper that ignited this whole fucking mess, that blew my life into smithereens.

It had been the date in the bottom corner of the video footage from Garrett's police interview about the gas station stop-off that did it, rather than anything he said in the interview itself. Well, not just that – it was a combination of things up until that point, but it was the date that sparked the idea. If my theory was right, though, and I prayed to God it wasn't, I needed to check things through, needed to be certain, to speak to Paige – I had a genuine reason this time – but when I called her again that afternoon, she didn't pick up. I held my breath, listened to her cell phone ring out, listened to her voicemail once more: 'Hey, it's Paige, leave a message! Or don't!'

This time, though, I didn't hang up.

'Hey. It's me. Again. I need to ask you something. Call me back. *Please.*'

31

Now

I open and close my mouth. '*You* gave Casey the necklace she's wearing in the photo?' I hold out the one Luke's just passed me. '*This* is the other half of it?'

If he's telling the truth, that means Brooke never had the matching half to Casey's.

'I got it for her first month we were dating,' Luke says. 'I don't wear my half – it's not exactly my style – but I carry it with me, all the time.'

'So there's no reason Brooke would have the other half? Casey's half?'

He laughs. 'Fuck, no. Brooke told you she's got it?'

'More than that,' I say. 'I've seen her wearing it. I asked her about it – saw Casey wearing what I thought was the other half in the Halloween photo. Brooke said it was a friendship necklace – she and Casey had half each – but she lost her half so Casey gave her hers.'

'You gotta be fuckin' kidding me, man.' He puts his head in his hands. 'I mean, fuck, who'd do that? It's got mine and Casey's names on the back.'

I turn the pendant over, and sure enough, *Luke & Casey forever* is engraved in tiny writing. It's the kind of soppy thing an infatuated twelve-year-old comes up with, but it proves Luke's not lying.

'You don't think there's any chance Casey gave her it?'

Luke, head still in hands, shakes it slowly side to side. 'No way. Brooke musta stolen it.'

I don't disagree. It does seem unlikely Casey would have given Brooke a necklace engraved with the names of her and her ex-boyfriend.

That night, I lie in bed unable to sleep. As Luke was leaving, I asked him point blank: if *he* didn't have anything to do with his ex's disappearance, who did? After the revelation about Casey's necklace, I half expected him to point the finger at Brooke – though stealing from her best friend, if that's what she did, doesn't make her a murderer, it doesn't look great, either – but instead, halfway out the door, he turned, fixed me straight in the eye.

'I heard around town that when the cops talked to your brother after Casey disappeared, he had scratches on him,' he said.

I swallowed. 'He'd had a fight with his girlfriend earlier that same day, but besides, the cops've cleared him.' Even as I said it, doubt had begun to creep in again.

'So what are you gonna to do now?' Luke asked.

'About the gas station footage?' I still hadn't decided. 'I don't know,' I told him honestly.

'And Brooke? The necklace?'

I didn't know that either. 'Even if I confront her about it, she'll probably deny it,' I said. 'Sure, she'll admit you gave it to Casey, that it wasn't a friendship necklace, that she never had the other half, but that doesn't mean she won't stick to her story that Casey gave her it, and there's no proof she actually stole it.'

Bruce is lying on top of the duvet, across my legs, weighing them down. The scar on my head is sore and itchy. But as uncomfortable as all these things are, none of them are the reason I can't sleep. Because the more I discover about Casey – the people in her life – the more questions remain. And far from the suspect pool narrowing, it just keeps getting bigger.

Despite Luke's denial, and despite the fact that for some reason I feel like he was telling me the truth, I can't overlook the fact that he was in town the night Casey disappeared. I also can't overlook the fact that he has a history of violence and drove halfway across the country supposedly just to talk to his ex – an ex he hadn't seen in over a year, an ex who'd moved to another state, left behind friends, family in a bid to get away from him. Luke's only in the clear because, thanks to his cell phone data, he has an alibi, but I've managed to drive a truck through that alibi. All he has left is his word that he didn't leave his cell phone at the motel on purpose; his word that he didn't know Casey's address. Maybe he knew where she lived all along, turned up at her place before she got home that night, waited outside in his truck. Maybe he saw Garrett drop her off and that incensed him, so he confronted her after Garrett left and they started to argue, things got physical. Or maybe Casey had already gone to bed – that would explain the porch light being off – and Luke somehow gained access, killed her in her own home then disposed of her body.

And then there's Brooke. There was something off about her even before the necklace revelation. Did the police even check her movements the night Casey vanished? Do *they* consider her a suspect? Again I only have her word for it that she went straight home after leaving Buddy's. But she was angry. Upset. Her friendship with Casey hanging by a thread. It sounded like Casey had had enough of her; sounded like Brooke was envious and resentful of Casey in equal measure.

Brooke also lied, who knows how many times; and if Luke was right, that Casey wouldn't have given her her necklace, then Brooke must somehow have stolen it, sometime between when the Halloween photo was taken (Casey was still wearing it then) and when they parted ways at Buddy's later that night. I've no way of proving it, though.

So why, I ask myself, given my suspicions about Brooke, what I've learned about Luke being in town the night of Casey's disappearance, can I still not shake the thought that there's a Garrett-shaped shadow looming over all of this? Why can't I stop thinking about those scratches, the ones Luke and Brooke both mentioned, the ones Garrett allegedly had after Casey vanished? But even if Garrett was all scratched up, there's another explanation: he and Taylor got into a fight earlier that day – Taylor told me. Brooke said she didn't think Garrett had the scratches when she saw him at Buddy's that night, but this whole time she's been going out of her way to implicate my brother. If only, I think, there was a way of finding out whether he had them before Casey went missing. But even if I track down every single patron at Buddy's that night, among all the Halloween costumes and with all the drinking I doubt anyone would remember.

I'm finally drifting off to sleep when I wake with a start, sit up so fast I feel dizzy. Further down the bed, still on my legs, Bruce starts to purr. *Why didn't I think of it earlier?*

'There might be a way to find out if Garrett had those scratches before Casey disappeared,' I tell Bruce. 'There just might.'

But first, the matter of Mum's funeral.

It's a small, sombre affair at the local crematorium, just me, Dad, Mum's literary agent, who's flown in from New York, and Lucky and Krauseneck, hovering at the back on high alert. There'll be no wake, but there's talk of a memorial service in a few months' time in Mum's native Scotland. This is what happens, I suppose, when the murder victim's son is on the run, wanted for the killing.

As the three of us sit in the first row of pews in the otherwise unoccupied chapel, I half expect Garrett to burst in, late of course, like a gatecrasher at a wedding; half expect to hear nails on the underside of a coffin lid. Thankfully, neither of these things happens, though I'm not sure if I'd have noticed if they did. I can hear the officiant talking, but I don't know what he's saying. I bite the inside of my cheek so hard I taste blood; fix my gaze on a spot – a lily in the bouquet on Mum's casket – focus on it so intensely I'm surprised it doesn't spontaneously combust. And all I can think, over and over again, is *Mum's body's inside that coffin*, as if the more I repeat it, the more it might sink in.

I hate lilies.

After the service, Mum's agent bids us an awkward farewell in the garden of remembrance, says she's got a flight to catch. I guide Dad to one side and we take a seat on a bench, despite the snow falling thick and fast. Dad unwinds his scarf, drapes it round my neck, and I pull it up so it covers my head. Lucky and Krauseneck watch from a distance like we're mad, and I intermittently eye the two satellite trucks parked outside the gates. I'm certain they weren't there when we arrived.

There's something I have to ask Dad, something important, but before I can, he reaches into his pocket, pulls from it a photograph. 'I thought you might like this,' he says, handing it to me. 'I was going through some of your mum's things, found it in her purse.'

It's wallet-sized, a photo I've not seen before: Garrett and me as children. Judging by our ages – I look about ten, Garrett eight – it was taken in the UK, at a birthday party, it seems. Garrett's wearing a paper Burger King crown, so askew it almost covers his eyes. In typical exuberant Garrett fashion, he's sticking his tongue out at the camera, holding his hands aloft, fingers splayed, while I stand beside him looking on in fond amusement. I feel a wave of nostalgia so strong it almost takes my breath away; am surprised, partly that Mum carried a photo of us both – not just Garrett – but also at how happy Garrett and I look. How normal. *Where did it all go wrong?*

But this isn't about Mum, or Garrett. Not now. Not directly. I can't get sidetracked.

I pocket the photo. 'I have to ask you something,' I say to Dad.

'Ask me anything,' he replies. He's smiling, but he looks broken, so broken I almost chicken out.

'Lucky told me something,' I begin. 'He said police cleared you – in relation to Mum.' I leave it at that, though he knows what I mean.

Dad clears his throat, brushes snowflakes from his hair with a leather-gloved hand. 'That's right, they did.'

'But he also said something,' I go on, 'about you having lied to them.'

'Oh,' he says.

'I don't get it. Why would you lie?'

There's a pause. Dad looks up, over to where Lucky and Krauseneck are standing. They shift on the spot, rub their hands together, trying to keep warm, and I wonder if Lucky's guessed what we're talking about.

Dad sighs. 'There's no easy way to tell you this,' he says, and my heart sinks. 'But before I do, I have to start by saying that I loved – I *love* – your mum.'

Having managed not to cry during the service, my eyes fill with tears.

'It was her dream to move here, but, well, I guess *I* wasn't ready to leave the city, the job I love. Which is why we compromised: I got the apartment, lived and worked in the Springs during the week. I suppose we thought it would make us value the time we spent together more. But I guess in the end it had the opposite effect.'

'You grew further apart.'

He nods. 'It just sort of happened. Your mum was here, writing, and I was there, working. And more and more I'd find myself making excuses not to come home on the weekends – the drive was too long, I was needed at the hospital . . .'

'Mum didn't mind?'

He pulls a face. 'Didn't seem to. You know how she liked her space. And Garrett was always around somewhere.' He smiles wistfully at this, like he's forgotten everything that's happened, like how Garrett always being around isn't the reason we are where we are: on this bench, in this garden, at this crematorium. But then, like Mum, when it comes to Garrett, Dad's always had blinders on, even if he's not as vocal about it.

'So what does all this have to do with you lying to the police?'

'Ah. Well, you see, at the same time your mum and I were growing further apart, I, well I—'

'Don't tell me,' I say. 'You met someone else.'

Dad looks down at his hands.

'Who?'

'It doesn't matter.'

'Of course it matters.' I close my eyes, wonder if Mum knew; wonder, if she did, if that's what Dad told her, too – that it didn't matter – wonder if that's what he told her the first time he cheated on her, when I was four and Garrett two and he had an affair with someone he met at work. I only found out about *that* recently, from Garrett – could tell my brother took great pleasure imparting the information – came to terms with it the only way I knew how, by justifying it: it was a one-off, a mistake, Mum could be difficult. But Mum was still alive then . . .

'It's Betsey,' Dad says.

'*Betsey?!*' I say her name so loudly that even though they're some way off, Lucky and Krauseneck jolt to attention. 'Your secretary Betsey?'

He nods.

'Oh my God!' I throw up my hands. 'You're such a fucking cliché!' It suddenly occurs to me to wonder if Betsey was the real reason behind Dad's decision not to come back to Heartsick until the funeral. 'Like it's not bad enough Mum's dead, I'm in hospital, but you send this woman out to buy me underwear? That's gross, Dad, really.'

He starts to say something, but I stop him.

'And that's why you lied to police? You were with *this woman* the night Mum died?'

Dad gives another sheepish nod. 'I didn't think it would matter. I was in Colorado Springs – I didn't lie about that. But I told the police I was at my apartment, alone, when really I was—'

'Please. Spare me the details.' I may not have been close to Mum, but I feel so betrayed on her behalf. Then I wonder if it's not that I feel betrayed for her, but, selfishly, for myself.

'No,' he says. There's a desperation in his voice. 'It's not what you think. Betsey and I were at a restaurant in the city. Someone saw us together, plus, I guess when the police checked, my phone didn't back up where I said I was. They confronted me about it, so I came clean.'

'Christ, what do you want, a medal?!'

'Steppy, please, you have to understand. Your mother and I, we were living separate—'

'Don't say it,' I tell him. 'Do not say you were living separate lives.'

That's the excuse Travis used to rationalise his leaving me for my best friend. I stand, remove Dad's scarf, hand it to him. 'I can't do this any more.'

As I stormed through the crematorium gates inches from Lucky, he reached out. 'What the hell happened?'

I shrugged his hand away, said, 'I asked Dad, like you suggested,' didn't stop till I reached Jenna's car. I drove off without looking back, having barely cleared the windshield of snow, before parking up in a quiet spot a couple of blocks away and bursting into tears.

But I have to keep busy, it's the only thing keeping me sane, and now I'm back in Buddy's parking lot, checking my reflection in the rear-view mirror. My phone keeps pinging with messages from Dad and Lucky, so I put it on silent, abandon it in the cup holder before climbing out. Buddy's doesn't open till four – it's only three fifteen – but there's a single car in the parking lot, which I hope belongs to Evan. There are lights on inside, but the front door's locked, so I hammer on it until I get a response.

'Hey,' says Evan, like my presence there is entirely normal, though I see him look me up and down, take in my all-black attire. 'Didn't think I'd be seeing you again any time soon. You work out what those numbers are yet?'

'Huh?' Then I realise: the numbers on the matchbook. With everything else that's gone on, I've almost forgotten about them. 'No,' I tell him breathlessly, 'not the numbers. But I need to see the video footage again. The bit where Garrett and Casey are leaving. Tell me you've still got it?'

He hesitates just for a second and my heart sinks. But then he says, 'Course I do. I hung onto it just in case. Come on in.'

And for the first time today, I feel a spark of hope.

Back in the office, we squeeze in front of the laptop as Evan brings up the footage from Halloween and presses play. There's Brooke and Garrett chatting again, then Brooke and Casey arguing, Brooke storming off. But although the quality of the footage isn't bad, Garrett's some distance from the camera. He's wearing a long-sleeved sweater – no hope of seeing his wrists – and he's too far away to see his face clearly enough.

'Can you fast-forward,' I ask Evan, 'to the bit where they're leaving?'

'Sure.'

As his hand goes to the mouse pad, my eyes flick automatically to the other side of the split screen, the camera that covers the door.

'There!' I say, pointing at it. Evan pauses the tape right as Garrett and Casey approach, and they're frozen in time.

'I still can't see.'

Though they're closer to the camera and the picture's okay, it's caught Garrett at the wrong angle – he's glancing down – and with the plastic Halloween mask on top of his head . . .

'Can you make it go again, but slower?'

'I think so.' Evan fiddles with the mouse once more and the footage starts up again. Casey and Garrett are walking towards the camera, Casey's beautiful face – she's in front of Garrett, blocking his – in fine focus. Just a couple more steps . . .

But right at the crucial moment – still in slow motion – she turns to Garrett, smiling, playfully swats that stupid fucking Halloween mask down over his face.

'*Shit.*' I drop my head.

Evan pauses the footage again. 'Not good?'

I look back up at the screen, shake my head. 'No.'

But then I notice something else. Something I didn't see before. Something I wouldn't even have thought to look for. Around Casey's neck, gleaming against her tanned skin, is a silver necklace. Not any old necklace, but a necklace with a heart pendant, a half-heart, to be precise, the jagged edge down one side clear to see; the necklace Luke gave her. The one that matches his half.

The one Brooke told me Casey gifted her earlier on Halloween.

32

Then

It was early evening, Paige hadn't returned my call, and I was pacing the cabin, trying to get things straight in my head.

Garrett had married Taylor a couple of weeks after Casey disappeared; a couple of *days* after he was questioned by police about a phone call he made to Taylor on Halloween, right after he said he'd dropped Casey safely home. Whichever way I tried to spin it, one thought kept creeping into my head uninvited: a spouse can't be compelled to testify in court against their other half. *Taylor couldn't be forced to testify against Garrett.* I'd long since given up trying to work out what went on in my brother's head, but whatever his motivation for tying the knot, even if it *was* entirely innocent, it had been a pretty dumb move, one I could see internet sleuths having a field day over once the news broke.

I sighed, sat down next to Bruce. *You can be pretty dumb, Garrett, but you're not* that *dumb.* That's what I'd told my brother. Not dumb enough to plan to abduct a girl then be the last person seen with her. Too dumb to be able to get away with it unless it was premeditated.

Whatever, it didn't really matter because, dodgy-looking phone call to Taylor aside, my brother's alibi was unshakeable.

Bruce purred loudly and I scratched his head.

'Almost too unshakeable,' I said under my breath.

Because maybe that was it. Maybe my brother wasn't dumb at all. Maybe he was smarter than I gave him credit for. Smarter than anyone gave him credit for. And maybe he'd had help.

I thought of the date in the corner of the police interview footage again. If the numbers on the matchbook were what I suspected, then not only was Garrett smarter than I gave him credit for, he was also more dangerous. I took out the matchbook, laid it on the table in front of me, then grabbed a scrap of paper and a pen, wrote the numbers out again, this time like they were dates:

03.27.09

29.12.15

01.09.16

Now it seemed obvious. I mean, I'd always wondered if they might be. But the middle one – the middle one didn't work. There *was* no 29.12 – no twenty-ninth month. But – I slipped my watch from my wrist – there was a twelfth one.

Though Travis and I weren't into grand gestures, after I'd finished making *Dark Corners*, he'd got me a watch for my birthday. We'd not seen each other in a couple of weeks – I'd been travelling cross-country, doing round after round of interviews, Travis stuck in New York – so he'd booked us a table at a restaurant I'd always wanted to go to. The watch he'd picked out was obscenely expensive (his dad, who had a taste for pricey timepieces, helped him choose it), and whilst there was no denying it was beautiful, it cost far more than

Travis or I would ever usually spend on each other, to the point I felt embarrassed about it. I grew to love the watch, though – still wear it, despite everything – but it was the inscription I treasured most of all: *Our sliding door moment*, Travis had had engraved on the back, a reference to how we met – a New Year's Eve party neither of us was supposed to be at – along with the date, *31.12.06*. It was a nice touch, pretty romantic for someone who didn't do romance, but it was that date – I turned the watch over in my hand – that now made me realise something. Well, not so much the date, but the format. You see, though Travis and I each had one British parent, Travis was born and raised in the US, lived there all his life with the exception of his time at uni. He was used to, and used, the American date format: mm.dd.yy. Whereas I, who'd spent a large portion of my childhood and early teens in the UK – only attended high school sophomore through senior year, before returning to the UK for uni – much preferred the British format. And that was why, when he had the watch engraved, he'd done the date the British way, *31.12.06* – 31 December, 2006 – a cute little in-joke between us, a nod from Travis: *I get you*.

So, coming back to the matchbook, what if the numbers *were* dates, significant ones, and what if – just like the date on the back of my watch – there was a reason the middle date on the matchbook was formatted like this? Garrett was, after all, half British. He knew how the date thing worked: in US format there's no such date as 29.12.15, but in UK format there is: 29 December, 2015. What if it wasn't cute, like Travis's date touch, but something more sinister? What if, in its own sick way, it too was an in-joke, a nod to something only Garrett would get? The thought made me feel ill, however much of a long shot it might be.

A long shot until I considered we were talking about my brother.

I logged into Facebook, opened up Garrett's profile, searched his friends and found Taylor. I was going to message her, but her cell phone number was on her page, so before I could talk myself out of it, I'd picked up my phone and dialled.

She answered after only two rings. 'Hello?'

'Hi, Taylor, it's Steppy, Garrett's sister.' There was silence on the line, so, like an idiot, I added, 'We met at Thanksgiving—'

'I know who you are.' Her voice wasn't cold, but it wasn't exactly friendly either.

'So, uh, I was wondering if I could ask you something, about that night?'

'Thanksgiving?'

'No. The night Casey Carter disappeared. Garrett called you. From a gas station?' There was a clicking sound on the line. I thought she'd hung up. 'Taylor?'

'I can't talk right now,' she said.

'Oh, okay. Well, uh, maybe we could meet? I'm staying just out of town, a cabin—'

'Text me the address,' she said, and hung up.

I did as instructed, adding a message telling her I'd be around the rest of the evening – she could drop by whenever she wanted – but didn't hold out much hope.

I flopped back on the couch. 'God, it's so frustrating,' I told Bruce. I tipped my head back. 'When it comes to my brother, all these girls – Casey, Taylor, Paige – they all hold a piece of the puzzle, but I'll be damned if I know how to get them, let alone fit them together.'

But there was someone else, I realised. Someone who might be willing to talk. Someone who'd already proven willing. She'd contacted Brooke, after all.

I grabbed my cell phone again and brought up the email address

Brooke had given me. The one for Rebecca Johnson, Amy Johnson's sister.

I was still torn. Reaching out to Rebecca, a complete stranger, when someone had already been tried and convicted of her sister's murder, was something I was reluctant to do. But although there was something about Brooke I didn't wholly trust, there must have been some truth in what she'd told me about my brother's connection to Amy: Brooke had been in possession of Rebecca Johnson's email address. She must have got it from somewhere.

And if my hunch was right, about the matchbook numbers, their significance . . .

Hands shaking, I began to type. Was there was any evidence that my brother knew Amy? Was there any evidence he was the last person seen with her before she vanished, just like he'd been the last person seen with Casey Carter?

I had to know, even if, deep down, I wasn't sure I wanted to, and before I knew it, I'd finished the email. Closed my eyes. Clicked send.

Beside me, Bruce looked up at me, purring proudly.

'No going back now,' I told him.

It was too late for that.

33

Now

'Can I come in?' I ask wearily, when Brooke opens the door of Casey's condo.

Casey's smiling face stares back at me from Brooke's T-shirt. 'I don't think so.' She doesn't budge.

It's the first time I've seen her since the vigil, so I shouldn't be surprised. Still, I hoped we could do this civilly, but since it doesn't seem we can, I come straight out with it. 'I know you lied.'

'I didn't,' she says, even though I've not yet told her what I'm accusing her of lying about.

I point at the silver necklace round her neck, the half-heart pendant hanging right above the *#FindCaseyCarter* slogan on her T-shirt. 'You never had the other half,' I say, 'because it isn't a friendship necklace. Casey got this necklace from Luke. *He* has the other half.'

Brooke barely misses a beat, says, 'All right, so it's not a friendship necklace. Casey *did* give me it, though. Said she didn't want it any more, it reminded her too much of Luke.'

'And after you had the fight with Casey on Halloween, left Buddy's, you went straight home? Didn't see her again that night?'

'Yes, I went straight home, and no' – she rolls her eyes – 'I didn't see her again. I told you all this already.'

This is exactly what I thought she was going to say, so I've come prepared, straight from Buddy's. I hold out the A4 printout. It's not the best – Evan did it for me on the office printer – but it's good enough: a still of Casey and Garrett leaving Buddy's.

'What exactly am I supposed to be looking at?' Brooke asks.

I point at Casey's necklace. 'Garrett and Casey leave Buddy's at eleven thirty-nine p.m.' I indicate the time stamp on the image. 'But Casey's still wearing her necklace.' Brooke turns white. 'The half you said she gave you earlier that night. Except she couldn't have, because the same video shows you leaving Buddy's twenty-six minutes earlier. So if the last time you saw Casey was when you stormed out of Buddy's, and you went straight home, how come you ended up with the necklace?'

Brooke starts to cry.

'Can I come in now?' I ask.

We're in the kitchen and Brooke's still sniffling. Her tears look genuine and I can't help but feel a bit sorry for her.

'Here.' I pass her a tissue, a small conciliatory gesture. 'I just want the truth, Brooke. Did you come here that night after you left Buddy's and wait for Casey to get home? Did you confront her when she did, have another argument?'

'*No*,' she says forcefully. She takes a seat opposite me at the breakfast bar, blows her nose. I catch sight of the photo of Casey and Brooke on the refrigerator, the high-school-age one in the *If friends were flowers . . .* frame.

'So how'd you get the necklace?' I press. 'If you've nothing to hide, tell me what happened.'

'I found it,' she says. 'Okay?'

'Where?'

'Here. That night.' She looks down.

'After Buddy's, you mean? So you did come here, wait for Casey to get back?'

'No,' she says, frustrated. 'I went home first, to my place. I texted Casey a couple times, tried phoning her, but she didn't reply. I guessed she was still at the bar with your brother. I was angry, sure, and upset – sick of the way she treated me. But I just wanted to talk. Honest.'

'So what did you do?'

'I guess I stewed for a bit – like maybe an hour? It was late, I was still drunk. It was stupid, I know, but I decided to drive over here. She wasn't home.'

'What time was this?'

'I don't know,' she admits. 'Maybe, like, sometime after midnight?'

'Was her car here?'

'No.'

'So what did you do?'

'I knocked at the door, but there was no answer. So I sat in my car for a bit. I wasn't thinking straight. Like, at first, when I arrived and she wasn't here, I assumed she'd gone home with your brother. But then I realised about her car – like, it was weird it wasn't here. I mean, assuming she'd left the bar with your brother, there were only two options: either they'd gone back to his place or hers. Either way, Casey's car should've been in her driveway, right?'

I nod.

'The street's real quiet,' she goes on, 'so I sit, wait a bit longer. Then I realise something else . . .'

'What?'

'Porch light's on.'

'Wait – it's *on*? But the neighbour across the street, Hank, said it was off the next morning. That's what made everyone think Casey got home safely, had gone to bed, disappeared sometime during the night or early next morning.'

Brooke looks down again. 'I switched it off,' she mumbles.

I'm not sure I've heard right. 'You what?'

'I switched it off,' she repeats, a little louder. 'I switched off the porch light.'

'But . . . but why? How?' This changes everything, I realise. If Brooke's telling the truth, then Casey either didn't get home at all that night, or got home but hadn't gone to bed before whatever happened to her occurred. 'I thought you didn't go inside? You don't have a key.' I pause. 'You don't have a key, right, Brooke?'

She avoids my eye. 'A few weeks before she vanished,' she says, 'like, the month before or something, Casey lost her apartment key, so the landlord got her another.'

'Okay . . .'

'Then, a couple weeks later, after she gets her new key, I find her old one at my place.'

'So you kept it? Didn't tell her?'

'She'd already paid the landlord for the new one,' Brooke says. 'What difference would it have made?'

A big difference, I think, potentially. Not to mention it's pretty creepy. But I nod. 'So you let yourself in that night?'

'I didn't touch anything,' Brooke says. 'I just wanted to make sure everything was all right. I only came as far as the hallway.'

'Did you see anything?'

'The hall table?' she says, like a question.

'What about it?'

'Casey's flower crown was on it, the one she was wearing that night.'

I nod. Lucky said Casey's Halloween headband was found by the door, like she'd come in, taken it straight off.

'And her necklace?'

'I mean, it was obvious she wasn't home, place was giving me the creeps. I was just about to leave when I found it on the floor in the hallway, sorta hidden under the edge of the table.' Brooke hangs her head. 'I took it.'

'Stole it, you mean.' Even though that's what Brooke did, I didn't mean it to sound so accusatory.

'I didn't *steal* it,' she shot back. 'I found it. I was going to look after it for her, till I saw her. The catch was broken, so I—'

'The catch was broken?'

'Uh-huh.' She nods. 'It was easy enough to fix . . .' She holds the pendant up, twists the chain round so I can see the catch.

'Did you take anything else?'

'God, no,' she says, insulted, like stealing your friend's necklace is understandable, anything else a bridge too far. 'Honest. I didn't touch a thing; got the hell out.'

'And that's when you switched off the porch light?'

She nods. 'Guess I was worried one of her neighbours would see me leaving, so I turned it off and left.'

'And when Casey's mom called you next day, you didn't tell her what happened? Or the police?'

'I didn't want to get in any trouble.' She bites her lip. 'I mean, at first I didn't think anything was wrong, just thought she'd gone home with your brother.'

'But her car,' I say, 'the necklace . . .'

'I was angry. Wasn't thinking straight. When she didn't turn up and shit started to get real, well, it was too late. I was scared. If I'd told the cops what happened, they might not have believed me, might have thought *I* had something to do with her disappearance.'

Later that night, I'm sitting in the cabin with Bruce, wondering if it's too late to call Lucky. I'm staring at Casey's pendant on the coffee table. Brooke gave me it before I left, and I sealed it in a Ziploc bag, even though she'd had it almost six weeks and any forensic evidence will be compromised.

I stroke Bruce absently and think about what Brooke told me. I'm not sure if I believe she would have been able to resist the temptation to check out the rest of Casey's condo when she let herself in that night. But why not admit it? Her admission that she found Casey's necklace and took it, that she'd been the one who switched off the porch light, was far worse.

And assuming the porch light admission was true, which meant Casey most probably didn't go to bed that night, that meant, technically, my brother *could* have been involved. But he couldn't have, could he? Because the whole porch light thing doesn't change the cell phone evidence: my brother's still in the clear. His phone tracked him from Buddy's, to Casey's, to the gas station, then our parents' house. He was there the rest of the night. The data doesn't lie.

Or does it?

Because it did in Luke's case.

I get the matchbook out again, its string of numbers on the underside of the flap in Mum's writing. I'd almost forgotten about it until Evan brought it up when I stopped by Buddy's earlier. Now, I lay it on the table next to Casey's necklace. The two are connected, I'm sure; not directly, maybe, but . . .

I turn the necklace over, squint at it through the Ziploc bag. It has the same inscription on the back as Luke's half, *Luke & Casey forever*, but I notice now that Luke has also had a date inscribed, presumably the date he and Casey met: *07.06.11*. Something clicks into place, like it's always been there, buried in the recesses of my memory.

I grab my laptop and log into my emails, bring up the one from Rebecca Johnson, scan it furiously until I find what I'm looking for: *Amy went missing on 28.12.15.* That's what the email says.

Shoving my laptop aside, I get a pen and a piece of paper, write out the numbers on the matchbook, this time like they're dates.

03.27.09

29.12.15

01.09.??

I use question marks for the last two digits, the ones I can't see for the smear of dried blood, but even so, it doesn't matter. Because I'd bet my bottom dollar I can guess what those two digits are: I'll bet they're one and six. And I'll bet they represent 2016.

And that's when, with utter horror, I realise what Garrett has done, how Mum helped him. Helped him get away with murder.

There's such a roaring in my ears, I don't hear the car engine outside. Don't hear tyres crunching over snow. Don't even hear the footsteps climbing the porch steps. But I do hear the knock at the cabin door, and when I open it, my brother is standing there.

'Hey, Step,' he says. 'You look like shit.'

34

Then

I was trying to locate my phone charger when Paige finally called back. I'd spent the last hour or so fretting, alternating between checking my phone and refreshing my email inbox.

When my phone rang at last and I saw Paige's name flash up, I was almost too afraid to answer, my first thought that it might be Travis again.

'Hello?' I held my breath.

'Steppy?'

I exhaled. 'Paige.'

'You keep calling,' she said. She sounded fed up. 'What is it?'

'I wanted to say . . .' My voice broke. I stopped, gathered myself – the last thing I intended was for Paige to think I was looking for sympathy. 'I wanted to say,' I began again, 'that I'm sorry. I know what my brother did to you.'

The line was bad, Paige hadn't said anything and I wondered if she was still there. I felt stupid at having poured my heart out, guilty for feeling relieved that I'd got it off my chest.

'Paige?'

'I'm here,' she replied. 'Is that it?'

'What?'

'Is this why you've been calling me? You wanted to apologise, tell me you know what Garrett did to me?'

'No,' I said. 'Yes. That and I miss you.' She didn't reply again, and I got the feeling she was about to hang up. 'Paige,' I said. 'Wait – the date . . .'

'What date?'

'I'm sorry to ask, make you go back there. But the date it happened, the date my brother . . .'

'The date your brother choked me out and raped me?'

I swallowed. It had been bad enough hearing it from Travis.

'January ninth,' she said simply.

'Not the eighth?'

'It was the eighth we all went out, Friday, Josh's birthday,' Paige explained. 'But what happened with your brother? That specifically? It was the early hours of Saturday. The ninth.'

I had the slip of paper in front of me, the one on which I'd written the string of numbers as dates. '01.09.16.'

I didn't realise I'd said it aloud until Paige went, 'What?'

'Nothing,' I told her.

There was a noise. The sound of a car outside. I looked up, saw a sweep of headlights through the blinds. Taylor. It had to be.

'Steppy?' came Paige's voice from the other end of the phone.

'I've gotta go,' I told her quickly. 'I'm sorry. But Paige?'

Silence, then, 'Yes?'

'I've got a cat' – I snuck over to the window – 'his name's Bruce.'

'*A cat?* Is everything okay, Steppy?' She sounded worried, like a real friend would, like she would have all those months ago when we used to be best friends.

'I don't have time to explain,' I said, parting the blind with my fingers. 'But you love cats. If anything happens to me – anything – promise me you'll take him.'

'But Steppy . . .'

I peered through the blind into the darkness outside, saw my brother's Jeep, saw the driver's-side door start to open. I let the blind snap shut, turned from the window. *'Promise.'*

'Okay, I promise, but—'

I hung up, turned back to the window, peeked outside again, my heart almost beating out of my chest. A figure was climbing from the Jeep. Not Taylor, but Garrett. *Shit.*

I scuttled back to the coffee table, slammed my laptop shut, then grabbed the matchbook, slipped it into the pocket of my jeans. I looked around, heard footsteps climbing the porch steps, a knock at the door.

'Steppy?'

For a second, I froze. Bruce, who until seconds ago had been washing himself, froze too. Our eyes met.

There came another knock, louder this time. 'I know you're in there, Step. Your car's outside, there's lights on.' I could almost hear Garrett rolling his eyes.

'Just a sec!' I shouted back.

I took a last look around – nothing I didn't want him seeing – then, with a deep breath, walked calmly to the door, steeled myself, opened it. 'Hey, Garrett,' I said, probably too brightly. 'Everything okay?'

Without answering or waiting to be invited, he pushed his way inside and closed the door. We were alone together.

'You tell me,' he said.

I watched his eyes wander over the room, alight on the coffee table, the scrap of paper – the one I'd written the matchbook numbers on in date form, had left lying in full view. *How had I missed it?* I held my breath, but thankfully, Garrett didn't seem to register it – or realise its significance – and his gaze kept on roving, settled finally on Bruce.

I met Bruce's eye, glanced towards the stairs, and he took my hint, darted up to the bedroom.

Garrett turned back to me, tipped his head. 'Well?'

'Look,' I said. 'Something's obviously bothering you, but I'm not a mind-reader. You're going to have to spell it out.'

'Okay,' he said. '*Okay.*'

I was suddenly conscious of how tall he was, conscious that he was between me and the door, conscious of the fact that I couldn't outrun him . . .

'Taylor,' he said suddenly.

'Sorry?' I caught sight of my cell phone on the coffee table, wondered if I could get to it before Garrett.

'My wife, Taylor. You met her at Thanksgiving? You must remember – you've been phoning her. I mean, dammit, Step. You said you were going to stop digging.'

'I did,' I said, trying to sound calm. 'Stop digging, I mean.' As I spoke, I inched closer to the coffee table, keeping my eyes on Garrett's. 'I gave Taylor a call, sure. But I thought, like, now that we're sisters-in-law, I should make an effort. Get to know her.'

'So you weren't trying to get information on me?'

I wondered how much he knew, what Taylor had told him. How much, if anything, he'd overheard. 'Course not,' I lied.

He crossed to the window, parted the blinds, peering through them like I'd done minutes before.

I was close enough to the table now, so with Garrett distracted, I picked up my phone, switched it to silent and pressed record, said a silent prayer that for once I had enough battery . . .

Garrett turned.

'Hey,' I said. 'You're obviously upset.' It took all my composure and acting skills, but I managed a smile, took a seat on the couch. 'Let's talk about it.' As I spoke, I slipped my cell phone down between my leg and the side of the couch. Somewhere my brother wouldn't see it.

He nodded, more composed, put his own cell phone down. Dragging a chair over from the other side of the room, he set it opposite me, the coffee table between us, coffee table and Garrett between me and the door.

'So,' he began calmly. Too calm. 'Here's what I have a problem with.'

Having thought I'd figured it all out, it suddenly occurred to me that that was just the half of it, that I'd no idea what my brother was truly capable of. I felt my hands begin to shake, gripped the sofa cushions either side of me to steady them.

Just then, from outside, came the sound of a car horn – Garrett's Jeep. I jumped, and Garrett turned towards the sound. The horn beeped once more, then again, a second later, longer this time, then again and again and again.

'Fuck's sake!' Garret threw up his hands, like that was all the explanation required. 'Wait here,' he instructed me, and got up, stormed out the door, leaving it wide open.

I waited a moment, then followed as far as the door, peered round it, saw Garrett by the open passenger door of the Jeep, remonstrating with someone inside. I could hear raised voices – my brother and Taylor's – so I pushed the cabin door to and stood for a second. What should I do? Dial 911? But what would I say? By the time they got here . . .

And that was when I noticed it: Garrett's cell phone. He'd left it on the table.

Quickly, all the while screaming at myself inside not to, I grabbed his phone, slipped the matchbook with its string of numbers from my pocket, laid it on the table in front of me. My hands were shaking so badly I almost dropped the phone, managed to swipe the screen, saw the message, *Enter PIN*, entered the long number in Mum's writing on the matchbook – *032709291215010916* – all the time praying, *please don't be right, please don't be right, please don't be right*.

I hit *OK*, felt a strange combination of disappointment and relief when an *Incorrect PIN* message flashed up on screen. My hands were sweating. I could still hear Garrett and Taylor arguing, was sure I heard her shout something like *Fuckin' try me!* I tried the number again – it was long, after all, and with shaking hands it was perfectly possible I'd made a mistake – but it still didn't work. *Incorrect PIN*.

That's it, I thought. I was wrong. I put the phone down.

'. . . that fucking night!' I heard Taylor scream, and my brother shouted something back, something I couldn't make out; and then, like a bolt from the blue, it hit me. If I was right about the numbers being dates, right about the dates' significance . . .

I picked Garrett's phone back up, swiped the screen a third time. A strange sense of calm descended over me as I entered the numbers on the matchbook one more time, *this* time with six extra digits on the end: *103116*.

The phone's home screen lit up – I was in! – and right then, I knew exactly what my brother was capable of, knew exactly what he'd done. The long number on the matchbook, the one in Mum's handwriting, was the passcode for his phone. *Mum had Garrett's phone passcode!* Some killers, like Larry Polk, kept something belonging to their victims. Trophies. It could be a necklace, an item of clothing, a photograph. My brother, it turned out, kept trophies too. But Garrett's trophies weren't *things* – material possessions – though they meant just as much to him. He kept dates, significant ones, had strung them together to create a passcode no one would ever guess, except thanks to the fact that he'd told it to Mum, and she'd written it down, *I* had guessed it. And now, but for a few small details, I knew my brother had killed Casey Carter, knew he'd had help covering it up, that he'd falsified an alibi using his phone. Then afterwards – a final sick twist – he'd updated his phone passcode, added the date he'd done whatever he did to Casey: *10.31.16*. October 31, 2016.

The simple fact that the code worked told me everything I needed to know.

But knowing wasn't enough. I needed proof. Besides, though I knew what – or, more accurately, who – two of the other dates stood for – Amy Johnson and Paige – that left one date I'd yet to figure out: *03.27.09*. What had happened in March 2009? What awful thing did my brother do on that date all those years ago?

Outside, I could still hear Taylor and Garrett arguing, could only hope he'd be distracted a little longer. My hands had begun to tremble again as I swiped through his phone till I found what I was looking for. Files. Lots of them. I didn't have time to open them – didn't want to – but I recognised the file names. File names that were dates. Significant ones. Dates now seared in my memory as surely as they would be in Garrett's, though for different reasons.

The first night I'd arrived at the cabin, needing to charge my cell phone when I'd mislaid my charger, I'd discovered a bundle of USB leads in a kitchen drawer while I was looking for a replacement. Leaping from the couch, I dashed over to the kitchen, yanked open the drawer, grabbed a handful of leads, jammed them into the USB port on Garrett's cell phone one after another until I found one that fitted. Then I raced back to the couch, opened my laptop, plugged the other end of the cable into it. Outside, my brother and Taylor were still arguing, but I knew I probably didn't have long. As the laptop whirred into action, I opened up the contents of Garrett's phone on it, dragged the relevant files onto my desktop.

My head pounded as I watched the timer bar count slowly upwards. As the last small portion started to fill, I heard Garrett's feet on the porch steps.

35

Now

'Aren't you gonna invite me in?' my brother asks.

I shrug like I've nothing to lose and stand aside, though he's already pushed his way past. Though he's only been gone a couple of weeks, he's lost weight. 'I'm not the only one who looks like shit,' I tell him, which gives me some satisfaction.

He reaches out to touch the scar on my head and I pull away.

'No *thank you* for saving your life?'

I ignore him, ask, 'What happened, Garrett? How did we end up here?'

He scoffs. 'You mean, like *here* here? Right now? Or life in general?'

To be honest, I'm not sure.

He's wandering casually round the living room, but he pauses when he sees the photo on the coffee table, the one Dad gave me after Mum's funeral. He picks it up, cocks his head.

I nod at it. 'We were happy,' I say. 'Once.'

Garrett looks at me funny, like I'm speaking a foreign language, and I wonder if the happy times ever existed, feel my childhood crumble.

I swallow. 'When did you get back?' I ask, voice small. Not *Why did you run?* That I'm sure I already know.

'This evening,' he replies. 'Went to mine and Tay's, but we got into it. She told me to leave.'

'Why come back now?'

He shrugs, says, 'I've nothing to hide,' which is weird, because he's acting like a man who has: going from window to window, peeking outside, closing the blinds. 'I mean' – he looks right at me – 'I didn't kill Mum. You know that, right?'

He says it so simply, sounds so believable, that for a moment I'm thrown. Could he be telling the truth? My head's pounding. 'I know you killed Casey,' I tell him.

He laughs. 'You and the whole internet. There's just the small problem of the cell phone evidence. Or did this' – he taps his head, indicating my scar – 'make you forget?'

'No,' I say, quietly but firmly. I may not remember anything of the past few weeks, but this I do know. 'I know *how* you killed her. How you got away with it.'

'Good for you.' He wanders over to the kitchen and opens the refrigerator, helps himself to a bottle of beer before returning to the couch, sitting down like an average Joe about to watch sports on TV. 'Enlighten me,' he says, self-assured and cocky as ever.

Until I pull the matchbook from my pocket.

I sit down opposite him, place the matchbook, open, between us on the table, watch his face change as he reads the numbers.

'Where'd you get this?'

'I can't remember,' I answer truthfully. 'All I know is it was on me the night of my car accident. But even though I don't know where I got it from, I do know what these numbers mean: they're dates.' I watch the colour drain from his face. 'You just have to break them down. These last two . . .' I indicate the final two digits, the ones obscured by blood, 'I'll bet that's a one and a six. 2016.' Garrett leans back in his seat, takes a swig of beer, doesn't know whether to be resigned or impressed; I begin pointing at each group of digits in turn, like a teacher at a tiny chalkboard, starting with the most recent. 'We've got Paige, then Amy Johnson. Nice touch, by the way, doing Amy's date in the British format because she was British.'

I see a smile flicker over Garrett's face. He just can't help himself.

'And these first six numbers?' I keep going. 'I bet, if I were to check, that's Madison McKinley. You remember Madison, don't you?' I don't give him time to reply. 'Well, I spoke with her parents. They told me what you did to her all those years ago. And I'd also like to bet that all together like this – one long string? – these dates make a passcode. The passcode to your phone.' I stretch out my open palm. 'Want to let me try?'

Garrett's phone is in his hand, but he doesn't give it to me. I didn't expect him to. 'So what if it is?' he says. 'Doesn't mean anything.'

I see the tiny muscle in the corner of his right eye begin to tic, and so even though my head's splitting now and all I want to do is reach for my pain meds, I know I have to keep going. 'These numbers' – I pick up the matchbook again – 'they're sick trophies.' I can tell from his face that I'm right. 'I'm guessing that the night Casey disappeared, you drove her home from Buddy's – feel free to jump in any time if I'm wrong – but when you got there, you were expecting something more. Maybe she invited you in, maybe she didn't. Either way, things got out of hand. Did it happen in the hallway, Garrett? Is that why Brooke found this?' I hold up the half-heart pendant in the little baggie, Casey's necklace, the one Brooke gave me, the one she found in Casey's hallway.

Garrett shakes his head. 'Fuckin' Taylor. She was supposed to check, make sure nothing looked out of place.'

'Taylor.' I nod slowly. 'I guessed she must've been involved. I mean, I knew you had to have had help – not just from Mum. So after you do whatever to Casey – strangle her, I bet – you panic. You know you were seen leaving the bar with her, that if anything happens to her, the police's first stop will be you. So what do you do?'

'I get out of there quickly.' He tilts his head at me, widens his eyes. 'What would you've done, Step?'

'I'd've fessed up,' I say, not missing a beat, 'told the truth. But that's the difference between us.'

'Really?' He smirks. 'I think if we're honest, Step, we're more alike than you care to think.'

'I'm nothing like you,' I snap. His words unsettle me, though I don't know why, since they're untrue. 'You decided to cover the whole thing up. I'm guessing that first you carry Casey's body to her car – you don't leave that to Taylor – put it in the trunk.'

'Not quite,' Garrett says. '*First* I go back to my own car, grab some gloves. It happened right inside the door' – I know that by *it* he means him killing Casey – 'and luckily I hadn't touched anything.' No fingerprints or DNA. Lucky said as much. 'After I glove up, *then* I carry her body to her trunk. Casey kept her car keys by the door, so they weren't hard to find.'

'The street's quiet,' I say, 'it's late, no one sees you. I'm guessing the whole thing only takes a few minutes. Then you get in your Jeep, head to Mum and Dad's. But you're panicked. You've left Casey's body in the trunk of her car. She'll be found soon enough if you don't do something. So you stop at the gas station. But here . . . well, here's where you have to help me out, Garrett.'

He looks at me questioningly.

'Did you stop to use the payphone hoping the cops wouldn't find out, or because you genuinely thought if you called Taylor from your cell phone, given that you argued earlier that day, she'd see your name come up, wouldn't answer?'

'Bit of both, I guess,' he admits. 'I needed to make sure she picked up, sure, and I knew if I called from my cell phone she probably wouldn't. I also guessed the cops would find out, one way or the other, that I stopped at the gas station, used the payphone. I mean, I knew the first thing they'd do was track my phone. I also knew about that thing – the thing you go on about in your podcast? How it got that guy you helped catch? Google Location History. I knew it was switched on on my phone, that they could track me like a sat nav.'

So Garrett did listen to *Dark Corners* after all. The thought that he used what he'd learned from it to help him get away with murder makes me feel sick.

'Guess I thought there was no point admitting to using the payphone unless the cops found out about it, so I kept my mouth shut. I mean, why make life harder for myself?'

'Right,' I say. 'But the police did find out, so – what? – you told them it was a booty call?'

He laughs. 'It had to be believable.'

'So when you called Taylor from the payphone,' I continue, 'what did you tell her? That you gave some chick a ride home, things got out of hand, you killed her by accident?'

'Something like that.'

'You asked her for help.'

He nods.

'And loyal Taylor, who loves you so much, agrees.'

'I don't know if you know this,' Garrett says, 'but Taylor's apartment at the time – before we moved to the one we share now – was only a few blocks from Casey's condo.'

'What did you ask Taylor to do?'

'Wear dark clothing and gloves. Go to Casey's place quick as she fucking could, but on foot, not by car. I'd left the front door unlocked, Casey's keys right inside. So Taylor gets there, checks everything looks normal – was supposed to, anyhow – then takes the car keys, apartment keys, locks the front door behind her.'

'That was why she switched her cell phone off right after you called from the gas station.'

'Yeah. We told the cops it was because she didn't want me calling her again that night, but that was just an excuse. Really it was so they couldn't track her. When I phoned her from the gas station, I told her exactly where to go, where I'd meet her. She just had to trust me.'

'So it was Taylor who left Casey's headband – which I'm guessing came off in the struggle – on the table by the door? And the necklace – that must've been torn off in the struggle too, but you didn't even notice–'

'Must've,' he agrees. 'And Taylor must've missed it. Fuck.'

'And it's Taylor who drives Casey's car, her body in the trunk, up into the mountains?'

Garrett nods.

'You know that after Taylor left, Casey's friend Brooke came along – the other girl you were chatting to at Buddy's – switched off the porch light?'

Garrett laughs. 'I assumed it was Taylor. Brooke really did me a favour, making everyone think Casey had gotten home, gone to bed safe.'

'And it was Taylor who sent the text message from Casey's cell phone to her mom, from up in the mountains, almost two hours after you supposedly dropped her home?'

'Yup.'

'So what next? Taylor keeps driving – you told her where to dump the car.'

'Right. I told her to make sure she waited till she was well out of town to send the text, but not to send it anywhere near where she left the car. So after she sent the text, she switched Casey's phone off, kept driving to the spot where I'd told her to get rid of the body.'

My brother's callousness takes my breath away, send chills through me. He talks about disposing of Casey, helped by his girlfriend, like he's recounting a family picnic.

'So,' he goes on, 'that once the police *do* start looking for her, they'll be looking in the wrong place – they'll be going off where her phone last pinged. That's why it took 'em so long to find her car.'

'Meanwhile,' I say, 'you're tucked up in bed at Mum and Dad's.'

'Right. After I phoned Taylor from the gas station, I drove straight to the house. My cell phone proves it. I'm there the rest of the night.'

'Except you're not,' I tell him.

He grins, a big old stupid grin. 'How'd you work it out?'

'This.' I hold up the matchbook again. 'Once I figured out the numbers were dates – don't ask me how; maybe I already knew before my accident, it was at the back of my brain somewhere – I realised they were the passcode to your phone.'

'All sounds pretty far-fetched, if you ask me.'

'It does, doesn't it? But then there was Casey's ex, Luke.'

'What about him?'

'You know Luke was in Heartsick the night Casey disappeared?'

'But the cops said—'

'The cops checked Luke's phone,' I interrupt. 'Right. It was pinging off a tower near the motel he was checked into in Colorado Springs all night. Cell phone evidence doesn't lie.'

Garrett doesn't answer, because he knows it does. Can do, at least.

'Luke admitted to me that he'd left his phone at the motel,' I go on. 'Swore it was by accident. I guess in the end it doesn't really matter.

When the cops checked, it showed he was holed up there all night. Essentially gave him a false alibi. Just like yours. So what happened, Garrett? You show up at the house on Halloween — well, November first — tell Mum everything, and, like the devoted mother she is, the one who'd do anything for her son, she helps you cover up Casey's murder?'

'I gave her my passcode,' he says simply. 'She'd never've remembered it — the numbers meant nothing to her — so she wrote it down on the matchbook, spent the night on my phone, surfing the net, logging in and out of Facebook, even replying to any text messages.' He laughs. 'Genius when you think about it.'

'So Mum stays up all night, pretending to be you, while you — what?'

'While I,' he says grandly, 'sans phone, drive up into the mountains to my prearranged meeting spot with Taylor. It's the early hours, the roads are remote, deserted, and there she is, good ol' Taylor, waiting with Casey's car. She's already gotten rid of the body, so that's one less thing to do.'

'So. What next? You give Taylor a ride home? Drive off into the sunset together?'

'Sunrise,' he corrects me. 'But yeah, pretty much. We went back to Mum and Dad's. I had to get my phone, see. Mum made us breakfast, then me and Tay stayed holed up the rest of the day, nursing my Halloween hangover.'

'Fucking hell, Mum made you two *breakfast*?'

He shrugs, *whaddya-gonna-do?* 'It'd been a long night. We'd worked up an appetite.'

'Jesus, Garrett.' I glare at him, wonder what darkness goes on in his head. 'You could at least pretend you feel some remorse.'

'I didn't *mean* to kill her.' He gets to his feet. 'I'm not going to prison for it.'

I stand too, but there's nowhere to go – I'm up against the couch. I've been so invested in getting the truth out of my brother, I suddenly realise I haven't thought about what will happen once I do. My eyes dart around the room, looking for something – anything – I can use as a weapon, but I can't even see Dad's old cell phone. Nice one, Steppy.

I've only one choice, I decide. I have to buy time. And the way to do that is to keep Garrett talking. 'I'm guessing you didn't mean to kill Mum, either,' I say. 'Was she having second thoughts about protecting you? Was she worried she'd be charged as an accessory, tell you she was going to the police?'

For a split second I'm sure he's going to lunge at me, but it seems I've underestimated how much my brother loves the sound of his own voice, because instead, a slow smile spreads across his face. He opens his mouth to say something, but before he can, I hear the sound of car engines, police sirens, tyres over snow, vehicles screeching to a stop.

Garrett and I look at each other, and I close my eyes in relief, the pain in my head all-consuming.

Shit-shit-shit-shit-shit . . .

Don't-die-don't-die-don't-die . . .

Stay with me . . .

Jesus!

And though it's probably no more than a few seconds, when I open them again, I see the back door wide open, flurries of snow billowing in. Beyond that, nothing but the gaping darkness of the forest.

Garrett's gone.

36

Then

I only just had time to slam my laptop shut and yank the USB cord free from Garrett's cell phone before he appeared in the doorway.

'Everything okay?' I asked him.

'Taylor's in the car,' he replied, as though that explained everything.

I made a face like that was news to me, like I hadn't just heard their shouting match. 'You should invite her in.'

'Maybe next time.' He glanced at his watch. 'She's cranky. Needs almond milk. Wholefoods place closes early Sundays. It's a whole thing.'

You were fighting about almond milk? I wanted to ask, but instead I held out Garrett's phone. 'Don't forget this,' I said, a little too chipper, faked a smile.

He didn't take it straight away. Instead, he looked at me, trying to figure me out. I forced myself to hold my smile, his stare, and after what felt like minutes but was probably more like seconds, he snatched the phone from my hand. 'We'll talk later.'

Something in his words sounded vaguely threatening.

*

Once I saw the tail lights of Garrett's Jeep disappear into the trees, I shut the door and collapsed onto the sofa, my whole body shaking. Bruce, who'd emerged from his hiding place upstairs, hopped onto the couch beside me, purring in relief. I lay there for a moment, and when I finally sat up, I knew what I had to do.

Like a woman possessed, I jumped up, grabbed my keys, looked around for my cell phone, couldn't see it anywhere. Where did I have it last?

And then I thought of something: my laptop. What if Garrett came back while I was gone, worked out my password? It wouldn't be all that hard. I'd used the same one for years. Bruce watched as I sat down and opened the laptop, but before I changed my password, I thought of yet another thing. I looked round for my phone again, couldn't see it, so I logged into Facebook. Paige had unfriended me months ago, but I found her profile, opened up Messenger, began to type:

I meant what I said. I'm sorry.

I logged out. Changed the password on my laptop. Changed it to Garrett's password – the last one he'd ever think of trying – the one he was using for his cell phone right now, the one with the six extra numbers added on the end: the date of Casey's disappearance.

The date I was now certain he'd killed her.

After that, I pulled on my sneakers, grabbed the matchbook and my keys and headed out the door. On the porch, I stopped yet again, dashed back in, looked around for something to write on. My eyes alighted on the scrap of paper with the dates on, still on the coffee table, so I grabbed it, snatched up a pen and began to write in my smallest possible handwriting. When I'd finished, I tore the excess paper away, a flurry of confetti, and folded what was left until it was teeny-weeny. Then, unscrewing the little silver capsule on Bruce's collar – the one Jenna had told me about – I posted the tiny paper bullet inside, screwed it back shut.

With a last backward glance at Bruce, who purred encouragingly at me, I dashed out the door.

37

Now
Six months later

I'm back in New York. My wounds – the physical ones, at least – have healed nicely, the doctors say; my staples removed months ago. I still have a scar, a permanent cleft where my hair no longer grows, an ever-present reminder of that day so many lives changed forever.

The night Garrett returned to Heartsick was the last time I saw him.

Moments after he fled through the back door, police swarmed the place, but it was too late.

As I lay slumped on the sofa, an EMT checking me over, Lucky beside me, I asked him, 'How did you know Garrett was here?'

The cabin was abuzz, full of cops with their booming voices, stompy boots and crackling radios. Outside, I could hear tracker dogs barking in the forest, helicopters humming overhead. Everyone looking for my brother.

'Lucky guess,' Lucky said. 'Pun intended. Taylor's neighbours heard arguing coming from the apartment, called it in. Your brother was gone by the time we arrived, so we dispatched a couple cars up to your parents' place, but he wasn't there. Next best bet was here.'

Garrett hadn't got far. He was picked up the next day, weaving his way along the edge of the highway, trying to hitch out of town, practically hypothermic. Despite what he'd admitted to me the night before, when the police caught up with him he denied everything, lawyered up. There was still no sign of Casey's body. No proof she was even dead. Mum wasn't around to turn state's evidence and Taylor was refusing to talk, despite the fact that Garrett had beaten her so badly the night he returned, choked her to the point of unconsciousness, she ended up spending a week in hospital. Worse, and exactly as I'd suspected, as Garrett's wife she couldn't be forced to testify. All the same, the local DA charged him with Mum *and* Casey's murders, first and second degree respectively. He had motive, means and opportunity for Mum's; as for Casey's, I'd be the state's star witness, would testify as to how I'd worked it out, what Garrett confessed to me that night, about Mum using his phone to give him a false alibi. Garrett's cell phone was never found. He'd had it on him that last night when he fled the cabin – I'd seen it. But after that, well, who knows. Lucky reckoned he'd tossed it, in the river, probably, before the cops caught up with him next day.

As far as the DA was concerned, that didn't really matter. Short of Garrett being caught red-handed, it was as close to a slam dunk as she could get. Dad was torn, I could tell, but in the end, he'd had enough of supporting Garrett. Without pressure from Mum, he no longer needed to. He refused to pay for an attorney, and Garrett couldn't afford a lawyer on his own so ended up with a court-appointed one.

As the months wore on and winter finally gave way to spring, Garrett continued to languish in jail awaiting trial. But with the thaw, so too came the discovery of human remains. It was hikers who found them. Taylor, presumably afraid of the prison time she faced, at last agreed to cooperate, did a deal with prosecutors, told them everything.

Two days after that, I received a phone call from Dad.

'Garrett's dead,' he told me. 'I wanted you to hear it from me first, before the press gets hold of it.'

'Oh,' was all I said.

I didn't mourn my brother's loss, and that didn't make me a terrible person. Though sometimes I feel like one when I can't sleep, when I wake in the wee small hours of the morning, having made the mistake of not taking a sleeping pill.

Garrett was found dead in his prison cell. It looked like suicide – he'd hanged himself from a bunk, left a note confessing not only to Casey's murder, confirming the story I'd already told police, but also to Amy Johnson's. After his death, there was talk round town for weeks, conspiracy theories abounding online, because by sheer coincidence, Casey's brother, Cody, had been awaiting trial in the same jail, on unrelated drugs charges. He and Casey's mom had stuck around in Heartsick, stayed in the same shitty motel for months waiting for Garrett's trial to come to court, in the hope of seeing justice. I don't think Cody had anything to do with Garrett's death, or that if he did, it was at most his mere presence – that it triggered something in Garrett, a guilty conscience, perhaps. I think it's more likely that Garrett simply couldn't face the thought of spending the rest of his days behind bars.

The DA thought the same. At a press conference held the day after my brother's death, she confirmed what most people in Heartsick already knew: thanks to DNA, the human remains – found in a shallow grave, miles from where her car was abandoned – had been identified as Casey's, the cause of death homicide. Remnants of the clothing she'd been wearing on Halloween were found, and although her remains had been scattered by animals, miraculously, her fractured hyoid bone was recovered nearby. She'd been strangled. My brother was consistent in his tastes, if nothing else. As far as the DA was concerned, Garrett's death put a period at the end of the whole sorry affair: Mum and Casey's cases were now closed.

As for Amy Johnson, the DA confirmed that a copy of Garrett's letter had been provided to the Thai police. A campaign was already under way, supported by Amy's family, to release the local man everyone now knew had been wrongly convicted.

But although in his letter Garrett had provided a thorough and detailed account of what happened the night of Halloween, into the early hours of November 1, as well as on the Thai island of Koh Tao the previous December, there was no mention of Mum. I guessed there didn't need to be. Her murder required little explanation, and knowing what everyone knew now about Garrett's involvement in Casey's death, it was clear that whatever my brother's motive for killing Mum, it wouldn't have happened were it not for what he did to Casey.

I still doubted Mum would ever have turned Garrett in, although I wouldn't have put it past her to at least threaten to, hold over him what she knew. As far as Heartsick was concerned, however, it was enough to have answers. The shock that had initially gripped the town had changed to acceptance. A collective mourning. Now Heartsick was ready to move on, put the whole thing behind it. So was I: after a new influx of suggestions sparked by the last few weeks' revelations, I'd finally settled on a subject for season two of *Dark Corners*. It was not, despite what many listeners wanted, Casey Carter. That would be too close to home. Instead, I was off to Texas to investigate the 1997 disappearance of an eight-year-old girl.

Could *Dark Corners* season two live up to the first season? I doubted it. Those things so rarely do, but I was good with that. All I needed was to be working again, to keep busy.

I've been back at my New York apartment three weeks. It's twenty-two whole days since Bruce went to live with Paige and Travis. They came to collect him the day before I left the cabin; had driven all the way to Heartsick from Connecticut, though Travis waited in the car. Much as I'd have loved to keep Bruce, my tiny New York apartment wasn't suitable for a cat used to the great outdoors, and Paige and Travis had recently got a place together in a leafy suburb. When Paige arrived, she hugged me, and I apologised to her again for everything – or, more accurately, for being too cowardly to face my brother head-on, to confront him about what I'd always known, deep down, he did to her that night in New York.

'Can I ask you something?' I said as she was leaving.

She stopped halfway out the door, put the cat carrier down on the porch.

'When I called you the day of my accident, what did I say?'

'You were rambling,' Paige admitted. 'To be honest, you sounded pretty paranoid. But you told me you knew Garrett raped me; asked me to look after Bruce' – she tapped the carrier gently with her foot – 'if anything happened to you.'

Despite the fact that nothing *did* happen to me – inasmuch as I didn't die in the car accident – Paige has made good on her promise. She's been keeping me up to date on Bruce's progress, and today I received a small package in the mail. Inside, Bruce's sparkly red collar, along with a note.

Dear Steppy,

Bruce is doing really well and sends his love. We had him chipped and my mom bought him a new collar – tweed, it really suits him – so I thought maybe you'd like his old one to keep as a memento. You should treasure it. You know that silver thing on it is an ID capsule?

If I'm ever in New York, maybe we can meet for coffee.

Paige

I don't know if we ever will meet for coffee – I think I remind Paige too much of sad times – but knowing she's safe and happy is enough for me. And it turns out that she's right: that funny-looking silver bell attached to Bruce's collar? It's not a bell at all. I unscrew it easily, but it takes me several goes to retrieve the tiny piece of paper inside, and in the end, I only manage it with tweezers. The paper's been folded into a tight little bullet, and when at last I unfold it, I'm surprised to see my own handwriting.

03.27.09

29.12.15

01.09.16

I recognise the numbers immediately. They're dates, the ones that make up the long number on the matchbook: the dates my brother committed his heinous crimes.

But there's something else. A postscript beneath, also in my hand.

This no. 03270929121501091610311 6 (dates Garrett committed crimes) is the passcode to Garrett's phone, also now my laptop.

Proof on there.

'Holy shit,' I utter.

With the newly found code, I finally gain access to my laptop for the first time in months, find the desktop littered with videos I must have uploaded from Garrett's cell phone, apparently on the day of my accident. Garrett's dead, and everyone already knows what happened to Casey, but nonetheless I call Lucky, and he dispatches someone right away to collect the laptop.

Those videos are the final nail in my brother's coffin.

Public interest in the story has yet to die down, won't do any time soon once the press get a hold of the scoop on those videos, but opinion on me has changed. Now, I'm a hero again: not only did I help solve the mystery of Casey Carter's disappearance and my own mum's murder, I put my brother behind bars, not to mention that I was willing to testify against him at trial.

Tomorrow I have an early flight to Texas, to begin recording season two of *All the Dark Corners*. Tonight, amid half-packed suitcases, piles of clothes, toiletries and recording equipment, I settle in front of the TV with a glass of wine. My sit-down interview with Keith Morrison, part of a *Dateline* episode on my brother, his trail of destruction, airs tonight.

'They were the perfect family,' croons that oh-so familiar voice – Keith's voice – the one that's as likely to lull a baby to sleep as it is to instil fear into the heart of the most hardened criminal. 'Until they weren't.' Cut to an aerial shot of Heartsick, which must be library footage, because the trees are in leaf in beautiful fall colours. 'Because then came the missing girl.' Cut to Keith, leaning against the door frame of Buddy's Bar, arms folded. 'Rumours about *other* girls, a murder, too. The common link? For one true crime podcaster, boy, was the answer ever too close to home . . .'

My face flashes up on screen, and though I look okay – I'm sitting poised, perfectly still, hair grown back, make-up done nicely – I cringe. Seeing myself on TV is something I don't think I'll ever get used to.

Cut again to Keith, who leans forward, hand on chin, fixes me with those enquiring eyes, asks, 'How's it feel to hear people say you're the only good one in your family?'

The camera cuts back to me, and, though blink and you'd miss it, I see myself hesitate under the weight of his stare, like somehow his insightful narration and probing questions make him a human lie detector. Like he can see straight through anyone not being wholly honest.

Then I watch myself smile modestly, laugh self-deprecatingly. I look relaxed, but not inappropriately so. 'Well, Keith, that's not saying much,' I tell him. 'But nobody's perfect. We've all got a dark side.'

38

November 27, 2016: the night of the accident

After Garrett leaves the cabin, after I Facebook-message Paige, change the password to my laptop, grab the matchbook, pull my sneakers on and snatch up my keys, hastily write the message to Paige and secrete it in Bruce's collar, I head out the door.

The road to my parents' is dark and deserted, and once I leave the highway, I don't pass another living soul. I make the journey in record speed, haven't told Mum I'm coming, want the element of surprise. When she opens the door, it's fair to say she isn't exactly happy to see me.

'Thanksgiving dinner,' is the first thing I say.

'What about it?' She turns, and I follow her inside.

'You acted like you'd never met Taylor before,' I tell her. We're in the kitchen, the breakfast bar between us. I slam down my keys. '*So this*' – I imitate her – '*is the lovely Taylor.*'

'I hadn't met her before,' Mum says coolly. 'Don't know what on earth you're talking about.'

'Really?' I ask. 'Because I'm sure you had met her. Scratch that – I *know* you had, which is why you didn't size her up when you were introduced; how you knew exactly how she took her coffee. You poured it for her that night – added Splenda, almond milk – without even asking.'

'Is that all you've got?' Mum sneers. 'Splenda and almond milk?'

'Not all I've got.' I fish in my pocket, pull out the matchbook. 'Did Garrett bring Taylor here the morning after he killed Casey? The morning after she helped him dispose of Casey's body; after you used this' – I open the matchbook, thrust it at her, numbers in her writing visible – 'to spend the night on Garrett's phone here, give him a false alibi?'

At the sight of the matchbook, Mum's face drops. And although until that point I've been pretty certain, in that instant I know, know I'm right, know there's no doubt, and everything comes tumbling out. I tell her what I've figured out: what the numbers on the matchbook signify; how I pieced it all together.

But if I hope this will be the turning point, that she'll break down, confess, agree to go to the police, hand herself and Garrett in, I'm mistaken.

She composes herself. 'A matchbook with some numbers on? Sounds pretty far-fetched, even for an armchair detective.'

I hesitate, thrown, afraid that if I tell her what I've managed to do – gain access to Garrett's phone, upload his sick videos to my laptop – she'll call him then and there and he'll go and destroy it.

So instead I keep my mouth shut, stand there dumbly, and Mum says haughtily, 'I think we're done, you should leave,' turns her back on me, walks out the kitchen.

But whether she knows it or not, she's already yanked my chain too much, so I go after her, down the basement staircase, follow her to her office, where, inside, she arches an eyebrow as if to say, *You still here?*

We argue, and I think she says something about loyalty, about me being intent on destroying my family, grabs my wrist, attempts to escort me out, and the matchbook – still in my hand – falls to the floor.

I flip – 'Don't you put your hands on me!' – blurt out about Amy Johnson; how I also know, from the dates that make up Garrett's passcode, that there's a fourth, mystery girl (I'm guessing those videos I've uploaded may hold the key to her identity).

'You know about Paige?' I say, a question but not a question. 'You know Garrett raped her?'

Mum stops, still holding my wrist, laughs in my face. 'Paige? Really? That girl's a sloppy drunk.'

At that, Garrett's words when we talked on Thanksgiving echoing in my head, I lunge at Mum – *lunge* – because I know he's told her, know she's parroting what he said to me that night.

Everything's pretty hazy after that. One thing I do know is that the time I mentioned earlier? The only time when I truly lost it, after Garrett threw the wooden owl at me and I shoved him so hard he fell and broke his wrist? Turns out that's *not* the only time I truly lost it. Because the moment Paige's name leaves Mum's lips, I see red, grab the closest thing to hand – the wooden owl, a silent witness on the corner of her desk – strike her with it, hard, keep on striking until I've nothing left.

It doesn't take long for it to all be over. I don't want it to sound like I don't regret it. I sink to my knees, kneel over Mum's body, check for signs of life – a pulse, breathing, anything – all the while talking to her, crying, pleading.

Shit-shit-shit-shit-shit . . .

Don't-die-don't-die-don't-die . . .

Stay with me . . .

Jesus!

But there's nothing, and that's when instinct takes over and I realise I can't stick around, so I leave her where she is and, careful not to touch anything on the way, wash the blood off my hands and face in the nearest bathroom, Garrett's en suite – poetic justice – wash the owl as best I can too, scrub it with bathroom cleaner. My clothing's covered in blood, but there's little I can do about that, and I'm halfway up the stairs before I remember the matchbook – *where is it?* On the office floor, I realise, race back, find it, don't dare look at Mum's body, still where I left it, a lifeless shape in my peripheral vision.

Back upstairs, I grab my keys from the breakfast bar, my cell phone, too, then, leaving the front door wide open, I race out to my car, jump inside and hightail it out of there. Don't look back.

It's not until I'm almost on the home stretch, having driven back down the mountain at breakneck speed, that Dad – though I don't know it's him at the time – calls Mum's cell. I hear the ringtone – Mum's, not mine – feel a hot, prickling sensation all over, feel the blood drain from my face, realise my mistake, like a strange out-of-body experience: in my haste to flee the scene, I grabbed Mum's phone, not mine – we have the same model! Panicked, I pull a U-turn then and there, in the middle of the road, a reckless manoeuvre but I have no choice – I have to get back up to the house, return Mum's cell phone before anyone realises what's happened.

And that's when I see them, headlights rounding a corner, heading towards me through the dark – another car, coming down the mountain as I make my way back up it – and I'm so startled, so panicked, driving so fast, I don't make the bend . . .

Epilogue

Now

I genuinely don't remember anything after that. Certainly nothing of the accident itself – not the aftermath, the rescue, the McKinleys or the first responders. Not even my brother, who chanced upon the scene on his way down the mountain after finding Mum dead at the house, exactly as he said he did.

What I've managed to piece together – from what I've been told, what I've worked out for myself – is this: the McKinleys, by the grace of God, reached my parents' place shortly after I left it, though didn't stop. They kept on driving, headed down the mountain, just in time to see my car lose control and go off the road. Meanwhile, Garrett – who'd just arrived at my parents' from the same direction as the McKinleys – found Mum and panicked. He called my cell phone, then made the abortive 911 call, the call in which he didn't wait to speak to an operator but made the mistake of venting to himself before hanging up: a masterstroke of self-incrimination. He then fled the house, again in the same direction as the McKinleys, chancing across them at the scene of my accident. After helping Mr McKinley pull me from my car, he left the crash site. Switching off his phone so he couldn't be traced, he made a quick pit stop at his and Taylor's apartment before, fearing he'd be fitted up for Mum's murder – though he hadn't killed her or stolen her cell phone, he had helped himself to cash from the scene as she lay dead – leaving town.

I, meanwhile – taken by ambulance to Heartsick Hospital, then transferred by air to the city – was never considered a suspect. Not only did I lack motive, I lacked means and opportunity: as far as everyone was concerned, I'd been at the cabin until Garrett called – my cell phone data proved it – and was seen by the McKinleys heading up the mountain towards my parents' house right before I went off the road. Any blood already on my clothing – Mum's blood – was masked by my own from my accident. Head wounds bleed. A lot. Mum's cell phone, which I'd accidentally grabbed as I fled the house, was destroyed, reduced to nothing more than a melted lump of plastic. Because it was the only phone on me that night, and the same model as my own, everyone – including me – assumed it was mine. The fact that it was destroyed in the crash shortly after Dad called it, which also coincided roughly with the time Garrett chanced upon the accident scene, meant the police assumed Garrett had stolen Mum's phone along with the cash he took, before switching it off, along with his own, in order to avoid being traced. I suppose you could say the whole thing was one big happy accident.

An accident I remember nothing of.

Before I go any further, I want to make it clear that as well as having no memory of the accident itself, I genuinely remembered nothing of the lead-up to it. Nothing of the preceding few days in Heartsick. Nothing of the day itself. Not even killing Mum.

It wasn't until very recently that I knew anything at all, not until after I returned to New York and received Paige's letter containing Bruce's collar. Well, okay, if I'm truly honest, I knew three weeks before that that something didn't quite add up. I just didn't realise the significance of it at the time.

It was my penultimate day at the cabin. Paige and Travis had not long left and I was spring-cleaning before my departure, trying to keep busy between bouts of crying over Bruce. So when I discovered it slipped down the side of the couch cushion, completely hidden – someplace no one ever looks unless they're spring-cleaning – it took a second to register what it actually was. I mean, yes, I knew right away that it was a cell phone, just not right away that it was *my* cell phone, the one I'd arrived with from New York all those months ago. The battery was long dead, of course, so it wasn't until I dug out my old charger, powered it up and entered my PIN that I knew for sure.

In the days and weeks after I returned to New York, despite various doctors warning it might never happen, memories slowly started returning. My retrograde amnesia, it turned out, wasn't permanent, though I maintained the narrative that it was, that I couldn't remember a thing.

It came as flashes here and there, like clips from a movie. I remembered my long drive from New York to Heartsick; remembered being at my parents' for Thanksgiving dinner, meeting Taylor for the first time. I remembered bumping into Brooke outside the motel; Jesse at the gas station; Hank across the street from Casey's place.

But it was Paige's letter, tipping Bruce's collar out of the envelope into my hand, opening the capsule, reading the note I'd written her that finally broke the dam.

You see, the list of dates, along with my brother's passcode, wasn't all the scrap of paper contained. On the other side, also in my hand, was a second note.

Nov 27, 7.30 p.m. Paige, Garrett killed Casey. Going to confront Mum. If anything happens to me, you know who did it. Pls look after Bruce. I miss you. Steppy

I'm guessing Paige must have read it. What I don't know is whether she worked out what really happened that night. I wonder about that sometimes; wonder more whether Garrett knew what had happened, whether *he'd* worked it out. After all, he had some of the puzzle pieces, knew he didn't kill Mum, even if no one else did, even if the whole town – the whole world, including me, if I'm honest – thought he had. And when I think back to the last night I ever saw him, when he turned up at the cabin, admitted what he'd done to Casey, I think about what he said about us being more alike than I cared to think, hear his words: *I didn't kill Mum. You know that, right?*

Then there was the voicemail. You see, although the phone records showed a call between Garrett and me the night of the twenty-seventh, when he called me from our parents', this was not in fact the minute-long conversation it appeared to be, but Garrett leaving me a voicemail. And unbeknownst to anyone, shortly after he left me that voicemail, back at the cabin, still on silent and inadvertently slipped between the couch cushions – where I'd secreted it trying to record my brother; a recording, it turned out, that was all but inaudible – my phone finally died. Of course, once I discovered it and charged it up, I listened to the message my brother had left me, but it was nothing earth-shattering. In fact, it was much the same as the incriminating 911 recording, a minute or so of him rambling: *What've you done? Shit-shit-shit.* I can't know for sure, but I don't think he was talking to himself; I think he was asking me. I got rid of my phone after that, of course. Chucked it in the Hudson on my return to New York. It was the only piece of evidence left tying me to Mum's murder.

Apart from the matchbook. More specifically, the smears of blood inside it. Again, I can't be sure, but knowing what I now know, I realise that blood probably belonged to Mum. When my car went off the road, the matchbook was in my back pocket, and the butt of my jeans was one of the only areas of my clothing left relatively unbloodied, since I was seated when the accident occurred. So I reckon the blood was already on there, spatter from when it lay open on the office floor as I killed Mum. Obviously I didn't realise this at the time I handed the matchbook – evidence – over to Lucky that night at the cabin, the last night I saw Garrett. I don't lose sleep over it, though. That blood, I'm quite sure, will never be tested – there's no need. I'm pretty sure the matchbook's still sitting in an evidence box, though, somewhere in the bowels of Heartsick PD, awaiting a trial that, with Garrett dead, will never come.

As for why, if Garrett suspected I killed Mum, he didn't rat me out, I don't have an answer for that either. Sometimes, when I lie awake at night, tracing my fingers over my scar, I wonder if, in his own twisted way, he was trying to protect me. He knew he'd killed Casey, after all. Once he heard her body had been discovered, he probably realised that even if he continued to protest his innocence when it came to Mum's murder, with his own wife and sister willing to testify against him, the weight of evidence would be too much. But there's also part of me that thinks my brother never did a selfless thing in his life, so perhaps his motivations will have to remain one of life's little mysteries. And I'm good with that.

Not that I don't feel guilty about the whole thing, haven't thought about coming forward – I have a conscience – but really, what good would it do? Mum's gone. Garrett's gone. Everything's tied up so neatly. My confession won't change anything. Not for the good.

But maybe it's not so much the fact that I killed my own mother that's so troubling, more that I'm content to live with it. And as I watch my *Dateline* interview, as Keith Morrison, hand on chin, poses the question 'How's it feel to hear people say you're the only good one in your family?', I know in that blink-and-you'll-miss-it moment, the one before I arrange my face into a suitable expression, laugh, say, 'Well, Keith, that's not saying much. But nobody's perfect. We've all got a dark side,' what I really want to add is *Maybe I'm just better at hiding mine.*

Maybe that's what makes me the darkest Corner of all.

Acknowledgements

Two books in less than two years. I can't quite believe it. It goes without saying that I couldn't have done it without my editor, Bea. Thank you, Bea, for your time, wisdom and guidance. Likewise, thank you, Jane Selley. Where would I be without your keen copyeditor's eye?

To Marina, the best agent. Thank you for your calmness, support, and always knowing the right thing to say at the right time. You are a super-agent.

As ever, to my family, for all their support. Thank you, Mum, for all the read-throughs (and the being read to!). Thank you Fi, my favourite – only! – beta reader. And Dad – thanks for getting all your friends to read book one!

To Ali Lowe, who is not only a wonderful writer but a lovely human being. Thank you for the quote for book one, and also for reaching out to me when you did: your words of encouragement were just what I needed.

To Dr Simon Nightingale and Dr Richard Shepherd. Simon, thank you for the crash course (no pun intended) when it came to all things head-injury-related, and for answering my extensive list of questions with patience, good humour and enthusiasm (but not for guessing the plot twist. Without having even read it). Dr Shepherd, thank you for being so generous with your time and knowledge, and for humouring what I'm sure were the most basic dead-body-related questions, without making me feel like they were. It's every true crime fan's dream to speak to one of Britain's top forensic pathologists, so thank you also Niamh O'Grady and Marina for brokering that contact. It goes without saying that any mistakes when it comes to head injuries and dead bodies – or anything else, for that matter – are entirely my own.

Thank you, New Writing North, especially Kathryn Tann, Rebecca Wilkie and Grace Keane. No one champions their own like Northerners. No one champions Northern writers like New Writing North.

To Alysoun Owen and Clare Povey of Writers' & Artists' Yearbook. Thank you for the advice you gave me all those years ago, Alysoun, and for the opportunities you and Clare have given me now.

To all the booksellers and librarians who are so passionate about what they do, but special thanks to Helen, Heather and team at Forum Books, Corbridge; and Sharron, Katie and team at Waterstones, Gateshead. To see my book in print is one thing; to see it on your shelves, and know I have your support, is quite another.

Katie Oliver, aka my unofficial PR. What can I say, other than I'm so grateful for the support you've shown me during what I know has been the most difficult time for you and your family. Thank you so much.

Finally, to the one and only Keith Morrison. Thank you for being such a good sport and giving me your blessing. The people at Dateline are right: you really are the nicest guy in the world.

'A tense, propulsive and twisty story . . . I was utterly
drawn to Boweridge and its simmering secrets'
Ali Lowe

HOW LONG CAN A SMALL TOWN BURY ITS PAST?

Summer, 1972. Sister Francesca Pepitone was found strangled in a parking
lot on the outskirts of Boweridge.

A week later, seventeen-year-old Minna Larson disappeared.
No one has seen or heard from her since.

The cases were never linked, and neither was solved. For some,
it was a scar that never healed. Others simply forgot.

Now, over forty years later, Minna's niece Maggie learns that days before
vanishing, Minna was telling people she knew who had murdered Sister
Fran, and that she had the evidence to prove it.

Except no one believed her because there was one thing
everyone could agree on . . .
Minna Lies.

Available to order

HEADLINE